MADDENING LOVE

They were on the balcony when the music began. Marshall turned to Renee and asked, "May I have this waltz?"

"But of course, kind sir," she drawled for effect, and laughingly went into his arms.

But instead of whirling her away, he merely stood gazing down at her. The light of the moon made her skin glow and her dark eyes luminous. He lowered his head and kissed her. It was a gentle, chaste kiss that nearly drove Renee mad. She pulled him closer and their kisses grew more passionate.

Voices from the house brought Renee back to reality and she moved away from him. She was bewildered by the emotions she felt; all she knew was that she loved him.

RAPTURE'S RAGE

BOBBI SMITH

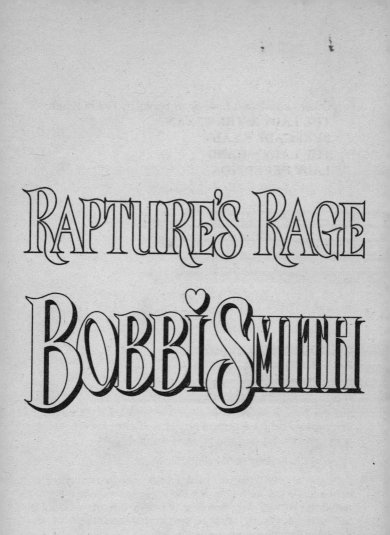

LOVE SPELL BOOKS ◆ NEW YORK CITY

LOVE SPELL®

November 1997

Published by

Dorchester Publishing Co., Inc.
276 Fifth Avenue
New York, NY 10001

ISBN 0-505-52238-1

For Mom & Dad
Jan, Jim & Bill

Prologue One
Anne
Philadelphia, Spring 1837

Margaret Chase observed her daughter quietly. Anne looked radiant as she stood at the open french doors gazing out at the flowering garden. She wore a white satin empire gown, embroidered intricately in gold, of the latest fashion. Her honey blonde hair was pulled up and away from her face with just a few loose curls to soften the style. Outwardly, Anne Chase-Parker seemed the picture of serene beauty, but within a great battle raged. Nervously, she turned to her mother who was seated in a comfortable wingchair casually sipping tea.

"Is it wrong to feel this way so soon? I never thought I could care for anyone else after Robert—but this is so different. Monsieur Fontaine is so . . ." Anne paused searching for the right word to describe the man whom she loved beyond all reason.

"Wonderful?" Margaret Chase finished for her daughter.

"Well, yes," Anne stated somewhat defiantly, moving to sit in the chair opposite her mother's. "He's like someone out of a dream. . . . He's so kind and gentle."

7

"Just how well do you know this young Mr. Fontaine?"

"I first met him at the Bancroft's three weeks ago and since then he's managed to arrange invitations for himself and his friend Alain Chenaut to all the important functions. So we have met quite frequently."

"And I'm given to understand that Rose Anderson is giving this 'intimate' dinner just for Mr. Fontaine?"

"Yes. Rose knew his mother many years ago when she lived in New Orleans. She's given him her stamp of approval and you know what a stickler for the amenities she is! But, I feel so guilty about going. Especially when I know that he will be there and I can hardly wait to see him again," Anne paused, flushed and slightly breathless.

"I knew there was something different about you lately. Now I know what it is," Margaret concluded, smiling slightly at her daughter.

"Are you laughing at me, Mother? I assure you this is no laughing matter. Why, if the Parkers hear of this, I–I–I just don't know what they'd do."

"No, my darling, I would never laugh at you. But I would be happy for you. It's wonderful to see you smiling again. That is, when I do catch a peek of you smiling and not sitting around worrying all the time!"

"Then you mean you approve of my acquaintance? You don't think I'm wrong . . . that my feelings are wrong?"

How can feelings be wrong? And after all, it has been over two years since Robert died. I think it's time that you began to live again. You are a young woman, there is no reason for you to spend the rest of your life alone, and Elizabeth could use a father figure." Margaret paused, observing her daughter quietly for a minute. "Really, Anne, to ease your mind, I have talked to Rose at length about Roger Fontaine. He is eminently suitable, thoroughly a gentleman and, indeed, wealthy beyond all expectations. If it is marriage with him you desire, I wholeheartedly support you."

"Oh, thank you, Mother! I was so afraid that I was being selfish," Anne exclaimed as she hugged her Mother excitedly.

"Nonsense. You've been out of mourning for quite some time now. And as far as the Parkers are concerned, I'll take care of any problems you may have there. Now, off with you! I'm sure your Roger is looking for you anxiously!"

"But, Roger, for you to fall in love so suddenly . . . it is hard for me to believe!" Alain Chenaut laughed, his Creole accent becoming more pronounced with each additional before-dinner drink.

"Alain, I have known her for almost three weeks and I know that she is the woman for me!"

"But how can you tell? There have been so many ladies, eh, Roger?" Alain smirked, remembering countless escapades in which they had both been involved. "You say that she is a widow and has a small child? Roger, that is a ready-made family!"

"All I can say is that you do not know her yet. She is the most wonderful woman I have ever met," Roger drifted off into silence remembering the way Anne Chase-Parker felt in his arms when they danced.

"Roger, my friend, you need not daydream any

longer," Alain announced nodding toward the door where Anne stood conversing with Rose Anderson and her husband Charles.

Roger froze, his drink at his lips. It seemed to him that at that moment time had stopped. He felt totally alone. His entire being focused on the petite blonde who stood, unaware of him, at the doorway engaged in animated conversation.

"Roger!" stated Alain softly. "I don't believe I've ever seen you this excited about a woman before."

"Ah, but Alain, she is not just any woman. She is the woman I am going to marry. Before we return home she will be my wife."

"I hope, mon ami, that I do not grow old and gray waiting for our return trip to New Orleans."

Anne and Rose were close friends despite the age difference and it was a relief for Anne to be distracted for a few minutes. Before Rose had come to greet her, Anne had spied Roger standing to one side of the parlor with his friend and traveling companion Alain Chenaut. He looked magnificent to her, tall and black-haired. His carefully tied cravat belied the four ruined ones back in his hotel room. His snug-fitting double breasted black coat and trousers emphasized his wide shouldered, narrow-hipped physique. Anne appreciated Rose's light chatter for it kept her from rushing to him. Charles excused himself and went back to entertain his friends as Rose took her arm and led her into the sitting room.

"He arrived quite on time and has been watching for you ever since," Rose confided with some amusement.

"Rose, I do appreciate your having this dinner

party. I always enjoy myself so much here," Anne returned smiling.

"Well, let's hope that this evening is no exception. Charles and I just invited our closest friends, all of whom you know, I'm sure. Martin and Helen Taylor and Raymond and Althea Summerfield. Althea obligingly brought her daughter Frances along, so Alain could have a dinner companion. It should be a very comfortable evening," Rose commented. "Especially since none of us like Felicity Parker!"

Anne smothered a lighthearted giggle, "Now *that* I truly do appreciate!"

"Come, let's join your young man now," Rose smiled as she led Anne to where Roger and Alain were standing.

They were quite a contrasting pair, these two single young men from Louisiana. Roger was over six feet tall, lean and darkly handsome, while Alain was short and soon to be on the heavy side if he did not watch his diet. One thing they shared in common, however, was ownership of vast amounts of land along the rich Mississippi River coast. They were very successful businessmen. Yes, Rose was as pleased as Margaret Chase that these two had met and fallen in love.

"Here she is, Roger, just as I promised you," Rose said gaily as she handed Anne to him.

"Thank you, Rose," he said warmly as he bent to kiss Anne's hand.

The contact of his warm lips on her cold hand sent shivers up her spine and she blushed at her own reaction.

"Good evening, Mrs. Parker," Alain bowed to Anne.

"It's good to see you again, Monsieur Chenaut." Anne spoke to Chenaut but her eyes were on Roger.

"Alain, will you come with me? There is a lovely young woman I want you to meet."

Alain took Rose's arm, and they moved into the study where the others were gathered.

"It's good to see you again, Anne."

"I'm glad to see you too, Roger," Anne spoke softly, blushing at her own boldness.

Roger laughed delightedly, "I'm glad you have not changed. You are the only woman I've ever met who says exactly what she thinks. It is indeed refreshing."

Anne was laughing now, too, for the first time in ages, as she realized the truth of his words.

The rest of the evening passed smoothly and far too quickly for Anne and Roger. Everyone attending approved of the handsome couple they made, the tall dark Creole and the petite fair blonde. After the final dishes were cleared away, the ladies retired to the sitting room and the men went off to the study for the after-dinner brandies and cigars. The conversation was on business. Usually Roger was very attentive where money was concerned, but tonight he could not bring himself to concentrate. His mind as well as his eyes were on the small blonde widow who had captured his heart. He could see her across the hall sitting on the love seat in the parlor. Roger smiled to himself. A love seat, how appropriate! He had already decided that as soon as he could maneuver her into a private place, in a suitable setting of course, he would propose.

"Roger?"

"My pardons, Charles, my thoughts were

elsewhere," he answered, a trifle embarrassed at having been caught daydreaming.

"Obviously," Alain agreed sardonically and proceeded to drag him back into the dealings at hand.

Within the hour the other married couples agreed that it was time to depart and Alain had courteously agreed to accompany Frances and her parents to their home.

"There is no reason why you should leave yet," Charles invited.

"Thank you, I was hoping for a few minutes alone with Anne. It's been three weeks and we have yet to have an unchaperoned moment."

"I understand, things were even stricter when I began courting Rose. Times have changed but not enough, and perhaps for the young ladies, that is good?"

"On that account you are definitely correct, Charles!" Roger agreed amicably.

Rose was pleased to see Roger invite Anne for a stroll in the garden, which now in early May was in full bloom. It would be quite romantic and she sighed as she remembered the days of her courtship with Charles in New Orleans.

"Sighing, my love?" Charles asked pulling her into his arms. "Are you sad about something?"

"Heavens, no, Charles!" Rose insisted. "I was just remembering our first moonlight stroll."

"My thoughts exactly," he assured her.

"We were certainly romantic in those days."

"Were? My dear, we still are!" Charles kissed her heartily. "I only hope that Roger has the same luck I did."

Rose smiled and rested her head on his shoulder.

Outside in the cool evening air, Anne walked quietly by Roger's side.

"You are so quiet now. Why the change? You nearly talked me to death at dinner," he teased, just to get a reaction out of her.

She glanced up at him almost angrily until she saw his smile and her expression softened. Her eyes were round and luminous in the bright moonlight.

"Sometimes I just enjoy the serenity of a moment without the necessity of talk," she replied softly, her face upturned, her lips moist and parted.

Roger realized that if ever he had seen a woman who needed kissing it was Anne at this moment, but there were things that he had to say first.

"Anne, we must talk." Looking around, he spied a small wrought iron bench beneath a tree. "Come."

Taking her hand, he led her to the bench and sat, pulling her down next to him.

"What is it that is so important, Roger?" she questioned, her heart pounding. She had wanted him to kiss her. She needed the reassurance that she was still a desirable woman.

"I must say these things so that you know I am not toying with you." He paused. "But now that I have you here my speech is forgotten. I have rehearsed in my mind all that I would say to you since that first time we met, but here I am and I am having such trouble. I need you. I love you. I want to make you my wife." He ended abruptly, too abruptly, and immediately apologized. "I'm sorry." Laughing, he took her hand. "I've never felt this way before and have never had to say all these important things. But I feel that you understand my ineptness. Perhaps if the words flowed too smoothly you would doubt their sincerity."

Anne's eyes filled with tears and she dabbed at them nervously.

"But you are crying? Have I made you unhappy or hurt you in any way?" Roger was stunned. He had not expected his declarations of undying love to be answered with tears.

"I'm happy, that's why there are tears."

"So you will marry me then? Soon?"

"Yes, yes of course. We can discuss this with Mother in the morning and she will help us with all the arrangements. I will be honored to be your wife, Roger Fontaine."

He smiled down at her, relieved. Then he stood and pulled her to him, "You'll never regret this Anne, I promise you that I will make you happy."

Their lips met and they were lost in the wonder of each other.

The arrangements were made and a small wedding was held at the Chase home just ten days later. Their happiness was marred only by the vicious opposition to their marriage by her in-laws, the Parkers. They were infuriated by the fact that she would marry so soon and to a distasteful papist from the swamp-filled Mississippi Delta. They tried everything in their power to stop the wedding but to no avail. Even the promise from Anne that little Elizabeth would return for regular visits did nothing to appease them. All of their efforts came to nought as the Andersons and Mrs.

Chase were quite well qualified to fend off their attempts. So it was in the June of 1837 that the newly wedded Roger and Anne Fontaine returned to his home in Louisiana with Anne's lovely four year old daughter, Elizabeth Anne Parker.

Their life together at L'Aimant, the Fontaine plantation on the Mississippi north of New Orleans, was idyllic. The big house, that Roger had always wanted to build was under full construction now with Anne providing details that she wanted. It would be a house of love, a large home with room for many children. Roger had *garconniers* constructed in hopes that these extra wings on the house would one day house all of his sons, even though they had not yet made an appearance. Anne bloomed in the relaxing southern climate. The friendliness of the neighbors, albeit distant ones, and the comfort of her new life made Anne more content than she had ever been. Roger's solicitous manner during the day enchanted both mother and daughter. Elizabeth was soon calling him Papa and climbing onto his lap at every opportunity. At night, Anne lost much sleep as his constant demands kept her awake and ecstatic. Never had she felt so loved and so cherished. And so, it was with great joy that she told him on their first Christmas together that they would have their own baby during the following summer.

Roger was in heaven. A son! Soon he would truly be a father. Not that he didn't love Elizabeth. God knows she was just like her mother. A delicate blonde beauty who would be incomparable as the years went by. But to have one's own offspring. That was truly the meaning of life. He had the work on the new house speeded up so that Anne would be settled in plenty of time for her confinement.

L'Aimant house was completed in February. Made of cypress and whitewashed brick it stood three stories high and was built to last for generations. Eight massive pillars graced the front and french doors opened onto the upper and lower galleries from all the rooms. The main halls were wide and airy and the ceilings were twenty feet high. Each room had its own marble fireplace. The chandeliers were of crystal and brass. Almost all of the furnishings Roger had ordered in Europe and were exquisite.

Roger supervised the planting on the grounds, massing magnolia and dogwood near the house so that in the following springs the air would be fragrant with their scent. Anne spent the last few months of her pregnancy putting the final touches on her home. She laughed now when she thought of the Parkers and their declaration that they didn't want their only grandchild raised on a farm in the swamps. This house was far more glorious than the estate the Parkers owned near Philadelphia. Roger doted on her and by his own decision, did not attempt to make love to her during her final three months. Not that she wasn't still tempting but his thoughts were all centered on his first heir soon to be introduced to the world.

Renee Fontaine arrived in late June, much to the pleasure of her parents. A son would have been nice but, ah, this little one with hair like her father's and eyes like her mother's . . . she would be a beauty any man would be proud to claim. Renee's birth was an easy one for Anne and within weeks she was up and about running the house. Her joy was great as she watched little Elizabeth play with her new sister.

Then in late August, Anne complained of a headache and took to her bed, thinking it nothing serious. By the time Roger returned from the fields she was running a high fever and before the doctor could arrive from town she had slipped into unconsciousness. It was the dreaded yellow fever. He moved the children to the *garconniers* for protection and stayed by Anne's bedside night and day. She never regained consciousness and died quietly four days later, leaving Roger inconsolable.

He spent the days after the funeral wandering through the house oblivious to everything and everyone. Chenaut did what he could but he was little help to Roger who remained alone day after day, leaving the children to their mammy and the fields to the overseer. His life was over. There was nothing left for him. This land had taken his beloved. He would sell it and move away, maybe to France where a gentleman could do nothing but drink his days away with no cares, no worries. It was at the peak of this depression, a few months after Anne's death, that Chenaut forced his way into the shuttered house. The home was a wreck, the rooms were all dark and neglected. Although it was early morning he found Roger in his bedroom drinking.

"Roger, you must get control of yourself."

"But why, my friend? My life is over," he stated flatly.

"You fool, don't you realize what's going to happen?" Chenaut was unusually disturbed about something.

"What are you talking about? You should have a

drink, then nothing will bother you either."

Roger pushed his half empty bottle at his friend.

"Roger! The Parkers are in Baton Rouge. They've come to get Elizabeth. You must prepare yourself for they will be here this afternoon. You can't let them see you this way."

Roger stumbled to the window blinded by his tears, "What do I care? When I look at Elizabeth the pain. . . ."

"Have you once thought of the children or their grief?" Alain exploded. "All this time you have kept yourself isolated here you haven't once thought of what poor little Elizabeth is going through or worse yet, your own child. You must put this anguish aside and take charge of your life. You cannot stay locked in Anne's room waiting for her return. She is not coming!"

"*No!*" Roger screamed and hurled the bottle at Chenaut's head. "Get out! I won't listen to you!"

Chenaut ducked the bottle and it crashed against the wall, splattering whiskey over the wallpaper that Anne had so carefully selected.

"Roger, she is dead! You can't bring her back. *Mon ami* . . . you must see to your own daughter. She needs you. L'Aimant needs you. Surely you still hold these two special things dear to you?"

Roger stood swaying slightly in the middle of the bedroom. He stared blankly at Chenaut who opened the door and called to the servants. A bath was arranged and the children were moved back to their rooms. Chenaut took command and by the time the Parkers arrived Roger was in control.

The Parkers came with the lawyers they had hired

and took Elizabeth away, cursing Roger for ever bringing Anne and Elizabeth to Louisiana. How could he do this to their grandchild? Leave her without her mother! But no matter now. They would take her back to Philadelphia where she would be raised according to their means, which were considerable. He was not to concern himself with Elizabeth again. They had no desire to hear from him again. The scene was short and Chenaut knew that there was no legal recourse. Five year old Elizabeth understood none of this and was carried screaming to the carriage, begging her 'Papa' to not let them take her. He knew that he had to give Elizabeth up, Chenaut had convinced him of that, but he still had Renee. She would never leave him and he would build his life around her now.

Roger looked at Chenaut with sane eyes for the first time in months, "Chenaut, I thank you for letting me know they were coming. I could not have borne it if they had found me in the condition you did this morning."

"It's nothing. Are you better now?"

"I will be all right. Things will not be the same ever again and I must realize that. But I have my child. My gift from Anne. I will raise her to be as special as her mother."

Chenaut put his arm around Roger's shoulders and together they went into the house to see his child for the first time since the funeral.

Prologue Two
Elizabeth
St. Louis - Fall 1851

"Oh, Mother, I'm so excited!" eleven year old Dorrie Westlake exclaimed as she saw the carriage turn through the gates of the Westlake estate, Cedarhill."

"I am, too," Martha Westlake turned to her young daughter. "It's so hard to believe. Marshall has finally come home—and married, too!"

"I hope she's nice. Do you think she'll like me? She sounds so worldly . . . Elizabeth Anne Parker of the Philadelphia Parkers!"

"I'm sure she's nice or Marshall would not have married her."

"That's true," Dorrie agreed, she'd always trusted her oldest brother's judgment and his choice of a wife must surely be perfect.

"George! Jim! Here they are, hurry!" Martha called as the carriage neared the end of the tree-shaded lane.

As it pulled to a stop in the portico of the white pillared home, George Westlake and his youngest son, James, appeared next to Martha and Dorrie. The carriage door swung wide and Marshall Westlake stepped down.

"Oh, Marshall!" Martha threw her arms around him and gave him a big hug. "It's so good to have you home. Where is she?"

"Right here, Mother," Marshall turned to the open carriage and handed down his bride, introducing her to his family.

Elizabeth Anne Parker Westlake was a lovely young woman. Not quite eighteen, she stood a little over five feet tall in contrast to her husband's six feet two. Her figure was petite and her hair was blonde, a light honeyed color. She gazed up at Marshall with undisguised adoration for a moment before she turned to meet her in-laws.

"Welcome, Elizabeth, it's wonderful to finally meet you. Marshall's written so often about you that we feel we know you already."

"Thank you. It's such a relief to finally be here. Why, you must be Dorrie."

Dorrie extended her hand timidly but before Elizabeth could take it, Marsh swept his only sister into his warm embrace and kissed her loudly.

"Oh, you big ox, let me down!" she squealed, loving every moment. She had missed him badly during the year he had been in Philadelphia completing his law studies.

"You don't know how much I missed you, little one," he countered and she threw her arms around him hugging him close.

"Me too, Marshall."

He set her down gently and stepped back to look her over, "When I left you were just a little girl and now you're almost grown. Jim's been keeping a close watch over you, hasn't he?" Marsh teased.

Dorrie blushed profusely and turned to her mother as Marshall ushered Elizabeth into the house.

"George . . . Jim get the baggage down. What are you two staring at?"

Husband and son grinned at Martha, "She's quite a looker."

George smiled up at his son as Jim made to throw down the bags, "That she is, Jimmy, and Marshall's happy. That's all I care about."

Later that evening, after Elizabeth retired, Marsh sat up late with his father drinking and relaxing by the fire in the study.

"Are you sure your bride doesn't mind your being here with me?"

"Of course not, Father. She's exhausted after all the traveling and the excitement of finally getting here. I'm sure she's fast asleep by now. Besides, I've really been looking forward to this time alone with you. It's been so long since we had a chance to talk."

"I was worried, since you've just married and all . . ."

"Father, it's been almost eight weeks now."

"Ah, so you're an old married man, already?" George chuckled.

Both men smiled, "I hope she'll be happy here. I know Philadelphia is a lot more sophisticated than St. Louis but after I get my practice established there will be no end to the invitations. She's really excited about meeting people in town."

"Good. She seems like a wonderful girl. I hope you'll be happy together."

"Thank you."

"She really didn't mind not having a big wedding?"

"On the contrary. Her parents died when she was a child and then her grandfather a few years after that. So there was only her grandmother and she's been in ill health for some time now."

"I see. We were more than a little puzzled when your letter came after the wedding. Martha and I had looked forward to the occasion."

"I'm sorry. I didn't think it important at the time."

"No need to apologize as long as you're content."

It was much later, well past midnight, when Marsh made his hazy way to his bedroom. Amusedly he thought to himself that this would be the first time he ever slept with a woman in his own bed under his parents' roof. The thought of trying that without nuptials brought a smile to his face. The holy state of wedlock sure made a lot of things correct and acceptable.

His room was dark when he entered. Everything was just as he'd left it, so he had no problem shedding his clothes in the dark and finding his way under the covers. Elizabeth lay quietly beside him and he thought her asleep until he reached to pull her to him.

"How could you, Marshall Westlake? How could you?!" she demanded angrily moving away from him quickly.

Dumbfounded, he could only stare at her outline in the dark. His brain more than a little numb from the brandies he'd shared with his father.

Elizabeth watched him from beneath lowered lashes and felt a cold fury growing within her. She would not, could not, share him. She had only vague recollections of her parents. Robert Parker, she remembered not at all, his image in her mind had been built for her by her grandmother's continual stories of him. Of her Mother, the lovely Anne, little had been said once her maternal grandmother had died. Grandmother Parker never spoke her name, she had always been described as "that woman" your father married. To all purposes, Elizabeth remembered only Roger Fontaine as her father. But in that memory burned the fact that men would not stay with you. They would desert you at the first opportunity. After all had not her grandfather died just two years after he had dragged her back from Roger's? Even her Grandmother Parker's behavior had contributed to that belief. For after grandfather's death she had wailed continuously about how she had been abandoned with such a great responsibility.

Presented with this evidence at the tender age of eight Elizabeth had decided that men were not to be trusted, no matter how much it appeared that they cared for you. She had learned early in life that she must never give her heart and soul to any man. Elizabeth had made the mistake only once with Roger and the message had been reinforced later with a vengeance. She had grown up with a servant boy named Patrick who was five years older than she and at the tender age of thirteen he had initiated her into the rites of what she considered love and he considered lust. They had carried on discreetly enough until her grandmother had caught them. Patrick had been run off the premises for good. Of course for him it had been a lark, but again she had been taught a terrible lesson. No one could ever be allowed to become important to her again. She could do quite well with no deep emotional entanglements, she convinced herself.

A few years later, she made her debut and was courted by many men but she had not enjoyed any of them. Then at age seventeen, Marshall Westlake from St. Louis had arrived in town. Marshall had been completely different from the other young men of her acquaintance. He was ruggedly handsome and totally indifferent to her charms. She had ignored him, too, in the beginning, but as time passed Elizabeth became intrigued. She decided that he would be an interesting challenge and she made sure that he was invited to the ball that was being given by her best friend the following weekend. He came and she conquered. Using all of her feminine wiles and the most outrageous designs she soon had him courting seriously and after three months he proposed. Elizabeth accepted, knowing that although she would never be happy with any man, Marshall came the closest to satisfying her. They agreed to marry right away before he had to return home. The wedding was small with only her grandmother and a few close friends in attendance. They made love for the first time on their wedding night and his surprise at her lack of virginity was hidden by the darkness of the room. Later, he had not mentioned it for he was too much of a gentleman and too enamored with her. After all, he decided, what had happened before he met her was none of his affair. It did not diminish his feelings for her although he could not help but wonder which of her beaux had bedded her before him. Elizabeth was secretly pleased that he had not mentioned it. She had made up a plausible story of how her innocence had been lost for she knew she could never be honest with him, no matter how much he said he loved her. After all, had not Roger and her grandfather said all the same things and yet they had left her. . . .

They turned his return trip to St. Louis into their honeymoon and had sailed from Philadelphia to New Orleans instead of going overland. After enjoying that cosmopolitan city, they arranged transportation upriver aboard one of his family's steamboats. The Westlake Line was one of the most successful lines making the run between St. Louis and New Orleans. As time went by Elizabeth relaxed and enjoyed the trip, relieved that Marshall made no mention of her deflowered state.

Now, here she was in the very situation she hoped never to find herself in, sharing him with other people.

"How could I what?" he was asking her and she jerked back to the present.

"Ooooh! You haven't given me a thought since we got here! All you've cared about is your precious family!"

He sat up slowly and lit a candle by the bed. Turning to her, he then realized that she'd been crying.

"Darling . . ." he said softly pulling her to him. "What did I do? I thought you had long since gone to sleep. I didn't know you were waiting for me."

"I just don't know how you could leave me all alone here in this house where I don't know anyone but you. You were so busy with your own pleasures you didn't give me a second thought," she hissed at him.

He had ignored her and deserted her to be with his father and if she was to have any peace at all, he would have to be hers completely with no outside interference. That meant his family. She had made her plan while she waited for him to come to bed. Never again would she feel second to anyone in his life.

"Ah, but you're wrong. I thought of you all evening. I couldn't wait to come up here to you," he mumbled drunkenly, unbuttoning the top buttons of her lace and silk gown to expose the tops of her breasts. He bent his head and kissed the smooth skin. Elizabeth felt only anger as he tried to subdue her mood with his lovemaking.

"That's all you want from me!" she raged and with all the power she could muster she shoved him away.

Marshall's eyes blazed as he glared at her, his mind finally clearing, "Don't ever shove me away from you again!"

"I'll do anything I like where my body is concerned," she stated smugly, refastening the tiny pearl buttons of her nightdress.

"That I know," he replied bitterly.

Elizabeth gasped in surprise at the crudeness in his voice. "I'm sure I don't know what you mean."

"My dear, your absence of maidenhead was enough for me to know that you always do as you please."

Elizabeth turned away from him, her cheeks stained red with embarrassment, "If you knew . . ."

"Don't say anything. It's not necessary. I love you and I want you. Now come here."

"Marshall, I love you, too," she answered quietly, the shock of his statement having turned her jealous rage to cold fear. "But, we have no privacy here."

"No privacy? We are alone, are we not?"

"Now, but who knows what can be heard in the next room?" she explained, deciding to change her tactics. She moved from the bed and standing let the gown slip, "Marshall, I do want you but I don't want to worry about who's going to hear us. Do you understand?"

He didn't answer but watched her with much interest as she let the gown fall to the floor. He leaned back casually against the headboard as she posed in front of him. He felt himself harden as his eyes roamed over her shapely figure.

"You are lovely, my dear. Come here."

She moved within an arm's reach of him and he grasped her around her waist drawing her across his lap. Elizabeth lay limply in his arms as he pressed soft kisses against her throat. Although she loved Marshall in her own special way, she found no enjoyment in his embrace. She had never enjoyed the physical part of love and could just barely conceal her feelings of distaste as he lowered his head to her breasts. She had managed to make him believe that she felt excited by his manipulations and so she continued her charade, holding him close and groaned in what she thought was a good imitation of passion. He rolled with her then and moved to fill her.

"Please, can we have our own home, soon? Just so we can be alone?" she pleaded, knowing that this was the moment he would grant her anything she asked for.

"We'll start looking tomorrow, love," he murmured as his mouth found hers and she began to match his rhythm in hopes that he would soon be finished.

It wasn't the next day but by the end of the month Marsh had managed to buy a fashionable brick house just west of the business district on Lucas Place. Elizabeth was not overly impressed with her new home but she knew that it was infinitely better than living way out in the country with her in-laws.

The next months passed somewhat peacefully for them. He was totally enamored with her and what he thought she was and she was busily making her presence known in the upper strata of St. Louis society. Elizabeth had no trouble getting invited to all the right parties; just being a Westlake insured that. Marshall's law practice grew rapidly and so did their income. It was at this point in time that Elizabeth was told the most dreaded news she was ever to hear.

"Congratulations, Mrs. Westlake, your baby should be here sometime in July."

She had cringed inwardly when the doctor had said those few words, she had only come because she hadn't been feeling well. It had never occurred to her that she could be pregnant. He had continued on with banalities about how pleased her husband would be, never realizing that she was on the verge of hysteria. She could only set a smile upon her face and blindly make her way home. How terrible! Just when she was making headway. Just when she was about to become the most desired person on the social scene, Marshall had to do this to her. It was all his fault. Yes, it definitely was. She would put an end to this stupidity once and for all. Never again would she put up with his embrace. He would get this child but never another. All the way home she cursed him. And then she cursed her need for him. For she did need him, near her, supporting and caring for her. But she was only going through this once. She would not suffer through nine misshapen months and then the agony of childbirth ever again. He would have to promise not to touch her again.

When Marshall arrived home that evening, he found her abed. A cloth covered her eyes and she looked very pale.

"Elizabeth, what's the matter?" he asked as he sat on the bed beside her.

"I'm ill," she declared moving away from him. "And you have no one but yourself to blame."

"What is it?" he questioned again running his fingers gently through her long flowing hair. He turned her face to him to kiss her but she jerked away.

"Marshall, I swear I shall die. It's all your fault!"

"What is all my fault?" he demanded, growing annoyed.

"I had to visit Dr. Freemont today."

"Then you really are sick?" worry clouded his face.

"You'll probably think it's wonderful. . . ."

"How could you believe me to be so cruel?" he interrupted. "If you are ill I doubt that I would be happy. You are my wife, the most important person in this world to me."

"Not for long," she murmured. The fear of losing his affection to some screaming baby unnerved her.

"Tell me."

"I'm pregnant," she stated flatly. "Dr. Freemont says the baby will be here some time in the late summer."

A look of wonder crossed his face. Marshall loved children and the thought of a child of their own filled him with delight. "You're right. I do think it's wonderful!" he said, kissing her thoroughly.

Watching the expression on his face, Elizabeth knew that this child growing inside of her was a threat to her newfound happiness and it had to be eliminated. She was lost in her thoughts as he rambled on about how they would drive out to his parents' house this very evening and tell them the good news. Vaguely, Elizabeth heard Marshall ordering the carriage brought around and she realized she'd been daydreaming.

"Elizabeth, are you ready yet? If we leave right away, we can be to Cedarhill in time for dinner," he called as he went into the hall.

"I'll be right there," she answered sweetly, rising from the bed.

Yes, she would let him believe that all was well, she would bide her time, but at the first opportunity she would rid herself of this burden in her body and then they would be happy. She knew it.

Luckily, Marshall believed her change of heart in regard to her delicate condition. The idea that she truly didn't want a baby never occurred to him. If it had he would have dismissed it as ridiculous. Elizabeth was a wonderful woman and motherhood would only enhance her loveliness.

Elizabeth, meanwhile, was plotting carefully to make the loss look accidental. She still remembered all too well the terrible concoction her grandmother had obtained and administered to her, after her involvement with Patrick, that had brought on her monthly flux. Somehow, she would take the same thing and be rid of this pregnancy so she could carry on with her life. A month passed before she finally had the opportunity. Marshall had gone to St. Charles on business and would be gone overnight. After sending her maid, Mary, to the chemist to get the potion, she closeted herself in the bedroom with the poisonous medicine and rapidly gulped down a double dose. She reasoned that if a single dose worked well in the first month a stronger dose would be needed because she was farther along this time. Then, she climbed into the bed certain that by morning her problem would be resolved.

Morning found her doubled over with cramps and violently ill. Mary summoned the doctor who arrived too late to be of much help. The baby was lost and Elizabeth was hemorrhaging badly. When Marshall finally arrived at the riverfront, he was greeted by Mary who hysterically told him what had happened. They rushed to the house to find Elizabeth pale and still, with Dr. Freemont hovering over her.

The doctor drew Marshall out into the hall and closed the door.

"What happened?" Marshall questioned frantically, worry creasing his brow. "Did she have an accident?"

"It was no accident, Mr. Westlake. Your wife deliberately induced this miscarriage by drinking this," he said solemnly holding up the bottle for Marsh to see.

"My God! But why? She seemed so happy . . ."

"She's been incoherent all morning. I couldn't make any sense out of what she said."

"Will she be all right?"

"I don't know . . . the bleeding . . . it's slowed but not enough. I really must get back."

"I have to see her!"

"All right, but no excitement. She must stay calm." They entered quietly—cautiously.

Elizabeth was awake, aware of them. Marshall sat easily on the bed and took her hand in his. It felt cold and lifeless.

"Elizabeth," her name came from him in a hoarse whisper.

She was still for a moment and then she sneered at him, "So you've come."

"I just got here. Mary met me at the boat."

"It's your fault you know."

"Elizabeth, don't . . ."

"Don't!" she screeched at him in a final desperate burst of fury. "Do you think I want to die?"

"Then why?" he asked. "Why did you do this to yourself? To us?" Tears filled his eyes. "I love you."

"Hah! All you could think of was the baby! You didn't want me anymore. I thought if it was just me again you would be happy. You would stay," her voice grew weaker and softer and Marshall heard the doctor mutter a curse from the foot of the bed where he was working feverishly to control the bleeding.

"Stay? What do you mean?"

"They left me, all of them . . ." she whimpered.

"Who left you?" he demanded, feeling her slipping away and thinking irrationally that if he made her angry enough . . . "Who? Elizabeth, answer me!"

She was looking at him blankly now, "If only you understood. I never needed anyone but you. But you . . . you needed everyone."

"No," he groaned leaning over her, searching for some sign of recognition in her face. "I never needed anyone but you. I've always needed you."

"But not enough. You would have left me, too. Just like they all did," she murmured.

"I . . ."

Her eyes closed and her head fell back against her pillow.

"Elizabeth!" he whispered and then shouting, "Elizabeth — Elizabeth — Dr. Freemont!"

"I'm sorry, Mr. Westlake. The bleeding . . . it just couldn't be controlled," Dr. Freemont stood quietly, unable to say more to the young man who sat quietly now, holding his wife's limp form in his arms.

Chapter One

The last glow of the setting sun turned the blue sky to a pink-streaked canopy and the mile wide river to liquid gold. It was a breathtaking scene as the white gingerbread bedecked *Elizabeth Anne*—pride of the Westlake Lines out of St. Louis—churned her way north toward home this fall of 1856. She was a massive sternwheeler and one of the most elegant to ply her trade on the Mississippi from St. Louis to New Orleans. After departing Memphis early in the day and a later stop at Cairo she was now heading straight for home hoping to dock the next afternoon.

Aboard the steamer in the ornate ladies cabin, Renee Fontaine was unaware of the conversations being carried on around her. To all outward appearances she was intent on her needlepoint, her head slightly bent to task, her fingers busily stitching. But in truth, her mind was far away. In her thoughts, it was early last spring, not late October. She was home—at L'Aimant, her family's plantation—with her father. The trees were in bloom all white and pink and the fields were green with new growth. They were sitting on the low bluff near the house watching the river as it flowed by on its way to New Orleans and the Gulf. Renee had spent many hours there reading or just thinking. It was her favorite place, there under the willow. But this particular day with her father had been glorious, for he had told her that she would have her first ball at L'Aimant in June. It was time. She had hugged him delightedly.

"Renee, are you all right?" The concerned voice belonged to Mrs. Bigelow, her chaperone for the journey."

"What?" Renee looked up questioningly at the plump gray-haired matron sitting across from her.

"My dear, you look positively pale. Are you feeling well?"

"Yes," she stammered, forcing herself back to the present—to reality. "But if you don't mind, I think I'll go back to my cabin and freshen up a bit before dinner."

"Of course. I'll have the Major come for you a little later."

The major and Mrs. Bigelow had agreed, at the request of her father's closest friend, Alain Chenaut, to accompany Renee to St. Louis to meet her aunt. They were traveling north, too, for the Major had just been assigned new duties at Jefferson Barracks, the post a little south of town. Childless, Mrs. Bigelow had been hesitant at first to accept the responsibility, but after their initial meeting Frieda Bigelow had looked forward to the trip. Renee had impressed her with her maturity despite her youthful innocence. The combination had brought out all the latent maternal instincts in her and Frieda had been smothering Renee with attention and concern ever since they had departed New Orleans three days earlier.

"Poor child," Mrs. Bigelow remarked to Mrs. Coleman who was sitting next to her. She's had nothing but heartache these past few months. Her father died of the fever and now she's all alone save the aunt she has in St. Louis."

Mrs. Coleman nodded in sympathetic understanding.

Renee entered her stateroom and fell across the bed, tears burning in her eyes. It was all catching up with her now, these past weeks. She had managed to protect herself from the deep pain of loss by pretending it hadn't happened and she'd succeeded until suddenly, there in the ladies cabin, the realization overcame her. Papa was dead! And he'd died so suddenly. One day late in August he had been fine and the next he was burning up with fever. There had been nothing she could do to save him. Nothing. Finally the long held back tears began, as she remembered her father in his delirium calling out for his beloved Anne. Renee had stayed by his bedside constantly but he hadn't spoken to her. Only to and about Anne. The thought of her mother brought new sobbing. Anne Chase Fontaine had died so long ago that Renee had no memory of her at all. And though Roger Fontaine had been a devoted father, Renee had always felt the lack of her mother. Finally, she quieted. She sat up slowly on the bed rubbing her eyes like a small child. Her face was hot and flushed and her hair had tumbled loose from its pins, the heavy black mass cascading down her back in unruly waves. She brushed aside a curl from her tear-dampened cheek and looked dully around her. In those terrible days after the funeral a protective stupor had surrounded her, ignoring the vast complexities of it all, Renee had gone through the mechanics of settling estate matters in an unnerving calm. Everyone who called commended her on her bravery and poise, while they waited patiently to hear rumors of her finally breaking down under the strain. But there had been no gossip coming forth from L'Aimant; Renee was carrying on and in a manner of which her father would have been proud. Now, eight weeks later, she knew that the pretending was over. Tomorrow she would begin a new life in St. Louis—one that did not include her father or her beloved home in Louisiana. Tomorrow, Renee Fontaine would take up permanent residence with her paternal aunt: Aunt Elise, a woman she hadn't seen in ten years.

Renee rose from the bed and made her way to the small dressing table. She sat down wearily, gazing at the tear-ravaged oval face looking back. Her dark hair in disarray gave her a wild look and her blue eyes, usually her best feature, were puffy and red. Searching miserably, he finally found a small cloth and dampening it in the cold water from the basin, she bathed her flushed face. When she sat again to inspect herself the wild-eyed look was gone; Renee saw only a pale frightened girl. Pulling the rest of the pins from her hair she began to brush it viciously, angry at herself for finally weakening. Papa had taught her to be in control of herself at all times.

"Ladies never reveal their true thoughts!" He had insisted.

"But don't my feelings count? What I think is important too!" She had retorted.

"That they do, ma petite, but men don't like that.

You should tell them what they want to hear."

"That's dishonest! Why can't people just tell the truth to each other?"

"Because life is not like that. You'll see," was all he had answered cryptically.

Renee smiled tremulously, she had learned her lesson well. Except for today she'd been in complete control. Papa would have been proud of her. And by the time the Major called for her to go to supper, Renee Fontaine was once again a demure young lady in mourning.

The meal was magnificent as usual, Westlake Steamers were renowned for their excellent food as well as their skilled river pilots.

The general topic of conversation turned to St. Louis. Everyone insisted it was the place to be for the winter season. It was an established town with a French soul and a southern heart. St. Louis was growing by leaps and bounds and would surely soon be the major inland port if it wasn't already! She heard giggles from the other girls nearby when they spoke of all the eligible soldiers who'd be in town for the season.

"Let's keep in touch after we settle in, shall we Renee?" implored Frieda, looking more than a trifle sad at the thought of never seeing her again.

"Of course, Mrs. Bigelow," Renee smiled warmly. "You've been a great comfort to me-these past few days."

Chester Bigelow patted her hand comfortingly, "You know you're more than welcome to stay with us."

He was genuinely fond of this young girl who had suffered such a loss just a short while before.

"Thank you, Major Bigelow. You're both so kind." She blinked back tears that flooded her eyes. "I think I shall be content with my aunt. We must visit though as often as possible."

"Of course, but are you just going to be content?" Frieda asked. "Surely, with time, you will learn to be happy there."

"Yes, I'm sorry, I didn't mean to sound so sad," she replied to Frieda's query, but in her heart Renee knew that the only happiness and security she'd ever known lay buried with her Papa at L'Aimant.

"Good evening, Major." A man's voice sounded from behind Renee causing her to jump in surprise.

"Captain Westlake! So glad you could join us on this final evening." The major rose, extending his hand to a tall, broad-shouldered, fair-haired man. "I don't believe you've met Mrs. Bigelow and our traveling companion, Miss Renee Fontaine. Ladies, this is our Captain—James Westlake."

The man nodded his greeting to Frieda and turned his attention to Renee. As his eyes met hers, a look of astonishment crossed his face and he was left speechless. The Major looked from the captain to Renee in consternation.

"Captain?"

"My apologies, Miss Fontaine—Major Bigelow," he finally said, his gaze still on Renee. "But Miss Fontaine bears a remarkable resemblance to someone I once knew. I hope I didn't put you ill at ease?"

Renee flushed deeply under his scrutiny, "No, Captain, but I do hope that was meant as a compliment!"

"Most assuredly, Miss Fontaine."

They all laughed as the tension dissipated and the captain joined their party. The conversation remained general, but Renee was very conscious of his dark eyes upon her, watching her every move.

"Miss Fontaine, is this your first visit to St. Louis?"

"Yes, Captain. In fact I've never been this far north before."

Jim Westlake grinned at her, "It's certainly easy to tell that you've never been to St. Louis before. There are more than a few upstanding citizens who'd be downright outraged at being considered 'northern.'"

"I'm sorry. I don't really know much about it at all," she ended quietly.

"Renee is coming north to her aunt's. Perhaps you know her aunt, Elise Fontaine?"

"Elise? Of course. She's a close friend of my mother's. They went to school together many years ago and still keep in touch." He turned his attention back to the slender, dark-haired beauty sitting next to Mrs. Bigelow. "Will you be staying long?"

"Yes. Permanently, sir. My father just passed away and I've no relations back home. Aunt Elise has graciously opened her home to me."

"I hope you'll be happy; Elise Fontaine is a wonderful woman." He rose a bit nervously. "Now, if you'll excuse me, I must attend to my duties. Major—ladies."

He made a courtly bow and then exited the grand salon in long, self-confident strides, nodding his greetings to the other passengers.

Once freed from the restraining atmosphere in the dining cabin, Jim let out a long troubled sigh and leaned heavily against an upright post. The resemblance was remarkable. He wondered why no one else had noticed it, especially with the full oil portrait at the end of the grand salon. More than likely their staterooms were at the opposite end of the ship. Jim rubbed his forehead, deep in thought. The hair was much darker and he was sure that she was much taller . . . maybe I'm imagining things, he decided. After all, it had been over five years ago. Frowning at nothing in particular, he made his way down the deserted gallery to the stairs and went up to the pilot house.

Chapter Two

A misty, icy drizzle fell from the dark threatening clouds that blanketed the riverfront as the Elizabeth Anne searched for docking space. The trim white packets were everywhere, arriving, departing, loading, unloading. It was a scene of complete chaos to the unaccustomed traveler but to the Westlake riverboat men it was home, a glorious sight. As far as one could see in either direction, the levee merchandise was piled high on the cobblestones awaiting shipment. Carriages were lined up, too, waiting patiently to pick up new arrivals.

Renee watched nervously from the promenade deck hoping that the miserable weather wasn't a forecast of her future life here. She shivered violently as a gust of wind blew the damp mist in her face and she pulled her light mantle more tightly around her. Louisiana weather had not prepared her for this kind of cold. If it stayed this bad—or Heaven forbid—got any colder she knew she'd need some warmer gowns and a better cloak. She saw Frieda Bigelow emerge from her cabin and Renee hurried to join her.

"Isn't this marvelous, Renee? It's so exciting!" exclaimed Frieda taking her hand. "Now don't you fret. Your aunt knows you're due at any time. The

Major's going to get us a carriage as soon as we're safely docked and we'll go straight to your Aunt Elise's home without delay. I'm sure she'll have a servant who can come down for your trunks later. This is no weather for us to be exposed to for any length of time!"

They descended the stairs to the main deck and made their way cautiously past the freight that was to be unloaded.

"Ladies," Captain Westlake came upon them as they waited timidly for the Major's return. "I'm sorry the weather has spoiled our arrival, but I do hope the rest of your trip was satisfactory."

"It was wonderful, sir. We've enjoyed it tremendously," Frieda assured him. "I do find river travel most enjoyable. Don't you agree, Renee?"

Renee murmured an agreeable answer as she tried to avoid the Captain's probing eyes. She was nervous enough worrying about her upcoming encounter with her aunt without wondering who he was comparing her to.

"Is the Major getting a carriage for you?"

"Yes, he left some minutes ago."

"I was wondering Miss Fontaine, if I might visit you after you've settled in?"

Renee was taken aback by his request and looking to Frieda for guidance, was relieved when Mrs. Bigelow took over the conversation.

"I'm sure that would be fine with Miss Fontaine's aunt, as you are a friend of the family, sir."

Jim grinned at the chaperone's reply, "Wonderful, I'll look forward to it."

"Oh! Here comes Chester now! Come on, Renee, we

must hurry. Thank you, Captain."

"Thank you, ladies, for gracing my ship with your lovely presence," he bowed to them quickly, smiling widely at their blushes.

Mrs. Bigelow and Renee started down the ramp in the sleetlike drizzle, the carriage had stopped some distance away due to the mountains of merchandise on the levee. They made their way cautiously over the slippery cobblestones. As they finally reached the conveyance and Frieda made to enter, a strong gust of wind blew Renee's bonnet off. Unthinking, she turned and chased after it. But twisting her ankle on the wet uneven ground, she fell heavily. The horse was upon her before she realized and she threw a protective arm up over her face. Suddenly, she was jerked, none too gently, to the side of the horse's path. The horse shied and reared at the commotion.

Renee was aware of Mrs. Bigelow's shrieks and the horses wheezing but she only heard the deep voice cutting through her dizziness.

"Are you all right?" the big man said gruffly, setting her to her feet before him. "You must be crazy to try a stunt like that today of all days!"

Renee gasped at the sudden shock of pain that ran up her leg from her injured ankle. The man put his arm back around her then, supporting her, and turned to the carriage some distance away, "It's okay, the lady only twisted her ankle."

Then as he helped her walk back to the carriage Renee put her hand to her head as she swayed more heavily against him, her head spinning.

"Are you sure you're all right?" he asked harshly as he caught her against him.

Renee looked up then, trying to focus on the man who stood above her. Her eyes were wide and dilated, her hair rain darkened and straggling wetly about her pale face. The man had pulled his slouch hat low over his forehead to protect himself from the rain. His black brows were drawn together and down, giving his face a harsh look. His mouth was set in a firm line and he had at least a full days growth of black beard, making him seem even more menacing. She started to speak to say that she must have hit her head, when she saw his eyes widen in shock. He let go of her abruptly and stepped back as if he could not bear to touch her. Luckily, Major Bigelow arrived at that time to support her.

"Who are you?" the man asked coldly—quietly.

Before she could answer, she was bombarded with questions from the Major.

"Are you hurt, my dear?" he asked as she leaned against him.

"I—I don't know," she said weakly.

"We must get you out of this rain. Mrs. Bigelow is quite frantic with worry. I made her wait in the carriage. If this gentleman—" the Major looked up but the tall dark stranger was gone, without a word.

The ride to Aunt Elise's seemed an eternity. Renee sat, teeth chattering, in her soaked coat and dress. Her clothes were covered with river mud and her ankle throbbed painfully. The Major wrapped her in his coat, but she was too chilled to notice.

"Where did the man go, Chester? We really must thank him," demanded Frieda.

"I don't know, he was gone when I looked up. Probably just one of those men who hire out for work

47

when the boats come in."

"I suppose, but it was a brave thing he did."

"Indeed," Chester looked at Renee sitting silently next to his wife.

Renee was biting her lip in an effort not to cry. Had she been of lesser constitution she would have fainted by now, the pain in her leg was so bad. But she willed herself not to think of it and sat half in a stupor listening to the voices that seemed so far away. All she could find to focus on was the memory of that hard impersonal voice demanding to know who she was.

When the carriage stopped in front of Aunt Elise's impressive home, Renee was carried inside and taken directly to a front bedroom. The doctor was sent for and Aunt Elise made sure that Renee was resting comfortably before she went downstairs to join the Bigelows for a cup of tea.

Elise sat on the edge of the chair, her back straight, her manner the picture of decorum. Although she had celebrated her forty-fifth birthday, she could still pass for thirty-five and she knew it. Her dark hair was pulled back into a bun at the nape of her neck and despite the severity of the style, on Elise it was very becoming. Her eyes were brown, her cheekbones high and her mouth was small but expressive. She stood a tiny five feet tall and was appropriately proportioned. She was in all respects a lovely sophisticated woman and Major Bigelow wondered idly why she'd never married.

"Major, may I offer you something other than tea? A bourbon, perhaps?"

"Miss Fontaine, that would be greatly appreciated. That was quite an ordeal we just went through."

48

"Please, tell me all," she said after directing Celia, her maid, to bring the Major a bourbon.

Frieda related the story, ending breathlessly with the mysterious disappearing stranger.

"And you have no idea where he went?" Elise asked with surprise.

"No, none. Chester got there right after he'd saved her and before he could thank him the man was gone. He pulled her right out from under the horse's hooves!"

"And you didn't get a chance to speak with him at all?"

"No, Miss Fontaine. I'm sure Renee did but she's so upset, she really hasn't said much."

"I can't thank you enough. Would you like to spend the night here and continue on to the barracks tomorrow?" she offered.

"Thank you, but we must get there tonight—orders you know."

"Well, let's please stay in touch. My niece would no doubt like to thank you in person, but I think it best if we let her rest now. We'll plan to have dinner soon."

"Wonderful. Tell Renee if there's anything we can do to just let us know."

"I shall. Thanks again," Elise said as they departed. Her carriage was taking them back to the levee so they could arrange transportation south of the city and then it was returning with Renee's trunks.

Turning to the stairs, she looked up nervously and wondered just how her young niece was doing. She had been a pitiful sight as the Major had carried her up the staircase. Elise had dispatched her personal maid to ensure Renee's comfort while she had bid the

Bigelows farewell. Now, the doctor was here and as soon as he finished his examination they would at last be able to visit. Elise smoothed her gown as she heard the doctor leave Renee's room and start down the hall to the stairs.

"Ah, Elise, you have a lovely niece," Dr. Montgomery stated as he descended the stairs to meet her in the foyer. "She'll be fine in a few days. She's got a bad sprain and she must have hit her head when she fell, but it's nothing serious."

"Oh, I'm so glad. That was quite an exciting arrival she had. May I go up to her now?"

"Of course. Just make sure that she stays in bed and gets a lot of rest for the next couple of days. I'll see myself out."

Elise mounted the stairway slowly with measured tread, anxious about her first encounter with Renee in over ten years. She knocked softly and entered the spacious bedroom.

Renee was settled on the bed covered by a huge down filled comforter. She looked quite childlike, her hair had been washed and plaited and pinned on top of her head. Her large round eyes followed her Aunt's movements into the room expectantly. Elise dismissed Celia and then turned to Renee.

"My dear," she smiled sitting in the chair next to the bed. "We are off to quite an exciting start, yes?"

"Yes, Aunt Elise," Renee replied meekly.

"According to the doctor a few days in bed will do wonders for you."

"Yes, Ma'am, I am still a little dizzy."

"Well, as long as you stay comfortably in bed for a while I'm sure that will pass," Elise took her hand and

50

kissed her cheek. "Rest now. We'll have much time these next few days for catching up."

She stood to leave and looking down at Renee again, she smiled, "You're most lovely. We'll talk tomorrow. Now you must sleep and rest. I'll check on you later."

"Yes, Aunt Elise," she answered snuggling down, grateful that there had been no questions, "And, oh, Aunt Elise?"

Elise turned from the door, "Yes?"

"Thank you."

"You're most welcome. Rest now," she said and quietly left the room.

Renee closed her eyes. It seemed a great weight had been lifted from her shoulders. She could be content here. She could be warm and safe and—her eyes opened. What was it he had said? It was getting muddled in her mind. He wanted to know who I was, she remembered. That was it. Well I certainly am glad I didn't tell him, he seemed most disreputable. Not quite the kind of man Papa would have approved of, or Aunt Elise. She fell asleep thinking of the penetrating deep voice and the strong arms that had pulled her to safety.

Chapter Three

Mounting the gangplank in long angry strides he looked about, his eyes narrowed.

"Where's the Captain?" he thundered to a roosta-boot unloading crates.

"Upstairs, suh, last I saw him."

He grunted in reply and took the steps two at a time. As he entered the main cabin he could hear voices at the far end and recognized one as Jim Westlake. He strode down the length of the boat, glancing only briefly at the portrait of the slender fair-haired girl and then slammed into the saloon.

"Give me a double, Ollie. Jim, how the hell are you?" Marshall relaxed into the chair across the table from his younger brother.

Ollie, the bartender and old family friend, quickly brought him his double whiskey.

"How are you, Marsh? You're looking a bit under the weather," the old man chuckled gesturing to Marshall's soaked clothing.

Marsh laughed and threw his drenched hat at Ollie, "I've been 'under the weather' all right! But this ought to help!" he downed half his drink and then sighed, leaning back, stretching his long legs before him.

"When did you get back?" Jim asked as he surveyed his brother.

"I came in on the K.C. Star early this morning. Packy met me and took the horse on out to the house. Father should be pleased with this one. Best piece of horse flesh I've seen in a long while.

"Does Father think you were on business?"

"Yeah, I told Packy to hide the stud in the north pasture but if the weather stays this bad we'll have to give it to him early. Maybe tonight, since you're here."

"Sounds good to me. I'll only be here until Friday, then we've got to head back downriver. I've contracted for a full load at Memphis, and it should be ready to go on Saturday."

Ollie stood behind the bar, putting things in order before he left. Leave it to these two to find the perfect present for their father's sixtieth birthday. He smiled to himself. He had worked for the Westlakes for thirty years now and knew the family quite well. He always marvelled at how two boys raised the same had turned out so different.

They had both learned the river trade young and had worked with their father to help build the business that now was so successful, but only Jim had the river in his blood. Marsh had gone to the books and successfully completed his law studies. He'd been practicing for over five years, and was well established in town. Jim had stayed with the boats, learning everything he could from everyone he could until his father gave him the *Elizabeth Anne* to captain four years ago. Jim was a ladies' man, too, leaving hearts throbbing all up and down the ole Miss, but that older boy had always been serious-minded. He had married and settled down once a few years ago, in fact his wife had been this boat's namesake. Too bad she had died so soon, they hadn't been married all that long. Ollie finally finished up his duties and came around the bar to the two younger men.

"I'll be goin' now, Jimmy."

"Fine, Ollie. Listen why don't you come out to the house for the birthday party? I'm sure Father would be glad to see you."

"Great idea, Jim," Marsh agreed.

"Sure. What time?"

"Let's make it tonight about 6:30. I don't want that horse outside all night."

So Ollie left the steamer for a day on the town, renewing old acquaintances.

Marshall helped himself to another bourbon and settled back in the chair, elbows on the table. Jim eyed him cautiously; it was quite out of character for his brother to drink this heavily so early in the day.

"What's troubling you? It's a little early for such heavy drinking."

"I don't really know. I've been up all night . . ." he paused, resting his head in his hands wearily. "There was almost a bad accident on the levee."

"What happened?" Jim straightened, more attentive. "Anybody hurt?"

"No, thank God. I happened to be in the right place at the right time," he paused again, taking a long drink. "Young girl—slipped and fell—almost got run down too. I grabbed her just in time."

"Then you're the hero of the day!" Jim grinned, his concern diminishing.

"That's not all," Marshall choked out. "Unless I'm totally drunk . . . I could have sworn . . ." he shook his head slowly.

Before he could finish, Jim did for him. "She looked a lot like Elizabeth, right?"

Marsh looked up, startled, "How did you know?"

"She came upriver with me. I met her on board . . . she was all right? Are you sure?"

"Yes. She seemed all right. Who is she?" Marshall could say no more. The whiskey was taking effect and he didn't want to start thinking—not about Elizabeth, not now. He'd finally put it all behind him, or so he'd thought. But the sight of that face had cut through him like a knife.

"She's Elise Fontaine's niece. Her father just died and she's come north to live with Elise." When Marshall didn't speak, Jim went on. "I should be done here in another hour or so. Why don't you wait and we'll ride home together?"

"Sure, can I help?"

"Not with anything I know of. Andrews is supervising the unloading; we won't load again until Friday morning. I just want to check the accounts before I leave." Jim rose. "Take it easy on the liquor. I'll be back in a little while."

As Jim left the room, Marsh leaned back in his chair, his mind wandering. He was glad to be home; the trip to pick up the horse had taken longer than he expected. He pondered the oddity of fate that he was in that certain place today to save the girl. He hoped she wasn't hurt too badly. He knew he should have stayed to help but he couldn't. He liked to be in control of himself at all times and the shock of seeing her had unnerved him. He was better now, calmer. He decided to look the boat over. It was a third his, as he'd invested equally with his Father and Jim. He got his hat from the bar, soggy though it was, and went out into the grand salon. She was a beauty, this steamer. The skylights in the main cabin were of colored glass and on a brighter day, rainbow colors would be shining off the high gloss white walls and the crystal and gold chandeliers. The mirror at the stern reflected the entire cabin and Marshall, standing alone at the opposite end, noticed his reflection. Ollie had been right, he did look disgraceful, hardly a prosperous attorney—more like a riverfront rowdy. His dark blue shirt was wet and plastered to him like a second skin, as were his dark snug fitting pants. His black hair was still damp and curling slightly now as it slowly dried. Even the beard surprised him, he'd just shaved yesterday morning and he didn't realize how unkempt he looked with a full day's growth. He understood now the girl's expression of fear when she'd looked up at him.

Turning to make his way amid the tables he faced inadvertently the portrait of Elizabeth. It had been painted shortly after their wedding five years ago. She looked lovely in it, her blonde hair had been pulled away from her face and fell to her shoulders in ringlets. She wore a low cut, full skirted evening gown of light blue satin that matched her eyes and around her neck was the diamond solitaire necklace he'd given her as a wedding present. Marshall rubbed a hand wearily over his eyes and continued outside to find his brother. He felt sure the ride home would help clear his mind of things he definitely didn't want to remember.

Chapter Four

George Westlake sat before the massive stone fireplace, a contented man. The evening had just ended and it had been wonderful. He smiled as he remembered the beautiful stallion the boys had presented to him. Martha, Dorrie, Jim and Ollie had long since retired and now he relaxed savoring these moments of peace. He studied his oldest son while Marsh refilled their glasses from the crystal decanter. Of his three children, Marshall was the most like himself and he was suitably proud of him. A few hours earlier though, he would have been hard put to claim either of his sons. They both had been mud spattered and drenched when they arrived at Cedarhill.

"So your business trip was not all business?"

"No," Marsh chuckled. "But I needed some rest and the trip was most enjoyable."

"I've been telling you to slow down, or better yet, why don't you take on a partner?" George asked. "Junior, of course!"

"I'll give it some serious thought. It certainly would give me more free time . . ." he let the sentence die, wondering if he really wanted any free time.

"I know Juliana would certainly enjoy seeing more of you," George kept his face carefully blank as

Marshall glanced at him quickly. "Did you let her know you were back?"

"No," he answered flatly, a vision of Juliana filling his mind. The night before he left she had pouted because he was going and when her little girl act had failed, she had screeched at him like a fishwife. She was a lovely woman, but he'd told her in the beginning that he would not marry and he meant it. Still, she continued her calculated pursuit. She'd become so demanding that Marshall had welcomed the two week sojourn to buy the horse. He had taken the time alone to sort out his feelings. Juliana was quite beautiful and the belle of St. Louis society . . . at least until today. Until he had stared down into those round eyes, so wide with terror and complete helplessness. All thoughts of Juliana had been banished. In his mind, now, was a girl with child-like innocence, wide eyed and pale. A girl who looked so much like Elizabeth that it had stunned him—and yet there had been a difference. He had realized it later on the ride to the house . . . Elizabeth had never been defenseless.

"What's on your mind?"

Marshall looked up and realized that he'd been staring into the fire.

"You thinking about Elizabeth?"

"Am I that easy to read?" he asked annoyed.

"Not to anyone else. Jim told me about the girl on the levee. Who was she?"

"Jim says she's Elise Fontaine's niece," Marshall stopped and took a drink. "It really shook me up, seeing her. . . . She's very young. The resemblance was uncanny but her hair is much darker."

"I wonder if Elise will notice?"

"Probably not. She only met Elizabeth once or twice socially.

"You're right. Don't you think you should send an inquiry as to her state of health?"

"I thought about it," he laughed softly. "I even picked up the bonnet she'd been chasing when she fell. It's ruined, but I thought she might want it back."

"There's your opportunity," George stopped, remembering his latest encounter with Juliana. "But I don't think Juliana will like the idea."

"It's really none of her business," he said coldly.

"Just thought it was worth mentioning. She can be quite captivating. Why just last week at the Clayton's party she almost convinced me that you would be married by Christmas!" George's eyes twinkled as he saw how Marshall reacted.

"I'm afraid Juliana's in for a disappointment," he said blandly. "I told her at the outset how I felt about marrying again."

"And how do you feel?"

"I don't want to."

George was stunned, but didn't show it.

"If that is your final decision, you had better tell Juliana before she buys a wedding gown." George laughed.

"You're right. That's one of the reasons why I took the trip. I had to decide what I really wanted to do."

It was hours later—almost dawn before father and son retired. George now understood for the first time Marsh's reluctance to become deeply involved with another woman. Elizabeth had left her mark on him and it was not one of love and trust. George regretted bitterly that the spoiled woman his son had married five years ago could have been so cruel and selfish. But Marsh did not have his objective opinion of the events that took place. Even five years later, he truly believed that he had been responsible. That guilt, although deeply concealed, had been aired for the first time this night. Marshall had told his father everything, holding nothing back. George had tried to convince him that what she'd done was sick and not something a normal, loving woman would do. But Marshall had blamed himself for so long that no rational reasoning from his father would help. George sensed this and knew that he must do everything in his power to free his son from his personal, self-imposed hell.

Chapter Five

The late morning sun was so bright that it filtered through the heavy green velvet drapes in Renee's bedroom filling the room with green shadows. She was awake but lying quietly, remembering the excitement of yesterday. Sighing, she stretched and almost cried out as she felt once more the pain of the ankle. Struggling upright she decided that at least her head felt much better and the effects of the chill were gone. Carefully sliding to the edge of the four-poster bed, she managed to stand on her good leg and hopped over to the window, throwing open the drapes.

She wasn't sure what she expected to find—another day like yesterday, she supposed. Renee was pleasantly surprised, for outside the sun was shining and the trees were various shades of yellow and bright orange. As she watched the traffic below, a carriage stopped in front. A man got out carrying a beautifully wrapped package and came straight to Elise's door. After delivering it, he drove swiftly away and she wondered idly what was in the present.

Only a few moments passed before she heard a soft knock at the door and Aunt Elise came swishing in. If possible, she seemed even more petite in her full-skirted day dresses. Renee was still standing by the window precariously balancing on her good foot.

"Good morning, Aunt Elise."

"What ever are you doing up?" she went to Renee immediately and helped her back to bed supporting most of her weight. "I am to assume you are much better this morning?" Elise asked carefully tucking her back into bed.

"Yes, much!" Renee answered enthusiastically. "Except for my ankle."

"Ah, the wonderful recuperative powers of youth!" Elise sighed. "Do you have another gown or bed jacket you would like to wear?"

"Yes. It's there in the second drawer, Celia put it away last night."

Elise found a pretty pale peach bed jacket and helped Renee into it.

"That's a lovely color for you. You'll look even better in it once you get some color back in your cheeks. Oh, by the way, a package came for you just a minute ago."

Elise went back out and came in with the same parcel Renee had seen delivered earlier.

"Yes, it says here on the note that came with it—Renee Fontaine c/o Elise Fontaine. I'm sure it's private."

"Oh," Renee paused breathlessly. "You mean it's not from you? Then it must be from the Bigelows."

With the impatience of an eager child, she ripped off the wrapping. Pulling off the lid, she found her crumpled, mud-stained hat. Her eyes opened in astonishment. Renee wasn't sure if she wanted to laugh or cry. Tears came to her eyes regardless and she searched on the bed for the envelope. Opening it she found a short note within:

Miss Fontaine,

My sincere apologies for my abrupt departure yesterday. I hope this note finds you in good health. I did find your hat and thought you might wish to have it back.

Sincerely,
Marshall Westlake

Renee's mouth formed an "Oh" and she looked up at her aunt wonderingly.

"What is it, dear?"

"This note, it's signed by someone named Marshall Westlake. Do you know him?" Renee asked, handing the message to Elise to read.

"So, he's your mystery man!" Elise laughed after reading the note.

"Who is he?' she asked. "The captain's name on the boat was Westlake, too. Are they related?"

"Yes, Renee. Marshall and the captain, his name is Jim, are both sons of my friend, Martha. Marshall's the oldest, he's got a law practice right here in town."

"But he looked so—so disreputable!" she shivered remembering the hardness of him and the smell of whiskey and horses. "Oh . . . you should have seen him!"

"Well, knowing Marsh, there must have been a good reason. Perhaps later when you're feeling better you can write a short thank you note to let him know you are well."

"Yes, of course. If you think it's proper."

"I think it would be most appropriate."

They smiled together then, pleased to know at last who the mystery man was. Later, in the afternoon Elise brought her pen and paper and Renee composed a short response to Marshall Westlake's note.

"Is he really a lawyer?"

"Yes, one of the best. His mother and I are very good friends. Perhaps you'll meet her soon. Martha's daughter is just about your age. We'll send the note to his office, though; I understand he spends most of his time there."

"Where does his family live?"

"They have a big estate north of town. It's quite a drive, about two hours. That's why Marshall has his office and rooms here."

Elise sent the note off promptly the next morning. With Celia's help Renee negotiated the stairs for the first time Friday morning and had just settled in the parlor when she heard someone at the door. Celia went to answer it and Renee could only hear part of the conversation.

"One moment, sir. I'll get Miss Elise for you."

After summoning Elise, Celia came into the parlor, smiling widely.

"Who is it?" Renee whispered conspiratorily.

"I think he's here to see you. It's a good thing you're able to get out of bed today," Celia disappeared into the back hall and Renee was alone listening to her aunt greet the unknown man in the foyer.

"Why, Jim, how pleasant!" Elise's voice was sincere as she greeted him. "Come in and sit down. Renee told me that she came up on the *Elizabeth Anne*. Did you hear about her accident?"

"Marshall told me. That's why I thought I'd come

by and make sure everything was all right."

"Well, as you can see, she's up and moving, albeit a little painfully." Elise smiled as she led Jim Westlake into the parlor.

His gaze warmed as he saw her seated on the settee. "It's nice to see you again, Miss Fontaine."

"You too, Captain."

"I think the formalities may be dispensed with, Jim. This is Renee, and Renee, this is Jim. My best friend's wayward son."

"You're looking well, Renee."

"Thank you. It's kind of you to stop by."

"Nonsense. I visit beautiful women every chance I get, ask Elise." He grinned, sitting down across from her in an overstuffed chair.

Elise laughed easily with Jim, and Renee was relieved to know that he was a friend of the family.

"Would you care for a drink, perhaps a cup of coffee? It's a little early for anything stronger, don't you think?"

"You're right about that. I've got a lot to do today. I'm leaving for Memphis this afternoon, so I thought I'd just take a few minutes to visit."

"How was your father's birthday? Martha told me that you had something special planned but she didn't know what."

"It was great. Marshall and I bought a stud for him and I think he was surprised. It was quite a celebration."

"Well, I'm glad you finally surprised him with something. He's the hardest man to catch unawares. Just like his sons . . ." She laughed. "Coffee all right with you? Renee?"

"Fine," Jim agreed.

"Yes, please."

As Elise left the room to get the coffee, Jim turned his attention to Renee.

"I'm glad that my brother was there to keep you from serious injury."

"It was frightening," she replied meeting his gaze. "One moment I had perfect footing and the next I was falling with no way to catch myself. It's a good thing that he was there. Did you know that he sent me my hat? That's what I was chasing after when I fell."

"He did mention it," Jim smiled.

"It's quite beyond repair, but at least when I look at it now, I'll remember to be more careful on cobblestones!"

"Good. You're far too lovely for such mishaps."

Renee blushed and Jim's gaze swept over her, taking in everything, her paleness, the dark hollows beneath her eyes, but even in this state she attracted him. The loose fitting black dress she wore was definitely unbecoming, but as a man of the world he could look beyond that to the time when she would be free of such restraining social customs and could enjoy her youth. He determined then and there that he was going to be the man who would introduce her to St. Louis society whenever her period of mourning was over.

"Do you always travel with the boat?" Renee asked noting his serious expression and not guessing the thoughts behind it.

"I'm the captain and part owner, so it is my responsibility. My pilots have the hard job, though; I just make sure everything goes all right," he grinned, minimizing his importance.

"Have you been a captain for very long?"

"For over four years. I've never had the desire to do anything else. Why?"

"For some reason, when I think of the captain of a ship, I feature a burly old man, with whiskers and a pipe," she laughed.

"Aging me, are you? Well, I have to admit I was one of the youngest captains on the river. I may be only twenty-six, but I've earned my job. It wasn't given to me lightly. I knew when I was still in short pants that I wanted to be on the river."

"Here we are," Elise said as she and Celia came in carrying trays laden with silver coffee service and croissants. "Have you been having a nice visit?"

"I was just telling Renee about my struggle to the top in the shipping world."

"I trust you didn't bore her, Jim," Elise teased.

"Actually, Aunt Elise, I find it fascinating. I used to watch the boats going by at home and wonder about all the exciting places they'd been."

"It is exciting, but it has its drawbacks too. Not much is ever said about how unattractive it can be if the steamer you're on is carrying a large load of livestock. Sometimes the smell . . ." he paused, his expression telling all, as Elise handed him his cup of coffee.

"I can just imagine, I suppose we were lucky this trip," Renee laughed.

"It was a peaceful, uneventful voyage, except for your misfortune. No snags, no fires, and a full cargo, it was quite profitable, actually."

"I'll bet George is happy about that," Elise said

filling her own cup after serving Renee and sitting next to her.

"Absolutely, with the four boats we've got running now, Father's made his mark in the world and can retire quietly to the country. Marshall handles all of the problems that come up while I'm gone and the rest of them I take care of when I get back. Of course, the *Elizabeth Anne* is our biggest and our best. She's lasted over four years now and is still the finest lady on the Mississippi."

"She is elegant. I was quite impressed with your boat."

"Thank you. Perhaps you'll travel on her again one day. I know it will be a pleasure to have you aboard," he smiled directly at her and she glanced away, breaking the contact. "Well, ladies, I'm afraid that I must go, if I'm to keep my schedule. Thank you, Elise, for your hospitality."

Elise rose with Jim but he turned to Renee before leaving the room.

"I trust you'll be well while I'm away and I may take the liberty of calling on you again?" he addressed them both but his eyes were only for Renee.

"That would be lovely, Jim," Elise encouraged. "We'll look forward to it."

"Yes, that would be nice," Renee agreed, trying not to sound too eager.

"Fine. Perhaps we can take in an exposition in town?"

"Do you feel that would be suitable?" Renee deferred to Elise.

"As long as we go in the afternoon, it will be quite proper. We'll look forward to your visit, Jim. Thank you."

She showed Jim to the door and bade him a cheerful farewell, before returning to Renee, who was still confined to her seat.

"What an attractive young man, don't you think?"

"Yes, he is. And you know him so well, do you get to visit with his family often?"

"It's awkward with Martha living way out in the country, but every time she comes to town we have luncheon and I go out to their house for an extended visit every year. We're quite close. We went to the academy together in New Orleans when we were girls and have kept in touch ever since."

"How wonderful. I don't have any close friends. We were so isolated at L'Aimant it was impossible and Father insisted that I study with a tutor."

"I'm sure though that your relationship with him was special."

"Yes, it was. We were very close," Renee tried to shrug off the sense of loss that haunted her constantly now.

Elise, sensing her sadness, gathered Renee into her arms and held her while she cried, "I'm so sorry, little one. If only I could make your unhappiness go away."

"Thank you," Renee said in a muffled voice against her aunt's shoulder. "Just having you near is a great help. I'm not usually so weak. It just comes over me sometimes and I have to let it out. I really held up well for a long time until it dawned on me that he was really gone."

Elise patted her comfortingly as Renee gained her composure.

"There, I'm all better now," Renee said trying to smile.

"I know. It will take a while, but the pain will ease eventually. Until then, just remember that I'm here, and if you need anything you have only to ask."

With that quiet understanding, they sat in companionable silence for a while, enjoying the founding of a deep and lasting relationship.

Chapter Six

It was two days later before Marsh returned to town and set about going through his mail. He had just started his correspondence when the office door opened wide and Juliana Chandler swept in, scowling at him.

"You're back, at last," she stated, perching on the edge of his desk. "I'm glad I had father bring me downtown today. I wouldn't have known if I hadn't seen your horse out front."

"I got back Wednesday, early."

"And you didn't come to see me?" she asked pouting.

"I had business to attend to. I was sure you'd be occupied."

Juliana rose and went to stand behind his chair. She leaned over him and kissed his neck. He was surrounded by a cloud of her perfume, it was a heavy cloying scent. He picked up an envelope to open as she moved behind him and now Marshall looked down and noticed the handwriting. So did Juliana.

"Love letters? From someone besides me?" Juliana snatched the note from his hand before he could move.

"Juliana, I want that letter."

She moved away ripping the envelope and reading the enclosed short message.

"Not important," she said handing it back, ignoring the black look he gave her.

Marshall didn't read the note, he merely folded it and put it in his vest pocket, then looked up at her.

"So, at last I have your attention," she giggled.

"Yes, Julie, you have it," he replied, bored.

"No, 'I missed you' kiss?" she moved to him and pulled him up to her. "I missed you."

Juliana pressed against him and pulled his head down to her, kissing him long and passionately. She felt no response in him and drew back a little perplexed.

"What's wrong?" her voice was soft and concerned.

"Nothing," he replied, removing her arms from him. "It's afternoon and we're standing in the middle of my office."

"Oh," she blushed, realizing the truth in his words. "I'm sorry. I'll expect you for dinner tonight."

"Fine. I should be done here about six."

"Good," she walked slowly to the door. "See you then."

Marshall sat back down after she'd disappeared out the door. He stared blankly after her for a moment. She was a gorgeous woman and he'd always been partial to blondes. He'd see her tonight and let her know that his feelings hadn't changed. He enjoyed her but he was not about to marry again. His decision made, he turned back to his desk and pulled out the note. It was short and sweet, thanking him for his help and thoughtfulness and hoping to thank him in person some day. He grimaced and turned to throw it into the fire in the stove behind him. Sweet, he thought as he watched it burn. They all seemed sweet, at first. He knew that meeting her was inevitable, but he had no desire to rush it. He was satisfied with the way his life was going now. His practice was successful and he could find relief and forgetfulness with Juliana. Although he would have to convince her that there was no future for them. No, Renee Fontaine had no place in his life, he was sure of that.

Marshall arrived on time at the Chandler home. The maid showed him in and directed him, not to the dining room, but upstairs to Juliana's bedroom suite. She greeted him with a kiss and then turned modeling the floor length, sheer negligee for him.

"Do you like it? I bought it this afternoon with tonight in mind," she walked into his arms and hugged him. "Father left for Jefferson City on business. We won't be interrrupted."

Marshall bent to kiss her but she moved away to the small candlelit table.

"I thought you might be hungry."

"I am'" he said eyeing her. He could see the outline of her firm lush body through the nightdress. Her large, full breasts pressed eagerly against the soft material, the peaks hard from the contact. Juliana had been blessed with a marvelous figure and she knew it. She always enjoyed Marsh's reaction to her. She could tell he wanted her and she smiled knowingly.

"Let's have dinner. You can tell me all about your trip later."

It was much later when they finally had time to

talk. Julie lay in his arms, satiated.

"You're different," she remarked.

"Oh?"

"What happened while you were gone?" she asked as she rolled on top of him and kissed him lightly.

"Why?"

"You're so—not exactly indifferent, but unconcerned."

"Juliana, I think you're imagining things."

"No, I'm not. If we are going to be married you'd . . ." she didn't have a chance to finish.

"What!" he roared. "Married!?"

He threw her off of him easily and got up. "I told you long ago there'd be no marriage. Did I ever encourage you to think I'd changed my mind?"

"Why—I—uh—" Juliana sat on the bed, her mouth open. "I thought since we—" she gestered lamely toward the bed.

"My dear, the fact that we've made love does not mean we're betrothed."

"But—I was a virgin!" she insisted.

"Virgin?" he snorted in derision. "I'm not stupid, Juliana."

She was silenced by his tone, for of course he was right. She had hoped he wouldn't care.

"Do you have anything else to say?" he asked.

"But what about us?"

"Us?" he walked to the chair and began to pull on his clothes. There is no us."

"What?"

"You're trying to pin me down. You're trying to tie me to you with sex and it won't work," he answered. "If there is going to be an 'us' then it's going to be on

74

my terms. Not yours."

"What do you want from me?"

"Nothing. And I want you to feel the same way. Don't demand things of me that I can't give."

"But I love you."

He looked at her briefly as he buttoned his shirt. Her body was pale in the candlelight and her soft blonde hair fell in waves to her shoulders. She was beautiful but he knew her thoughts. The discovery of her conniving ways and possessiveness had made it easy for him to push her from his mind.

"What are 'your terms'?" Juliana asked nervously.

"You just heard them. I'll see you when I want to and not before. I don't love you, Juliana. We enjoy each other. Let's leave it at that."

She was silent, eyes downcast.

"Good night," he said softly and closed the door on his way out.

Chapter Seven

Weeks passed in a slow comfortable way. Indian summer departed rapidly and Thanksgiving was spent quietly at Elise's. Soon it was a very cold December. Renee's ankle had healed and she soon was accompanying her aunt on shopping sprees to Veranda Row and other small shops in town. Elise insisted on purchasing Renee a complete new wardrobe for Christmas. Not only did they order her practical mourning dresses but also new spring gowns. Elise had already decided that she would present Renee to society in March . . . six months was long enough for a young girl to mourn and it would be wonderful to see her in something besides black. It was on one of these shopping excursions that they ran into Marshall. They were entering Saundlein's Emporium when they met him on his way out.

"Marsh! It's so nice to see you."

"Hello, Elise. How are you?" His voice was as deep as Renee remembered.

She looked up at him as he turned his attention to her. All of her imaginings had not prepared her for the striking figure he made. His height, black hair and dark eyes she remembered, but without the beard and old hat he seemed entirely different. She'd never envisioned him quite as handsome as he really was. Marshall was dressed impeccably this time in navy trousers, highly polished boots and a navy greatcoat.

"Marsh, this is my niece, Renee. Renee this is note-writing Marshall Westlake."

"How do you do?" Renee said extending her hand.

He took it and met her eyes for the first time since he'd saved her over a month before.

"It's my pleasure, Miss Fontaine."

"Renee, please," she insisted. "I'm so happy to finally meet you and to thank you again for everything."

"You're more than welcome," he smiled but his eyes were somehow cold.

"Marsh, I've been meaning to invite you to dinner and this is the perfect opportunity. When can you come? Tonight?" Elise asked.

"Tonight would be fine, Elise," he replied.

"Good. We'll have more opportunity to visit then. Is seven o'clock convenient?"

"Yes. I'll see you ladies tonight then. Elise, Renee," he tipped his hat and left the store.

Damn! It had taken every ounce of self control he had to keep from gawking at her. He didn't know how it was possible for two women, who were not related, to look so much alike. Renee was much taller and their coloring was different, but their faces. . . . He hoped he could make it through dinner this evening. Angrily, he cursed himself for not thinking of an excuse fast enough. He certainly didn't want to foster a relationship with Renee Fontaine.

At twenty minutes of seven Renee entered Elise's room to wait as she completed her toilette.

"Are you excited?" Elise asked innocently.

Renee, who was standing at the window, turned to Elise, "No, not really. It will be nice to get to know him, though. I think he's most attractive."

"That he is, and one of the most sought-after bachelors in town. Of course, there are a few others. You'll meet them later."

"Oh?"

"After your period of mourning ends, you'll enter society as you should," Elise declared as she rose from her chair at her dressing table. Her gown was of deep red satin with a square cut bodice and bell sleeves. She had braided her hair and wound it artfully about the top of her head.

"Elise, you look lovely."

"Thank you. You do too . . ."

"I know that I don't look attractive but . . ."

"Renee, darling, don't say such things. You're beautiful."

Renee blushed at her aunt's compliment.

"Come now, we must be downstairs to greet Marshall. We wouldn't want him to be uncomfortable," Elise said ushering Renee out into the hall.

Marsh arrived promptly at seven and dinner was served right away.

"How's your mother? Have you been to Cedarhill lately?" Elise asked as they finished dessert.

"She's fine," Marshall answered. "I was out last week for Thanksgiving. Jim and Ollie made it in."

"Well, it's nice that you could all be together for the holiday," Renee added.

"Yes, it was," he directed to Renee. "Usually Jim

doesn't get to stay in town that long. In fact it's very seldom that we're all together anymore. The last time before Thanksgiving was the night you arrived."

"It must feel wonderful to be surrounded by family," Renee observed quietly.

Marshall glanced at her sharply. He had noticed the wistfulness in her tone and immediately felt ashamed for having brought up family relationships.

"We're family, my dear," Elise said patting her hand tenderly.

"I know," Renee smiled. "But I still miss Papa very much, especially with Christmas coming."

"Yes, the holidays are difficult when you've recently lost someone," Marsh agreed.

"Let's change the topic," Elise said cheerfully. "Martha has invited us out for a visit in January."

"I'm sure Dorrie will enjoy that."

"I'm looking forward to meeting your sister. Elise tells me we'll have a lot in common."

"Oh?"

"She said Dorrie rides all the time and her debut is coming up."

"Yes, that's an accurate description of my little sister. She's quite an equestrienne. And as far as her ball goes, that's the only topic of conversation allowed in her presence, lately," Marshall laughed.

"I remember how excited I was last spring," Renee concurred.

"So you've made your debut already?" Marsh inquired.

"Last June. It was wonderful."

"Then maybe you can help Mother and Dorrie with their plans."

"That's a wonderful idea," Elise agreed. "We'll discuss it during our visit."

"Elise, I hate to end a lovely evening, but I must."

"We understand, of course. We're just very glad you could come."

"Yes, It's quite nice to know I was rescued by a successful attorney and not a waterfront hand!"

"I have to admit, I was not at my best that day. I'd just gotten back from a horse buying trip."

"Well that certainly explains Renee's description of her mysterious hero," Elise said teasingly.

They all laughed together.

"Thanks for the evening," he said as he kissed Elise on the cheek and then bent over Renee's hand. "Renee, good night."

"Good night, Marshall," they called as he made his way down the front stairs to his waiting horse. Then, they watched from the door until he had ridden out of sight.

It was a cold blustery mid-December day when Jim stopped by in hopes of catching them both at home.

"Thanks, Celia, it's freezing out there," he said jovially as he hurried into the main hall. "Are they home?"

They are, right here in the front parlor by the fireplace."

"That's the wisest place to be on a day like this!" he replied as he shed his coat and hat and made his way into the room.

"Jim, how nice of you to stop by," Elise greeted him, rising to take his hand.

"Ladies, I'm just sorry that it's been so long but business has been booming. There hadn't been a quiet moment, except for Thanksgiving, since I saw you last. I trust your holiday was enjoyable?"

"We spent a quiet day together. Quite pleasant. It's wonderful news that you're doing so well."

"Yes, I've no complaints at all. Could I. . . ?"

"Don't even bother to finish. I'll pour you a scotch right away. It'll help warm you, I think," Elise smiled as Jim sat near the roaring fire.

"I definitely need that, although the fire and the company of two such lovely ladies warms my heart indeed."

"It wasn't your heart that I thought needed warming," Elise laughed at him and he smiled at Renee's blush.

"How have you been, Renee?" he asked solicitously. "Are you up and about comfortably now?"

"I'm fine. Elise has been showing me the sights and we've done some shopping in town."

"Well, I hope you two haven't taken in the Exposition at the St. Louis Museum? I saw their ad in the paper and thought it would be just the place for us to go. That is if you're available tomorrow?"

"That sounds wonderful! I saw their advertisement too. They certainly have a variety of displays," Renee agreed.

Elise watched happily at Renee's ease of conversation with Jim, glad that she had found a friend.

"I think that would be lovely. What time do you suggest?" Elise asked Jim as she handed him his drink.

"I'll pick you up about three if that's convenient?"

he said taking the offered drink.

"Fine. We'll be ready. What did the paper say was on display?" Elise questioned. "I'm afraid I missed the article."

"Reptiles, birds, quadrupeds and best—a real mummy!" Renee related.

Jim was more than pleased with her enthusiasm. These small glimpses of what she would be when her mourning period was over gave him heart toward his objective. Though he had found Elizabeth beautiful all those years ago, Renee was just as attractive in a more realistic way. He thought idly that Elizabeth wouldn't haunt him so if he didn't see her likeness every day on board the boat. The portrait more than did her justice. She looked positively angelic and he knew that she had been anything but.

"Great, then it's settled," he rose, putting down his empty glass.

"Must you leave so soon?" Elise asked. "Won't you stay for dinner?"

"Thank you for the kind offer, but no, not tonight. I just got in town this morning and there is much paper work to do. I would love to tomorrow, though if the offer is open?"

"That will be just wonderful. I'll tell Celia to plan for dinner for about six in the evening. That will give us plenty of time to view the exposition and get back here to eat."

"Fine. I'll see you both tomorrow then," he bade them good night and showed himself out.

Renee snuggled beneath the laprug, trying to find some warmth in the brougham that Jim had hired for the afternoon. Although the sun was shining brightly, the temperature was frigid and comfort was hard to find out of doors. Wrapped securely in her new furlined cape and her hands stuffed into her fur muff, she waited shivering for Elise to join her. Finally, when all were settled, they moved off at a brisk pace for their outing. Beneath lowered lashes, she observed Jim who was intent on his conversation with Elise. His light brown hair was hidden beneath a stylish beaver hat and his greatcoat surrounded him warmly. He sat at ease in the cold carriage, seemingly indifferent to the freezing temperatures.

"Aren't you cold?" Renee asked, as there was a lull in the conversation.

He quirked an eyebrow at her grinning, "Actually, no. I love it. I've always been a cold weather person."

"I don't think Renee is enjoying her first St. Louis winter," Elise teased.

"It is a bit chillier than at home, I'll have to admit," she laughed.

"I can attest to that," Jim added. "Sometimes there is quite a temperature difference when we start downriver this time of year. What's cold in Louisiana is considered mild here."

"I can believe that!"

"It took me a while to adjust, but I enjoy the different seasons here. Spring seems so much more appreciated after you've been seeing snow for months on end," Elise said tucking the laprug more tightly around her.

"I know I'll appreciate it this year," Renee smiled.

"You've got quite a way to go," Jim said. "February is a real killer in these parts."

"Worse than this?"

"I'm afraid so," Elise sympathized.

Renee muffled her exaggerated groan into her muff as she warmed her face.

Jim watched her with amusement. She looked so young today, her cheeks were pink from the cold and her eyes sparkled with the excitement of the day.

Shortly, they stopped at the museum, just opposite the Court House downtown. The St. Louis Museum was already bustling with people. Offering Elise and Renee each an arm, he escorted them inside. After shedding their coats, they moved off to see the various displays. Occasionally, Renee would move ahead to examine an exhibit in more detail and Jim would watch her with warm eyes. Even in the dreaded black dresses, he was amazed at the attractive picture she made. He tried to visualize what she would look like in a low cut flowing gown with her cheeks flushed from dancing with him. . . . Elise brought his attention back to the present with a strategically asked question and he turned his gaze away from Renee's trim figure.

Renee was enjoying her first outing in male company since her father's death. She had always been comfortable with men, having spent most of her life in only her father's company. She was accustomed to male oriented conversations and was at home in any discussion, be it politics or business. Glancing back at Jim and Elise she found them deep in conversation and took another opportunity to appraise him objectively. His bottle green jacket fit him superbly across the wide breadth of his shoulders and tight tailored trousers of the same cloth clung to his long muscular legs. His waistcoat was of pale green silk, embroidered in dark green and his white cravat was carefully tied. Her mind wandered briefly, comparing him to his elusive brother. Somehow, having spent only slightly more time in Jim's company she felt as if she had known him all of her life. Marshall, however, was a whole other story. He was hard to get to know and his demeanor was one of aloof indifference. No wonder the women wanted him, she thought amusedly. They were handsome men, but each in a different way. Classically, Renee felt Marshall was the better looking of the two. His features were more chiseled, they might even be considered harsh by some, but she knew that a smile from him would light up an entire room. Jim, on the other hand, was rarely without a smile. He was fairer than his brother, but with the same Westlake eyes, piercing and knowing. Above average in height, they were both in superb physical condition, wide shouldered and narrow hipped. As Renee watched his movements, he glanced up and caught her staring at him. He grinned at her and winked outrageously and she blushed, hoping that no one else had seen his ploy. Smiling back at him, she moved to join them as they continued their tour.

"So Marshall came by for dinner already?" Jim asked sipping his after-dinner brandy, a few hours later.

"Yes, we met him at Saundlein's and he accepted my invitation for that evening," Elise explained as they sat comfortably snug by the fire in the front parlor. "He mentioned that you were seldom in town for any length of time."

"I'm afraid I asked for it when I made the choice for a life on the river. It's a never-ending trip from here to New Orleans and back. It's rare when I can take the time to get out to Cedarhill."

"When do you head back?" Renee asked.

"Tomorrow late in the day," he answered.

"It certainly doesn't give you much free time."

"I like it this way. I've got a lot I want to accomplish and one lifetime just doesn't seem long enough," he smiled. "Being a success at my job is only the first of my goals."

"But you are a success at that already," Renee stated.

"Thank you," he grinned. "I'll be successful at this when I've managed to save enough money to buy my own boat, or at least buy Marshall and Father out of their shares."

"I think that's admirable of you, Jim," Elise said seriously.

"Marsh made it on his own without any family help. Now I have to do the same thing. Once I'm my own boat owner, I'll have proved that I'm my own man."

"I didn't know that you had any doubts," Elise said.

Jim's smile was whimsical, "None whatsoever, in my mind, but some of the older captains on the river aren't exactly supportive of my age and connections."

"They're probably just jealous that they didn't get an early start like you did," Renee supported.

"Very true, but still it makes for an uncomfortable position in my trade. The admiration of ones' peers is always coveted," he stated what he thought was a simple truth.

A fleeting thought crossed Renee's mind that she was sure Marshall Westlake never gave a single thought to what his 'peers' cared about. For some reason that struck her as a very noble trait. Had she been born a man, she was certain that she would only please herself, to do what she thought was necessary, not what her acquaintances dictated was right.

Jim, noticing the look of consternation that crossed Renee's face after his last statement, wondered at her thoughts. But rather than question her, he rose and promised to see them in January, if not sooner. Then wishing them a pleasant holiday, he made his departure.

Chapter Eight

The holidays came quickly and were over just as quickly. Elise and Renee spent them quietly at home, enjoying each other. They were most compatible and Renee found in Elise the female guidance she had always lacked. They attended a few holiday teas, preferring to remain at home in deference to Renee, who could not yet bring herself to attend any other festivities.

Then it was January and there was a flurry of activities as they prepared for their sojourn at Cedarhill with the Westlakes. It would be Renee's first introduction to her aunt's best friend. The thought that she would soon meet someone her own age made Renee inexplicably happy. She knew she would enjoy spending time with someone who shared her own interests. They arrived for their stay, the second week in January, after a very cold drive out from the city. The warmth of the great house was appreciated as George and Martha welcomed the two warmly dressed women indoors. They were ushered quickly into the parlor where they shed their coats and muffs and relaxed in front of a roaring fire in the vast fireplace.

"George, Martha, I'd like you to meet Renee," Elise introduced Renee.

As Martha turned her attention to her friends' niece, her eyes widened in surprise. Jim had said there was a resemblance a few months before but she had no idea that it would be this close. Covering her emotions rapidly, she called to George who was still in the hall.

"George, come and meet Renee."

As George entered, he too was struck by the likeness but hid his feelings and came to take her hand. They sat around the fire and were served steaming cups of hot chocolate to chase away the chill, while Martha went upstairs in search of Dorrie. Shortly, she came down accompanied by her daughter. She had the height of the Westlakes and their dark good looks and at her first smile her friendship with Renee was born. Soon, they were off discussing the coming spring and the activities that would take place.

"Did you notice the resemblance, Elise?" Martha asked after the girls had disappeared upstairs.

"Resemblance?"

"Renee's to Elizabeth. The boys noticed the first time they saw her."

"Oh, my, no. I hadn't thought . . . Now that you mention it, though, it is far more obvious. Unusual, isn't it?" Elise asked worriedly.

"Do you think it's worth mentioning? I wouldn't want to put her ill at ease."

"No, I don't see the point. Marsh won't be here and it would only make her self conscious."

"I definitely agree," George put in. "She's a lovely young lady and I think with all the unhappiness she's had lately, she doesn't need any more at this time."

The ladies nodded their accord, sipping their drinks.

"Elizabeth was not a pleasant person and despite her beauty I don't think anyone would want to be compared to her," George finished obliquely.

"I hope Dorrie doesn't say anything," Martha said worriedly.

"Don't worry about that, dear. I spoke with her briefly before you arrived, Elise. She remembered Jim mentioning it back when the accident occurred."

"Well, good," Martha said obviously relieved. She knew Renee was what she appeared to be, a sweet innocent and she didn't want to see her hurt in any way.

Chapter Nine

Marshall's law practice was a prosperous one and for the past five years he had devoted nearly all his waking hours to it as the best antidote for the poison of Elizabeth's death. But now, on the long January nights, as he tried to rest in the back room of his office, his mind was flooded with thoughts of her. Theirs had been a turbulent marriage. Especially after she'd found out she was pregnant. He remembered well her tirades. He had assured her that he loved her, or so he thought, until he came back from the business trip to find she had destroyed his whole world. Except for his mother and Dorrie he had no trust for women. He could feel the cold anger growing inside him as visions of those last hours with Elizabeth ran through his mind. He jerked upright, startled as someone hammered at his office door. He rose quickly and left the dark room, grateful for the interruption.

Deputy John Randolph was waiting patiently as Marshall opened the door.

"John!" Marsh was surprised as he held the door wide, "Little late for a social call. I hope it's not anything serious."

"Bad news. Thought you should know right away," John said as he went to stand by the warmth of the stove. "Wes Maguire's loose. Broke out sometime last week and I just got word tonight."

Marshall took the telegram John offered and sat at his desk to read it.

"I'd better let my father know right away."

"That's why I came over this late. Maguire's a mean man. It's been four years since you sent him up but I doubt he's forgotten you."

"I only wish he had," Marshall replied, remembering the courtroom scene when Maguire was dragged away cursing and threatening the Westlakes for their part in his conviction. "How about a drink to help warm you, John?"

"Thanks, Marsh, but I have to get back. If there's any further word, I'll let you know right away."

"Appreciate it, John," Marshall closed and locked the door after the deputy had gone. So Maguire was out. He had to warn his father first. In town, he was safe, but living out in the country as they did, his family was vulnerable. He gathered what he needed for a few days' visit and set out for home. The cold fresh air kept him awake on the long ride. When he got to the house, he let himself in quietly.

Spying a light in the study, he started in but stopped suddenly in the doorway. Sitting in a massive wing chair before the fire was Renee. She hadn't heard him, so he took a moment to study her as she read by the firelight. He had thought of her often these past weeks since he'd had dinner at Elise's, but always in comparison with Elizabeth. Now, seated as she was there was little resemblance to his dead wife. Her dark hair fell about her shoulders in loose curls as she bent over the book. She wore a dressing gown of pale green that covered her completely yet stimulated the imagination. He had to suppress his thoughts, not wanting to get involved with her for all the wrong reasons and yet here she was in his own home. He shook his head to clear it and then spoke.

"Renee?" he asked quietly.

She jumped at the sound of his deep voice and fumbling the book, looked up in surprise.

"I'm sorry. I didn't mean to scare you. I expected to find my father here."

"I—um—couldn't sleep and he offered me the use of his library earlier—so—" she said haltingly and then, suddenly aware of her state of undress and his dark eyes on her, she blushed.

"Please, don't be embarrassed."

Renee was very conscious of her heart beating wildly. She wasn't sure if it was from the shock of being disturbed or just because he was here. She had never been alone with a man before and yet here she was with the man she had dreamed of constantly since her arrival.

"Um, well, I guess I'd better go to my room," she said rising quickly and exposing a long slim leg in the process.

"There's no need for you to leave. I'll just go on up."

"No. Marshall. This is your home. It's time I get to sleep," Renee insisted.

He moved into the room then, walking toward her, so that she would have to pass by him on her way out. He casually tossed his saddlebags onto the chair she had just left and as she moved by he grasped her arm and pulled her to him.

"Don't go, not yet," the words were choked out before he even thought.

At the feel of her against him, he bent his head and kissed her. His kiss was brutal, hard and demanding until he felt her struggle. He softened then, remembering just who she was. As his mouth began a gentle exploration of hers, Renee felt her resistance weaken. She had never been kissed like this before. He had scared her at first but now he was tender as she knew he could be. As his tongue parted her lips, she started, but the sensation was so pleasant that she timidly met him in that intimate caress and relaxed against him. Suddenly she was free of his embrace, standing alone.

"Good night, Renee," he said harshly, as he turned from her and stalked to the fireplace.

She put her hand to her lips as she stared at his back, not sure at all that the kiss had happened. She then hurried from the room in a flurry of nightdress, embarrassed by his sudden dismissal. When Marshall turned, hoping she'd still be there, he found the room empty. A feeling of relief swept through him. He had forgotten that Elise and Renee would be here in his rush to warn his father about Maguire. Now, here he was, just where he didn't want to be. There was no helping it. This was an emergency. He went to the cabinet with the liquors and poured himself a double bourbon. He would need it on this night. Debating on whether to wake his father or not, he succeeded in pushing Renee from his mind, but only temporarily. As he mounted the stairs later, after deciding to wait until morning to tell his father the bad news, a fleeting image of wide innocent blue eyes and soft green gown came to him. Marshall entered his room at the far end of the hall and lay down fully clothed. He knew sleep would not come easily this night, if at all.

It was afternoon when Dorrie and Renee reined their horses in at the top of the bluff. They sat quietly watching the brown river as it carried the chunks of ice downstream.

"Does it seem different to you?"

"Absolutely, I've never seen ice in it before," Renee answered.

This was the first time that they had ridden as far as the river. The scenery and the weather were different but the river was basically the same—wide, muddy and deceptively lazy.

"I've got a favorite spot at home, too, only our bluff isn't nearly so high as this," she gestured, indicating the view.

"It sounds wonderful."

"Yes, it is—was—" she blinked back sudden tears.

"I'm sorry. I didn't mean to—oh, look, Marshall's coming," she pointed excitedly, glad to change the subject. "I guess he must have finally finished his business with father."

He rode up at a gallop, stopping abruptly by them, his expression ominous.

"Hi!" Dorrie greeted her oldest brother. "What are you doing out here?"

"Mother was worried, she asked me to check on you," he replied gruffly, not looking at them. "Why did you come way out here?"

"Renee wanted to see the river, but I'm sorry we

came. It made her homesick."

Marsh glanced at Renee then and saw the tears she was hurriedly wiping away.

"I'm just being silly," she stated, trying to smile.

"It's never silly to miss your home," he said kindly. Then turning his horse, "Ladies, we'd better get back, it's getting late. Father said Jim will be out to the house tonight."

"Oh, good. By the way, what were you talking to Papa about all that time? You were in the study all morning!" Dorrie asked.

"That young lady, is none of your business," he answered bluntly.

"Oh," she replied, more than a little hurt and surprised at the coldness in his voice.

"I guess we'd better get back. I wouldn't want your mother to worry unnecessarily," Renee said to break the uneasiness.

"You're right, Renee," Dorrie said and they headed back with Marshall trailing behind. "Race you!" and digging her heals into her horse's sides, Dorrie galloped off.

Renee urged her mount on and was soon racing after Dorrie. Marshall held his stallion back but kept pace easily. Suddenly, Renee's horse went down and she fell heavily and lay still. Marsh yelled for Dorrie, but she had already disappeared down the path. Throwing himself from his saddle, he ran to her.

"Renee!" he gasped, rolling her over carefully. He brushed her hair back, worrying at her pale face. "Renee!"

She groaned soflty, putting a hand to her head and focused on him.

"Marshall—" she murmured, trying to read his expression.

"What?" he asked abruptly.

"Nothing I'm all right. How's my horse?"

"She's favoring her leg but she'll be fine," he helped her stand after a moment, keeping his arm around her.

"Think you can ride now?"

"In a minute," she answered, still leaning against him and enjoying the comfort. It seemed so long since she'd had someone to lean on.

He helped her up and after gathering the reins to her horse, he mounted in front of her instructing her to hold on tight. Renee encircled him with her arms and rested her cheek against his back as they started toward the house with her mount following behind. Dorrie was watching for them anxiously at the stables.

"What happened?"

"My horse fell," she answered as Marsh stopped and slid off. He turned to her then and helped her dismount.

Renee was sorry that the ride was over but she landed lightly and smiled up her thanks to him.

"You're not hurt, are you? Look at you!" Dorrie exclaimed taking Renee's arm and leading her off to the house. "Let's go take care of you. Marsh'll see to the horses."

"Thanks," Renee called just as they disappeared into the house and Marshall smiled for the first time that day as he watched them.

Renee stood, hands on hips, before her wardrobe. She had relaxed in the tub until the water turned cold to relieve her aches and pains from the fall this afternoon and now she was feeling considerably better of the body. She was, however, sad for the first time that she could not wear one of the lovely gowns Elise had bought for her. She felt so feminine tonight and knowing that both Marshall and Jim would be there for dinner was added incentive to look her best. With a sigh, in deference to her father, she pulled out a black, high-necked, long-sleeved gown. It was only proper that she wear this, she knew, but she did so want to be pretty this evening. Dejectedly, with the help of the maid, she put on the plain, dark dress and was soon on her way down to dinner.

Renee and Dorrie both managed to finish dressing at the same time and came downstairs together. Entering the dining room, Renee was greeted by a boisterous chorus.

"How do you feel? Are you all right?"

"I'm just a little stiff and sore," she replied, smiling wryly.

"I'm beginning to think you're accident prone," Jim commented, laughing.

"I'm not accident prone, I'm just too much in a hurry. My father used to complain all the time that I was always in a rush!"

Marshall didn't move away from his position by the hearth when she entered the room. He merely watched her as she chatted with his brother and sister, feeling slightly irritated by the easy camaraderie among the three of them. He moved to refill his whiskey glass, only as an excuse to keep himself from staring at her too long.

Dinner was ready to be served so they all took their

seats. The meal was a pleasant one, with the Westlake men regaling Elise and Renee with the tales of their escapades and daring in the early days of establishing the Westlake line. It was a festive evening and Renee enjoyed the affection of this warm family group. When dinner was over, it was still too early to retire so they went into the parlor to relax. Martha played the piano for them and Dorrie challenged Renee to a game of backgammon, unaware that Roger Fontaine had tutored his offspring well at such pursuits. The game was a lively one but there was no doubt who the winner would be after the first few moves. Jim was suitably impressed by Renee's ability and declined the challenge of a match, so Dorrie unceremoniously dragged Marshall from a deep discussion with his father to play Renee.

"He's the best we've got to offer," Dorrie boasted, then teasingly to Marshall she added. "You can't let her get away with beating me so badly! After all, you taught me everything I know!"

Marshall laughed, his mood lightening, as he seated himself opposite Renee at the small cherrywood table.

"Shall we roll to see who goes first?" Renee asked.

"No need, ladies first," Marsh insisted graciously.

But it wasn't too much later that he regretted his gallantry as he watched her finish off her play, trouncing him soundly.

Eyes sparkling Renee watched him as he stood, "Thank you for the game."

He gave her a twisted grin that seemed to take her breath away, "No need to thank me, I showed mercy tonight. I didn't want to spoil your undefeated record."

They all laughed at his reply and the evening ended amicably, as the ladies and George retired for the night.

Chapter Ten

The carriage raced down the street at breakneck speed. Within sat a furious and fuming Juliana Chandler. It was after nine o'clock. She was over an hour late. How dare he! Marsh had told her he would pick her up before eight and they would attend the De Grande ball together. She had thought him just detained, at first, but by 8:30 Juliana had been concerned and so she had sent her maid to his office. He was gone! Gone! Here she was, abandoned on the night of the first big social event of the year! The carriage jerked to a stop and she descended with the help of her coachman. Regally, her back straight and head held high, she entered the De Grande mansion. Luckily, she was greeted at the door by Philip De Grande, only son and heir to his father's millions.

"Julie, you look wonderful. Where's Marsh?" he asked glancing behind her out the door to her carriage.

"He's been detained. He didn't know how soon he could get away, so he suggested I come on alone," she lied smoothly.

Looking up into Philip's handsome face, she smiled. He was attractive enough, she rationalized—not ruggedly good looking like Marshall but passable.

"Would you like to take care of me tonight?" she flirted.

Philip gazed down at her for a moment, amused, "Darlin', I'd escort you through the gates of Hell."

Juliana gasped but did not change expression, aware of the other guests observing them.

"Come, come, my dear, I've made no secret of my true feelings for you. And you don't have to play games with me," he whispered.

"You're right," she answered, looking him straight in the eye. "We've known each other too long for that."

They walked into the ballroom, smiling and greeting all their acquaintances. The orchestra began a waltz and Philip led her expertly around the floor.

"So where is he really?"

"I don't know. The bastard!" she hissed.

Philip threw back his head and laughed loudly, "Now that's the Juliana I know and love."

She was silent.

"Julie, my dear, how often have I told you that you should forget Westlake and marry me?"

"Oh, pooh," she retorted. "You don't love me."

"You're mistaken, darling, and the sooner you realize you've no future with him, the sooner we can make our plans."

"Marsh will marry me," she said stubbornly.

"Now on that point you're wrong, too. At least, not with this new girl in town."

"What new girl?" she demanded.

"Why, Elise Fontaine's niece, Renee."

"Renee Fontaine? That sounds familiar . . . that note!" she exclaimed.

"What note?"

"Oh, nothing, Philip."

"Ah, so they have met! Mark my words. You've no chance with him now for sure."

She glared at him dangerously.

"How can you be so sure?"

"I happened to run into Renee Fontaine one day when she was out with Elise."

"So?"

"She bears a startling resemblance to Marsh's dear departed Elizabeth."

"What?"

"Please, Julie, don't be so obvious. Everyone's watching. You know what a great looking couple we make."

"Philip! Don't be so casual about something so important to me."

"All right! All right!" he answered lightly as the waltz ended and he led her to the punch bowl.

"Tell me all you know," she requested, sipping her champagne punch.

"But, of course. Naturally, there'll be a price to pay!"

"Philip!"

"Later, later. I'll collect. But for now . . . Renee's from Louisiana, a little south of Baton Rouge. She's come to live with Elise because her father died last fall."

"What about her mother?"

"Dead, too, according to the local gossip."

"Oh. So she's here permanently then?"

"I suppose so. She still has a plantation down there being run by some friend of the family."

"She has money?"

"Most definitely. But the most astounding thing—although nobody noticed it but me—is how much she looks like Elizabeth."

Juliana did not like this at all. One thing she didn't need was competition with Marsh, especially someone who would remind him of his dead wife.

Philip watched the change of expression on Julie's face. Her eyes were cold and hard as they narrowed in thought.

"Now, enough disquieting news for this evening. May I suggest we dance and enjoy ourselves?"

"Of course, Philip. You've been most helpful and I do enjoy your company. But what is the payment you'll expect?"

"I haven't decided yet, but as soon as I do, you'll know," he answered cryptically and they joined the dancers in a schottische.

Chapter Eleven

"I must say, Marsh, you seem in good spirits for just finding out about Maguire," Jim stated as they sat up late talking that evening. The others had retired earlier, leaving the two brothers alone.

"How so, Jim?" Marshall looked up questioningly.

"This is the most relaxed I've seen you in years. Our young guest upstairs couldn't be the reason for your change, could she?"

"What makes you think that?" he growled, draining his drink.

"Well, for one thing, you monopolized her at dinner, and secondly, you've been downright glum since she went up to bed." When he didn't respond to his baiting, Jim went on. "She is perfectly delightful. Nothing like Elizabeth."

"Just what do you mean by that?"

"Well," Jim said, sitting opposite Marshall. "You know how much Elizabeth hated family . . ."

"Yes, yes." He raised his hand to silence any further discussion on the subject.

"Then you'll admit Renee is quite special?"

"She is special."

"Has it been difficult for you?" Jim asked. "Being

around her?"

"I haven't been that much. This visit was an accident. I'd forgotten they would be here. If I'd remembered, I wouldn't have come. I would have just sent a message."

"That hard, huh? Does she know?"

"No."

"Don't you think she deserves to know?"

"Why?"

"I think she's rather taken with you."

Marshall snorted in derision, "I doubt that."

"On the contrary. According to Mother, Renee thinks the world of you and she doesn't want Renee hurt."

"I didn't realize. She's so young . . ." he paused. "Jim, you're the only one I can say this to; I don't want to get involved with her. I don't want to see her for all the wrong reasons."

"What wrong reasons? If you find her an attractive woman, where's the harm?"

"Woman? She's hardly more than a child."

"Elizabeth was the same age when you married her."

"That was different."

"Why? Because you were away from home and lonely?"

"No."

"Then, why not? See her. She might be just what you need."

"How do you know what I need?" he raged, slamming his glass down. "Do you think I need that kind of torture? No, thank you. I'll stay the way I am. I may not be pleasant company all the time, as you say, but at least I can live with myself!"

Marshall rose angily and stalked to the window.

"I'm sorry you feel this way. I didn't know that you still had so much pain," Jim spoke truthfully, quietly.

"It's all right, Jim," Marshall turned to his brother, and in that moment Jim could see all of the anguish and doubt Marsh carried with him on his face. "I'm dealing with it as best I can. Renee is a lovely young woman and I can't deny I find her attractive but I'm hesitant to let myself think anything could come of these feelings. I don't want to use her. I don't want to take advantage of her innocence to prove Elizabeth is no longer important to me."

"I understand. I'll speak of it no more, but Marshall?"

"What?"

"You'll have no objection if I see her?"

Marshall paused and studied Jim for a moment, "I have no right to object." The cryptic answer that he gave even surprised himself.

"Fine, now to change the subject will you be riding back with me in the morning?"

"Yes, the earlier the better."

"Agreed. I'm going to bed now. You coming?"

"No, not yet," he replied heavily, pouring himself another drink.

"All right, I'll see you at sunup and we'll head back," Jim left the room quietly.

"Good night," Marsh called as Jim disappeared up the stairs.

Renee paced her bedroom unhappily; here it was midnight and she couldn't sleep. According to Mr.

Westlake, they were in serious danger until this man, Maguire, was recaptured. He hadn't explained too much, just that Maguire had a grudge against Marshall and had sworn to hurt him or his family. To Renee and Dorrie that meant no more rides in the country and they were greatly disappointed. Living in the city had been a great change for Renee and she relished these few days she could spend outdoors. Coming here had given her a taste of freedom again. She regretted having to give it up so soon, but Mr. Westlake and Marshall had insisted that they stay indoors for the remainder of his visit. She sat down on her bed frustrated, worrying. The thought that he might be in danger upset her. Marsh had said he was riding to town the next morning and already she felt an emptiness and a dread that something could happen to him on those long miles. Renee went to the fireplace and put on another small log. She stared into the crackling reborn flames, not seeing them but seeing herself at dinner with Marshall. He had been on her right, with Jim on her left, near George at the head of the table and his mood seemed quite relaxed and carefree for a change. Now, it had been over an hour ago since she'd heard the last footsteps come up the stairs and here she was still wide awake and still thinking of him.

She snatched up her wrapper and moved to the door. Maybe if she got a book she'd be able to fall asleep. Carrying her lamp, she made her way back downstairs. The fire in the study was a mass of glowing embers and it cast great shadows about the room as she slipped quietly in. Making her way to the book shelves, she selected a volume of poetry and started back out. Then she saw him, sitting in the overstuffed wingchair, an empty glass in his hand.

"Renee," he said softly. "You couldn't sleep?"

Renee could almost have sworn that he sounded sad, but his face, hidden in the shadows, betrayed nothing.

"I, um," she swallowed nervously, knowing that she had wanted him to be here, glad that he was. "I thought I'd read a little."

"So I see," he remarked coming to stand before her. "Byron?"

"Yes, he's one of my favorites," Renee said numbly, knowing she should leave. She felt heat flush through her and she wished he would kiss her again as he'd done last night.

"Mine, too," he turned to the small table where the decanters were. "Would you like a drink, brandy, perhaps?"

"Yes, please," she answered, wondering at her own boldness. Then gathering her robe closely around her, she sat on the sofa. Often, when her father was alive, they would sit up late talking and Renee somehow felt that same closeness with Marshall.

He refilled his glass and poured her a snifter of brandy. Glancing over at her he watched as she pulled her wrapper more tightly about her. He smiled inwardly, amused by her nervousness. His resolve to avoid her had faded during the past hour with each refill from the bourbon bottle. She was beautiful and he wanted her.

"Here," he offered her the liquor and sat down next to her.

"Thank you," she said softly, taking a sip and

feeling its warmth relax her. "Father and I often sat up late like this. . . ."

"I hope you're not comparing me to your father?" he asked in mock horror.

"No—" she protested, putting her hand on his arm to reassure him. She was in his arms then, crushed to his chest, his mouth covering hers in a repeat of the passionate kiss he'd given her the night before.

Renee gave herself up to the erotic sensations sweeping through her. Her arms slipped around his neck in an innocent offering of herself as she pressed against him. His lips left hers and searched out the sweetness of her throat, as his hands parted her robe and caressed her through her silken gown. He pressed her down on to the sofa slowly, so as not to frighten her, as he continued his practiced, careful exploration. Renee was weak with unexplained delight. She knew she should stop him but it felt so wonderful to have his body upon hers as he kissed her. His hand slid beneath her gown and she started abruptly at the heat of his touch on her bare flesh.

"Oh . . . no . . . don't!" she cried. "Please don't."

At the sound of her words, reality came back to him in painful clarity. He raised his head to look down at her and his eyes narrowed at the thought of what he had almost done to her. To her, Renee, the young girl who had made him laugh for the first time in ages this evening. Marshall moved away from her smoothly and sat at the end of the sofa farthest from her. He picked up his glass carelessly and finished his drink in one swallow.

Renee lay stiffly where he'd left her. She was too numb to move and a great unknown frustration welled up within her. She didn't know what it was, just that it throbbed unbearably and she wanted him back upon her, holding her and kissing her. She felt a tear slide down her cheek and blinked to try to clear her eyes. Realizing that he was watching her, she made a feeble attempt to pull her robe together.

"I hope I didn't hurt you," he said evenly.

"You didn't," she replied, sitting up. Suddenly, she was angry at him for his arrogant indifference. All evening he had been so kind and thoughtful. Now, he had dismissed her again just like last night. She rose abruptly glaring at him but he returned her look mockingly.

"Good night," she said and left the room with as much dignity as she could muster.

Marshall sighed deeply when he finally heard her bedroom door close. He didn't understand her at all, but far worse, he didn't understand himself anymore. For so long he hadn't wanted or needed anyone. Now, he wasn't so sure. He stood and made his way slowly upstairs, casting a hungry look at her door as he went down the hall. Glad that he was returning to the city early the next morning, Marshall stretched out on his bed and was soon sleeping the deep sleep of the 'over-imbided'.

Renee had taken extra care with her toilette this morning and had worked with her hair until she was totally satisfied with the results. She'd spent long hours last night thinking of Marshall Westlake and she was going to show him that she couldn't be so easily discarded. She'd make him want her! Renee had naively decided, after much plotting, to make him desire her the same way she had wanted him last night. Her plans had mellowed somewhat from her original death wish for him. Smiling and happy, she entered the dining room a little after eight to find George, Martha, Dorrie and Elise breakfasting. The places for Marshall and Jim were all too obviously empty.

"Good morning, Renee," Elise greeted her. "We have some exciting news for you."

"Oh?" she tried to sound casual as she sipped her hot tea and reached for a croissant.

"Yes, before Marsh and Jim left this morning they mentioned that it might be safer if Martha and Dorrie stayed in town with you until Maguire is back behind bars," George explained.

"That sounds wonderful!" Renee agreed, hiding her disappointment at Marshall's absence. But as she thought about the proposal she realized that if Dorrie and Martha were in residence then Marshall and Jim would be coming to visit regularly and that thought made her day considerably brighter.

The move into town took only an extra day and soon Renee and Dorrie were a twosome at all the stores and dress shops. There had been no further word about Maguire and after a few weeks the original tension had melted away and their thoughts turned to spring and Dorrie's coming out ball.

The *Elizabeth Anne* churned south on the smooth-flowing Mississippi River. Now that they were south of Memphis, the river was free of ice and navigation was normal. Jim strolled the promenade deck greeting the occasional passengers he met and surveying the

112

passing river banks. Instead of the riotous green growth of the warmer months, everything seemed brown and lifeless. He sensed a restless discontent in himself and knew an unusual eagerness to be home. His mind, which he had disciplined over the years to concentrate only on business during trips, was being clouded with thoughts of Renee. It was irritating to him to discover that she could interfere with his normal daily routine. As he dwelled on it though, he was pleased that his parents had decided to move into town with the news of Maguire's escape. Not only would it give him extra opportunity to see Renee, but he also remembered the threats that Wes Maguire had leveled at his brother all those years ago. Marshall had successfully prosecuted the case against Maguire and George had testified against him, too. Maguire had murdered a man on one of the Westlake boats and George still a working captain at the time had witnessed it. With George's firm testimony and his own astute use of the facts, Marshall had proven that it had been murder, not self-defense as Maguire had claimed. The jury cooperated, found him guilty and sent him off to the penitentiary. They had thought that he was gone forever . . . but now . . . he was out and Jim was sure returning with vengeance in mind. Maguire had sworn before the whole court as they took him away that one day Marsh would pay and pay dearly. Yes, it was good that the family was ensconced in town and that the sheriff was aware of the dangers involved. Thoughts of Renee intruded again. Since Marshall had expressed no interest in pursuing her, Jim felt that he had an open field where she was concerned. There would be no other men coming to call until spring when her mourning period for her father would be over. By then, he deduced, he would be firmly established in her affections. A sudden thought jarred him. Why was he even worried about it? He had never taken this much time to plan any of his conquests before. In fact, he had stayed far away from the eligible, marriageable ones. Preferring faster company and no obligations, Jim had steered clear of all entanglements with young ladies of family. Yet, here he was planning a seduction. That word didn't sit well in his mind. Certainly, she was not a candidate for any such attempts from him. He only knew that he wanted to hold her in his arms and have her completely to himself. The thought that he might be falling in love with her shocked him. He had never felt this way about a young woman before and he was confused. He made a mental note to pay a visit to his good friend Angelique LaBruyere when they arrived in New Orleans. Perhaps she would make him forget such foolishness as the thoughts of love and marriage. She had always helped him clear his mind of troubled thoughts in the past. A smile momentarily appeared on his face at the thought of Angelique's comforting arms, then it disappeared to be replaced by a frown of concentration. He entered the pilot house, with his expression serious, giving wonder to his on duty pilot who rarely saw his boss without a smile.

When New Orleans finally hove into sight, Jim was eager and ready for the trip to his favorite fancy establishment. He completed his work quickly and accurately, then leaving Ollie in charge, he beat a hasty retreat to Angelique's place of business.

At thirty-six, Angelique LaBruyere was a well

established business woman. Well known and respected in her trade, she had a great appreciation for her select clientele and felt obligated to give them only the best. She employed just a few young women and they were carefully chosen and trained to please the men who frequented her house. Situated in a comfortable part of town, away from the trash that went with the riverfront, it was always a special evening for the man who decided to visit.

She greeted Jim profusely, as her doorman ushered him into the main salon after taking his cloak and hat. Jim swept her into a warm embrace and kissed her heartily before following her to the bar.

"To what do I owe this honor?" she asked handing him his drink, a scotch as usual. "Have you missed me perhaps?"

Jim smiled widely at her as she moved from behind the bar to stand next to him, "You know I miss you. There's no one else on the river like you."

Angelique watched his face as he spoke and noted the small troubled frown there.

"I can tell just by your expression that tonight you are lying to me. Who could have caught your attention so well that here in my presence she still invades your thoughts?" Angelique asked.

"That's why I came. I knew if anyone could help me, it would be you," he grinned and casually pulled her against him.

"Wouldn't you like another drink before we get too involved here?"

"No," he answered. "As a matter of fact, I think I've had quite enough."

"Good, then let us retire upstairs. This is a lovely

room," she stated glancing around at the classically furnished sitting room. There was no red wallpaper or loud music over at Angelique's. "But as you very well know, my own apartment is much more comfortable and much more private."

Moving away from him slightly, she turned to another woman in the room. "Marie, you will be in charge this evening. I am not to be disturbed until the morning. Is that understood?"

"Yes, ma'am," came the surprised reply. It was exceedingly rare that Miss Angelique devoted her own time to a customer; this one must be special.

"Good," she turned to Jim and took his arm. "Shall we go? I do believe you know the way."

Laughing, he led her into the hall and up the carpeted stairs to the back of the tastefully decorated house, where her own private rooms were located. After entering and securing the door to prevent any unpleasant surprises, Angelique came to him and kissed him lingeringly.

"Are you in a hurry?" she asked helping him shed his coat and loosen his neckcloth.

"No, just getting comfortable. How have you been?"

"Fine. Business has been excellent. As a businessman yourself you can appreciate it when things are moving smoothly and profitably. I have two new young women working for me now and they are both extremely talented and successful at what they do. Perhaps you'd like to see them?"

"No. No thanks. You're all the woman I need. There's no need to bring in anyone else. Come here," Jim could feel his body stir as she moved closer to him, her familiar perfume exciting him.

He had been visiting Angelique for almost twelve years now and they understood each others desires. Many a time she had entertained the fantasy that if she had stayed a good girl she could have married a man like Jim Westlake, but what use were dreams? She much preferred business and dealing with men on their own level. Somehow this profession gave her that opportunity. They seemed to respect her judgment and expertise and did not challenge her authority. She liked being their equal and would not deal with any men who could not accept that.

Running her hands down his broad back, she revelled in the feel of his hard muscles beneath the silk shirt that he wore. Helping him with his studs she soon had it loosened and off. He waited patiently for her, somehow sensing that this night she would be the aggressor. Observing her she moved to spread his shirt over a chair and he couldn't help but admire the sight she made. Still a youthful woman, she was a quadroon of unusual coloring. Her hair was burnished gold, made even more arresting by her fair golden complexion. Her yellow/brown eyes always indicated her mood and could be warm as cafe au lait or frozen into chips of gold. Trim and graceful, Jim had often wondered why she had not taken the easy way out and become some man's placee, but such topics were forbidden between them. Neither spoke of their respective families. Except for the knowledge that he was unmarried, she knew little about him personally. All she needed to know was that he was a good lover and excellent company. With that, she was most pleased.

Knowing that she was taking the lead removed the pressure from Jim and he settled back on the full bed comfortably to watch Angelique shed her gown and come to him in her own good time. Her undressing for him had become a ritual in all their years and he enjoyed her slow seductive movements as she finally stood naked before him. The sight of her fired his lust to even greater proportions. He pulled her to him and clasp her full length to his body, so she could feel the need he had for her. Responding with a throaty chuckle, she quickly mounted him and brought him to a fast satisfying climax, then lying next to him, caressing his chest, she smiled as his breathing calmed.

"Now, perhaps, you won't be in such a hurry?"

"You're right about that. And since we have the entire night to take our time, I think this is going to be a very pleasant evening after all."

"You had doubts?" she asked slightly offended.

Renee's fleeting image entered his mind and he was truly sorry that she was not the woman lying next to him at that very moment.

"None whatsoever," he lied, and Angelique knew it.

Hours later as the early morning sun crept into the sky, Angelique watched him dressing, her eyes hard and golden.

"That will be $250, Mr. Westlake," she said icily.

Jim stopped buttoning his shirt and glanced at her questioningly. For some years now their nights together had been for mutual enjoyment, but right now Angelique was all business and he didn't understand her reasoning.

At his silence, she continued, "You used me tonight. You were not in fact making love to me, you were using me as you would use any whore from the levee. There was no affection for me in your arms tonight. I do not waste my time usually with paying customers, but I have made you, sir, the exception for tonight only."

Knowing full well that her accusations were right, he didn't attempt to persuade her differently. He merely unfolded the amount and placed it on her dresser. As he pulled on his jacket, he turned back to the bed.

"Goodbye, Angelique," he said softly, and she was left stunned by his unspoken admission.

Jim was back on board the *Elizabeth Anne* before the sun had fully arisen. He felt neither rested nor physically relieved. Forgetting about sleep for the moment, he threw himself into his work and kept busy until late afternoon when he finished his contracting. Finally he had time to get some sleep. It had been distracting to him that after the initial engagement with Angelique he had been unable to get Renee out of his mind. Being the shrewd woman that she was Angelique had practically read his thoughts. It was disconcerting to find out that the most exciting woman in his life had lost out in favor of dreams of a sweet innocent who knew nothing of her effect on him. Cursing, he undressed and climbed into his bunk after making sure that Ollie knew not to disturb him.

Jim was glad to see the last of Ste. Genevieve. They had just refueled and hopefully were ready for a nonstop trip to St. Louis. Backing out to midstream, the *Elizabeth Anne* headed north on the last short jaunt to home.

The return trip had taken much longer than expected for Jim had managed to pick up a load of cotton at Memphis. That, plus his full load of cabin passengers, pleased him. A profitable trip could ease many a captain's discomforts and he was not that distracted that he'd lost all of his good business sense. He strolled the promenade deck, hands in the pockets of his heavy blue coat, watching the early winter darkness overtake the river. He enjoyed these frigid months and the briskness of the cold night invigorated him. Ascending to the pilot house, he decided to check in with the pilot before going into the grand salon for dinner with the passengers.

The man was of average height and average looks, but despite that, he'd taken great pains to conceal himself. Heavy coat, warm scarf, even spectacles had been added to insure his remaining unnoticed. He'd stayed in his cabin since boarding at Ste. Genevieve and intended to remain there until it was time. Now, dressed in ordinary clothing with the feature-concealing eyeglasses discarded he looked more like himself. Frank Maguire sat on the bed in the tiny eight by eight foot cabin waiting. He had waited a long time for this moment and he could wait a few minutes longer. Glancing at his timepiece, he noted that it would be another few hours yet, but that didn't matter to him at all. Besides, he had to make his move at the designated spot or he'd be left high and dry, or more high and wet, he mused and laughed evilly at his own jest. He had managed to get on board, dressed as a respectable businessman, and now he was comfortably settled in a luxury cabin on the Westlake's best steamer, eager to begin the first of many revenge plans that his brother had planned for them since his escape from the pen. He stood and stretched leisurely, then placing his suitcase carefully on the floor next to the bunk, he lay down on the small bed and closed his eyes. It wouldn't be long now, with a few moments of rest, he could handle anything.

Closing his cabin door, Jim went down the companionway to eat. The meal promised to be less than exciting for him. Tonight, he was eating with a family who were on their first step of a journey to California. He had heard it all before, the reasons for leaving the Mississippi Valley, but none of it appealed to him. Fertile cropland, large cities, small towns and every ethnic group you could imagine could be found right here. Though he'd always be polite with those eager to leave, no promise of gold or other riches could tear him from the river. He would never leave the place he considered home and the Mississippi was his home.

Dinner was an elegant one and the chefs had as usual created perfection. Jim excused himself from his table and moved down the length of the cabin, noting with pride the sparkling crystal chandeliers, Elizabeth's portrait, the exquisite furnishings and the full length mirror that reflected all of it in a glistening splendor of lights. He was at ease in his surroundings. Confident, proud, capable, these were the adjectives used by people who travelled on his boat. The Westlake lines were successful and the boat and its captain reflected that success. Pausing to pull on his gloves, he left the salon to double check his boat.

Frank sat up, checked his watch and knew that the time was right. It was completely dark outside and the dining room was crowded with people. Carefully, he opened the large case he had carried with him on board and took out the contents, two large containers of oil and a quantity of matches. He piled the bedclothes together in the middle of the bunk. Then closing the interior transom, he soaked the covers in oil and put a match to them. They flared to life easily and after fanning it momentarily, he watched with satisfaction as it grew, hungrily lapping at the cabin wall. Casually gathering the rest of the oil and matches, he exited the room by way of the outside door. He walked easily down the promenade deck to the companionway. His next stop was the cotton on the lower deck. Hopefully, the fire upstairs would be discovered first and while everyone was busy with that one he could start a major blaze down here, where it really mattered, close to the boilers. If the boilers got too hot, then there was a chance that the whole ship would blow, and that was what the Maguire brothers decided was the best idea. They would hit the Westlakes where it hurt, in the pocketbook. Without their main moneymaking boat, they would be hard put to do anything, any more.

Frank walked along smoothly and didn't pick up his pace until he heard distantly someone yell, "Oh, my God! Fire!"

At top speed, then, Frank started down to the bales of cotton and dousing them with the oil, he lighted the matches and threw them into the pile. Flames shot upward and Frank jumped back, surprised by the ferocity of it. He heard footsteps bounding down the steps behind him and turned to see Jim Westlake.

"What the hell are you doing!" Jim thundered as he dove at Frank from the last step.

Frank sidestepped him and Jim hit the deck rolling. As he regained his balance, Frank laughed at him and jumped overboard, striking out for shore in long confident strokes.

Jim hesitated momentarily, the desire to follow the madman who was trying to destroy his boat was nearly overwhelming. But reason won out and he turned his attention to the growing blaze. Giving no thought to his own danger, he grabbed bale after bale of burning cotton and heaved it over the railing. Bellowing for help from the men working in the boiler room, he continued his valiant effort. Paying no mind to his smoldering coat and gloves, he didn't feel the pain as the scorching heat burned his hands and arms. All that mattered was saving the boat. He had worked all his life to have her and he wouldn't give her up, he couldn't. It seemed an eternity before help came with buckets of water to preserve what wasn't already fired. He continued to throw the now glowing bales into the river until he was sure it was all gone. Breathless and coughing from the heavy smoke, Jim didn't pause in his efforts, he headed back to the upper deck, hearing the commotion and dreading the worst. Passengers were crowding everywhere, women and children were screaming and cowering against the rails, afraid to descend because of the smoke and flames below, and afraid to go inside because of the tremendous blaze in the stateroom.

"Captain Westlake! You must save us!"

"Sir, beach this boat at once! Most of us can't swim!" the terrified voices of unknown passengers demanded of him.

Jim glared at them as he raced by, heading for the area where the smoke and flames billowed from an open stateroom door. The first mate and engineer had already begun to fight the fire, dragging the water barrels kept on deck closer so they could throw buckets of it onto the blistering conflagration. Jim joined the effort and along with the men from below they worked feverishly to contain it. When finally it was deemed under control, Jim leaned against the railing grasping it to hold himself upright. The smoke had finally gotten to him and he rested there against an upright post, the voices fading away and only one sounded in his mind.

"Get him to Texas! Be careful of his arms! Get out of the way! One of you men calm these passengers down! Give 'em free whiskey or something! It's only a few more hours to St. Louis, everything's under control now!"

"Look at the captain!" a horrified female voice exclaimed with awe and revulsion. "Will he be all right?"

"I don't know yet, please let us through," Ollie replied gruffly, somehow supporting Jim up the companionway to the Texas with the help of two of the deck hands.

The men opened the door to Jim's private cabin and got him inside and onto his bunk before leaving him in Ollie's care. Jim was barely aware of what was

124

happening. Leaving him momentarily, Ollie soon returned with a large bottle of bourbon and two glasses.

"Ollie, the boat . . . ?" he struggled to sit up, but fell back exhaustedly.

"Fire's out. Drink this," Ollie said firmly.

"Did you check . . ." Jim continued after taking a sip.

"Don't worry. Take a big swallow, this is the best thing for you right now," he commanded, knowing how stubborn this Westlake could be.

Ollie helped him drink as much as he could and then made him comfortable again, so he could remove his ruined clothing and see how bad the burns really were.

Frank Maguire pulled himself out of the freezing water and up onto the river bank. He couldn't tell from here if the fires were spreading or not, but at least he had started them and it would give the Westlakes something to think about. He rested, panting heavily from the swim. Soon, behind him, he could hear the horses approaching.

"It looks pretty lively out there, Frank," Wes greeted his brother.

"It sure was, Westlake caught me in the act on the main deck. Got away in time and left a nice fire burning just for him."

"I think you done us proud," Wes said with great feeling. "Here's them dry clothes. Figure you'd need them right about now."

"You're right about that. It ain't exactly July out here tonight!"

"Well, hurry up and change. We got some celebratin' to do."

"Did you send the message?"

"I sure did."

The brothers grinned slyly at each other and then Frank moved off into the woods to change before heading out for a night of carousing.

George Westlake paced Marshall's office nervously. "What do you think it means?"

"I don't know, but I'm afraid it has something to do with Jim and the *Elizabeth Anne* . . . he's already so over due . . ." Marshall said looking up, fingering the note that had been mysteriously delivered to him only a few hours before.

George growled, "What time have you got?"

Marsh pulled out his pocket watch, "It's after ten."

"Well, I hope Martha's not worried about your unusual missive to me. It isn't often that you send someone over to bring me down here to the office."

"I doubt that she'd even think it had anything to do with Maguire."

"Read it to me again. I'm still confused . . ."

Marshall unfolded the note, "Westlake — This is just the first of many surprises we have in store for you. Wait for the next . . . Maguire."

They both looked blankly at each other.

"Maybe we ought to ride down to the riverfront and see if there's been any news of the *Elizabeth Anne*."

"It can't hurt. Just let me lock up here and I'll be right with you."

"Ollie, when we came running out, he was already

throwing them blazin' bales over the rail all by himself!" the deck hand said admiringly. "He's gonna be all right, ain't he?"

Ollie had just come down to survey the damage to the main salon and the stateroom.

"I'll know more tomorrow when I can get him to a doctor in town. Looks pretty serious to me, but I don't know that much about burns. How badly damaged is the ship?" he asked following the man into the burned out cabin.

"We lost about a third of the cotton, to both the fire and smoke. The one stateroom here is a total loss but wait'll you see what happened in here."

The moved through the rubble into the main cabin.

"They must have stampeded! Was anyone hurt?" Ollie questioned, stunned by the sight before him.

"No. Just scared, that's all. Think it'll take very long to fix her back up?"

Ollie's gaze took in the overturned tables, the smashed crystal and china and the serious damage done by the smoke. Even the beautiful mirror at the far end of the salon had been shattered by a chair hastily thrown against it during the evacuation.

"It'll take a while, but Jimmy'll have her running again good as new," then sadly, a little defeated he turned. "By the way, how did the fires start?"

"I don't rightly know, although we heard the boss yellin' at somebody when the flames first started down on deck . . . I guess we'll find out when he feels like talking again. Just let him know that everything's working and we'll be home in a few more hours."

Ollie nodded and left, making his way slowly to Jim's cabin.

George and Marshall scoured the riverfront, hoping to find someone who'd seen the *Elizabeth Anne* somewhere downriver. At last, after an hour of searching, they located the *Belle Marie* out of Memphis, whose Captain Jake Mason had indeed seen Jim at that port. They were relieved when he told them that Jim had contracted for a load there and that that was probably the reason for his delay. The two Westlake men headed back to Elise's house. Martha met them at the door, openly curious about their whereabouts for the past few hours.

"Is Jim in yet?" she asked after they explained that they had had business down at the levee.

"No, not yet. But according to Jake Mason on the *Belle Marie*, Jim managed to pick up a load of cotton down the line and that's why he's so late."

Martha took that explanation at face value and then moved into the parlor. Renee, Dorrie, and Elise were well pleased to see George and Marshall back. Things had seemed too quiet without George's company this evening and they welcomed them warmly.

Declining the hot chocolate that the ladies were drinking, they got large snifters of brandy and settled in close to the warm hearth.

"I look for Jim to get here any time in the next twelve hours," George said just to make conversation.

Marsh smiled as he stood at the mantel, elbow negligently resting on it, snifter in hand, "He probably got every freight shipment between here and New Orleans. I don't think he's lost money on that boat yet."

"You have a lot of respect for your brother's

business sense, don't you?" Renee asked, watching Marsh's every move. The indifference he'd shown her since that night at Cedarhill was wearing on her nerves. She could still feel his mouth on hers and the breathless way she felt after his kiss. How could he have forgotten it so easily?

"He's an astute businessman," Marsh replied and was grateful when his mother carried on the conversation. Sometime later, Marshall left to return to his office, but not before quietly promising his father that he would check again for Jim. The note from Maguire weighing heavily on their minds.

It was after two a.m. when they finally docked. Ollie took care of all immediate business after first sending a roustabout for the doctor. Then he returned to the Captain's cabin and awaited his arrival. He settled next to Jim's bunk on a hardback chair and waited. Less than a half an hour later Dr. Freemont arrived, more than a little irritated at having been awakened in the middle of the night.

"Ollie, you had trouble?" he inquired, setting his bag on the small washstand and shedding his heavy coat.

"Fires, two of 'em, but we managed to put them out."

"What happened to Jim?"

"Burned his arms throwing some burning cotton overboard."

"How long has he been unconscious?"

"I think he's more passed out than unconscious. First thing I did was bring on the whiskey and I dosed him real good, too."

"How long ago did all this happen?"

"Around seven."

The doctor didn't speak again but set about examining Jim's hands and arms. After a few long minutes, he looked up into Ollie's expectant face.

"They aren't as bad as they look actually. Not that it isn't going to hurt him. He'll have a lot of pain, but there doesn't appear to be any permanent damage done."

"Good."

"Keep him down for a few weeks, and make sure that he takes good care of himself."

"I'll make sure of that," Ollie stated firmly.

Dr. Freemont was grateful that Jim was unaware of what he was doing as he applied the medicine and bandages to his injured limbs.

"Make sure to apply this salve twice a day and keep clean wrappings on him."

"He ain't gonna like this," muttered Ollie, knowing Jim.

"If he wants to get back to work as quickly as possible, he'll just have to take it easy for a while. Doctor's orders," Dr. Freemont smiled.

"Thanks, Doc," Ollie shook the physician's hand and walked him out on deck.

"No need to walk me down, Ollie, you look like you could use some rest, too. I left the bottle of laudanum for him on the washstand in his cabin. Only let him use it if the pain becomes too unbearable. I'll check back with you in a few days."

"Fine. But I'm gonna get him off this boat as soon as I can. We've got a lot of repairs to do and if he's anywhere near, he'll be trying to run the whole show."

"That's a sound idea. Where can I find you then?"

"At Elise Fontaine's house; his family's staying there."

"I'll check back on him there, then. Good night."

Ollie watched as the doctor moved off down the stairs and disappeared on the promenade deck.

Marshall rode silently along the riverfront trying to pick up news of any recent arrivals. He wasn't sure what it was he expected to learn, but hopefully the *Elizabeth Anne* making town would be worth talking about.

"Yup, that's what I jest heard. That they managed to put them both out is a miracle, I'd say . . ." a dockhand leaning against a pile of merchandise confided to a friend.

Marshall interrupted them without a thought, "Which steamer?"

"Down on the end, south of here . . . the *Elizabeth Anne* I think she's a Westlake boat."

Marsh paled at the news and without thanking the men, he turned his horse and raced off in the direction indicated by the men. It was a long ride but he finally located her and throwing his reins to a waiting roustabout, he ran up the gangplank. The blackened main deck greeted him first. There was no one about, so he went up to the promenade and went into the main salon in hopes of finding his brother or Ollie. The sight that greeted him left him speechless. It was a shambles. Even after hours of cleaning up by the crew, the room was still almost a total loss. Furniture was ruined, the mirror smashed and the smoke damage appalling. He walked cautiously to the origin of the fire anxious to see just how much of the boat had actually burned. The cabin where the blaze had started was a blackened shell. There was nothing at all salvageable in the burned-out room. He left the scene wondering where Jim and Ollie were and if they were all right. As he reached the Texas, Ollie was just exiting Jim's room.

"Marsh, I'm glad you're here," Ollie greeted him quietly, extending his hand in a firm shake. "You've seen it all?"

"I'm afraid so, the main deck, salon and the one stateroom?"

"That's all of it and frankly that's too much for me."

Marshall didn't answer, they were both quiet as they thought of the near tragedy that had just been averted aboard this steamer.

"If it had gone on a few minutes longer without being detected, we wouldn't be here right now," Ollie said in honest grimness as they walked to the railing and stared out at the swiftly flowing darkness of the river.

"I can tell. Where's Jim?"

Ollie cast a furtive glance at his captain's closed cabin door and didn't have time to reply when Marshall moved hurriedly toward it.

"He's hurt?"

"Now, Marsh, the doctor's already been here. He'll be just fine in a few weeks. . . ."

"A few weeks . . . what happened?"

"He was alone when he discovered the fire in the cotton downstairs and threw the bales overboard to keep it from spreading over the boat . . . then the blaze in that cabin had to be put out and you know he ain't one to stand back and let his crew do a job he wouldn't do himself . . ."

"Ollie . . ." Marsh interrupted menacingly.

"He burned his arms and hands when he was moving those damn bales. Freemont already bandaged him up and I got him so drunked up that he ain't feelin anything right now."

"Think we should get him off the boat? Maybe take him out to Elise's house? He'd be better off if Mother and Dorrie were around to watch him and keep him out of trouble."

"My thoughts exactly, but I was going to wait until he woke up on his own accord. No use stirring him up until it's necessary."

"You're right about that. Listen, why don't you go get some rest and I'll sit up with him. I don't think Father has to know anything this late at night. We'll wait until tomorrow to tell him."

"Fine, but call me if you need anything. There's whiskey in there and the doc left laudanum, too, if he gets really bad. You want anything now?"

"No, I'll be fine. See you in the morning."

Ollie moved off toward his own cabin and Marsh quietly went into Jim's. Jim lay still and pale on his bunk. His bandaged arms and hands rested grotesquely on top of the blankets. Moving to the chair by the bed, Marsh settled in for a long and tedious night.

It was almost dawn when Marshall came awake suddenly. Jim was groaning in his sleep. He turned and lay a gentle hand on his brother's shoulder.

"Jim?"

"Marsh?" Jim opened his eyes wearily and looked up

at his brother. "When did you get here? Where's Ollie? How's the boat?"

"Slow down, everything's going to be fine. I got here right after the doctor and I agreed to stay with you so Ollie could get some rest."

"The doctor?" he raised one arm experimentally and saw it encased in bandages.

"Don't move around too much. According to the doctor you're going to hurt like hell for a while. I'd like to move you to Elise's house when you feel you can get up. You'll get more rest there."

"Elise's! I don't want to go there. My place is here . . ."

"For all that I agree with you under ordinary circumstances, this is not ordinary. The Doc's orders were to keep you quiet and make you rest, so that's what you're going to do."

Jim pondered that quietly, "How bad is the boat?"

"It should be ready to go about the same time you are."

"Good," he lay back quietly.

"I'll line us up a carriage and we'll see about getting you out of here."

Marshall left Jim grumbling as he went in search of transportation for them.

The early morning knock at the door brought Celia worriedly to the front of the house. Opening the door, she was confronted with Marshall and Ollie supporting Jim between them.

"You'd better wake my father, Celia," Marshall instructed as they moved into the parlor and she hurried upstairs to do his bidding, passing Dorrie and

Renee on their way down, who had heard the noise and were checking to see what was wrong.

"Celia, what's happened?"

"I don't really know, but it looks like your brother's been hurt," she whispered as she moved past them.

Dorrie looked worriedly at Renee and they both ran downstairs, mindless of wearing only their dressing gowns. They followed the sound of the men's voices into the parlor.

"Marsh?" Dorrie asked.

"What happened? Is Marshall hurt?" Renee asked, her face pale as she followed Dorrie into the room.

Marshall looked up from lowering Jim carefully onto the sofa. His eyes met Renee's for a long searing moment before he replied.

"I'm fine, but Jim's had an accident on board," he tore his gaze away from hers and turned as he took off his coat.

"What's happened? All Celia said was that it looked like Jim had been injured," George bellowed as he came into the room at a run, buttoning his hastily donned shirt.

"Good morning," Jim said weakly, giving his father a half-smile, before Ollie or Marsh could explain.

"What happened to you?" George demanded, as he took in his son's bandaged arms.

"Just a small fire," he tried to sound nonchalant, but the effort cost him much and he leaned back against the sofa and closed his eyes.

"Someone set two fires on board just a little north of Ste. Gen. Luckily, Jimmy caught him in the act or we wouldn't be here right now. He took to throwing those burning bales off the boat all by himself. Helped put

135

out the fire on the upper deck, too, before the smoke got to him. Doc's already seen him and said the best thing for him was rest. So I thought it was best to get him off the *Elizabeth*."

"You're right, Ollie. How bad are his burns?"

"You know, it's really entertaining to be talked about as if I wasn't here," Jim said sarcastically, opening one eye to peer at his father.

"You rest," George commanded and Jim closed his eye again.

Martha came into the room, then, tying her flowing warm robe about her and gasped, "I heard you from in the hall! So this is what all that mystery was about last night! I knew something was going on. Why didn't you tell me?" she demanded of Marshall and George.

"Mother, we didn't know for sure what was going on, just that Jim was late and we were worried, that's all."

She gave them both a frosty glare and took charge of the situation, "Celia, prepare Dorrie's room for Jim. I want him in bed as soon as possible."

"Yes, ma'am," she replied. "Shall I wake Miss Elise?"

"Please, this is after all her house and we've brought all of this 'excitement' with us. I'm sure that she'd want to know what was going on under her own roof."

Martha sat next to Jim, "What did the doctor say? How soon will you be back to normal?"

"I'm not sure, Ollie did all the talking. I was pretty groggy at the time. He managed to get me pretty well drunk in the few hours it took to get here from Ste. Genevieve."

"It's probably the wisest thing he ever did. I'm sure

"you would have been in a lot of pain if he hadn't."

"That's for sure," Ollie agreed. "And peeling those gloves and your jacket off were no mean trick. I'm just glad he was out while I had to do that. I know I'm no match for his strength if he decided to use it on me."

Jim grinned at Ollie, "I didn't feel a thing. Maybe you missed your calling all these years. You should have been a nursemaid!"

Ollie snorted indignantly at him, "You ought to just sit there and be quiet."

Celia returned and let them know that the bedroom was ready for him.

"Jim's been hurt?" Elise asked entering the room behind Celia.

"There was a fire . . ." Renee explained and Elise gasped as she saw his bandaged arms.

"You'll be just fine, won't you?"

"Absolutely, I should be good as new in just a few weeks," he said with bravado that sounded a little false.

"How's your boat?" George asked.

Ollie replied, "I'll tell you all about that later. We don't have the complete damage reports yet and as soon as I get them I'll let you know."

"Since the bedroom's ready, why don't we get him upstairs, Ollie?" Marsh said moving to Jim's side and with Ollie's help they carefully got Jim to his feet.

Martha led the way upstairs and opened the door to the freshly made up room for them.

"Marshall, I'd appreciate it if you'd get him undressed," she said with authority as she turned back the covers on the bed.

Jim came to sit on the edge of it and Marsh helped him out of his clothes before settling him back on the pillows.

"Are you hungry?" his mother asked, as she bustled about the room putting his things away.

"No, not a bit. I'm afraid that I'm still suffering the results of Ollie's first and most practical method of nursing."

"I'll let you rest then, but I do want you to eat something this afternoon. I'll have Dorrie check on you later to see if there's anything you need."

"Thanks," he answered and then closed his eyes wearily.

Downstairs, there was a heated discussion in the dining room as they went over the excitement of the previous night.

"It was," Marshall insisted, his eyes blazing.

"It was what?" she asked as she took her seat and poured a cup of tea.

"Well, Mother, you might as well know the whole story," Marsh began. "Last night, a note was delivered to me from Maguire. It taunted us with the knowledge that they'd done something to hurt us, but it didn't say what."

"Maguire?" Renee asked, the word coming from her in a breathless whisper.

Marsh looked at her as she put the pieces of the night just ended together.

"Yes, Maguire. Somehow one of them got on board the *Elizabeth Anne* and set those fires deliberately. Thank God the cotton didn't have a chance to burn more than it did."

"Jim managed to get both of the fires out but the

damage to the grand salon is considerable," Ollie added. "We're gonna have a lot of repairs to do in these next few weeks while he's laid up," Ollie gestured upstairs.

"After breakfast, I think I'd best survey the boat and see what needs to be done. We can get that contracted out today with any luck and have her ready to go when Jim is," George said. "But what do we do about Maguire? Evidently this is just the first of many such attempts to disrupt our lifes. We can't stay here, cooped up like scared animals!" He slammed his hand down on the table, jostling everyone's cups of tea and coffee.

"I'll take the letter to John and see what he can come up with. I'm sure they'll lay low for a time. It wouldn't be too smart to try another too soon since he knows we'll be overly cautious from now on."

George nodded his agreement. An uneasy silence fell over the table and when Celia entered the room to serve breakfast she found everyone quiet and the atmosphere gloomy.

After George, Ollie and Marshall left to inspect the boat and visit John Randolph, Renee broke the tension of the moment.

"Since Jim's going to be here for a while, is it all right if Dorrie and I share a room?"

"I think that's a fantastic idea," Dorrie smiled brightly. "It'll be just like being sisters!"

"Good," Elise agreed. "I have to admit, I've never had this many houseguests at once before and I was wondering where everyone was going to sleep."

"I'll go check on Jimmy and get my things ready to move into Renee's room," Dorrie said anxiously.

"Be quiet, just in case he's still sleeping. I don't want his rest disturbed, young lady."

"Yes, mother," Dorrie answered and she and Renee hurried upstairs together.

Renee waited for Dorrie in her bedroom, thinking it improper for her to be in a single man's bedroom and set about making room for Dorrie's belongings in her chest and closet. When they had talked at Cedarhill about the danger involved with Maguire she had never in her wildest imaginings ever thought anything would come of it, yet here Jim was seriously injured. It gave her cause to worry; Marshall was even more vulnerable than Jim and she hadn't ceased being concerned about him since that first morning at his home. But he had been treating her so coolly since that night together in George's study . . . she almost felt as if she'd dreamed it all. How she'd loved the feel of his arms around her and the heat of his body next to hers. Loved?! Love him? Did she? Could she? When every other woman in St. Louis no doubt wanted him too? She stood immobile, staring into space as she let her feelings run rampant for a few moments. Yes, she loved him, but she couldn't let him know. Not yet. Hadn't her father tried to explain it all to her once, so long ago and she had argued with him about honesty. But she knew now what he'd meant. If she told him the truth she'd scare him away from her. No, she must go slowly and try not to be too obvious about the state of her heart.

When Dorrie came back in a few minutes later to let her know that Jim was still resting, they decided to wait downstairs until he'd awakened.

It was a full three days before Jim felt well enough

to venture downstairs to visit. Dr. Freemont had come to check his injuries in the morning and had pronounced him fit enough to move around a bit. Indoors only though, he insisted knowing Jim's desire to return to his ship. Scowling at this restriction, Jim grudgingly agreed and was satisfied to just get out of bed for a while. After he'd made himself comfortable Elise and Martha told him that they were going out for the afternoon but Dorrie and Renee would be home if he needed anything. His thoughts brightened considerably at the thought of seeing Renee again. He'd not missed the sight of her in her pale peach robe the morning of his injury and he'd thought of little else these past few days when he'd been awake. Every word Angelique had hurled at him had been true, he had been using her. She'd been a replacement for the woman he desired but couldn't have—yet. But fate had been kind, he decided. Being stuck in this house had its advantages if he were to be alone with her at least some of the time. His eyes sparkled at the thought.

"You look like you're up to something, Jimmy Westlake," Dorrie teased as she and Renee joined him

"Jim, I'm so glad you're feeling better," Renee said earnestly.

"Thanks, but just seeing you—two—has already put me well on the road to recovery."

Dorrie laughed at his banter, never suspecting him of being serious, "can we get you anything?"

"No, I'm fine. Just keep me company for a while. What's happening in the outside world?"

"Nothing good," Renee said bleakly. "There's been no news about Maguire at all."

"Don't worry. He won't get away with anything else. We'll be ready for him. I've already discussed getting guards on the boat with Father and Marshall and they think it's a good idea. Now, all we have to do is figure out how to protect you."

"Us?" they questioned in unison.

"Who knows how warped their thinking is? We've got to be prepared for any eventuality!"

Dorrie shivered. "It never occured to me that he'd want to hurt us. I thought he was just angry with Papa and Marshall."

"Dorrie, how better to hurt us than to injure someone we love?" his glance took in Renee, too. "The man is an animal and I won't rest until he's behind bars again!"

"I see," she replied meekly. "Renee would you like some tea?"

"Yes, thanks."

"I'll get it. You entertain our captive audience for me for a minute."

"I'd love to."

After Dorrie left Renee moved to the small bookcase and looked through the novels there.

"Would you like me to read to you?"

"Whatever. I'm not hard to please. After being flat on my back all this time, anything will be a diversion."

She chose a penny romance and grinning wickedly seated herself across from him.

"I thought you could use a little diversion, so I've selected very light literature here. Ready?" she asked keeping the book hidden.

"I suppose, but make it good. From the look on your face this had better be some special piece."

"Oh, it is!" she laughed. "It's entitled—are you ready?—the *Loves of Janie Hart* and it comes to me well recommended by Celia who assured me that it's just wonderful!"

"What?!" he burst out laughing.

"It's a penny romance; haven't you ever looked at one?" she asked innocently.

"I'm afraid I missed this one," he commented drily. "Please begin, I am really interested in Janie's loves and if Celia recommends it then it must be good."

"Fine. I knew you'd applaud my choice. Let's see—," she said turning pages. "Here we are . . ."

She began the sad tale of the young English chambermaid who'd loved and lost with not only the Lord of the Manor but a groom and the butler as well. By the time Renee had finished reading, they were all nearly hysterical with laughter. Dorrie had rejoined them during the course of Janie's trials and had found it just as amusing as Renee and Jim.

"That made my day!" Jim sighed, weary from laughing so hard. "Now at last, I understand how women really think and feel."

"Believe me, Jim, if you take this as a gospel for women's emotions, you're going to be in for a big surprise. I think Janie was a trifle more . . . Dorrie what's the phrase I need?"

"Try 'free with her favors', I believe that's how I heard Mother describe . . ."

"Describe who?" Jim asked, suddenly very interested.

"Oh, nobody," Dorrie tried to sound casual, realizing what she'd just about blurted out.

"I'm serious Dorrie, I can't believe Mother said any

such thing. Are you sure that's what you heard?"

"Yes! She was talking to Father and I overheard what they said . . ."

"Well? Don't leave us in suspense . . . who was it?"

Dorrie's eyes twinkled, she glanced to Renee first and then to her brother, "All right, I'll tell you, but you must swear yourselves to secrecy."

"I swear," Jim teased and Renee echoed him, but she wasn't really interested.

"Well," Dorrie glanced around suspiciously. "It was when Marshall was gone on that horse buying trip . . . and Mother and Father had gone to a dinner party. When they came home they were discussing Juliana and Mother made the remark that she didn't think Marshall would ever marry her because she was much too free with her favors!"

Before Jim could start laughing, a voice cold and sarcastic boomed at them from the doorway, freezing them motionless in their seats.

"Is this all you have to do all day? Discuss my personal affairs?" Marsh spoke evenly, as he stood in the parlor doorway, still wearing his heavy coat. "I came to find Father but obviously he isn't here. So, if you'll excuse me, I'll be on my way."

He turned and was gone in an instant, leaving Dorrie totally stricken and near tears.

"Oh, Jimmy!" she cried and moved to the sofa next to him, crying.

Jim gathered her to him as best he could without bumping his arms and spoke soothingly to her, "Don't worry. It was harmless. He just didn't hear the whole conversation. That's all."

"But what will he think of me? You know I don't say

144

mean things behind his back. I love him!"

"I know that. You'll just have to let the storm pass," Jim sympathized, knowing how his little sister idolized Marshall. "He'll come around."

Renee sat silently through the entire scene, wondering what she could possibly say to make things any better. Finally, Dorrie felt a little better and rubbed at her eyes, trying to regain control.

"I'm sorry, Renee."

"Don't worry about it. That was a pretty devastating cut he just delivered. It's just a shame that he missed the story!" She smiled and Jim, remembering Janie's trials, started laughing again.

"Maybe we could write one about Dorrie; it seems like she's always up to something!" he teased her.

Dinner was a quiet affair that night. Jim still declined to eat with the family, so it was just George and the women who enjoyed the sumptuous meal that Elise's cook had prepared. During the dessert, Dorrie casually mentioned to her father that Marshall had come by looking for him earlier in the day.

"Yes, I stopped by his office on my way home."

"Was there a problem about Maguire?"

"No, nothing to do with him. Marshall needed my advice on some matters concerning the *Elizabeth Anne*."

"Oh." They issued a collective sigh of relief.

"By the way, Marsh said that the boat's cleaned up enough that you could come aboard tomorrow, if you'd like, that is."

"I don't know . . ." Dorrie hedged, not eager to face her oldest brother.

"Martha and I have an appointment with the

145

dressmaker, but Renee and Dorrie may join you," Elise said.

"That sounds like fun," Renee agreed giving Dorrie a reassuring smile. "I'd enjoy a trip down to the river."

"All right, we'll go with you Father. What time do you want to leave?"

"Let's make it early, what do you say? About ten?"

"We'll be ready," Renee said pleased.

"I think I'll go tell Jimmy that we're going. Maybe he'll want us to bring him something back from the boat." Dorrie excused herself from the table and went up to visit Jim.

She knocked loudly and entered at his call to come in.

"Well, little sister, what brings you up here to my personal cage?"

"It's not that bad, is it?" Dorrie asked, coming to sit by him on the edge of his bed.

"It's worse than bad, it's . . ."

"Don't say it!" she laughed at him. "How do you feel? Outside of being bored, that is."

"I'll live," he said without enthusiasm.

"Hurts?"

"Like hell, if you really want to know the truth. And I'm so damned weak. Just those few hours downstairs completely wore me out."

"I guess the doctor knew what he was talking about when he told you to get a lot of rest."

"I know, but I've never been down this long before. It's quite a blow at my age to discover that I'm mortal just like everyone else. Enough about me, what's up?"

"Renee and I are going down to see the *Elizabeth Anne* tomorrow morning, Marsh told Father that we were welcome to come take a look around . . ."

"Scared to go?" he grinned knowingly.

"You know I am. And you won't be there to run interference for me!"

"Don't concern yourself. If he was still angry, you can bet he'd never have invited you aboard."

"Are you sure?"

"Positive."

Dorrie relaxed visibly, "That's good to know. Can we bring you anything back? Is there anything in your cabin you could use?"

"Just my ledgers. They're in my desk drawer. Think you can manage that?"

"I certainly hope so," she grinned. "They shouldn't be too hard to find."

Noting his pale coloring and the sudden grimness of his expression she added, "Do you want some of that medicine that Dr. Freemont left for you?"

"No," he answered almost angrily. "No, I don't want to use that stuff at all. I'll feel better in the morning . . ."

"If you're sure you're going to be all right," she said hesitantly.

"Sure—good night," he replied turning his face from her and Dorrie left the room quietly.

The next morning was bright yet cold and they all dressed warmly for their venture down to the river front. They were appalled by the damage done on the main deck and George hastily explained that little had been repaired there so far. Most of the work was being done in the main salon, it being the very heart of the *Elizabeth Anne*. As they entered the room from the far end, they were saddened by the sight that greeted them. All of the furniture and decorative touches had been removed, including the portrait of Elizabeth. It seemed cavernous to Renee as she and Dorrie watched the workmen painting and polishing, trying to remove the effects of the smoke.

"It must have been terrible," Renee muttered.

"We're lucky that no one was injured," Marshall's voice came from behind them as he joined their group. "We've been working in here constantly for three days now and you can tell what kind of progress we've been making—slow."

Dorrie looked up at him a little timidly, but he was frowning about something and turned to his father to make a remark on some of the workmanship being done.

"I promised Jim I'd get the ledgers out of his desk for him, I'll be right back, Renee," and with tears in her eyes she almost ran from the room.

"George! Look at this!" Ollie's voice called from the bar and George moved off to see his old friend.

Renee turned to Marshall and found him studying her, his expression coolly assessing. It unnerved her a bit but she spoke anyway, "Could I speak with you alone for a moment?"

His eyebrow quirked, "I believe we are alone."

"This is private and I'd like to talk to you about it before Dorrie gets back," she insisted, her cheeks reddening at his taunting tone.

"Come on, we can use the clerk's office," he led her outside and into the private office where the steamer's business was conducted. Closing the door behind him, he folded his arms across his chest, "Well?"

She had her back to him but still took offense at his tone, "I just wanted to apologize for what you heard yesterday morning, but it wasn't what you thought . . ."

"Oh, really?" he replied sarcastically.

"No," she felt suddenly braver and turned to face him, "You see I'd been . . ."

"There's no need to explain. I heard the laughter and Dorrie's comment about Juliana," he stated tersely.

"But we weren't laughing at you or anything to do with you! I'd just read a story to Jim and we were laughing about that. I was trying to think of a word that described the heroine and Dorrie came up with it. Jim was startled to find out that she even knew such a phrase and asked her where she'd heard it. That's all!" she watched his closed expression, her heart sinking. If anything she'd made things worse. "Well, I'm sorry and I just didn't want you to be angry with Dorrie. She was very upset last night and didn't even want to come here today. She was worried that you'd still be angry . . ."

"And what about you?"

"Me?"

"Weren't you afraid of me?"

"No," she answered with certainty and then more worriedly, "Should I be?"

She was in his arms then, safe and warm, his mouth descended but hesitated above hers, "You're sure?"

Unconsciously, her arms reached up to him and pulled his head down, giving him his answer and he smiled slightly before meeting her lips. Renee felt breathless at the tender inviting caress of his mouth. He pulled her more closely to him, irritated by the nuisance of her heavy cloak between them. Deftly, his fingers released the catch and it fell to the floor unheeded.

"You feel so good to me," he murmured against her lips, as his hands ran down her spine and molded her hips against his. She gasped at the sensation this close contact with him aroused in her and sought his kiss again, matching his desire with her own. Keeping her pinned against him with one hand, the other sought the softness of her breast and she arched her back at the heat of his touch. Some logical part of her mind kept telling her to stop him, but the exquisite sensations that he was arousing in her were overwhelming. "I love him," her passionate nature argued with her sensible counterpart. Her emotional side won as he loosened her bodice and slid his hand within to caress her flesh. As he fondled her intimately, she moaned softly against his mouth and instinctively moved her hips closer to him, wanting to feel the hardness of him against her, to somehow fill the aching she felt within. He lifted glittering eyes to hers as he broke away from her kiss.

"I want you more than I've ever wanted any woman," he said softly before kissing her again.

She didn't answer, not quite sure what he meant but saddened that he hadn't declared his love. A part of her had frozen at his words and the heat she had felt for him moments before was rapidly cooling. So he wanted her, did he? Probably to make her into a woman just like that Juliana Chandler, whoever she was! Indignation arose and she would have broken away except for the voices coming from out on deck.

"Have you seen Marshall?" George's voice called

from somewhere above them to a deckhand below.

"No, suh," came the reply.

Marsh stepped back from her immediately and drew a deep breath. Renee stood silently watching him bring himself under control.

"We'd better go," he remarked quietly.

"Just like that!" she cried, stunned at what had almost happened to her. "I suppose you think I'm one of those women who are free with their favors, now."

"Hardly," he replied wryly, half-smiling.

"How dare you laugh at me!" she stormed at him.

"I'm not laughing or even amused right now," he answered her coldly. "If you'll calm down, I'll fix your dress for you. I wouldn't want anyone to get the wrong impression if they were to walk in right now."

"Oh," was all she could say and she struggled to refasten the dress.

"I'll do it," he said and did, quickly and efficiently.

"Thank you," she picked up her cloak and wrapped it around herself feeling more protected from him with it on. "I'll go now."

"Just wait a minute," his voice was harsh. "You're still flushed from crying. I'll go first and you can follow in a few moments."

"All right."

He moved to the door and opened it. Then turning, he smiled at her, "Don't worry about Dorrie. I'll talk to her." And with that he was gone.

A little while later, Renee met everyone in the pilothouse. The view of the levee was magnificent from there and the line of steamers stretched in both directions as far as the eye could see.

"It's easy to see how it could have happened,"

Dorrie was saying.

"What?" Renee asked.

"The fire back in 1849."

"Was it bad?"

"It was horrible. The steamer *White Cloud* caught fire and before it was all over twenty three boats were lost, not to mention all the buildings that were destroyed on the levee," George explained.

"So it wasn't just warehouses?"

"No, many businesses were wiped out. We've improved our fire fighting capabilities since then, so hopefully there'll never be a repeat.

Renee was silent trying to imagine the entire levee in flames, knowing that it must have been an awesome sight. She was glad too to have something to distract her from Marshall's disturbing presence. She was all too well aware of his deep voice as he went over plans for the boat's repairs with his father. Nervously, she moved away from him to take in the view from the opposite side of the room and Dorrie followed her.

"Did you get Jim's ledgers?"

"Sure did, I left them downstairs so we can pick them up whenever we leave."

"Good."

"We'll meet you both downstairs," George called to them as he and Marsh left the cabin.

"What did you say to Marshall?" Dorrie asked when they had finally disappeared from sight.

"Why?" she asked, disturbed by the question.

"He was so sweet when he found me a few minutes ago. He said that you had explained everything. Thanks," she hugged her impulsively. "You're braver than I am."

152

"I am?"

"I'd never have had the nerve to face him. When he's angry he terrifies me!" she confided.

"Well, he doesn't scare me."

"That's good. Anytime he's mad at me from now on, you can handle it!"

Renee smiled. No, she wasn't afraid of Marshall, she was afraid of herself. All he had to do was touch her and she was lost. She didn't know how she would manage it, but she had to stay away from him. He might want her, but he didn't love her. She had to hide her real feelings from him, she had to.

"I guess we'd better meet them," Renee finally replied and moved off toward the door.

"Right and I want to get those ledgers too before we leave."

They left the pilothouse and rejoined Marshall and George on the main deck after retrieving the books for Jim. Their trip home was uneventful and Jim was more than pleased to have his books so he could go over the figures from his last trip. And indeed, they did spend the next few days reviewing the information. Dorrie and Renee took turns flipping the pages for Jim and making the necessary notes for later when he'd be back at work. The task was not all drudgery and Renee came to enjoy even more Jim's sense of humor and his good natured personality. They bantered easily, exchanged quips and laughed at their own cleverness. It was a pleasant time, made even more pleasant by the fact that Renee was able to avoid Marshall. Although his visits at the house were by no means regular, he did stop on a few occasions and Renee managed to slip away undetected.

Finally, the following week, the doctor announced that Jim was ready to have his hands unwrapped. They were sufficiently healed, that if he took extra care with them he could do without the awkward wrappings. Jim was delighted. He had had much trouble adapting to having help with everything from buttoning his shirts to eating. And he felt sure that his mother was just as tired of taking care of him. He was not at all pleased with the sight that greeted him when the bandages were finally removed. His hands were still red and swollen and tender to the touch, but at least he appreciated the mobility it gave him. He could now at least dress unassisted and eat his meals with the family downstairs. He was happy to note that Renee seemed delighted to see him as he joined them at the dinner table and that she was not at all upset by the state of his hands.

"How long until Dr. Freemont takes the rest of the dressings off?" George asked.

"Depending on how my hands are healing, probably next week and then I can get back to work the following Monday."

"That's wonderful," Renee said, happy for him. She knew from their conversations just how much being on the river meant to him.

He felt warmed by the tenderness he saw in her eyes and was eager to be about his pursuit of her. He smiled back, "I know. I'm beginning to feel like I'm in drydock . . . not that I mind with all the pretty women around, but I do have a ship to run."

Actually, he mused, he hadn't longed much for the river the past week. Try as he might to distract his thoughts with his ledgers and other business, Renee was constantly on his mind. The scent of her perfume, an elusive spicy scent, always seemed close to him. Even when she'd gone from the room it lingered and many were the nights when he'd tossed and turned, trying to push her from his thoughts.

The meal was a gay one, everyone happy that Jim was well on his way to recovery. After the dishes were cleared away, George and Jim went into the library across the hall and settled down with a brandy while the women drank their coffee in the dining room. Celia answered the knock at the door a few minutes later and ushered in Marshall, who looked to be slightly frozen.

"It's getting terrible out there," he complained as he shed his heavy coat, and after greeting the ladies he disappeared into the library.

"They're talking business again," Martha remarked. "Anytime you get those three together they don't talk about anything else."

"It's understandable, though," Elise said. "It is their livelihood."

"I know. The steamers do pay the bills and quite admirably too, I might add," Martha said, her eyes twinkling. "But just once it would be nice to know that they found us as attractive as some white, filigreed sternwheeler!"

Everyone laughed, "It could be worse, mother, they could be down at the riverfront!"

"That's true, that's true," she sighed. "Shall we join them? I think they've had enough time alone. They need some gentler companionship."

"Decided to keep us company, have you?" George teased as they entered the library.

"We gave up waiting for an invitation," Martha responded. "I know how you can get talking about business and forget the rest of the world, so the rest of the world decided to join you."

"Marshall just brought us good news," George said hugging his wife and kissing her on the cheek. "The boat will be ready the week after next. So Jim and the *Elizabeth Anne* can both get back to work at the same time."

"That's wonderful," all agreed.

When Martha and Elise called it a night an hour or so later, Jim excused himself, too. It had been a long, exciting day for him, and he felt himself tiring. Dorrie stayed behind to talk with her father and brother a little longer, but Renee was eager to be gone from Marshall's disturbing presence. She had felt his dark eyes upon her during the course of the evening and she had grown agitated. Finally, a few minutes after the others had gone she said goodnight and started up to bed. Hurrying blindly, she reached the head of the stairs wanting only to go to her room and relax. Not looking where she was going, she ran directly into Jim. He had remembered something important that he had forgotten to tell Marsh and was coming back down. He grasped her to him to keep her upright, the pain in his hands draining his face of color.

"Jim! I'm sorry, I didn't see you," she gasped. "Are you hurt?"

"I'm fine," he said loosening his grip a bit, but not letting go. "Are you?"

"Of course, I'm just a bit startled, that's all. I didn't know you'd be coming back down."

"I was on my way to tell Marsh something, but it

can wait," he murmured.

"What?"

"Do you know how lovely you are?" he asked, his voice husky as he stared at her lips so close to his own.

She didn't reply, but stood helpless and slightly stunned by this attention from Jim. He went on, "There's something that I've been wanting to do and now seems the perfect time."

His arms went around her tenderly and his mouth moved over hers in a gentle warm exploration. Renee was too surprised to do anything and stood immobile while Jim kissed her in anything but a brotherly manner. As his tongue parted her lips, she was forced to respond and tried to push him away. Sensing her reluctance, he pulled back and gazed into her flushed face.

"You are so beautiful, I've wanted to do that for so long . . ." he was about to kiss her again when the door to the study opened and Marshall stepped out into the hall accidently glancing up the stairs.

At the sight of Renee in Jim's arms, he halted in midstride. His expression turned thunderous, but he said nothing. Instead, he turned to his father who was following him and guided him back into the room, closing the door firmly behind him.

Renee panicked. Whatever will Marshall think of me? She pushed at Jim and was freed immediately.

"I won't say that I'm sorry, because I'm not," he said grinning before she could speak.

She looked at him blankly for a moment and then ran on past him to her room. Jim watched her until she went in before continuing on to the study.

Renee threw herself on her bed. She was too upset

to cry and so she lay there for long sleepless hours, wondering what to do.

The following day, having worried herself into a nervous state, Renee decided to spend the day in bed resting. Everyone remarked at her absence from the table, but Jim felt that it had been his forwardness that had disturbed her so badly. He didn't regret the fact that he'd done it, not at all. He was just sorry that Marshall had caught them. Marsh sure had acted strangely. He'd been almost surly when Jim had entered the library. Surely, Marsh didn't object to his pursuit of Renee. After all, Marsh had said that he had no interest in her. No, Jim didn't know what had come over him but it had not been pleasant talking with him further that night. Possibly, he was concerned about Renee's reputation, so Jim decided he would make his declaration as soon as possible. Then no one would object to any show of affection between them. Once they were engaged, things would be different.

Renee spent the day sorting out her feelings. She had had no idea that Jim was attracted to her. She knew that they were close friends, but it hadn't dawned on her that he was physically attracted to her. Comparing their kisses had not been a contest. Jim's kiss had been . . . nice. Yes, that described it. Warm and nice. Not devastating like Marshall's but a comfortable gentle caress. There was no doubt at all in her mind that Marsh was the man for her. He could set her on fire with a mere look. And just being in the same room with him could make her want him. If only he felt the same way . . .

Marshall had deluged himself in work at his office.

The farther away from the *Elizabeth Anne* he stayed, the better. Everytime he passed the clerk's office, he felt an overwhelming desire to enter and relive what had happened there. And, as far as going to Elise's, that was out. He was well off to stay away from there, too. If Renee was in love with Jim, then that was fine. After all, he had told Jim that he had no interest in her. Why then had he been surprised to find Jim courting her? How many times had she been in Jim's arms? The question haunted him and work was his only escape.

It was three full days later before Jim found the opportunity to talk to Renee alone. He summoned her into the study while the others were busy and closed the door behind them.

"I think you've been avoiding me," he smiled at her.

"You're right," she answered, giving him a smile in return and the warmth between them returned too.

"I just wanted you to know that I in no way wanted to compromise you the other night. The last thing I expected was for Marsh to come into the hall. Thank God, he's a gentleman."

"He didn't say anything?"

"Not a word, but I have to admit, he wasn't any too pleased with me."

"Oh," and she wondered if that was a sign of hope.

"Renee, this is so hard for me," he moved closer to her and taking her by her shoulders, drew her to him.

"I don't think this is a good idea, Jim."

"Renee, do you know what I want to say to you?" he watched her face, knowing that she was not aware of the turmoil within him. "I love you and I want you to be my wife."

"You love me?" she asked, dumbfounded.

"Very much. It's been terrible all these weeks having you so close, but not being able to touch you," he bent his head and kissed her lightly.

Renee started to move away from him and he let her go reluctantly, watching her move gracefully to the window.

"Jim, I . . ."

"Don't say anything just now. Think about it. We have all the time in the world to decide. I know that you're still in mourning for your father, so we don't have to marry until you feel you're ready."

"But I don't love you," she said painfully, knowing as the words came that they would hurt him. "Not the way a wife should love her husband."

He didn't reply, he just looked at her quietly. It had never occurred to him that she wouldn't fall in love with him. He'd always had every woman he'd wanted and he hadn't expected that she would be any different. They stared at each other, emotion tense between them.

"Is there someone else?" he asked.

When she didn't answer right away, he knew. And he remembered his mother remarking that Renee was attracted to Marsh when Jim had visited Cedarhill all those long weeks ago.

"So it's Marshall, is it?" he asked her, his voice toneless.

"Jim, I'm sorry. I care for you, I do. I think you're a wonderful man, but it's never gone deeper than that. You're my dearest friend . . ."

"Friend . . . That wasn't quite what I had in mind," he replied, his voice even but his emotions seething. "If you will excuse me?"

Renee watched helplessly as he left the room, not looking back.

Within two days Jim had moved out of the house, saying that he was needed on the boat when the final touches were put on. Renee felt relieved that he was gone. Knowing that she had hurt him had made her very uncomfortable in his presence. She had tried to avoid him, but that had not been as easy as avoiding Marshall. Jim had finally cornered her alone in the dining room the morning before he left.

"Renee?"

She jumped as he came up behind her quietly, "Jim, oh, you startled me."

"I wish things hadn't changed between us."

"Me, too."

"There's no point in denying that you've been avoiding me for the past few days and I can't say that I blame you. We have a very special relationship and I don't want to spoil it. That's the only reason that I'm leaving now. I think I can be more objective about you from a distance than I can when I see you everyday. Do you understand?" he asked, taking her arm and turning her to face him.

"I think so. I'm glad you're not angry."

"Never. I care too much about you."

She forced a smile, "I never intended to hurt you."

"I know that, too. Believe me, I know that," he leaned toward her and kissed her tenderly on the cheek. "He's a very lucky man, if he ever realizes it."

She blushed and said nothing as Jim turned and left her standing there alone.

"Well, I think it's wonderful that you're finally ready!" Martha beamed at her son across the dining room table.

"We leave tomorrow morning at 6 A.M.," Jim agreed, happy at last to be getting back to work. "The salon is perfect. Everything's been repaired or replaced, shined or painted. We've booked a full load of cabin passsengers and I've got guards on board around the clock."

"I just hope you don't need them," Renee commented, glad that they were still good friends and comfortable together.

Elise and Martha had planned this special dinner for Jim's last night in town. The repairs had progressed smoothly and the *Elizabeth Anne* was ready to go three days ahead of schedule.

"Me, either," Jim replied. "I don't know why, but I have the feeling that he isn't after the boats any more. When he realizes that she's back in business again I think he'll try something ever more daring."

"Like what?" Dorrie asked.

"Believe me, Dorrie, if I knew how his mind worked, he'd be back in jail by now," Jim said with great frustration. "It's nerve-wracking, isn't it? Never knowing when or if he's going to strike."

George and Marshall both grimaced.

"I try not to dwell on it, but it's always in the back of my mind," George grumbled.

"We'll just have to be cautious. All of us," Marsh said, his gaze directed to Dorrie. "Just watch around the house or when you go out shopping."

"We do," Dorrie insisted.

"Good. It can't hurt to be extra careful. And

maybe, before too long, they'll be caught."

"God, I hope so," Martha said sounding slightly upset. "I love being here with Elise, but I miss my own home."

"As soon as it's safe, we'll move back," George told her, trying to soothe her.

"Well, in spite of everything, it's time for me to get back to the boat," Jim sighed as he pushed away from the table. "Dinner was fine, Elise, thank you."

"I'm glad you came," Elise answered him.

"I'll see you all when I get back from New Orleans in a week or so," he stood and moved to the hall with everyone following.

Celia brought him his coat and as he shrugged into it, he spoke directly to Marshall, "You take care of them."

"Father and I will both be around. He does have to ride out to the house, but when he's not staying here, I'll have John check more frequently."

Jim nodded and turning to his mother, he kissed and hugged her, "You're an excellent nurse, I don't know how you put up with me."

She didn't answer, but hugged him tightly. Jim shook hands with his father and brother and turned to Elise, Dorrie and Renee.

"Goodbye Elise," he said kissing her cheek. "Dorrie, please be careful and Renee, you too."

"We will," they promised.

He gave Dorrie a brotherly hug and kiss and was about to take Renee's hand when an idea came to him. Smothering a roguish grin, he pulled her to him and would have kissed her on the mouth except for her quick action. What he'd planned to be an incentive to stir Marshall on, turned into a chaste peck on the cheek.

"Only trying to help," he murmured for her only and smiling, he left.

Chapter Twelve

The last Saturday in March was set as the date for Dorrie's ball. Since there was still concern about Maguire, Elise offered her home for the party and Martha gratefully accepted. So the planning began and excitement stirred the Fontaine household.

One evening, after Martha and Dorrie had retired, Elise and Renee sat quietly in the parlor reading.

"Renee," Elise said looking up from her book.

"Yes?"

"Are you happy here?"

Renee rose from her chair to sit by her aunt. She hugged her tightly, "Oh, Elise, in the beginning I never thought I could be. But I truly am."

"I'm so glad. I know how close you and your father were. I just hope you aren't too lonesome or homesick."

"I do miss L'Aimant terribly. But it is good to have you to talk with and with Dorrie here now there's never a dull moment."

"I know, I know!" Elise laughingly agreed. "It's been six months you know."

"Yes, six months," Renee repeated flatly.

"I've been thinking that perhaps Dorrie's ball could be your first here."

Renee smiled and her face lit in anticipation, "You don't think it'd be too soon?"

"No. You've shown your respect most admirably and now it's time to start a new and exciting time in your life. I'm sure, once everybody gets a look at you, there'll be plenty of young men coming to call."

"Well . . ."

"We shall see what happens. Tomorrow, we'll go order the most lovely gown in town for you."

"Wonderful! I really feel this first ball will be very special."

"Me, too."

The following day, they visited an exclusive dressmakers and ordered her gown from a picture in a book straight from Paris. After being assured it would be ready in plenty of time for the party, they headed home for lunch. As their carriage passed Marshall's office, they both saw him coming out with a petite blonde on his arm. He didn't notice their carriage as he carried on a conversation with the young woman.

"That was Juliana Chandler."

"Oh?" Renee tried to sound disinterested.

"Yes, quite. She's one of the belles of society. She and Marshall have been seeing each other for some time now, according to Martha."

"Why hasn't he married her?"

"From what I understand, he doesn't want to marry again."

"Again?" she asked, startled from her act of indifference.

"You didn't know?"

"Why, no."

"He was married to a girl from Philadelphia about

five years ago but she died not too long afterward. It was all very sad, as I recall."

"Oh," Renee replied meekly. "I had no idea. But why wouldn't he want to marry again?"

"I'm not sure. There's more to it, I would imagine, but not much was ever said."

"What was she like?"

"She was small and blonde, a lot like Juliana."

Renee felt silent, wondering at her chances with Marshall if he preferred petite blondes. Perhaps that explained his cool indifference to her now. He'd been just toying with her. If he'd stayed with Juliana Chandler this long, she must be the woman he really cares for. And yet, Renee still felt an overpowering desire for him as she remembered their heated intimate caresses and the words—"I want you more than I've ever wanted any woman."

It was two nights later that Marshall dropped by unexpectedly only to find that his parents and Elise had gone for the evening and the girls eating dinner alone. Renee was glad for Dorrie's presence when Marshall decided to stay and eat with them. Dorrie's bubbling personality easily dominated the conversation with her much-adored brother. All discussions seemed centered on her debut at the upcoming ball.

Renee listened half-heartedly to all the light-hearted repartee but seldom entered the conversation. Her mind wandered to her debut last June and she remembered dancing gaily with her father and Uncle Alain and a dozen or so young men from the parish. It had been a fairy tale evening and she hoped that the Westlake ball would be as exciting for her friend. She must have sighed out loud for Marshall was looking at her quizzically, one eyebrow raised in question.

"Don't you agree?" Dorrie was asking her, as she took another bite of her dinner.

"With what?" Renee asked.

Dorrie burst out laughing, "I told you she wasn't listening, Marsh!"

Renee colored, "Was I that obvious?"

"Oh, Renee, don't worry. I'm sure you're sick of hearing about my party!"

"Oh, no, not at all. It's going to be wonderful. I'm truly excited for you."

"Well, I'm happy for you, too! Don't you think it'll be great to see Renee in something besides mourning clothes?"

"Most assuredly," Marshall agreed, his eyes catching and holding hers.

"Thank you," Renee blushed and looked away.

"It's the truth," Dorrie declared. "You're much too pretty for black. Is Juliana coming with you?" Dorrie continued uninterruptedly.

"Yes. She'll be there," Marshall replied.

"Good. Renee hasn't met her yet. Juliana is so sophisticated."

Marshall looked at his sister amusedly.

"Oh, really?" Renee asked.

"Oh, yes. Why her parents—the Chandlers—were pillars of society."

"Were?"

"Her mother died a long time ago, but she and her father still entertain fabulously. They have a fantastic house. Right, Marsh?"

"Yes, they do socialize regularly," he answered, casting a dark look at Dorrie.

"I think it would be so exciting to live like that! A different party or dance every weekend," Dorrie sighed romantically. "Don't you?"

"Actually, Dorrie, if you do anything to excess it can get boring," Marshall replied, pushing away from the table.

"Is that the voice of experience speaking? You can be so depressing at times!"

He laughed at her then, glad to at least have diverted her from Juliana.

"It must be because you're so old!" Dorrie teased. "Don't you agree, Renee?"

"Absolutely," Renee laughed as they moved into the parlor, Marsh scowling at them both in jest.

"Well, if I'm so old, Miss Westlake, maybe I should plan on staying at home in my rocking chair instead of dancing with you all night," he returned in good humor.

Dorrie laughed again and threw her arms around him, hugging him tightly. A gesture which Renee wished she could do so naturally, she felt a pang of envy at the affection these two shared. As soon as she realized what she felt was jealousy, Renee was ashamed. Why should she be envious of Dorrie? Dorrie was a generous, warm-hearted girl and Marshall, well, she'd just have to learn how to be around him without wanting him so badly. Glancing at him, as he stood at the mantel, she knew he was a handsome man. His features were relaxed now as he joked with his sister and he looked almost boyish. The white silk shirt and dark snug-fitting pants he wore only increased his attractiveness.

"You make sure to save me your second dance, all

right?" he was asking Dorrie.

"Of course, but there are so many men that I've wanted to dance with like Philip DeGrande and Mark Clayton. Just wait till you meet them, Renee!"

Renee laughed lightly at Dorrie's excitement, "I can wait, I can wait!"

"I'm afraid you'll find that Philip and Mark are not the Prince Charmings your imagination has made them out to be," Marshall said.

"Well, don't ruin my dreams. Let me find out for myself."

"All right. I can't protect you forever," he sighed in mock frustration.

"And just what does my daughter need protecting from?" George bellowed from the front hall as he, Martha and Elise came in from their evening out.

"Just some of my acquaintances, Father."

"That's true enough," George joked as he clapped Marshall on the back. "It's good to see you, son. Been busy?"

"Very. Why are you in town?"

"Just came in to see your mother and check on the plans for Dorrie's party. From what I understand, it should be quite a success."

"We heard today from the Bigelows, they'll be coming and Alain Chenaut is planning to make the trip upriver, just to be at this ball," Elise said seating herself next to Renee.

"Who is Alain Chenaut?"

"My father's best friend," Renee answered smiling wistfully.

"That will be nice for you," Martha added. "I'm sure you've missed him. Elise was telling us tonight how close you are to him."

"Yes. He's very dear to me. I wouldn't have made it through those last weeks before I left home without him."

"Let's don't think about the sad times," Elise said patting Renee's hand affectionately.

"Of course not!" Renee smiled brightly. "It's only ten days to the ball and there's so much to do. Last minute details."

Chapter Thirteen

Marshall had quietly observed Renee's changing moods as the evening progressed. She could be childlike sometimes. One minute happy, the next sad, but always honestly so. There was nothing deceitful about her, he decided grudgingly. She was exactly what she seemed to be. These times together with his family had proven to him that her similarities to Elizabeth went no deeper than her appearance. She was a delicate, blossoming young woman who had been desperately hurt by her recent loss. He wondered if she thought of him at all. He remembered her reaction when he had stopped making love to her on the boat. She had been so worried about his opinion of her. He shook his head slightly, smiling. He also remembered well the lovely picture she'd made lying there half nude on the sofa, her long legs bared to his gaze. He redirected his attention to the conversation between his parents and pretended interest in what was being said.

When the ladies finally retired for the evening, George and Marshall settled down for a long visit.

"Have you been by often?"

"Actually, no," he answered firmly.

"Oh," George returned. "Because of business?"

"I have been busy," he said evasively.

"So you don't want to talk about it?"

"It?" he raised an eyebrow questioningly.

"We've always been honest with each other, son."

"Yes, we have, but there's nothing really to say. I was here for dinner a few weeks ago but other than that, I felt I should stay away."

"Have you talked to John Randolph lately?"

"Yes, just today in fact."

"And?"

"Well, Maguire and his gang were spotted in St. Charles last week, but they got away."

"That's getting close," George sighed. "Now I feel better about your mother and sister being here. For a while there I was feeling sorry for myself all alone out at Cedarhill, but now I'm glad. I don't want them in danger."

"They're safe here."

"Are you so sure? If you've been staying purposefully away . . ." George began angrily.

"Father, I told John and he's been keeping a close watch."

"Still, I'd feel a lot better if you'd personally stay."

"What?" Marshall asked incredulously.

"I've got to go back home for at least two more days, but I can be back by the weekend. I think you should stay here until I get back. With your Mother here, there'll be no room for gossip."

"Are you certain it's necessary? The idea is . . ."

"The idea is a good one. It's necessary," George said obstinately, ending the discussion. "I'll tell the ladies to expect you tomorrow afternoon."

Marshall grimaced inwardly. Just what he needed,

he thought sarcastically, to be thrown together with Renee. Tonight had been enough to try the patience of a saint. He was glad Dorrie had been there to relieve the tension. With each passing encounter, he was finding himself drawn to her more and more.

"All right," he agreed, knowing he had no other choice. "I'll bring my things over as soon as I get my work caught up and close the office."

"Fine. I'll wait for your arrival before I head home."

Marshall took his leave then and headed back to his office. He was in no frame of mind to sleep, so work seemed the best solution. As always. It was dawn before he tried to rest and then as soon as he dozed, the dreams bombarded him with images of Elizabeth. Elizabeth laughing and flirting, then her image changing until she stood before him, her face contorted with rage, her long blonde hair blowing wildly, a knife in her hand. In the dream she advanced on him shrieking—You're mine! I won't share you! Marshall tossed fitfully as she drew closer and raised the knife to strike. In the nightmarish slow motion, the blade descended but instead of cutting him she stabbed herself, laughing hideously. She moved away from him in the dream and he tried to run after her but his legs wouldn't move.

"Elizabeth! Don't leave me this way!" he shouted to her disappearing figure.

Then he was riding, the wind tearing at him and at last he seemed to be gaining on her. She was running ahead of him in a white hooded cloak. He reached out and snared her and pulled her across his horse in front of him.

"Elizabeth," he breathed, his heart lurching.

The woman pushed the hood back and tilted her face up to him.

"Renee!" he uttered in surprise. Her face seemed radiant in its innocence and he felt his breath catch in his throat. This was the woman to make him whole again, his soul knew it. He lowered his head and gently touched his lips to hers. . . .

He sat upright abruptly, rubbing a hand over his eyes. What time was it? What day? Marshall looked around his sleeping room, his mind still groggy. The sun was streaming in the one window and by the angle he guessed it to be past noon. He swung his long legs off the bed and rested his head in his hands elbows on his knees. It was coming back now, the vagueness fading the content of his mind's fantasy returning full force. He rose quickly as he remembered the conclusion. He felt shaken by the force of the dream and pulled on his clothes, anxious to be gone from the confinement of the small room.

Juliana raised her after dinner drink in salute to Philip as they sat opposite each other in the parlor of the Chandler mansion.

"So that's all you could find out?"

"Yes, my dear, but was it worth it? The price a mere evening with me?" he chuckled.

"Yes, Philip, it was worth it. It's reassuring to know that he's staying at the Fontaine's to protect his family, even if that girl is there, too. When do I get to see her?"

"I imagine at Dorrie Westlake's ball."

"Ugh! You mean I'll have to be nice to her?"

"Of course, you're a lady."

Juliana laughed lightly, "That's right. Have you heard anything about Maguire?"

"Just that he was spotted in St. Charles a while ago but hasn't been seen since."

"No wonder Marsh moved in with his mother. Mr. Westlake must be just frantic."

"I imagine," Philip said boredly, then leering at her. "Now, come here sweet. The evening is early and I want to get my money's worth."

Juliana rose casually and went to him, sitting on his lap.

"Yes, it is still very early," she agreed eagerly, her hands moving over his aggressively.

"Your father's out for the evening?"

"Of course, we have the whole house to ourselves."

"Good, let's go upstairs so we won't be interrupted."

Juliana moved from his lap and drew him up with her, running a finger down the front of his shirt.

"Are you sure you can wait that long?" she asked archly.

He looked at her questioningly, as she moved away and closed the sliding doors that led into the hallway. Mesmerized by the seductiveness of her intent, he followed her.

"I need a man, now," Juliana told him throatily as he took her in his arms.

Philip didn't realize that Juliana was using him. He was so in love with her, that all rational thought was lost to him. He fumbled with the buttons on her dress until she, almost angrily, led him to the sofa. Lying down, she pushed her skirts aside and urged him upon her.

"Please, I have to have you now," what seemed begging was in fact an order, and he moved upon her, eager to make contact with her exposed flesh. Eyes closed, Juliana strove for her release, her hands clawing at Philip's back as he thrust into her. Visions of another man and another time filled her mind as she finally gained what she'd sought. Philip, feeling Juliana's wild movements beneath him as she climaxed, let himself go and soon collapsed beside her, fulfilled and exhausted.

"You're wonderful, Juliana," he murmured, drowsily.

"So are you, Philip, but let's go upstairs, where we know we won't be disturbed," she was once more calculating and cold.

Philip rose, straightening his clothing, and smiled as he watched Juliana pull down her skirts and become, once again, the seemingly unattainable woman whom he desired. He opened the hallway doors and they ascended to her bedroom, unaware of the servant's eyes upon them.

"So you think it's funny, do you?" Marshall growled at smiling Renee.

"I would have thought you'd know enough not to play backgammon with her!" Dorrie laughed. "Beat you again, huh?"

"I may have lost the battle, but not the war!" he declared. Then flashing them both a warm smile, he rose from the game table.

"How long will this war last? You've lost three battles already!" Renee teased.

"I know, I know!"

"Dorrie? Don't losers usually have to pay up?"

"Absolutely!"

"What shall it be?" Renee looked up at Marsh, standing with his back to them, silhouetted against the window. Just watching him made her breathless and she blushed remembering his touch.

"I know!" Dorrie said intriguingly, giving Renee a conspiratorial glance, as Marshall turned to face them.

"Yes, dear sister? What torment have you devised for me?" he questioned, a smile playing about his lips.

"Well, Renee, don't you think that three dances at my ball would be recompense enough for the three losses at backgammon?"

"More than enough!" Renee laughed.

"But not just any three," Dorrie continued. "Three waltzes."

Renee's eyes widened questioningly and Marshall stifled a groan. Not that he didn't want to dance with Renee, but what was he to do with Juliana?

"What do you say?" Dorrie urged.

"Dorrie, it may be awkward . . . I mean . . . Miss Chandler will be his partner and . . ." Renee stuttered.

"No. No, it's not a problem, Renee," he said quickly, not wanting to embarrass her by hesitating. "Three waltzes it shall be. But just remember, there'll have to be payment made to me when I finally win," he added threateningly and left the room abruptly, leaving both young women staring after him.

Chapter Fourteen

The following week seemed to drag by for Renee. Marshall had moved back to his office and Elise's house seemed empty without him. The two days he'd stayed had been heaven and hell to Renee. He had constantly been near and seemingly took pleasure in being with her but they were never alone. On one hand, she was glad for his attention, especially when she'd catch him watching her, a soft unexplained look in his eyes. On the other hand, not once did he attempt to touch her or maneuver her for privacy. She couldn't understand how he could be so ardent one moment and the next be so 'brotherly.' She didn't know why, she only knew she was angry. She would have her chance at the ball. The infamous Juliana would be there. Subconsciously, Renee prepared for combat. Marshall was going to want her Saturday night, of that much she was sure.

Her one respite from dwelling over much on thoughts of Marshall was Alain Chenaut's arrival. It thrilled her to see her 'uncle' when he finally got to town on Friday. He spent his time at Elise's, relishing the attention poured on him by the females there. He and George struck an immediate friendship and time flew by. Alain had taken rooms at the Planters House, so after an exhausting day and evening he bid them all good night and kissed Renee before departing. They all retired then, tired yet happy and excited about the coming day.

Renee stood in her wrapper at her bedroom window gazing down at Elise's flowers below. The riotous color of the massed tulips and crocuses was fading as the shadows of late afternoon engulfed the garden. The slow passing day at last was drawing to a close and she knew that the hour was near for her to begin dressing. The day had been unseasonably warm and the evening promised more of the same. She could hardly believe that Saturday night was finally here. Turning to her full length mirror she twirled excitedly, watching her own reflection. Her cheeks were flushed with excitement and her freshly washed dark hair swirled about her shoulders in an abundance of soft loose curls. She opened her wardrobe and carefully took out her gown, enjoying the feel of the smooth silk. She momentarily thought of her father and how she wished he could be with her tonight. Uncle Alain's presence would help, she knew, for he would always be there whenever she needed him.

Elise and Martha had insisted she be in the receiving line, so there could be no late entrance. She must be ready at 7:30 to greet guests. Elise had said earlier that Marshall and Juliana would arrive ahead of time, too. Renee frowned at the thought of seeing him with another woman. It would not be easy to feign indifference, knowing how his presence could arouse her. This was her first opportunity to really enjoy herself since last summer and she was determined to do just that. Perhaps Uncle Alain could keep Juliana busy tonight while she had her waltzes with Marshall. Tonight, she would be enchanting and he would be hard put to tear himself away! Smiling, she sat at the dressing table and began to get ready.

"Juliana!" Marshall said startled. He stood naked to the waist at the wash basin in his room, having just finished shaving.

Juliana swept into the room on a cloud of her sensuous perfume, closing the door behind her, "Hello, darling."

"What the hell are you doing here?" he asked angrily, throwing his towel on the washstand and moving to the bed to get his shirt.

"Marsh, I just stopped by to find out what time you were picking me up," she remarked casually, moving to him and putting her arms around him as he bent to retrieve his shirt.

He gently turned to her but instead of the embrace she expected, he removed her arms and set her from him.

"Not now. I have too much to do."

"Like what?" she asked seductively as she sat down on the bed and gazed up at him longingly. "What could be more important than our love making?"

"For one thing, we have to be at Dorrie's ball before the other guests arrive."

Juliana grimaced, "Too bad. I'll miss not making an entrance."

"If it's inconvenient for you, I can arrange for you to come later," he said smoothly.

Her eyes narrowed, "No, I want to be with you.

181

Besides there'll be time for us later. Perhaps we could leave early?"

"Hardly. I'll be by about seven. Can you be ready? It's almost six now."

"I guess I really must hurry off, if I'm to be perfect for you," she turned to leave, then turned back to him wrapped her arms around his neck and before he could protest covered his mouth with hers. "Darling, I want you so."

Marsh accepted the kiss and embrace unemotionally. He had no time now and little feeling left for her. The desire he had felt for her in the beginning of their relationship had been destroyed by the lies she'd told and her persistent maneuverings to get him to the altar. He took her arms from around him and glared down at her but as he began to speak he noticed the open bedroom door and saw Jim standing there observantly.

"We have company, my dear," he said gruffly.

"Oh?" she turned and grinned slyly, mistaking the dark look and his tone for passion. "Why, Jim, how nice to see you. I must be off, if I'm to be ready by seven. Gentlemen."

After Juliana had gone from the office, Jim looked at Marshall questioningly. "Did I come back at a bad time?"

"No," Marshall sounded relieved. "I'm not seeing much of Juliana anymore."

"Is there a reason?" Jim asked cannily.

Marshall shrugged carelessly, dismissing the subject. "Who are you bringing tonight?"

"No one. There'll be plenty of single young ladies in attendance if I know Mother's guest list."

"Absolutely. Not to mention Dorrie, of course. I'll bet she's excited," they both laughed thinking of their little sister's anxiety, waiting for the hours to pass.

"How are you going to discourage Juliana? She seems quite convinced you'll marry her."

Marshall frowned, "I can handle her."

"I hope it goes easily for you," Jim paused. "Hell hath no fury. . . ."

"I know but there are times when subtleties don't work."

"Just don't wait too long."

They agreed on that and each set about getting ready.

Elise found Renee watching the street from her bedroom window when she entered her room a little past seven.

"Anyone arrive yet?"

"No," answered Renee nervously. "I was hoping Uncle Alain would be here early, but there's been no sign of him yet."

"What about Jim or Marshall?"

"No. No one."

"Well, they'll be here soon. Turn around now and let me see you."

Renee turned carefully to give Elise time to observe the gown they had selected together.

"Tonight you are a woman!" Elise declared, proud of her niece's appearance.

Renee's gown was devastatingly simple. It was a low cut gown, off shoulder in style, of peach grosgrain and cream lace. Elise had insisted on elegance for her, not the usual over-trimmed, bow-bedecked gowns that were gracing ballrooms lately. The result was stunning. She had pulled her hair up and away from her face and it was curled artfully with a peach ribbon entwined through it.

"Thank you, Elise," she laughed lightly. "I feel wonderful. I'm probably as excited as Dorrie!"

"Almost. Dorrie looks lovely, too," Elise said. "It's almost 7:30; are you ready to go down with me?"

"I guess. Have I forgotten anything?"

"No. You're perfect."

Renee smiled a trifle nervously as they left the room. They were halfway down the stairs, when the front door opened and Juliana Chandler came in, followed by Marshall.

Marshall attentively took Juliana's wrap and handed his own coat to the butler before he noticed the ladies on the staircase.

"Good evening, Marshall, Juliana," Elise called happily drawing their attention as she moved ahead to leave Renee alone on the steps.

Marshall froze as he glanced past Elise to Renee. His dark-eyed gaze took in every inch of her. Swallowing hard, his expression carefully blank, he turned back to Juliana and introduced them.

"Juliana, I'd like you to meet Renee Fontaine, Elise's niece from Louisiana. Renee, this is Juliana Chandler."

"Hello," Juliana said brightly as she turned to greet her. Her eyes grew cold as she surveyed the dress the newcomer wore. Then their eyes locked and each recognized the other as a worthy rival. Juliana was amazed by the resemblance Renee bore to Elizabeth Westlake. Uncanny. Yes, she decided, she would have

184

to keep a close watch on this 'southern' belle tonight.

Renee, remembering all the lessons her Mammy had taught her, floated down the remaining steps and in her most exaggerated drawl, dripping sweetness, she greeted them.

"Why, I've heard so much about you, Juliana. It's so nice to finally meet you. And Marshall, dahlin'," she smiled innocently and offered him her hand. "I swear it just seems like ages since I saw you last."

He raised an eyebrow at her as he bent over her hand. The contact between them was electric and Marsh frowned.

"You look lovely, Renee," he said sincerely and his mood darkened as he felt Juliana move closer and take his arm possessively.

Although her face betrayed none of it, Renee was taken aback by the scowling look on his face. She couldn't imagine what she had done to incur his wrath and then to watch Juliana fawning all over him was almost more than she could bear. Elise, much to her delight, was enjoying this little scene. Juliana looked positively livid and her discomfort added to Elise's enjoyment. Elise knew that Juliana needed a put-down and she also knew Renee was the one to do it, but poor Marshall! Just as Juliana started to speak, the door opened and Jim entered, resplendent in his new clothes.

"Good evening ladies, Marsh, good to see you," he greeted, handing his coat and hat to the butler. Then turning to Renee, "My dear, it's hard to believe that you are the same child who came upriver with me last fall. Tonight you are a vision."

"Thank you, Jim," she took his compliment with

practiced ease. Jim offered her his arm and led her off down the hall.

"You are gorgeous," he said softly. "Come, let's see how the ballroom looks. The guests won't be here for a while."

"I'd love to," she agreed. "You certainly look dashing this evening."

"Why, thank you," he grinned as they moved into the ballroom.

"Well, she certainly looks like Elizabeth!" Juliana said cattily after Jim and Renee had disappeared into the ballroom.

Marshall started at her remark but before he could speak Elise interposed quietly.

"Why, Juliana, you really think she looks like Elizabeth? We've never noticed, I mean Elizabeth was small and blonde like you. I really don't see the resemblance. In fact, Marshall has been seeing Renee for some time now and he's made no mention of it . . ."

Juliana was surprised by Elise's reply and fell silent temporarily as George and Martha came down together. They were dismayed at the sight of Juliana hanging on Marshall's arm.

"Where's Renee?"

"With Jimmy, in the ballroom," Elise answered.

"Oh," they said in unison and smiled widely at Elise as Marshall led Juliana away after Jim and Renee.

Chapter Fifteen

It was well after eight before everyone had arrived and promptly at 8:30 Dorrie made her grand entrance on her father's arm. Her youthful radiance was complemented by her white, full-skirted gown of tulle. It had a square neckline, tiny puff sleeves and was ornamented with pale pink bows. At her throat, she wore a single strand of pearls, a gift from her parents. The music began as soon as her entrance was complete and George led her onto the dance floor to begin the celebration. Slowly, the other dancers joined them. Dorrie spied Renee dancing with Alain while Marshall squired Juliana about the room and Jim danced with his mother.

"Father, this is wonderful!"

"Dorrie, honey, it's a joy to see you so lovely, although I must admit it ages me considerably to think my baby is old enough to marry now."

Dorrie laughed delightedly, "Oh, Papa! There's no need to worry about that. There are some very attractive men here tonight but none to compare to you."

George laughed at her and twirled her more quickly about the floor.

"Juliana certainly doesn't look happy tonight," she

noted as they moved past her brother and his partner.

"Between you and me, I think she's finally realized Marshall is not in love with her. And then seeing Renee—well, that unnerved her," George confided.

Dorrie smiled, "Good. I don't like Juliana at all. I just don't think you can trust her."

"Enough about her. Let's enjoy our evening."

"Fine," she agreed.

The second dance, a polka, began with Dorrie waiting impatiently for her brothers to decide who would have the honor. Finally, in a burst of irritation, she grabbed Marshall's hand.

"He's so much older than you, Jimmy. I'm afraid he won't have enough energy left for me later. Did you know he almost stayed home in his rocking chair tonight?" Dorrie confided loudly to Jim as Marsh led her away onto the floor.

Marsh guided her around the floor in dizzying circles until she begged him to slow down and promised no more old age jokes for the rest of the evening.

"Have you seen Renee yet?" she asked breathlessly as they changed directions again.

"Yes, when I arrived."

"Isn't she absolutely gorgeous? Who would have thought under all that black—" Dorrie let the sentence drop as she noticed him scanning the dance floor.

"Where's Juliana?"

"I don't know. I think with Philip DeGrande somewhere. Why?"

"I just wondered how soon you'll dance with Renee. They should be playing a waltz next. I made Papa insist on lots of waltzes tonight."

He glanced down at her, wondering if she really knew what a problem it would be to get away from Juliana this evening. Dorrie was gazing up at him guilelessly, seemingly unaware of the awkward situation he was in.

"Thank you, Jim, that was wonderful," Renee said as he led her back to Elise and Alain who were both beaming over the exquisite picture she made.

"Any time," he assured her as Marsh and Dorrie joined them.

"Here, Jim, she's all yours now," Marshall said handing Dorrie over.

The music began again, a slow lilting waltz and as Jim led Dorrie onto the floor she called softly to Marsh, "Pay up, big brother!"

He cast her a dangerous look and turned to Renee who was trying to ignore the whole scene.

"Renee, may I have the honor?" he asked quickly, noting Juliana's approach from across the floor.

"Marshall, it's not necessary. I won't hold you to anything so silly as that."

"You may rest assured that if I didn't wish to dance with you, I wouldn't. Shall we?" he stated abruptly, offering her his arm.

"Why, yes," she murmured politely and took his arm.

At the edge of the dance floor, he swept her into a warm embrace and they glided smoothly across the room oblivious to Juliana who had witnessed the whole scene. Renee knew it would be like this dancing with him, held tightly in his arms. He was graceful and she felt as though they were floating. When she finally looked up, she blushed to find him staring at her quizzically.

"Why so quiet?"

"I was just enjoying the music," she declared, her drawl gone.

"What happened to your accent?"

She glared up at him for she knew he was mocking her, "I didn't think it was necessary with you."

"Why before, then?"

"I needed to reassure myself," she answered quietly, feeling his arm tighten about her at her reply. He understood now, she knew.

They continued to move in silence, each lost in the reverie of the other's closeness.

"What do you think, Jimmy?" Dorrie asked as they too circled the room.

"I think you're right, little one, but we can't push them anymore and somehow I've got to keep Juliana away from Renee tonight."

"Um," Dorrie agreed. "I'll do what I can but I think Renee can take care of herself. With the build-up I gave her about Juliana, I'm sure she's aware of just how great Juliana thinks herself to be. And how serious she is about Marsh."

"Well, forewarned is forearmed. But still I'll dance with Julie as often as possible just to keep her quiet."

"Thanks. I want this to be an eventful evening, but not a disastrous one."

Juliana sipped her champagne and looked evenly at Philip, "I see what you mean, Philip."

"I knew you would. Just look how he's holding her, like there's no one else in the world. . . ." Philip said caustically.

"Oh, shut up!" Julie snapped.

"Believe me, all the tantrums in the world can't tear those two apart. The most logical thing in the world for you to do is to step aside gracefully."

Juliana started to shriek at Philip but stopped and turned back to the dance floor, her face frozen in a calm expression. He saw her blanch then, as they watched Marshall lower his head attentively to Renee and then laugh amusedly at something she said.

"That southern bitch!" Julie whispered venomously. "Philip, I shall play out this charade but never again will I put myself in such a position."

She drained her drink and turned to Philip who was eyeing her cautiously.

"Phil, let's dance, shall we? I do believe it would be heaven to be held in your strong arms, darling."

Philip smirked at his good fortune. He was still madly in love with Juliana and the sooner she got over Marshall Westlake the better for him.

When the waltz ended Renee and Dorrie were both claimed by eager young swains anxious to dance with the most beautiful ladies present. Marshall had gone to the bar after finally catching sight of Julie dancing with Philip. He met Jim there and they went outside on the terrace for a moment. The sky was cloudy now and the heavy scent of rain was in the air. They leaned against the balustrade, enjoying the music and the warmth of their night.

"Looks like Julie may be busy tonight," Jim said absently.

"I think she's busy every night," he snorted in derision.

Jim fell silent for a moment, then he grinned, "Dorrie told me about your dances with Renee."

"Damn!" he said with great annoyance. "Is nothing in my life private? Why am I saddled with a sister who not only fancies herself a matchmaker but is a busy-body gossip as well?"

"Take it easy. I just asked her what the 'pay-up' business was all about. I promise not another word. I'm sure you've got enough on your mind without any extra aggravation from us."

Marshall growled and drained his bourbon. Jim was inwardly amused at his brother's discomfort. For years, he had seemed mercenary where women were concerned. Now, Jim knew Marshall was once again aware of another's feelings and it was disturbing him.

"What are you going to do?"

Marshall looked at him sharply and then handed him his empty glass, "Right now, I'm going to claim Renee for waltz number two," and he left Jim standing alone, glasses in hand, on the terrace.

Juliana had observed Marshall leaving the room with his brother and had relaxed her carefree exterior for a moment. She received a multitude of offers to dance and dance she did, gaily and happily. Still Marsh did not return to her and Julie became increasingly irritable. George did nothing to soothe her when he danced with her, only saying that since this was a family affair, Marshall was helping to entertain the guests. She almost believed it until she saw him return from the terrace and go straight to

192

Renee. Philip was right and she had to acknowledge it now, but she would not make it easy for him. Juliana had felt the change in him this afternoon. Now, she knew her instincts had been correct. She headed on a collision course for Marshall, certain she could distract him. Suddenly, out of nowhere, Jim had taken her into his arms.

"Come, Julie, we haven't danced yet tonight," he coaxed as the waltz began and she could not refuse.

Renee had just returned to Elise and Alain after a rousing schottische with George when Marsh came to her. He seemed very tense and the expression he wore made her nervous.

"Well, my southern belle, are you ready for our second waltz?" he queried.

"If you are . . ." she replied looking at him shyly, afraid of his unknown moods and not wanting to seem too eager.

His expression seemed to darken at her reply and he led her out to the dance floor. Again, she was in his arms but this time he held her closer, almost crushed to him. It was a pleasant sensation to be moving as one and the warmth that his closeness always brought spread through her.

"Are you enjoying yourself?" he asked gently, watching her face.

"Oh, yes, Marshall," she answered breathlessly, the champagne making it much easier to speak her mind. The years of Mammy's tutoring were fading away. She knew instinctively now that with this man she could be herself.

"I'm glad," he answered sincerely. "These past few

months have been terrible for you, haven't they?"

"Did it show so very much?" she asked, upset that her depression might have affected others. "I tried so hard . . ."

"I know."

"You do? How?"

"I lost my wife, it's been five years now, but sometimes the pain . . ."

"I'm sorry."

"Why?"

"Because I wouldn't ever want you to be hurt," she answered honestly, then blushing at her own words, she turned her face away pretending interest in the other couples.

He was quiet then, enjoying the dance and the closeness of the moment. When the waltz ended, he took her to the refreshment table and got her more champagne punch and himself another bourbon. Dorrie joined them and soon Jim, Philip and Juliana had gathered about. Julie stayed carefully out of Marshall's reach, observing him with narrowed eyes. He finally came to her with a fresh drink, leaving Renee with Jim.

"I'm sorry I haven't been more attentive," he apologized dreading her waspish tongue.

Instead, she shrugged, "It's all right; this is, after all, a family affair and you must help entertain the other guests."

"Thank you for understanding. Have you been suitably entertained?"

"Of course. I haven't missed a dance yet," she said but then taking his arm. "But no one dances as well as you, darling."

He took her, somewhat stiffly, out onto the floor for the quadrille that was forming.

"Come, Renee," Philip urged and they, too, joined the others.

It was almost an hour later when Marshall finally made his way to his parents who were resting momentarily near the open double hall doors.

"Having a good time, son?" George asked noticing how relaxed he was.

"Of course. Did you doubt it?"

"Not for a moment, dear," Martha interrupted.

He looked curiously from parent to parent and then went out into the hall where he found Dorrie and Renee going upstairs. He moved in their direction.

"Leaving so soon?"

"No. We just thought we'd rest a bit before we eat," Dorrie explained.

"I was thinking the same thing but I was going out to the garden. Care to join me?"

"I won't but Renee will!" Dorrie exclaimed, before Renee could speak. "Wait here, I'll throw down a shawl for you."

Renee looked at Marshall without embarrassment and came back down the stairs. She hadn't talked with him for an hour and it had made her miserable. She smiled at the thought that at last he wanted to be alone with her.

Marshall caught the deftly thrown shawl and put it around her shoulders caressingly. Then taking her hand, they slipped out quickly before they were discovered by prying eyes. He led her to the half wall where he and Jim had earlier been.

"Isn't it lovely out here?"

"As long as the rain holds off," he mused as he saw a flash of distant lightning.

"I love storms, when I'm inside and safe that is!" she laughed.

He heard the music begin again, a waltz, and he turned to face her.

"May I have the honor?"

"But, of course, kind sir," she drawled for effect and laughingly went into his arms.

Instead of whirling her away, he merely stood gazing down at her. She met his searching eyes with an unspoken plea and he lowered his head and gently kissed her. A chaste kiss. A warm kiss. An affectionate kiss. It just about drove Renee mad. She wanted him to need her, to want her as she wanted him. Renee put her arms around his neck and pulled him more tightly to her. He was aroused by her encouragement as her lips parted under his. The liquor they had consumed that evening had heightened their awareness of their need for each other and this first embrace had confirmed what each had suspected all along. Voices from the house brought Renee back to reality and she moved away from him, bewildered by the force of the emotions she felt. Forgotten was her great plan; all she knew was that she loved him. The thought was frightening to her. Elise had told her that every girl in town wanted him; what chance did she have? With Juliana as competition, Renee felt unexplicably sad.

"Renee," his voice deepened. "I love you."

"What?" she choked out, her voice sounded strangled in her throat. She was sure that her jaw dropped in surprise. She could say no more.

He purposefully strode to her and kissed her again. She melted against him.

"And I love you," she whispered when the kiss ended.

He smiled at her then, "Will you marry me?"

"Marry you?" her eyes widened.

"Well?" he asked seemingly very sure of himself.

"Yes, oh, yes!" she cried hugging him tightly

"Wonderful," he murmured lowering his head to hers.

"See, Julie, I told you he was out here with her," Philip said quietly to Juliana, who was watching Marsh and Renee kiss with unconcealed jealousy.

"Is this why you brought me here? To watch that slut . . ."

"I would hardly say it's one-sided, dear. Come now let's go back to our dancing and merrymaking. Perhaps we should announce our engagement tonight?"

"No," she said brittlely. "We'll announce it at Papa's party next week." To herself she thought, that way he'll think he's lost me for good and try to make amends.

Philip sighed in vexation at her tenacity. She could be really annoying sometimes. They went back to the party leaving Marsh and Renee alone once again.

"When?" Marsh asked holding her away from him.

"When what?"

"When shall we get married? Do you want a big wedding?"

She looked at him with open adoration, "Marshall,

I don't care about a big wedding. I just want us to be together."

"Are you sure?"

"Of course. Without Father there's no point. As long as I have you, I shall be content."

"Then let's get married now, tonight."

"What?"

"We can leave now. I know where there's a parson who'll marry us tonight."

"But what about Juliana? And your family?"

"Leave that to me. Is there anything you'd like to take along?"

"Just a few things."

"Fine. I'll meet you back here in say five minutes?"

Her breath catching, she nodded assent and hurried inside. In a few short moments they both were back, Renee carrying her reticule.

"Ready?" he asked noting her small bag.

"Are you?"

"I want this more than I've ever wanted anything," he answered with conviction. "Are you afraid?"

"Yes."

"Don't be. I love you."

"I love you."

Hand in hand, conspiratorily, they circled around the house and found the Westlake carriage waiting for them.

"That was fast!" she laughed.

"I know some important people," he grinned.

"Like Danny, the head groom?" she smiled.

He winked at her and handed her into the vehicle.

"Parson Gordon's," he instructed the driver.

With a look of surprise, the servant acknowledge his

instructions and the carriage rolled away. Renee and Marsh faced each other across the carriage.

"Come here," he invited patting the seat next to him.

She went to him willingly and slid into the crook of his arm. He bent down and kissed her lightly.

"How far is it?"

"About an hour's drive. It's on the way to Cedarhill."

"Marshall!" she gasped.

"What?" he asked jumping at her tone.

"It never occurred to me before, but do you think it's safe?"

"Is what safe?" he was totally confused.

"Our being out here alone?"

"No, you're not safe. You'll never be safe when you are alone with me," he leered at her in jest and leaned over to kiss her again but she shoved him back.

"I don't mean safe from you. I mean . . ." she gulped, "Maguire."

"Don't worry, my love. The last place he'd look for me tonight would be in a carriage driving home."

"Oh, good," she sighed. "I wouldn't want anything to happen because of our recklessness."

"Our what?"

She blushed.

"Renee," he said seriously. "What I feel is not reckless. And what we are about to do tonight is not without thought. I wanted you since I first saw you on the levee."

"Oh," she managed.

He pulled her onto his lap and kissed her, his mouth hard with desire against hers. She was

199

breathless when the kiss ended and as his lips moved to her throat she felt the longing begin deep within her. The shawl she'd worn had fallen to the floor, leaving her shoulders bare. His breath was hot against her as he pressed kisses on the swell of her breasts above the low decolletage. With one gentle movement, he pushed the material away and freed her straining breasts from their confinement. She started at the first touch of his warm mouth at her breast but her anxiety was replaced by rapture as he continued his caresses. Renee felt the ache within her growing unbounded as she held his head to her savoring the feel of his lips upon her.

"Oh, Marshall, I love you," she whispered to him.

He raised his head and kissed her again longingly, wanting her to read in his kiss all the emotions that he could not put into words. There was no doubt in his mind that he was doing the right thing. He had not thought of Renee and Elizabeth in the same context since the days he'd spent at Elise's. She was an honest and forthright person. In his estimation, that was the most important thing above all else. He was done with conniving women and their duplicity. He would devote himself to her happiness. It did not occur to him that she would want to know more about Elizabeth. He felt it sufficient that he had told her of his marriage and that it was painful for him to speak of it. The whole episode was after all something he had no desire to remember or dwell upon. So, Marshall dismissed the physical resemblance as now an unimportant matter and thought only of the night to come when he would at last have her for his own.

Renee was enjoying Marshall's lovemaking for the

first time, without worry or guilt. She had to admit that as she'd watched him at the ball this evening, she had burned for his touch and now to have him holding her was more intoxicating than all the champagne she'd consumed. Marsh broke off the kiss and held her away from him. He adjusted the bodice so she was once again covered and reaching down for her shawl, he wrapped it securely about her.

"Why did you stop?" she asked earnestly.

He was amused by her innocence and gave her a lopsided grin. "My dear, unless you wish to consummate our nuptials before the fact, it's best we move apart for a bit," he said, moving her from his lap to the seat next to him.

She looked at him questioningly but followed his guidance. He moved uneasily in the seat and she wondered at his discomfort until glancing at him curiously she saw the bulge of his manhood against his tight dress pants. An embarrassed groan escaped her and she blushed profusely. Marshall, realizing what had caused her agitation, laughed loudly.

"As you can see, it would hardly be proper to greet the minister so endowed, my love," he said laughing at her lustily. "Come, sit next to me and I promise to control myself for the next few miles until we reach the chapel."

Forgetting her embarrassment, she laughed and sat next to him, careful to keep her hands to herself.

"Did you tell anyone where we were going?"

"No."

"No? Won't they worry? And what about Juliana?" her questions were innocent enough but the whole subject was one he did not wish to discuss.

"Don't be concerned. I told Jim that we were leaving. He's going to keep Juliana occupied," his expression was strained.

"But what about Elise?"

"I'm sure Jim will think of something."

"Good. Tomorrow everything will be fine, but I didn't want her to worry unduly tonight."

"That's very thoughtful of you and that's one of the reasons why I love you so much," his face was more relaxed now and he bent to kiss her.

"Oh, no!" she squealed and pushed him back. "We're almost there, aren't we?"

"Yes, but . . ." he muttered.

"You can wait just a little longer, can't you?" she teased. "Please. We don't want to embarrass ourselves."

"Ah . . ." he groaned exaggeratedly. "You're a hard taskmaster."

"Just following orders, sir."

"You're right, of course. It's just you're so tempting curled up here," he said leaning back against the seat, resignedly.

The carriage turned abruptly and she was flung more tightly against him.

"Well, we're here, pet," he said enthusiastically, as the carriage finally stopped and the driver hopped down and opened the door. "Wait for me here. I'll be right back!"

He jumped down and went up the path to the small house next to the chapel. Watching from the open carriage door, she saw a light appear in the window and soon the front door opened. In the quiet of the night she heard the murmur of voices, one she knew was Marshall's but she could not distinguish what was being said. There was a flash of lightning and the distant roll of thunder, yet the rain still held off. Marsh came back and handed her down.

"Parson Gordon is waiting."

"He doesn't mind?"

"Of course not. From what I understand, he does most of his business at night."

She laughed delightedly. He escorted her into the small candlelit chapel. In the next few minutes, her life was sealed with his. They became, in the eyes of God, one person.

Chapter Sixteen

"You may place the ring on her finger," Reverend Gordon said.

"I didn't have time," Marshall apologized.

But there was no need for physical proof of the wedding. The love with which the young girl beheld her new husband made the minister and his wife smile knowingly at each other.

"It's all right, Marshall."

He smiled at her half sadly. He felt in his heart that he was somehow cheating her of something very important. Reverend Gordon's voice continued with the short ceremony.

"You may kiss your bride, Mr. Westlake," he concluded.

And Marshall gave her a chaste peck.

"Congratulations!" Mrs. Gordon beamed going to Renee. "Mrs. Westlake!"

Renee smiled vaguely and returned Mrs. Gordon's pleasantries, yet for all the conversation, she was only aware of Marsh's nearness. The scent of him, the heat of his arm about her, the pressure of his hand at her waist were driving her to distraction. After the necessary papers had been signed, they made their way back down the short aisle to the double doors.

The lightning was flashing and it was pouring down. The wind was blowing in strong gusts. They stood huddled in the doorway momentarily.

"Ready?" Marsh asked as he pulled her shawl up over her hair.

"Not really," she answered dreading the cold chill of the wind-driven rain.

"Do you want to spend our wedding night here?" he questioned raising an eyebrow.

She smiled impishly, casting a look about her, "Well, the pews do look a bit uncomfortable."

He gave her a quick embrace and then swung her up into his arms.

"Marshall! Put me down ! You'll hurt yourself!"

"Hardly. Now hold on tight!" and he ran toward the carriage.

Throwing wide the carriage door, he put Renee inside and then went in search of their driver. Soon he joined her and they were on their way.

"We can spend the night at Cedarhill and return to town tomorrow if the rain lets up. I thought we would have more privacy there," he sounded so restrained that Renee threw him a sidelong glance.

"That will be fine. It's closer than town, isn't it?"

"Yes, only a few miles farther."

"Good. I think the sooner we get out of these wet clothes the better," she said nervously, picking at her wet bodice.

"That is exactly what I had in mind!" he watched her, his gaze heated, noting the hardening of her nipples against the cold wetness of her gown. "Would you like me to warm you a bit?"

She noted the strange light in his eyes and

apprehensively drew away.

"I shall be fine as soon as we reach Cedarhill."

"Come, Renee, sit by me," he coaxed, his voice husky with emotion.

She moved closer to him but she was still cold and miserably damp. He kissed her hair and she raised her lips to his.

"Mrs. Westlake," he murmured softly to her and Renee shivered, whether from emotion or the weather, she was not sure.

"My husband," she whispered to him as the kiss ended and as she snuggled against him, she was no longer aware of her physical discomforts. There was only the warmth of her heart.

They remained that way the rest of the trip, quiet and peaceful, at ease with each other.

When at last they arrived at Cedarhill, the entire house was dark. He carried her over the threshold and deposited her on her feet in the main hall. She followed him as he went into the library to build a fire. He set to the task and when at last a bright blaze flamed to life she sighed audibly.

He looked up from where he knelt feeding wood to the hungry fire.

"Tired?"

"Yes. I really think so. You have to admit it's been an exciting evening."

He chuckled and rose to embrace her, "Would a brandy warm you?"

"Yes, please."

Marsh moved away to the decanters and poured them each a snifter full. He handed her hers and toasted her silently. As he was about to take her in his arms, someone cleared their throat in the doorway and they jumped guiltily apart from habit as Martha's housekeeper Louise appeared.

"Why, Mr. Marshall, Miss Renee, what are you doing here?"

"Beginning our honeymoon," he said pulling Renee into his arms.

"That's wonderful! Congratulations! Can I get something for you?"

"No, we'll be fine. Thanks, Louise. You may go."

"Good night," she said happily and disappeared down the hall to the servants quarters.

Marshall gazed down at Rene, his eys sparkling, "I suppose you want to get out of these wet clothes?"

"I am most uncomfortable."

"There should be something in Dorrie's room that'll fit you. Shall I take you up and help you undress?"

"No!" she answered nervously. "I can manage. But what about yourself?"

"I have plenty of clothes in my room. Come, let's go up and change," he took her arm and they mounted the stairs together quietly, each dwelling on the hours ahead of them.

He left her at the door to Dorrie's room, lamp in hand, "I'll meet you downstairs."

She smiled timidly at him and disappeared inside. Marsh felt that familiar tightening within him and moved anxiously down the hall. His room was as he'd left it, those long weeks ago, in his panic to be gone. He understood now his hurry to leave with Jim at dawn that day. His feelings at that time had been too new, so real they had been painful and he'd fled from Cedarhill and Renee, thinking it the safest solution to his dilemma. He felt a moment of apprehension now as Elizabeth came to mind. They had spent their first night in St. Louis here and it had not been pleasant. He would make sure that there were no quarrels with Renee this evening to mar it. He changed into a comfortable white linen shirt and tan breeches and made his way downstairs. Noting the closed door to Dorrie's room, he knew that she was still occupied and went to the kitchen to get some food. He fixed a tray of cheeses and bread and took it to the study. He only had time enough to pour them each another brandy before he heard her on the stairs and went to the study door to greet her. He had thought it impossible for her to be more beautiful than she had been at the ball but he'd been wrong. She wore a deep red velvet dressing gown that buttoned high about her throat and clung to her figure sensuously. Her hair was brushed out and fell heavily about her face and shoulders.

"I'm sorry I took so long."

"You are well worth the wait," he replied admiring the splendid sight of her.

"Thank you."

"I brought some food from the kitchen in case you're hungry. Shall we sit by the fire for a while?"

"It sounds lovely. This study is my favorite room in the whole house."

She went ahead of him and he closed the door behind them.

"Is it still storming out?"

"The lightning has let up but it's still raining."

"Good. It seems so much more intimate when the weather confines you," Renee smiled at him.

They sat together on the couch sipping their brandy and listening to the rain pelting the windows.

"I'm not very hungry, Marshall, but if you are then please go ahead and eat."

"There's only one thing I'm hungry for and that's you," he told her softly and she blushed at his honesty. "Don't be embarrassed."

"I'm not so much embarrassed, as I am nervous," she answered setting her glass down and facing him. "I love you with all my heart. Just this morning I was wondering how I could possibly make it through tonight watching you with Juliana."

"Why were you worried?"

"Well, Dorrie said you'd been seeing her for a long time and how much Juliana loves you. . . ."

"Obviously, my little sister doesn't know everything. Renee . . ." he took both her hands in his and looked her straight in the eye. "I don't ever want anything to come between us. Let's vow to each other now that we'll always be honest, all right?"

"I would like that. I want you more than anything to be my friend."

"I am that. I like you very much. I enjoy being with you and you're the only woman I've ever met who could beat me at backgammon!" he hugged her tightly then kissed her sweetly.

She clung to him, her head resting on his shoulder.

"I love you," he murmured and she raised her lips to his in complete trusting surrender.

They moved together on the sofa straining against each other.

"Renee, shall we go upstairs?"

"Let's stay here by the fire. It seems so right."

He kissed her hungrily and then rose to lock the study doors. The thought occurred to him that he was glad they hadn't gone upstairs where . . . no, he wouldn't dwell on that. There was no more appropriate place for them to spend the night than here before the fire where they had come so close to loving before. He took her hand and pulled her up from the sofa into his arms.

"Warm enough, now?"

"Yes," she answered, pulling his head down to hers. The kiss was long and passionate and she could feel him hardening against her.

"I want you," he whispered as his lips sought her throat.

Renee felt a moment of apprehension, what did he intend to do? She knew little about what happened between a man and a woman. Only that it was part of marriage and children were the result. At L'Aimant she had been sheltered from it all and her father had certainly never broached the subject. The coldness of timidity was warring with the passion she felt as Marshall unbuttoned her robe and slid his hands within. She heard him gasp in his surprise to find her naked beneath the dressing gown.

Nervously, she pulled back, "I thought it would please you . . ."

"It certainly does, my love," he answered gruffly, pulling her down on the rug beside him, then slipping the robe from her shoulders. "You're more beautiful than I imagined."

His touch was light and yet exquisitely painful as he ran his hands over her. She shrank from him noticeably and he frowned.

"I'll not hurt you," he said with tenderness and he leaned over and kissed her softly. "Don't be afraid."

Renee watched him wide-eyed as he sat back up and took off his shirt exposing his tanned, heavy muscled torso to her gaze. Noting her reticence, he decided not to shed the rest of his clothes until she was ready for him. He didn't want to make her any more nervous than she was. Stretching out next to her, his back to the blaze he pulled her to him and began pressing tender soft kisses against her mouth. He felt her relax against him a little as her lips began seeking his, trying to stop the shortness of his kisses. When at last he moved his mouth on hers she was ready and he heard her moan as he kissed her deeply. She wanted him, all of him, she knew. The heat of him against her was erotic in the extreme. Renee moved tightly to him to absorb some of the warmth that poured from him. He shifted positions then, lowering his head to her breasts and Renee gasped as his warm wet mouth closed on one nipple. Delight coursed through her as he gently sucked and she arched her back, offering him more of her ample breasts. Marshall ran a hand down her hip and urged her legs apart, caressing her most intimate place. Renee moaned softly and moved freely against him. She was spellbound. She had never known the joy of complete arousal before. His every touch and kiss seemd to bring her closer to . . . to what? She wasn't sure but she knew it would be wonderful. It wasn't possible for her to think now, the ache Marshall had created in her body screamed for release and her hips seemed to grind against his hand of their own volition. Marshall was thrilled at her virginal eagerness. Well aware of Renee's passion he paced himself slowly to bring her to her first climax before he would mount her for his own release. He changed his rhythm and moved his mouth to her neck and shoulders before again caressing her full breasts with hot kisses.

Renee changed her movements to match his, straining against him as he carefully, teasingly brought her to her fullest pleasure. Renee shuddered as each shocking wave rushed through her. Distantly, she heard Marshall talking to her, soothing her as she came back to reality.

When she was relaxed again, he smiled down at her. Renee put her arms around his neck and hugged him close.

"I didn't realize . . ." she whispered.

"I know, my love."

She blushed prettily. He took her hand and guided it to her own sweet wet warmth.

"You're ready for me, now," he said hoarsely.

Renee jerked her hand away from herself embarrassed at touching her own body, but Marshall took her hand and kissed it.

"I need you, Renee," was all he could say as he bent to kiss her again.

She was sensuously languid against him, he moved away from her for a moment and when he came against her again her eyes flew open.

"Don't look so astonished," he teased. "We could hardly consummate this marriage if I kept my clothes on."

"But I . . ."

"Soon you'll know my body as well as you know your own," he said softly. He moved over her then and spread her legs gently. Her breath caught in her throat as she felt his hardness against her belly.

"What . . . what should I do?" she asked, wanting to please him and yet still afraid of the unknown.

"Just relax and kiss me," he answered and captured her lips with his.

His mouth seared hers as he caressed her. Renee was astonished to find herself responding to him again. She delightedly moved her hips against his and he moaned at the given invitation as old as time. He raised his hips and guided himself to her. Pressing forward slowly into her hot tightness.

"Marshall, it hurts!" she cried anxiously.

"I'm sorry—" he pulled back out to relieve the pressure and then moved to fill her again. This time in one smooth stroke. Renee moved painfully to get away from him, tears coming to her eyes but Marshall stilled her with his hands.

"Lie still. It will only hurt for a little while and I'll be gentle," he coaxed kissing her eyes that brimmed with unshed tears.

"But you're so big!" she declared.

"Why, thank you," he grinned down at her. "God, you are beautiful."

He brushed her hair back from her face and kissed her gently. At the same time, he fought with himself to keep from losing control as he began thrusting into her more deeply. Renee let her hands caress his hard muscled back and she slowly became aware that the pain had passed and she only felt a certain tightness as she held him within. Kissing him more ardently, she wriggled her hips and moved encouragingly. Marshall was conscious of her every move and when she finally was ready, he congratulated himself on his patience and began his rhythm. Anxious as he was for her, he knew it wouldn't take long for him to come.

"Move with me, sweet," he murmured to her as he felt himself about to climax within her.

Renee clung to his broad shoulders and lifted her hips to his as he thrust more rapidly into her. Suddenly she felt him tense and then clasp her to him tightly before he slowed and stopped. As he lay heavily upon her, she could feel his heart beating within his chest and knew instinctively that he, too, was satisfied by their lovemaking. After a moment, he shifted his body weight from her and lay to the side of her away from the fire.

"You're wonderful," he said and she smiled at him and pulled his head down for a quick kiss.

They were quiet for a long while, savoring the oneness of their new commitment.

"I never imagined being with you could be so marvelous. Let's stay here, like this forever . . ." she said softly, as she nestled against him in warm security.

"I like your train of thought, Mrs. Westlake," he murmured kissing her gently on the forehead.

"So do I," she smiled.

"But I don't think father's study is always this private," he grinned.

"That's true, but it's private right now," her smile turned a trifle wicked.

"That it is," he agreed, his mouth claiming hers in a flaming kiss that left her breathless.

She molded herself to him and surprisingly found him to be ready again.

"I definitely like the privacy here," she said kissing his chest and experimentally letting her hand stray down his lean stomach and then resting it on his hip casually.

"So do I," he admitted, guiding her errant hand to his hardened manhood. "Don't be shy. I enjoy your touch as much as I love touching you."

She shivered at his words, "I'm glad I please you."

"Oh, you do more than that," he muttered as he buried his face in her neck. "You are the answer to my dreams."

Encouraged, she guided him to her and he possessed her again, branding them both forever.

Chapter Seventeen

Elise looked worriedly about the room and finally caught sight of Alain making his way toward her through the crowd.

"Well?"

"No sign of her anywhere."

"Where could she have gone? I haven't seen her for at least a half an hour!"

"Relax, ma petite, I'm sure she's here somewhere," Alain replied putting a supporting arm about Elise.

"Dorrie!" Elise called waving to her as she danced by with Jim.

Dorrie noted the worried expression on Elise's face and said a few words to Jim, who led her back to Elise and Alain.

"What's wrong, Elise . . . Alain?" Jim asked, already knowing the answer.

Dorrie tried to look concerned but a smile threatened to break through.

"It's Renee, I can't find her anywhere," Elise answered nervously, wringing her hands.

Before Jim could answer, Juliana appeared, "Has anyone seen Marshall? I've just looked all over and I can't find him."

Jim groaned inwardly, "No, not lately, Julie, but

come, we'll search for him together."

As Jim led her away, Dorrie giggled and turned back to Elise who hadn't yet made the connection.

"Why are you laughing, Dorrie?"

"It's just so perfect!" she sighed romantically.

"What is?"

"Renee and I were going up to rest about half an hour ago and we met Marsh in the hall."

"Oh?" Alain said, his eyes twinkling.

"Well, the last time I saw them they were going outside into the garden."

"The garden?" Elise said nervously. "Did you look there, Alain?"

"Of course," he answered. "The first thing."

"Where could they be now?"

"Don't worry," Dorrie said confidently. "Jim said they left shortly after that."

"They left?" Elise paled. "But why?"

"But why, indeed, ma cherie," Alain chuckled. "I suppose our main problem now is Miss Chandler?"

"Right. Marshall told Jimmy to be sure to keep her occupied for him," Dorrie laughed loudly. "Poor Jimmy!"

Alain laughed with her but Elise looked stricken.

"Oh, how could she? Her first ball! Her reputation will just be a shambles."

Dorrie, with surprising maturity, put a hand on Elise's arm, "Please don't be upset, Elise. Marshall is a gentleman. He would never do anything to hurt Renee."

Elise patted Dorrie's hand and forced a smile, "I'm sure things will be fine. I just want her to be happy."

"She will be after tonight. I'm sure."

"Jim, do I get the feeling that you're trying to distract me from my purpose?"

"What do you mean, Juliana?"

"I mean, we were going to look for Marsh, remember?"

"Oh, him," Jim grinned at her.

"Yes, him," she declared, then changing her tactics she smiled at him beguilingly. He was devilishly handsome, and rich, too. "But if I must have a substitute, you're quite my choice."

"My pleasure," he answered smoothly.

"Shall we go out to the garden?"

"I think I'd rather dance," he replied quickly, sweeping her off onto the dance floor.

Jim had no intention of getting involved with this woman. She meant nothing but trouble. Inside Juliana was seething. How dare he? She knew now that Marshall had gone and most probably with that simpering substitute for his wife. But Jim's refusal to take her for a walk in the garden hurt even more. Philip would have jumped at the chance, but Jim had turned her down cold. She would show them. The Westlakes would pay for humiliating her! Juliana began to plot it all then, as she danced gracefully in Jim Westlake's arms.

Chapter Eighteen

Marshall came awake quickly. His eyes surveyed his bride resting peacefully next to him on the crowded sofa. Funny, he smiled, he didn't remember leaving the floor. It was almost dawn. He could hear the birds singing to greet the new day. The storm had passed. All was quiet. The fire had died sometime in the early hours and a chill had invaded the room. Carefully, he reached down to get her robe to cover her, but his slight movement woke her and her eyes flew open. Her blue eyes locked with his warm brown and she flushed remembering their torrid play of a few hours past.

"I was about to cover you with your robe but now that you're awake I can think of a better way to warm you."

"I can, too!" she giggled and drew him down to her.

He sat up quickly and pulled her onto his lap facing him. Then to her surprise, he guided her onto him. She sank down slowly, excited by the new position, watching his face as he entered her, enjoying the newly discovered power she had over him. He buried his face in her breasts as she rode him. His hands guided her movements expertly and they both moved together in final ecstasy. Renee lay limply against his shoulder.

"It shall be pleasant teaching you all the variations," he teased. "You're quite an apt pupil."

"You're quite a qualified teacher," she retorted. "I just wonder where you learned your lessons!"

"Jealous, sweet?"

"Positively," she replied seriously.

He hugged her tightly and moved her from his lap. "We'd best be up. If we start back soon, we could be at Elise's by ten or 10:30."

"All right," she said rising to get her robe. "Ouch!"

"What's wrong?" he asked worriedly.

"You said it would only hurt once, but Marshall, I'm quite sore!"

A one-sided smile came to his lips, "Shall I kiss it and make it better?"

"Marshall!" she squealed, outraged, and quickly moved away from him pulling on her robe.

He laughed heartily and rose to embrace her muttering, "Someday, someday."

Over an hour later, after pleasantly sharing a bath and breakfast, they were on their way back to town. The active night had taken its toll from the lovers. Renee slept securely on his shoulder but Marshall was afforded little rest as he tried to absorb the bumps for his bride. The road was more rutted than usual from the storm and the ride was quite rough and slow.

His original estimate revised, it was almost noon when they rolled to a stop at Elise's. Marshall woke Renee with a quick kiss and painfully straightened his tall lean frame. Stretching his cramped muscles, he finally climbed down, only to have Renee waiting excitedly for his help out.

"Getting old?" she teased, watching his slow movement.

"Not you too?" he asked, irritated at her humor. "While you were sleeping like a babe, I had a most uncomfortable time of it!"

"I'm sorry," she said in mock seriousness, sighing. "I suppose I'll just have to let you sleep tonight."

He pulled her from the coach and held her prisoner against his chest, "I think not, my dear."

She blushed quite prettily as he kissed her soundly and set her from him.

"Shall we?" he offered his arm.

"Yes, I think we'd better."

They were halfway up the stairs when the door flew open and Dorrie rushed out.

"I'm so glad you're back!" she cried with delight hugging Renee and then grabbing her left hand. "But—didn't you? Where's the ring?" she demanded before either could answer her question. "Marshall Westlake! How could you? I've defended you all night long and you didn't . . ."

Martha, Elise, George and Alain all stood in the doorway watching anxiously. Surely Marshall wouldn't have compromised Renee this way. Worry was etched on their faces.

"Dorrie, if you'll hush, we'll tell you all about last night and right after that we'll go pick out a ring of Renee's choice."

"Oh! You did?! You are?!"

"Yes, we did and we are," he answered laughing.

They went inside to explain it all and closed the door happily behind them.

"Juliana, you're in for a big surprise," Philip stated cryptically. "And I'm afraid all those rumors you've started since last night will make you look the fool."

"What are you talking about?" she demanded as she followed him from the front hall into the parlor.

"Sit down, this will not be pleasant for you."

Juliana sat abruptly on the edge of a chair.

"I just left Mayflower Jewelers."

"So?" she asked indifferently.

"My dear, Marsh was there with Renee. They eloped last night and they were picking out a wedding ring for her," he finished bluntly never taking his eyes from her face.

He watched as first she paled and then grew red with anger.

"In order to save your reputation and not have you branded a jealous gossip, I also made a purchase," he said smoothly and pulled a ring box from his vest pocket and handed it to Julie.

She took it with numb fingers and opened it. The ring Philip offered her was a single emerald surrounded by twinkling diamonds. It was gorgeous. Juliana raised her eyes to his, "You care this much, Philip?"

"More than that mere token. Will you marry me soon?"

Juliana considered this momentarily. She had no doubts that Philip wanted her but she had to extract her revenge on that little tramp from downriver. If she couldn't have Marsh, then no one could.

"Yes, Philip, but only on one condition."

"What's that?" he asked cautiously.

"I need your help. I will not be played for a fool."

"What do you want me to do?"

"Find Maguire. After you've located him let me

know. We're going to help him get the Westlakes."

"But Julie—that's insane. Maguire is a killer."

As she turned to Philip her eyes glittered dangerously, "I know that. Help me and I'll make sure you're never sorry."

Philip was nervous at the turn of the conversation.

"Shall we go upstairs? I'll show you how happy I can make you," Juliana invited, taking his hand and drawing him up the main staircase past a gaping maid. "I'm not to be disturbed, Alice. Philip and I have business to discuss."

"Yes, ma'am," Alice curtseyed and hurried from the hall.

Chapter Nineteen

"We'll only be a little while," Marshall said to Renee as he unlocked the door to his office. "I want to check a few things and then we can go back."

Renee smiled and seated herself opposite him as Marshall sat at his desk sorting through a stack of papers. Renee rose quietly, glad to move unobserved about the office as he concentrated on the documents. She hadn't been here before. The door to the back room was ajar so she went in, curious to see where he usually spent his days and nights. The back sleeping room was spartan, containing only a narrow bed, washstand and armoire. There were no pictures or adornments and Renee was relieved. It pleased her that Marshall had no reminder of his first wife. She knew little about her and in a way was glad. Renee was sure that she must have been a wonderful person for him to love her, so the less said the better. She sat carefully on the edge of the bed testing its softness.

Marsh found what he needed and glanced up only to find Renee gone. He rose quietly and traced her steps to the door smiling as he found her sitting on the bed.

"Waiting for me?" he asked huskily and she looked up in surprise.

"Yes, I was," she agreed, pushing her voluminous skirts out of the way and patting the mattress next to her.

He disappeared from her sight for a moment and Renee heard the door locked and the shades drawn. When he returned striding toward her with purpose she felt her heart flutter. He was so masculine, still in the white shirt and tight tan breeches that concealed so little from her gaze.

"You're ready so soon?" she asked wide-eyed, noticing the hardness of him as he sat down beside her.

"Always," he whispered against her lips and kissed her deeply. His mouth burning against hers. "Turn for me."

She presented him her back and he deftly unbuttoned her high-necked gown, slipping it from her shoulders. He stood and pulled her up pushing the bulky clothes from her and lifting her clear of the mound of petticoats and hoops. She helped him with her chemise and shivered as he ran his hands over her.

"You're so lovely," he said, holding her to his chest as he stretched out full length on his bed. "I love the feel of you against me, soft and smooth . . ."

Renee nestled close, pressing her hips to him, enjoying the feel of his maleness against her.

"Take your shirt off," she demanded, grinning up at him wickedly.

He took it off without comment and then followed with the rest of his clothes and moved back against her. She was ready for him and he mounted her quickly, claiming her once again for his own. Renee amazed herself at her eagerness for him. She wanted him deep within her, it was the only time she felt he was completely hers. Moving easily with him now, she explored his back and hips with sensuous caresses, feeling him shiver under her inexperienced touch. Marshall was thrilled to know Renee wanted him as much as he wanted her. Even in her virginal innocence, she had shown a willingness to him unencumbered by false motives or deceptions. There had been no doubt of her purity, her greatest gift to him. Renee was the woman he had looked for all his life and she would be his forever. He kissed her hungrily, seeking to draw her within him. She felt him tense as he neared climax and she held him more tightly when he finally rested against her.

"I'm sorry. I should have gone more slowly, but I needed you so badly . . ." he breathed huskily in her ear.

Renee didn't answer, she only smiled and kissed him, in reply. After a moment, Marshall eased his weight from her and lay on his side watching her, memorizing her face. She turned to him, a look of determination on her face, and he raised an eyebrow at her expression.

"I think it'll do quite well."

"What will?" he asked, baffled by her statement.

"Your office. We can stay here 'til we find our own home," there was a certain finality to her statement, although her eyes twinkled merrily.

"So this was all in the nature of an experiment?" he questioned. She nodded and he continued, "And I was your guinea pig?"

"No! Not you!" she laughed. "The bed!"

"It is much more comfortable with two," he agreed,

226

laughing. "Or it could be I just don't notice the lumps when I'm otherwise occupied."

He lowered his mouth to her pink-tipped breast and Renee felt the heat well up inside of her as his tongue moved over her sensitive flesh. She held his shoulders tightly as he continued his play, teasing her to new heights of abandonment until she finally collapsed against him, her tension released by his knowing hands and mouth. She lay against him languorously, their legs intertwined.

"You're sure the ring is what you want?"

"Absolutely," she murmured against the dark hair of his chest.

"As long as you're happy," he began and then noticing her calm easy breathing, he realized she'd drifted off to sleep.

Marshall relaxed against her, once again pleased by another unfolding facet of her. He had given her free choice of the rings a few hours earlier and she had chosen simply. A wide gold band unadorned but for their initials. The engraving was being done now and they were to pick it up on their way back to Elise's later this afternoon. He recalled their brief encounter with Philip, who had confided his own engagement to Juliana and they had congratulated him. He had been relieved that there would be no need for a scene with her. Obviously her engagement was not a rebound, since she could hardly have known he'd married Renee. Marshall let his gaze wander over his sleeping wife. She was lovely, her hair a wild tangle of curls about her creamy shoulders, her full breasts still hard tipped from their lovemaking, and her belly pressed against his thigh, warm and inviting. He felt himself harden at the thought of her willingness but pushed down his instincts. He would let her sleep, now, so she'd be rested for tonight, Marsh smiled to himself. He lay back and closed his eyes, wanting the release sleep would give him from his body's demands.

Renee came awake slowly; she was so hot, she was sweating and felt as though someone was holding her down. She blinked momentarily in the semi-darkness of the room and then remembered where she was. Marshall lay halfway atop her, his body heat and weight pressing her deeply into the bed. She didn't move but studied him curiously as though she'd never seen him before. His face turned toward her, a relaxed contentment showing on his features. She sighed happily, he was a handsome man and he loved her. How wonderful! Maybe she could convince him to travel to L'Aimant with her. She would love for him to see her home and walk the fields with her. She'd never wanted to leave in the first place, but a young lady could not remain unchaperoned on a large plantation. The thought of going home for a visit was exciting and she kissed Marsh's shoulder until he stirred and then came awake with a start.

"Hi," he said, kissing her lightly.

"Hi."

"It must be getting late, it's so dark in here," he observed, rolling away from her. "We'd best be getting back."

He sat on the edge of the bed and looked back at her. Her eyes were still heavy with sleep and her cheeks were flushed from his casual perusal. "I love you."

"I'm glad," she answered and hugged him tightly

from behind.

He grabbed her roughly and brought her across his lap as she squealed in delight, "Not now, darling. We have much to do." He kissed her soundly and put her from him.

"Marshall?" she asked as she tied her chemise and stepped into her petticoats.

"Yes?" his back was to her as he fastened his breeches.

"Would you go back to L'Aimant with me? Just for a visit? It could be our honeymoon."

He turned to look at her, her eyes were pleading with him.

"We'll see what I can arrange. It means a lot to you?"

"Yes," she replied quietly.

"Then, I'll try to plan it as soon as possible."

She hugged him excitedly and then set about finding the rest of her clothes.

It was dusk when they arrived back at Elise's. Dinner was ready when they came in, a sumptuous wedding feast that Martha and Elise had spent the entire afternoon planning. Alain had stayed on an extra day to celebrate and so had Jim. They were thrilled at the thoughtfulness of the meal and by the many toasts to their happiness. There were no protests when they made plans to stay at his office that night, only understanding smiles.

"Now that you've married, cherie, perhaps you could persuade your husband to come back to L'Aimant. It could use some attention," Alain asked.

"We've already discussed a trip, Alain," Marshall replied smiling at Renee. "As soon as I put my office into order, we shall travel south to see you."

"How wonderful! I am more than pleased at the prospect. Renee is like a daughter to me."

Renee gazed at Marshall in unconcealed adoration, "Thank you."

He grinned and raised her hand to his lips, the contact sending chills down her spine.

"My pleasure," his heated gaze giving her cause to blush. "See to your things now, so we may leave for the office."

"Yes. I'll hurry," she whispered as she excused herself from the dining table.

Dorrie went with her excitedly. Then the men adjourned to the study for a brandy, while Elise and Martha relaxed in the front parlor over coffee.

"Well, Marshall, what are your plans? Surely you can't live at the office indefinitely!" George queried, his eyes twinkling.

Marshall with glass in hand leaned against the mantel, "I thought I'd get my work in order tomorrow early and then Renee and I could spend a few days at Cedarhill, before we head down river."

"Do you think that's wise?" Jim asked concerned. "Where's Maguire?"

"I don't intend to take any chances. Besides you'll be the only ones who know where Renee and I are."

"When are you going south?"

"Probably Friday. Why?"

"I just didn't want you to spend your honeymoon with Rene aboard the *Elizabeth Anne*," George stated.

"You're right, of course."

"Who's *Elizabeth Anne?*" Alain asked curiously.

"Our best steamer—she's named for Marsh's first wife. In fact, you'll be aboard her tomorrow."

"Ah, yes, I see your point," Alain agreed.

"What boat is out of here Friday?"

"*Starbelle.* That is, if she's on time getting here."

"Good. We'll sail on her."

They finished their drinks in quiet comfort. George and Jim were happy to know that Marshall had finally found the peace and happiness he'd so desperately needed these last years.

"Do you love him?" Dorrie asked breathlessly.

"How could I not? He's wonderful."

"Well, you certainly hid it well."

"Honestly, Dorrie, we didn't really talk to each other until last night when you threw us together, " Renee paused in her packing. "I know I thought he was handsome and dashing and I was so jealous of your closeness with him. But before last night, I never dreamed that he seriously cared for me, other than as a friend of the family," Renee blushed as she remembered their encounters in the library at Cedarhill. "He treated me so oddly. One moment kind and the next with cold indifference . . ."

"I know, I know. He had to break through that protective wall he'd built around himself. Elizabeth meant so much to him when she died. . . . it's really best forgotten . . . Well, Marshall just didn't want anyone near him. I'm glad it's you. Let me see your ring before you run off to your 'honeymoon suite'," Dorrie laughed.

Renee proudly showed her the simple gold band with their initials.

"It's lovely."

"Thank you," Renee said as they hugged each other. "Dorrie?"

"Yes?"

"Someday, will you tell me about his first wife? No one's said much more than you did about her."

"Someday. But not now. Later, when there's more time."

"Thanks. I didn't want to bother him about her."

"I doubt if he could bring himself to tell you."

"Oh."

"Let's go. I'm sure he's ready to leave by now," Dorrie said as they picked up her two cases and started back downstairs.

Renee looked radiant. She had changed into a spring gown of buttercup yellow and had matching ribbons in her hair. Her cheeks were flushed and she glanced anxiously about the entrance hall for Marshall. She heard his laugh and then met his eyes as he led the group out of the study in search of their gentler companions.

"Here they are now," George announced to Jim and Alain who were trailing behind.

Marsh met her at the foot of the stairs and taking her bag from her, kissed her gently on the cheek.

"You look wonderful," he murmured for her ears only and taking her arm led her into the front parlor. Elise and Martha watched them both with unshed tears in their eyes.

"It's so romantic!" they sighed as they kissed them goodbye.

"Be happy, son," Martha whispered as Marsh hugged her tightly.

"I will, Mother," he answered, his eyes not leaving his bride as she said her goodbyes.

Then they were off for the office.

It was almost dawn when Philip stood at the foot of the bed facing Julie who stretched contentedly on her silken sheets.

"You'll come for me as soon as you learn something? I would meet with Maguire privately where no one knows me."

"If I can locate him tonight, I'll come for you. I don't imagine he wants to be found."

"It'll be worth his while, I'm sure," she stated watching Philip through slitted eyes. "I'm off to pay my respects to the newly wedded Westlakes today, so I'll know everything by the time you get back."

"Fine," Philip said with an ease he did not feel. "Until then."

He bowed shortly and left her chamber, the memory of their lusty night burned in his mind.

"Did you want to see Alain tomorrow before he leaves?" Marsh asked as they entered his office to settle in for the night.

"It would be fun to see him off, but if it interferes with your work there's no need . . ."

"My dear, my work will always be second to you."

She hugged him at the thoughtfulness of his offer, "Then, yes, let's both go to see him off. Did Jim say when he was departing?"

"At noon, I believe," he said kissing her lightly. "Let's get your things put away so we can relax."

"That's a wonderful idea," she agreed and went

into the bedroom with her smaller valise.

He followed in a moment after closing the office and aided her in her unpacking.

"Do you think I brought too many things?" she asked worriedly, noticing the size of his armoire.

"Absolutely," he grinned. "I rather fancy you as you were earlier this afternoon!"

A blush stained her cheeks, "Be serious for a moment!"

"But I am!" he insisted, laughing.

Renee was torn emotionally, her basic shyness still battling the innate wantonness she had discovered in Marshall's arms. She realized, of course, that he was her husband and she loved him. It seemed perfectly natural to want to be as close to him as possible. But having never been exposed to married life, she had no knowledge of such things.

Marshall read the confused look accurately. "What's troubling you? You looked so lost for a moment."

"Nothing," she muttered, not meeting his gaze.

His arms encircled her and he turned her face to him.

"You made a promise to me last night and I hold you to it now. If something is troubling you then share it with me," he demanded. His tone gave no quarter, but his expression was one of gentle concern.

"Well," she had trouble finding the correct words, "I just feel so strange all the time. I'm not used to . . ."

"Strange? How?" he interrupted.

"I just want to be near you, touching you . . . I've never felt this way before. So totally absorbed with another person," she answered finally, her voice soft.

"And this worries you?" he asked incredulously.

She nodded, resting her cheek against his chest.

"Renee, don't worry. I feel the same. With others around I listen for your voice, when we're apart I wait impatiently for you to come back; you are always in my thoughts. In fact you are my thoughts. It's well I'm closing the office for a few weeks. I'd get nothing done with you here to torment me," he smiled at the thought of trying to converse with a client knowing she was in the back room waiting for him. "No, it's nothing to worry about. It's love and your feelings are returned full measure."

"Then it's not wrong for me to want you so?" she asked with mischief in her eyes.

"Well, I'll have to give that some thought, " he replied teasingly, tightening his embrace and pressing her hips to his. "You at least can hide your desires. I'm not that fortunate, my dear."

His hands released her gown at the back and with her help she was soon in his arms in just her chemise.

"I believe you once said it was awkward to make love with your pants on," she said her hand toying with the buttons on his breeches.

"Yes, I believe I did mention that," he said his breath catching in his throat as her hands explored him.

"Am I shameless to desire you so?" she questioned, her eyes glowing.

"No, you are my wife and I love you. There is nothing to be ashamed of when you love someone," he bent and kissed her, capturing her hands. "If you continue your teasing though, I may be forced to show you how much fun it can be even when I'm dressed."

"Oh?" she asked in seeming innocence as she thrust her hips against him, thrilling at his hardness.

Marshall felt his legs weaken at her bold play. He released her hands and lifted her onto the washstand. Renee's eyes widened in surprise at her precarious position and she grasped at his shoulders. He freed himself from his breeches and lifting her hips pulled her slowly forward onto him. Renee shivered at the contact and relaxed against him, wrapping her legs about him.

He smiled down at her as she held tightly to him. Feeling his gaze upon her, she raised her eyes to his. There was no need for spoken words now. Their bodies told them all they needed to know about wanting and needing and fulfillment. Renee arched to him as he moved easily within her, a feeling of total abandonment overtaking her and she clung to him wanting to become a part of him. A part he could not live without, a part as necessary to his well-being as breathing or eating. He sensed her changed attitude. Her openness and her gift of her total self in her unrestrained movements. Marsh slowed his pace to enjoy her surrender. He knew now that she was his in body and in soul and he was pleased at the realization. The ache in his loins grew fevered and Marshall thrust more deeply into her welcoming tightness as he gained his release. When the heat of the moment had passed he held her gently to him and lowered himself onto the bed. His legs felt weak from the strain and the magic of her desire held him silent captive. Renee was resting quietly on his chest. She didn't want to move for all eternity. The reassurance that her need for him was normal and acceptable had lifted a great burden from her shoulders. She was free to love him, confident that he felt the same. Marshall rose from the bed momentarily to shed his clothes and then stretched out next to her again, drawing her against him and pulling a light cover over them.

"Are you comfortable?"

"Um," she answered sleepily with a slight nod of her head.

He didn't respond, but just held her closely as they drifted off to sleep together.

Chapter Twenty

Renee blinked in amazement at the brightness in the room. It was morning! She almost laughed but smothered it and shifted positions to watch her sleeping husband. His features were sleep-softened and he appeared younger in his relaxed state. She smiled warmly as she remembered their play of the night past. No wonder they'd slept late! Renee knew this morning a calm happiness that hadn't been hers for a long time. She sighed contentedly and snuggled back under the covers. Today they would go back to Cedarhill to spend a few days before taking the *Starbelle* to L'Aimant on Friday. She knew Marshall would love her home and she thrilled at the thought of returning. She missed the huge house, the flower-scented air and the fields green with new spring growth. It seemed all her dreams were coming true and they were all due to this man sleeping at her side. She lifted her hand and stared at the sign of their marriage and knew she would love him forever. Renee wanted to please him and keep him happy and idly she wondered how Elizabeth had done it. Surely, Elizabeth had been quite special if Marshall had loved her. She determinedly knew that somehow today she would learn the truth from Dorrie.

The opportunity presented itself before Renee really expected it. After seeing Alain off, Marshall and George stopped at his office and Elise and Martha went off shopping. Dorrie and Renee returned to Elise's to visit and relax. Dorrie went to change and Renee had just settled in with a cup of tea when Juliana arrived flashing her engagement ring and wishing her profuse best wishes. So it was, that for the first time Juliana confronted Renee without Marsh. Juliana played her role to the hilt, asking casually of their plans, learning of their proposed trip after a few days of honeymooning. Renee missed the tenseness about Julie and took her questions in stride, avoiding what she could, yet trying to be pleasant. Juliana rose to depart, having finished her tea, smiling at Renee.

"Thank you for your kindness. I only hope Philip and I find such happiness as you and Marsh have," she sighed breathlessly, but her eyes were cold as she surveyed the younger woman.

"Please, let's keep in touch. We're leaving the city tonight, but I'm sure we'll be back from L'Aimant in a few weeks."

"Wonderful! You'll be here in time for my wedding. You say you're leaving tonight? I didn't know the *Starbelle* was in."

"We're going to spend a few days alone in the country before we leave."

"Oh, that sounds so romantic!" Julia said moving easily into the hall.

"Leaving so soon, Juliana?" Dorrie asked as she descended the stairs.

"Yes, Dorrie, I have to meet Philip shortly. I just wanted to extend my best wishes. Too bad I missed Marsh."

"Yes, isn't it?" Dorrie replied sarcastically; Renee missed this but not Juliana.

Julie paused at the door, a burning hate filled her as she turned to the girl on the steps, so obvious in her dislike.

"You know, I'm really surprised that no one has noticed Renee's resemblance to Elizabeth," she saw Renee's eyes widen in shock and knew her remark had found its target. "The resemblance is just startling. Well, I must be off! Bye!"

With that, she was gone and Renee turned to face her sister-in-law.

"Dorrie," she stated quietly. "I think I need to know more about Elizabeth and now is the time."

Dorrie noted Renee's stricken pale face, "Let's go into the parlor."

"Is it true? Dorrie, I must know!" Renee stood tensely by the front window.

"There's more to it than that," Dorrie said worriedly.

"Then it is true!" Renee gave a small cry and sank down on a chair. Her eyes were huge in her face when she finally looked up at Dorrie. Straining for control, Renee managed a tremulous smile.

"That certainly explains our beginning," her voice faded.

"Don't be so quick to judge. True, there is a resemblance, but believe me, you two are nothing alike."

"I want to believe that . . . Dorrie, I love him so!" she gave a choking sigh. "Tell me about her. I really must know."

"All right," Dorrie said. "But first let me say I

240

haven't seen Marshall this happy in years. You're wonderful for him, he loves *you* and I know how you feel about him," she paused to catch her breath. "I'll tell you."

"Go on."

"Well, Marshall went to Philadelphia for his law studies and he met her there. Elizabeth Anne Parker. She was raised by her grandmother. Quite rich and quite spoiled. She was pretty enough . . . a lot like Juliana. Small, delicate, you know the type," Dorrie looked to Renee.

"Yes."

"That was Elizabeth. He brought her back when he was ready to start his practice. She refused to live with us at Cedarhill, insisted that he buy her a house on Lucas Place. As fast as he could, he moved her out. Oh, Renee, he was much younger then and wanted so to please her. They socialized a lot and he was so excited when she found out she was pregnant."

"A baby?"

"Oh, no . . . she miscarried. I think that's what caused her death. They didn't tell me a lot."

"Oh," Renee couldn't think. "Poor Marshall."

"It was pretty awful around here. He sold the house right away. That's when he moved into the office. He's been there ever since, dividing his time between Cedarhill and his work."

Renee sat quietly for a moment then rose and walked to the door, "Thanks, Dorrie. I just have to be alone for a while."

Dorrie watched miserably as her new sister-in-law went out into the garden.

Marsh grinned at his father's jest and they rode away from the office.

"No one was as surprised as I was," George was saying.

"I'm just glad there was no scene. Julie's a lovely woman but not one I'd care to spend my life with. I hope Phil is happy."

George wished Philip and Julie happiness, too. He was glad the pressure was off his son. He knew that Renee was perfect for him. They arrived at Elise's just in time for dinner. The ladies were waiting for them.

"How did your afternoon of work go? All caught up?" Martha asked as she kissed George and led him into the dining room. Renee started to follow Elise and Dorrie when Marsh stopped her.

"Surely you missed me more than that," he teased referring to the quick kiss she'd given him a moment before.

Pulling her into his arms, he lifted her chin and kissed her. She clung to him then, knowing that her love was deep and strong. The doubts of hours before dimmed in his passionate embrace. When he finally let her go her cheeks were flushed.

"Now you look better," he whispered as he followed her into the dining room. "You seemed a little pale before."

"Just tired, I guess," she lied.

"I wonder why?" he returned, quirking an eyebrow at her.

She blushed even more and quickly took her seat so dinner could begin. Dorrie watched them carefully and felt great relief at their ease together. She had been deathly afraid that Renee would change, once the truth was out, but watching them now she knew her worries were for nothing.

The evening passed slowly for Renee. She had so many thoughts crowding her mind that it was quite difficult for her to make polite conversation. If anyone noticed a difference in her, it wasn't mentioned and finally they left for the office.

It was a quiet night for them. Planning to leave early for Cedarhill, they packed and got everything ready before going to bed. Even their lovemaking this night was different. More leisurely, more tender, more aware of each other. Renee relished the attention he gave her.

Her excitement at finally going away with him was quite evident as she hurried him along in the morning. Convincing him she had no need for breakfast, they arrived at Cedarhill before ten. Renee was thrilled at the thought of the coming secluded days and nights.

"Which room shall we use?" she questioned as they started up the stairs to the wide second floor hall.

"Take your pick," he smiled agreeably. "But hurry, these bags are heavy!"

"Yours!" she stated emphatically, instinctively knowing that she wanted new memories made in that room.

She noticed the slight tensing of his expression which would have gone unnoticed if she had not known the cause. Tonight, Renee firmly decided, she would give him something better to remember about that room. Throwing the door wide, she went about his room opening windows and shutters until sunshine and fresh air filled it.

"I'll get some fresh linens and we'll be all ready," she said as she turned back the cover on his bed.

"Ready for what?" he asked slipping his arms around her from behind and hugging her tight against him.

"Why to sleep of course!" she laughed as his mouth sought the tenderness of her neck.

"If you're planning on sleeping tonight, perhaps we should wear ourselves out now."

Renee turned in his arms and drew his head down to hers, "What a wonderful idea!"

It was almost lunch time when they finally made their way to the kitchen. Louise had prepared food and left it for them with a note telling them dinner would be at seven sharp.

They ate in comfortable silence. Each replete in the other, yet Renee knew she had to broach the subject of Elizabeth soon, so she would be holding nothing back. They walked to the stables after eating and saddled their horses for a brisk ride.

"Tomorrow let's have a picnic!" she called as she trotted at his side.

"Fine. I know the perfect place."

"Where?"

"Oh, no. Not until tomorrow!"

The afternoon was utter perfection. They rode to the river again and rested there before heading home later in the afternoon.

Maguire lowered his rifle and signalled his brother.

"I don't think I'll do it now. I want to face him when he's alone."

"I don't know how we're gonna catch him alone. If

they're on their honeymoon, like that broad told ya, then I doubt he leaves her alone for a minute."

"Well, he's gotta come out alone sometime and when he does I'll be waiting," Maguire said smugly as he watched Marshall ride. "I'm gonna kill him but he's gonna know who's doin' it.'

"Let's get outta here and get somethin' to eat. They ain't goin' nowheres but to bed 'til Friday, anyways," he smirked.

Maguire and his brother crawled from their secluded spot and headed for their small hidden camp.

Marshall relaxed in the study with an after dinner brandy while Renee went upstairs to bathe. He sat at the desk and felt inexplicably tense. An uneasiness had settled over him on the ride back from the river and try as he might he couldn't shrug it off. He downed the drink and rose to pour a fresh one as someone knocked.

"Marsh? It's me, Packy."

"Come on in. What's wrong?" He knew it had to be important for the foreman to come to him this late in the evening.

Packy came in nervously, hat in hand, "Well, thought you oughta know we found some fresh tracks that don't belong to us out along the trail."

"How many?"

"Two horses."

He frowned. Now he understood the tenseness he'd felt all day, "You got anybody following them?"

"We did far as we could but we lost 'em in the creek."

"It could be Maguire, but I don't know how he could have found me here. . . . Double the guard on the house tonight and in the morning we'll ride out and see what else we can find."

When Packy had gone, Marsh paced nervously about the room. His main concern was protecting Renee, but he also knew that until Maguire was caught the Westlakes would not rest easy. The sound of Renee's footsteps in the hall turned his more somber thoughts and he forced the worried expression from his face as she came to stand in the study doorway.

"Was there someone here? I thought I heard the door."

"Just Packy. There are a few things he needs help with in the morning so I'm going to ride out with him early and we'll have our picnic a little later."

"Oh, all right," she murmured agreeably, sensing there was more to it but not wanting to push him. She went to him then hugging tightly and he held her close, enjoying her softness and the sweet scent of her perfume.

"Shall we go up?" she asked encouragingly, her eyes warm as she gazed up at him. "If you're leaving early you'll need some rest."

He moved to put out the lights and then they mounted the stairs together, neither intent on resting yet. All during her bath Renee had thought about Elizabeth and wondered why Juliana had thought it necessary to mention the resemblance. She had noticed the dislike between Dorrie and Juliana at the ball and supposed that Julie had said those things, not so much to hurt herself, but to embarrass Dorrie. It had all turned out for the best, Renee reasoned, for now a lot of Marshall's actions were quite understandable. Renee had come to the calm conclusion that Marsh had loved his first wife dearly, and the loss to him was such a tragedy that he was only now recovering from its effects. She firmly believed he loved her, too. Not for her resemblance to Elizabeth but for herself. Renee was now more determined than ever to replace his old memories with new ones. They entered his bedroom and closed the door behind them. The windows were still open and a faint breeze stirred the curtains. She had only a small lamp burning by the freshly made bed and a bath was waiting for him.

"I thought you might want to bathe this evening."

"Thank you, sweet," he said, kissing her lightly and shedding his jacket.

"You look so troubled," she stated quietly as she sat watching him from the large four poster bed.

He glanced at her quickly, "I do?"

"Yes. Very pensive."

"It's been a long day," he began evasively.

"Marshall Westlake, you promised we'd keep nothing from each other and if my instincts are correct, you're not telling me the truth about Packy's visit."

"You read me too well."

"So, what don't I know?"

"Some tracks were found that don't belong to anyone here. That's what we're going out to check in the morning."

"Maguire?" she asked fearfully.

"Maybe. I don't know. If it is, how did he find me

here? There's a lot I don't know and that's why I didn't want to bring it up before I had the answers."

"I understand," Renee shivered. "I will worry about you while you're gone."

"And I will think of you while I'm gone!" he grinned. "It shouldn't take long. We'll be off on our picnic before noon."

She smiled tremulously at him as he rose from the tub and quickly dried. Joining her in the bed, he pulled her to him and kissed her.

"Worries don't seem so terrible when you've someone to share them with," he said against her throat.

"I know, I feel that way, too," she sighed softly as his mouth caressed her neck. "I've been so alone, since Father died."

He pulled her under him and covered her body with his, claiming her in one movement. She looked at him wide-eyed with surprise by his action. Marshall was watching her, his eyes serious, his expression intent.

"I love you," he paused kissing her softly, slowly, in no hurry to complete the act he had begun so abruptly. "I will always be with you, you won't be lonely ever again."

She trembled at the fierceness with which he finished and felt a deep joy at the words he spoke. Renee offered herself to him then, bonding them more firmly in their love for one another.

When Renee finally awoke Marshall was gone and the sheets where he'd lain were cold. She smiled sleepily to herself at the thought of his leaving quietly so as not to disturb her. Stretching languidly, she rolled over to survey his room. It was strictly masculine, with a heavy armoire, desk and walls lined with books and guns.

It suited him and she wondered what Elizabeth thought when she'd been here. Dorrie said she'd not been happy and that seemed hard to understand if she was with the man she loved. Putting Elizabeth out of her mind, she got up and searched through the armoire for her new riding clothes. Dressing herself, she pulled her hair back with a ribbon and went to the kitchen for breakfast.

Louise was packing their picnic lunch when she entered.

"Good morning," she greeted Renee.

"Good morning, Louise. Have the men been gone long?"

"Oh, my yes. They should be back soon. Packy and Mr. Marshall left right at sun up," she said setting a cup of hot tea and a biscuit in front of Renee.

"Thanks," she said sipping the tea.

"Would you like anything else?"

"No, not now and judging from the size of that lunch you're packing I doubt I'll have any room left for dinner!"

"Well, you just enjoy yourselves. It's so nice having Mr. Marshall smiling and happy again."

"He wasn't before?"

"No, Miss Renee. He hasn't been this happy in a long time."

"I'm certainly going to try to keep him that way."

"Good," Louise said seriously.

Renee had to force herself not to question Louise further and she was greatly relieved when they heard the horses in front.

"They're back!" Renee went to greet him.

Marshall was already in the main hall when she came hurrying to meet him.

"Mornin' " she drawled and kissed him warmly.

"Been up long?" he asked as they started upstairs, their arms intertwined.

"Half an hour or so. Thank you for letting me sleep late. I'm sure I needed it."

He quirked an eyebrow at her demure expression and pulled her more tightly against him. She laughed delightedly.

"Louise is all ready fixing our lunch."

"Good. I'm hungry today and one of Louise's picnic lunches should just about fill me up." They entered the bedroom and he went to the washstand, pulling off his shirt. "We'll be off as soon as I wash."

"Fine. I'll get a clean shirt for you," she went to the armoire. "What did you find?"

"We tracked them up the creek bed heading north but lost them. Just two, whoever they were."

Renee handed him the clean shirt as he finished toweling dry.

"Do you think it's safe?"

"Reasonably so. It's a secluded spot. Not too many know about it and if anyone gets too near, we'll know."

"Sounds wonderful!"

"Let's go."

The place he'd picked was his favorite at Cedarhill. It was a secluded spot on the bank of a crystal clear, sandy-bottomed creek. After spreading their blanket on the grassy slope, Renee surveyed the surroundings. Marshall came up behind her and encircled her in his embrace.

"It is the most relaxing place I've ever found," Marshall told her, brushing her hair to one side and nuzzling her neck. "Did you see the waterfall?"

"No, where?"

Releasing her, he walked down to the bank and pointed upstream. Renee joined him at the water's edge and saw the small, splashing waterfall about fifty yards away.

"It's just beautiful," she remarked, hugging him.

"There's a pretty nice swimming hole there, too."

"Good. This is as close to heaven as I can get north of L'Aimant," she said softly as Marsh moved to the blanket with her and they sat down.

"Any place with you is heaven for me," he said pulling her into his arms.

"You are so romantic, Mr. Westlake. However am I going to resist you?" she teased.

"You're not!" he answered quickly undoing the buttons of her blouse.

"Marshall! Out here?"

"Why not? I chose this place with privacy in mind," he continued undressing her. "Let your hair down for me."

Renee pulled the ribbon from her hair and it tumbled loosely about her shoulders. Marshall slid her shirt from her and looked down at her.

"I've wanted to make love to you like this, in the sunlight," he ran his fingers through her hair. "You're beautiful."

She smiled up at him lazily, "This is a nice, quiet spot."

"Now don't get too relaxed," he smiled, kissing her tenderly. "You might fall asleep on me."

"No chance, sir. I've been waiting for you all morning and now that I've got you, I'm not going to waste one minute," she pulled him close, enjoying the roughness of his shirt against her bare breasts. "You make me feel so sexy."

He watched her expression, knowing that she wanted him and that she wasn't ashamed of it.

"How do you think you make me feel?" he asked, kissing her throat.

"Somehow, I think we have the same effect on each other," she said softly.

Marshall managed to free her from her riding skirt and pressed full length against her, his clothes preventing further intimacies for the moment.

"I'll undress in a few minutes," he explained. "But for now I just want to enjoy you."

Renee moved beneath him, loving the feel of his weight up on her and the undisguised hardness of him. Marshall smiled at her restlessness. He kissed her softly, his lips exploring hers, slowly, sensuously.

"I could come to really like this place," she said as their mouths parted and he shifted away for the moment to shed his clothes. "Maybe more than the study."

"Hopefully, we won't have to choose between them," he grinned. "It gets cold out here in January."

She didn't answer right away, but anxiously pulled him back to her. "I could keep you warm enough."

He trailed kisses from her throat to her breasts while his hands parted her thighs and readied her for his entry. Then they were one, coming together in a whirlwind of desire. Renee wrapped her legs around him and pulled him more deeply within. She sensed a completeness in their union as if he were the other half of her and together they were whole. She matched his thrusts and kissed him passionately, telling him with her body how much he meant to her. The rhythm of his body drove her mindlessly onward until, again, she reached that point of breathless ecstasy. And Marshall, knowing that he'd pleased her, gave in to his own desires and released deep within her his life-giving seed.

Moments later, they moved slightly apart. Neither spoke, for there was no need. Marsh studied her as she lay beside him with her eyes closed, her cheeks flushed and her hair in disarray from their lovemaking.

"You are a lovely sight," he said softly, as he moved to kiss her shoulder.

She turned her head and met his gaze, her love for him showing in her face.

"Thank you," she answered, kissing him gently on the mouth. "I think making love here will become a habit for us. It is so peaceful."

He lay back next to her again, closing his eyes, "Shall we rest for a while?"

"You go ahead, I'm hungry!" she said as she moved to unpack the lunch Louise had prepared.

Having second thoughts about sitting naked in the middle of the forest she reached for her shirt but Marshall grabbed her hand.

"Don't dress. I like you the way you are," he stated, grinning at her.

"Is it safe? I mean is anyone going to see us?"

"No. We'll know long before they get close, if anybody's coming."

"All right," she agreed, but not wholeheartedly.

Glancing around a bit nervously, she went back to setting out the food.

"Would you like some wine?"

"Louise thought of everything didn't she?" he asked raising up on one elbow to accept the glass Renee offered to him.

"Uh huh, are you sure you wouldn't be interested in something to eat? I don't want to take a chance on your strength giving out due to lack of nourishment."

"Lord knows, you're trying to wear me down with your constant demands on my body!" he grinned.

"Then eat up, I certainly don't want a weakling for a husband!"

They shared the meal, relaxing with the wine and savoring the freedom of being alone, together, in the woods.

"Now, are you ready to lie back and rest a while?" he asked as they finished off the last of the food.

"Absolutely, I'm stuffed."

"You don't look it," Marsh leered at her and pulled her against him, one hand on her hip holding her possessively.

She fought playfully for a minute and then gave in, resting her head on his shoulder.

"You make a very comfortable pillow, I meant to tell you that before," she sighed.

Turning toward her, Marshall caressed her length, "You can sleep on me anytime you want to."

"Thanks," she murmured, her eyes closed. "I'll take you up on that."

"Good," and he rested with her.

"They rode out alone, headed somewhere south of

the house."

"You're sure? And they went alone?"

"Yep. Just him and the gal. She sure is purty."

"Don't worry about that. We jest have to catch him unaware. I want to surprise him."

"All right. Let's ride."

Maguire and his brother Frank, rode in search of Marshall.

They slept for over an hour and when they awoke, the day had become unseasonably warm. Marshall moved to possess Renee again, but she was too quick for him and darted from his embrace.

"You'll have to catch me first!" she laughed running down to the edge of the stream.

She saw him chasing after her and ran into the water, shivering at its coldness.

"It's freezing in here! Why didn't you warn . . ." before she could finish he was beside her splashing her completely. "You bully!" she sputtered.

"I caught you!" he said triumphantly, pulling her against his chest and pressing her full length to him.

His hands slid down her back to her buttocks and he held her firmly to his hips, so she could feel his growing desire for her. By not struggling, he relaxed his grip and with a quick move she was free of him. Heedless of the cold water, Renee ran further upstream and reaching the deeper pool, swam away from him in strong, practiced strokes. Marshall came after her, eager to regain his prize. He gained on her easily, grabbing her foot and stopping her progress abruptly. Sputtering and laughing, she turned to him and threw her arms around his neck, forcing him to keep her afloat. Marshall treaded water for a moment and then, keeping one arm around Renee, made for the bank. While he concentrated on swimming, Renee clung to him enjoying the feel of his muscular body next to hers. As he neared the shallows, he gained his footing and dumped her playfully into the waist deep water. She came up splashing, bent on revenge, when he captured both her arms and pulled her to him.

"Don't you want to play anymore?" she asked, her eyes darkening as she realized his intent.

"Oh, I want to play, all right!" and his mouth found hers, open and demanding.

Renee strained closer to him as the chilling waters swirled sensuously about her hips.

"I'm not cold at all, are you?" she asked as she kissed the droplets of water from his neck.

"I haven't given it a thought," he replied and then, lifting her easily, he guided her legs around his waist.

Bracing himself against the current, he pressed into her slowly. She grasped him tightly, as the heat of her body drove him on, until at last, he found his fulfillment. Still clinging to him, Renee relaxed her grip and slid to her feet. They rested momentarily, encompassed in each other's arms. Then they moved slowly to the blanket, arms still around each other, and collapsed there to catch their breath.

"I must tell you that this has been the most eventful swim I've ever taken," Marshall smiled at her tenderly.

"I hope there will be a basis for comparison in the future," she replied, laughing.

"I'm sure we can arrange that."

She curled against him and they rested, enjoying the sound of the stream as it rushed, gurgling, past.

"They can't be far," Wes whispered, as he and Frank came upon a small waterfall.

"I don't hear nothin'," Frank answered.

"Keep your voice down!" his brother ordered quietly. "Noise travels on water!"

"Wes, look!" Frank pointed downstream where Marshall and Renee stood naked in the water, embracing.

"Get down!" Wes and Frank quickly hid in the brush.

"Did you see her?" Frank leered.

"We're not here for women, Frank," Wes told him sarcastically. "Only Westlake, and we got him now. For sure he ain't expecting company."

"What d'ya want to do?"

"First, we gotta get closer, so we can see what kinda set-up he's got. I'm sure he didn't come out here without a gun. So let's go easy. You ready?"

Frank nodded and followed his brother in a round-about direction toward the unsuspecting couple.

At the rustling sound in the bushes, Marshall came to his feet and drew his gun from the holster he'd placed nearby. Renee was shaken by his actions and grabbed the blanket around her.

"What is it?" she asked, terrified.

Before Marsh could answer, a doe ran out of the trees to stand on the bank. As no one moved, she drank elegantly from the stream and with a flick of her tail bounded across the water and out of sight.

Renee fell back helplessly on the blanket, "I think I just died of fright."

"You're not alone," he told her as he rejoined her and put the gun safely away.

They both lay there silently, their imaginations bringing the worst possibilities to mind.

"Want to walk up to the waterfall?"

"Sounds wonderful," Renee replied, eager to forget the previous moments of tension. "I'd better dress."

"It seems a shame to cover you up," he sighed heavily as he dressed, too.

She blushed at his compliment and he finished buttoning her blouse for her, caressing her, then bending down to kiss her breast through the soft linen fabric.

"A walk?" she asked teasingly and smiled at his look of vexation.

"I did mention that, didn't I?"

"Yes, you did. Which way?"

He took her hand and led her off through the bushes.

Wes looked at Frank as they came within sight of the clearing; having left their horses some distance back, they had approached on foot.

"They're here somewhere. Guess we'll just have to wait for him. Get the gun he's left there and we'll just sit a spell under the trees."

"Race you!" Renee called over her shoulder and ran ahead of Marsh back to the clearing. Not noticing the missing gun, she fell onto the blanket gasping for breath. Before she could move, a hand clasped over her mouth and she was dragged to her feet by a knife-wielding man. Twisting and kicking out did no good and she was jerked tightly against the man who held her, just as Marshall came out of the woods.

"Renee I . . ." he stopped in horror at the sight

before him. Wes Maguire holding her tightly, a knife at her throat. "Maguire . . . let her go."

"Why should I?" he snarled pressing the blade deeply against her.

"This is between us. Let her go. She can't hurt you."

"You're right about that," Wes chuckled. "How are you, Westlake?"

Marshall stared silently at Wes, his muscles tense as he waited for an opportunity to lunge.

Renee felt faint, the hands holding her were ruthless. Dazedly, she watched Marsh hoping for a quick rescue yet knowing that he had no weapon to use.

"What do you want?"

"That's simple," Wes replied, "Hey, Frank, Westlake wants to know what we want from him. You want to tell him, or shall I?"

"Aw, you go 'head, Wes," Frank called coming up along side of Wes, his gun aimed at Marshall's chest.

"I want to see you suffer, just like I done all those months. But there ain't gonna be no escape for you, like there was for me." he smiled. showing uneven black teeth.

"Let my wife go and I'll go with you."

"Let her go?" Frank asked. "Now, she's too purty to be left all alone out here in these woods. Ain't she, Wes?"

"She sure is. You like runnin' around naked, lady?" Wes asked and then grasped the front of her shirt and ripped it straight down. Before Renee could move, he had her pinned back against him, his hand cruelly tormenting her exposed breasts.

259

Blind rage tore at Marsh and he dove for Frank's gun. Wes, in one move, threw Renee to the ground and hit Marshall full force on the back of the neck. Marsh rolled limply off Frank as Renee screamed hysterically.

"You've killed him!"

"Not yet, we ain't. We got plans for him."

Sensing their distraction, Renee stumbled away trying to run to their horses. Wes heard her movements and went after her, laughing at her efforts.

"There ain't no use you tryin' 'cause I can get ya whenever I want!" he snickered, following her easily.

Low branches tore at her hair and clothes, scratching and ripping. She ran now without thought, knowing he was always there behind her watching and waiting. Panic seized her, reason fled. Help, she had to get help. She fell heavily over a half buried log and knew complete terror when she heard his steps in the underbrush. She lurched forward just as the shot rang out and fell heavily again, blood covering her face.

"What took so long?" Frank asked irritably. "I need help getting him on the horse."

"I did a little trackin' 'fore I had target practice," Wes grinned. "He tied up good and tight?"

"Yes."

"We'll throw a blanket over him just in case we run into anybody, which I don't plan on doin', but we gotta get outta here. Somebody may come a-lookin' for 'em."

"Right. Give me a hand with him and we'll get out of here."

Marshall's head was throbbing and the jolting pace

of the horse under his stomach only made the pain worse. He was gagged and felt suffocated under the heat of the blanket that completely covered him. He couldn't guess how long he'd been out. Judging from the grogginess he felt, he knew it was quite a while. Silently he hoped when Maguire pulled off the blanket that Renee would be there somewhere with him. They wouldn't have left her behind . . . that thought struck a deeper pain within him and he forced his mind to other things. Escape now was impossible. He was tied on the horse and from the direction of the voices around him he knew one was riding behind him and one in front. His only choice was to wait and hope that Packy missed them before it got too late in the day. Overnight would be hard tracking . . . his hold on consciousness slipped and blackness closed around him again.

Chapter Twenty-one

Pain. The pain was forcing her to wake. Wake. Hurry . . . Help . . . Her eyes opened and tried to focus. Pain. Sharp and blinding. Moaning, she put a hand to her head and withdrew it to find it bloody. Renee struggled to sit up, pushing hard at the ground that seemed to hold her against her will. Panic gripped her again. They still might be here! She looked around nervously but the woods were quiet. Quiet and peaceful. As if nothing had happened, none of the violence of an hour ago had happened at all. Dragging herself, she finally crawled to a tree and pulled herself upright, swaying dizzily. She closed her eyes and rested wearily against the rough bark of the trunk. Slowly a measure of steadiness returned to her limbs and Renee managed to look about. She wasn't far from the clearing, and with a concerted effort she knew she could make it, but what would she find? Marshall . . . she forced her feet to move, shuffling, jarring steps over uneven ground. Hurry. The thought of him in trouble, unconscious, needing her, drove her on. Finally she was there, panting, exhausted from the effort. Empty. Overturned basket. . . . Nothing else. Dazedly she sat staring about her, trying to understand what had happened. She swatted at the flies that pestered her and tried to remember.

"No . . . he ain't dead . . . We got plans for him . . ."

The words echoed in her mind. A rustling movement close by jerked her from the stupor she was in and she started as the noise came closer. Only the nicker of the horse relieved her fear as it wandered from the trees. Speaking softly she moved toward her mare and grabbed the reins. With some difficulty she pulled herself up and giving her her head let the horse take her home.

Falling, she was falling and there was no one to catch her. The ground was hard beneath her cheek and then blackness. Soft, blackness. There were voices. She couldn't distinguish who. High. Deep. Worried. Hands lifting. A moan came from her lips as she was moved into the house.

"Marshall!" was all she could say, it hurt. Her head hurt.

More urgent whisperings. Renee tried to open her eyes but they were too heavy. Peace.

She was running, Marsh was hurt. She had to get to the horses. She had to go for help. The bushes and trees blocked her headlong flight, she fell, moved ahead again and then pain. Blinding, sharp pain. A scream tore from her throat and she sat upright, shaking. Hands grasped her and held her.

"Marshall, I've got to get help for him!"

"Quiet. It's all right. Quiet."

Renee focused on the calm voice talking to her. Everything in her mind was blurring, a series of images all running together ending with the shot!

"Oh, my God!" Renee breathed looking up into Elise's and Martha's worried faces. She put a hand to her head and found it bandaged. "Marshall, did you find him? Is he all right?"

"Let me get George," Martha said quietly and hurried from the room leaving Elise to comfort her niece.

"Elise, have they found him?" Renee asked, her eyes brimming with tears.

"No, darling. They're not even sure of what happened. George is downstairs. He'll know what to do."

Elise pressed Renee back against the pillows.

"How long has it been?"

"Louise and Packy found you by the stable and sent for us right away. The doctor left about two hours ago. I guess you've been unconscious for about six hours. It's eleven o'clock."

"So long. Too long! They've got him! Did Packy search for him?"

"Who's got him?" George demanded, hurrying through the door.

"Oh, George," Renee cried. "It was Maguire!"

Disjointedly she told her story. Their walk, Maguire waiting for them, the struggle, Marshall lying there, running for help and then nothing, 'til now!

"Help him! You've got to find him!" she raised her tear-streaked face.

George looked pale and grim. "Give her the medicine the doctor left. I'll be in my study."

Renee balked at the sedative Elise gave her and tried to get up, only to fall back on the bed, her face tight with pain.

"I've got to find him, Elise. Where would Maguire have taken him? And why?" she asked nervously biting her lip to stem the hysteria she felt rising in her soul.

"Drink this. It'll calm you. George knows what to do. He's already talked to the sheriff and sent word downriver to Jim."

Renee nodded mutely and sipped the concoction the doctor had prescribed.

"Lie back and rest. You're very lucky to be alive. The bullet just grazed your head, if you'd moved even an inch you wouldn't be here now."

Renee fell back against the pillows and looked around. Marshall's room . . . why just last night they'd . . . tears flowed freely and she sobbed brokenly as Elise held her.

"Where is he? He's got to be all right! But where . . . where can he be?"

Chapter Twenty-two

Marshall sat back against a tree watching Wes and Frank eating. It was late. They'd ridden well past sundown. He watched the pair through hooded eyes, hoping for some indication of their plans. They hadn't spoken to him, just thrown him off his horse by this tree and went about their business. They built no campfire despite the late spring chill. They were afraid of being followed, Marsh reasoned and that was good. Renee surely had gone for help. He wondered how she was. He knew Maguire was brutal but he didn't think vicious enough to kill an unarmed woman. She must be safe . . . unease crept into his soul. He tried to erase the memory of Maguire with the knife at Renee's throat but always he saw her, standing there terrified. Resting his head back against the tree, he closed his eyes. Staying alive. That must be his main thought. He must stay alive. To get home. To get back to Renee.

Slowly Marsh became aware of the silence. Wes had bedded down and Frank sat some distance away, gun out, watching him. He knew now that they had no intention of feeding him so he got as comfortable as he could and tried to rest. He knew tomorrow was going to be a long day.

Frank watched Westlake shift positions trying to find some comfort on the grass. He smiled, but in the dark no one could see. If he thought he was hungry now, he'd better wait a few days. The plans they had for him were perfect.

They were up and getting ready to move out in what seemed like just a few hours. As they untied his feet so he could mount, Marsh managed to kick Frank in the stomach, but before he could run Wes was there and clubbed him with his rifle butt. Marshall fell heavily to his knees. Frank came at him, then, as Marsh shook his head to clear it.

"No more, Frank. We gotta move. Jes' don't be so stupid next time," Wes laughed.

Frank looked at his brother, hatred gleaming, "I won't."

"Good. Let's go!"

Four days of constant riding had taken its toll on the horses and the Maguires were relieved when they finally reached their destination undetected. The trip had been cold, rocky and wet and they were grateful for the fire that welcomed them. Marshall had recognized the general direction they'd been heading the last few days. Totally avoiding civilization, they had ridden to the southwest, stopping only for a few hours sleep each night. Now, they were secluded in a cave that anyone not familiar with the area would never find. The other five members of Maguire's gang were there and all were glad to see their boss. It was early afternoon when the horses were finally tethered and Marsh was led into the high-ceilinged main chamber.

"Who's your friend?" they guffawed.

"This is my prisoner," Wes stated proudly, prodding Marshall in the back with his rifle. "Turn around, prisoner, so I can untie your hands."

Marsh turned to his tormentor. Rage flowed through him. He had been beaten and starved and now was his only chance. If only he could get the rifle, he'd handled worse odds than this before. The five by the fire he reasoned to be drunk and Wes had to be tired and maybe a little slow. Wes casually untied his hands and Marsh paused watching him.

"Now, over to the wall."

He made to turn and then saw what Wes expected him to see. A short chain with cuffs attached to it, looped through an iron ring high in the wall.

"No!" the primeval scream tore from his throat as he launched himself at Wes. They rolled together across the rocky floor each trying to gain the advantage. Had the rifle not flown from Maguire's hands, his plan might have worked; as it was it landed near the fire and any chance of success was gone. Frank entered the cave to find his brother in a close match. Deciding Westlake needed to be taught a lesson, Frank joined the match. Marsh felt blood on his face as the two brothers overpowered him, but still he fought. Desperately. Blindly. Unaware, as the fists pummeled him and a well placed kick cracked his ribs. Marshall was glad when darkness finally closed in, giving him release from the pain and humiliation that engulfed him.

The water thrown on him was icy and jerked him back from the protection of unconsciousness.

"Wake up, you bastard," Wes hissed, throwing another bucket of water in his face.

Marsh turned his head slowly to one side as he tried to look at Wes. His vision was blurred, both eyes were swollen almost completely shut. His mouth was cut and bloodied. While he had been out, Wes and Frank had put him in the cuffs so that he now hung limply from a short chain while facing the wall. Marshall tried to support himself by standing but his knees buckled and again he was suspended by his arms. Pain stabbed him in the side when he moved and he drew a ragged breath.

"At last, you're movin'. Good. I want you to see what you're gonna get," Wes said with evident enjoyment. "Frank, bring that strap over here."

Frank brought his brother a jaggedly cut piece of leather attached to a wooden handle.

"See this? Recognize it? In a minute you're gonna feel it, just like I did. Everything that they did to me, I'm gonna do to you. 'Ceptin' you ain't gonna live to talk about it."

Marsh knew all about the strap and what it could do to a man. He'd read the reports on torture in the penitentiary. He knew now what Wes had in store for him. A long lingering taste of hell. Marsh's only hope was to pray for rescue. Surely, Renee had gone for help and the sheriff was on his way.

"If you're thinkin' that somebody's comin', forget it. We left so many false trails out there they won't ever find this place," he grinned.

Marshall ignored the taunt, there was no point in arguing. There was no way for him to escape what Wes had in mind for him right now. Fear twisted through him now. He knew he had to remain calm. He couldn't give in to the desire to cower and beg and save himself from the pain he knew was to come. That was exactly what they wanted. Determination gripped him and he only trembled slightly as Wes stood behind him. A sudden unexpected pain drew down his back as Wes cut his shirt from him and drew blood in the process.

"If you jump at that much, just think how it'll be when this strap takes ya," Wes snickered to Marsh.

Terror threatened. He knew Maguire was close behind him and yet there was nothing he could do. He couldn't turn enough on the short length of chain to face his captor, so he stood stolidly as possible awaiting Wes's next move.

"Scared? You should be. I was and, by God, I had every right to be."

The voices behind him grew silent and Marshall heard the strap whistle through the air. He jerked as the leather slammed into his bare back. Wes paused, savoring the feeling of power. As each stroke pounded into Marsh, Wes watched with amusement as he struggled for control.

At the prison, there had been no time, as blow after blow had fallen until the twenty he'd received had nearly killed him. Wes remembered, all too well, that feeling as the strap whistled through the air. He knew now that there was no instrument better for prolonged torment. A whip drew blood and the cuts usually healed cleanly. But the strap was designed for long term remembrance. It raised huge blisters that ulcerated and took months to heal. Wes could easily recall those days and nights in his cell trying to find comfort, weeks after the punishment had been given out.

"I think twenty lashes just like I got will do you for starters, Westlake," Wes spoke to Marsh's back.

Marsh didn't acknowledge, he couldn't. He waited dazedly, his teeth clenched for the next strike. His legs were growing weak again and he could barely stay erect. As Maguire brought the strap down for the fifteenth time, Marshall slumped forward without a sound. Wes threw more water on him but Marsh didn't revive.

Cursing, Maguire finished the last five strokes on an unfeeling victim and then went to the fire to drink with his brother. Tilting the whiskey bottle to his mouth, he chugged the potent brew.

"Feel better?" Frank asked.

Wes didn't answer.

"He didn't break. Did you really think he would?"

"I'll see him broke before I kill him," Wes said coldly. "And I know now just what will do it. Is that room ready in the back?"

"Yeah, all set. It's about the right size, nice and dark and only a slop bucket. He should do just fine in there, almost as good as you did in the pen," Frank said mercilessly.

"Well, let's get him outta here."

Frank unfastened one cuff and slid the chain through the ring while Wes lowered Marsh to the ground. After putting the manacles back on his already raw wrist, they dragged his inert form back to a small opening in the cave wall. It was only waist high and the room that opened beyond was small, about the size of a cell at the jail. Frank, taking a lantern with him, dragged Marsh through the hole. The going was slow, Marsh's body was dead weight.

"Wes, you comin' in?"

"Hell, no!" he answered quickly. "I spent enough of my time in solitary these past few years. Now I want him to know what it's like."

"All right. Gimme that bucket of water settin' there. He's gonna need that."

Wes shoved the half full bucket of water through the hole and a minute later Frank crawled back out.

"Where's the barricade?"

"Out in front. I'll get it."

Wes came back with a heavy barrier and sealed off the opening.

Marsh's first thought when he opened his eyes was that he had been blinded. He knew he wasn't dead. The pain was too great. He ran a hand gingerly over his face, wincing at the cuts and swelling. Oddly, he realized his back was numb. He knew enough to be grateful, it would pass all too soon. He shifted and levered himself weakly on an elbow, blinking. There was no change, only blackness. Somehow, he managed to sit and groggily shook his head. His side flamed to life as he had moved and it left him gasping. Slowly, after a minute's rest, he stood and groping about him, at last located the wall. There was no sound except for the clanking of his chains. Marsh wondered where Wes and Frank were. Surely, they were nearby watching.

"Maguire?" he croaked, but there was no answer, no response.

Marsh moved along the rocky wall, hoping to find the passage out. All he learned was the dimensions of the natural cell, barely six foot by four foot. He

272

located the buckets and sinking wearily to the floor he drank slowly. He started to lean back to rest against the wall but as the rocky surface made contact with his shoulder, it brought a strangled cry from his throat. Pain throbbed through him now. As if every nerve end had been awakened by that small contact.

A light flashed into the cell and Marsh raised his drooping head to stare blindly in the direction, relieved to find he wasn't sightless.

"He's movin'," Frank called to Wes.

Two faces peered at him through the opening.

"How do you like your new home?" Wes asked, not expecting an answer. "You'll get used to being all alone soon and it won't bother you much. You know," Wes went on, "I don't think there'll be anyone comin' for you now. Ya see, there wasn't anyone left to tell them."

Marsh glared at Wes suspiciously.

"Yes, she wasn't very fast. 'Course, we both had our fun with her first." Wes glanced at Frank. "She sure was nice and tight. Moaned real good, too. Think she liked us, Frank?"

"I think she loved us, Wes. Especially when I . . ."

Before he could finish Marshall lunged at him, but Frank easily knocked him to his back, successfully killing his drive. Marshall could not move as Frank stood over him.

"Here's your supper, make it last. We probably won't be back for a while," he sneered.

Marsh didn't open his eyes. It was impossible. Barely conscious, he felt something hit his stomach and then heard them leave and felt rather than saw the darkness surround him again.

Renee raped and then killed? He realized now that he'd been a fool to think that Maguire would let her go. God, what a fool he had been. The anger and frustration at his helplessness tore at him and mixing with his unceasing pain, brought sobs of anguish from him. He rolled halfway off his back to relieve some of the pressure and then collapsed, giving way to the welcoming blackness.

Chapter Twenty-three

Renee sat on the small settee in the front parlor of Elise's home. Her face was pale and her manner listless. Three weeks! Each one like the other. Sleepless nights, and when sleep finally did come those horrible dreams . . . she shuddered. No news. Nothing encouraging, at least. George and Jim had been gone for days, this time. Major Bigelow was with them now, plus the sheriff and a good sized posse but with each passing day her spirits lagged. How could God be so cruel? To give her love and then have it snatched from her again! First her mother, then Papa, but Marshall . . . in such a short time he had become her whole world. And now, now she had nothing . . . no one . . . Renee jerked her mind away from those thoughts. No! He wasn't dead! She would know it. Feel it. No, he wasn't dead. She looked up as Dorrie came back into the room with their tea.

"We may hear from Jimmy today. They've been gone over a week, now."

"They should send word soon," Renee paused to sip the hot brew. "How is your mother today?"

"She's much better. She's with Elise now."

"Good. I'm glad she's up and about today. I'm trying to be strong but it's so hard, especially when I think she blames me!" Renee choked out, at last voicing her fears.

Dorrie blanched at Renee's words, "Oh, God! Do you really feel that way?"

Renee nodded bleakly as her control crumbled and tears coursed down her cheeks. Dorrie ran from the room. Convinced she'd hit upon the truth and surprised Dorrie with her perception, Renee rose and went to the window to stare out blindly.

"Renee?" Martha's strained voice came from the doorway. "We need to talk."

Renee turned to face her mother-in-law as Martha closed the sliding doors to the entry hall.

"My dear, Dorrie just came to me with some very distressing news. I hope what she had to say was not true," Martha noting Renee's pallor urged her to sit and then joined her on the small sofa. "I'm sorry if I've been so wrapped up in my own worry that I seem to have overlooked your own," she took Renee's hands and squeezed them gently. "By no means do I feel that you are in any way responsible for this. . . ." her voice trailed off and her eyes clouded.

"But if we hadn't married, then we'd never been alone at Cedarhill . . . then Maguire could never have found him alone. I asked him if it was safe . . . He insisted it was . . . that there was no reason to be afraid. I should not have let him go there. He would have been just as happy here in town."

"Now there, you're wrong. Marshall loves Cedarhill. It's his favorite place to be. In town is only a necessity for business, if he wanted to be truly happy and relaxed then he would go to Cedarhill. And believe me, Renee if that's where he wanted to be, no one could have convinced him to change his plans!" Martha insisted, impulsively hugging the younger woman. "Please don't feel such guilt. If Marshall had any idea that Maguire was around he'd never have taken the chance. Somehow, Maguire found out where he was and that's how he surprised you both. Thank God, you weren't injured any worse than you were. You could have been killed!

"No, Renee, George and I love you dearly. You've become one of the family, one of us. We have to have faith and trust that he'll come home to us and soon."

"Mother!" Dorrie called rushing down the hall to the dining room. "Hurry! They're back!"

Martha, Renee and Elise all looked up from their meal.

"George is here?"

"I just saw them from my bedroom window, come on!" Dorrie ran to the front door and threw it open.

"Is Marshall with them?" Renee asked coming up behind her friend.

Dorrie's shoulders drooped as only George and Jim stopped in front of the house, "No. He's not."

Renee was almost overwhelmed by a mixed feeling of anger that they hadn't rescued him and relief that he hadn't been found dead. She leaned limply against the wall as Elise came to take her hand. Martha bustled past them and went out to greet her husband and son.

"How are you? I've missed you. Any news for us? This waiting has about driven us crazy."

"Fine, I'm fine," George said tiredly. "Jim, take the horses around back and I'll meet you inside."

Jim nodded wearily and leading his father's mount he rode behind the house to the stables. George hugged Martha briefly and followed her back inside, carrying his rifle and saddlebags.

"I'm glad you're back, Papa," Dorrie hugged him impulsively after taking his gear.

"Me, too, darlin'," he replied. "Elise, Renee you're both looking well."

"It's good to see you. We were worried. . . ."

"I'll tell you everything as soon as I sit down. Could Celia fix Jim and me something to eat? We haven't had a hot meal in the last four days," he asked, his face lined with exhaustion.

"Of course, I'll tell her," Elise said and moved off to the kitchen. "There's still hot coffee at the table."

"Good," he moved into the dining room with Martha at his side.

Renee came behind them with Dorrie, trying to control her eagerness to know about their search. Jim and Elise rejoined them as they poured the coffee and sat at the table. All was silent for a moment until Renee finally blurted out the question they all wanted answered.

"So you didn't find anything? Not even a clue?"

"Nothing. We checked all of the outlying towns, hoping to pick up some word of Maguire or some of his gang . . . but it seems they've disappeared. We searched all the more obvious places, but there's no sign of them. Wherever they went, they didn't want to be found," George told her.

"What are we going to do now?" Dorrie asked. "We've got to do something. I mean, we just can't sit here!"

"That's exactly what we're going to do," George said almost angrily.

"They've got to come out sometime," Jim interrupted. "They're going to have to get supplies and knowing what kind of animals they are, you know they can't go too long without drinking and whoring . . ."

George cast him a censoring look and Jim realized what he'd just said in mixed company. Renee had paled at his words as she remembered Wes' dirty, hurting hands upon her. Jim knew the condition Renee had been in when they'd found her. Though the Maguires hadn't raped her, it must have been traumatic for her and he regretted his words.

"I'm sorry," he spoke contritely.

"We all know what kind of men they are," said Martha relieving his discomfort.

"I wish I could have gone with you," Renee said. "I feel so useless."

"We all feel that way," her mother-in-law assured her. "You checked with all of the neighboring sheriffs? It's hard to believe that no one's seen or heard from them."

"I know, but that's where it stands right now," George finished his coffee and finally relaxed a little.

"They've all agreed to contact John Randolph if there's any news at all," Jim added. "Unless they've left the state, I'm sure we'll hear something pretty soon."

"What I haven't been able to figure out is why Wes didn't kill Marshall on the spot," George told them. "If he wanted him dead, and he already thought that he'd killed Renee, why kidnap him?"

"We'd surely have heard something by now if they

wanted a ransom," Jim added.

"All he said before I ran was that he had plans for him, that he wasn't dead yet," Renee told them unemotionally. She had relived that day so often in her mind that it no longer had the power to terrify her.

They looked helplessly at one another.

"Whatever it was, I can't help but feel that *yet* is the main word to keep in mind," George said, sounding defeated. "It's been almost a month with no word. I just can't imagine that Maguire's let him live this long. I just can't. . . ."

"But you're his father! You can't give up!" Renee countered on him.

"I'm just trying to be logical about this right now. I don't want to think that my oldest son is lying dead somewhere," George said, his voice breaking and everyone fell silent at the table. "But, my God, what chance do I have of believing otherwise? Maguire hates us. He swore he'd get even and what better way than to kill the very man who sent him to jail? I have been searching for him for almost three and a half weeks. There's been no sign of Marshall. None!"

"I won't believe he's dead. I would know it! I would!" Renee looked wildly at all of them and then ran from the room, trying not to cry in front of them.

Jim rose and hurried after her, but his father's words stopped him at the hall door.

"She needs to be alone to work this out, Jim. I don't mean to sound heartless, but it isn't fair to offer her false hope when I feel there isn't a chance. . ."

Martha looked at her exhausted husband and went to embrace him. Forgetting the meal he'd wanted, they left the dining room and retired to their room for the day.

Jim looked questioningly at Dorrie and Elise from the doorway where he stood.

"Is it really that hopeless, Jimmy?" Dorrie asked tearfully.

"I'm afraid so," he said sadly. "Can I get cleaned up and rest in your room for a while, Dorrie?"

His sister nodded and Jim went upstairs, too.

"Do you think I should see how Renee is?" Dorrie asked Elise.

"Let's leave her alone for a while. We'll check on her after lunch."

"All right," Dorrie agreed but she couldn't help but worry about Renee and how she would accept what George had told her.

Renee stared solemnly out her bedroom window. It was difficult for her to listen to the things George had told her. She steadfastly refused to believe it until she had proof. Until then, no matter what they might say, she would not waver in her faith that somewhere her husband was alive. She realized that they were only trying to help, but she was not ready to admit that the Maguires had won. Not those vile, evil men . . . She shivered as she remembered.

Dinner that night was early as there had been a general loss of appetite at lunch time. Dorrie visited with Renee earlier in the afternoon, but she had not been ready to share her thoughts. They agreed to go down to eat together, for Martha and George were taking their evening meal privately in their room. As they reached the foot of the stairs, Jim and Elise were already waiting for them in the dining room.

"I'm glad you're better," Jim remarked, relieved, as he rose to seat them.

Renee smiled at him warmly, her serenity restored, "I'm fine, really."

The meal was quiet, the conversation almost stilted, until she asked Jim point blank what the best course for finding Marshall would be now.

"Are you sure you want to talk about this?"

"Absolutely, it's on my mind constantly and trying not to talk about it only makes things more difficult for all of us."

"You're right about that," he told her. "Our only hope is that Maguire will come out of hiding. It's like father was saying this morning, we just have to sit and wait." When Renee didn't speak, he continued, "Did you get any rest this afternoon?"

"A little. It's much easier to relax now, knowing you and George are back and everything possible has been done."

Jim was glad that she wasn't depressed by the events of that morning, "I'm afraid Mother and Father aren't taking this as well as you are."

"I know. When Dorrie told me that they weren't coming down for dinner—" she seemed momentarily worried. "I'll speak with them in the morning. Maybe if they see that I haven't lost hope, that will help them."

Late that night, George and Martha lay in bed trying to find the sleep that eluded them.

"I hope Renee didn't think that I was deliberately being cruel."

"No, George. I'm sure she realizes that as each day passes, the hope we have grows smaller and smaller."

"Lord knows, I want him back! But how could he survive this long in Maguire's hands?" George spoke despairingly.

"I don't know. It's hard to accept things when you're dealing with an animal like Wes Maguire. We knew he was dangerous in the beginning. I guess all those years in jail only made him more vicious," although Martha wanted to believe Marshall was alive, she knew that George was trying to prepare her for the truth when it came. "You really don't think that there is any hope, do you?"

He shook his head as he looked at her bleakly, "I'm sorry."

Martha broke down then and cried all the tears she had kept inside. Her only prayers that night were that her son had not suffered at his tormentors' hands and that he had found peace.

Renee, too, was having trouble sleeping. The evening had passed slowly and everyone was glad when it was time to retire. But, now, she was in bed and she still couldn't unwind. Although she still held on to the thought that Marshall was alive, she felt emotionally numb. A disturbing notion had occurred to her tonight. Throwing off her lightweight cover she walked to the window and opened the heavy drapes. The night was black velvet and clear with a full moon so bright that it cast shadows about her room. The future was beginning now, and disturbed, she rested a hand on her belly. She hoped the thought that had come to her earlier was fact. She could be carrying his child. Marshall's child. A small, contented smile lit up her face. A son. A boy who would grow to be like his father. If for some reason Marshall did not return to her, she would have his child to love and nourish.

When he could force himself to think about it, Marsh was certain there was no way out except through the opening that Wes and Frank kept barricaded. He had spent endless hours during his first days of captivity trying to devise a means of escape but he knew his only chance was to go out the same way he had come in. And even if he made it out, there was still the rest of the gang to deal with. As rapidly as he was losing strength, he knew that if he were to break free it would have to be soon. A plan began to take shape in his mind, a slim hope that he could trick them into believing he was unconscious and then fight his way out. His chains could be both a hindrance and a help. If he could get either Frank or Wes around the neck with his arm shackles, then there was a possibility that he could make it. Marsh waited. The hour would come when they would finally open up and he would be ready. His back still caused him pain but it was nothing compared to the agony his mind was enduring. He had to try. Not to would be admitting defeat and he would not give himself up to them, no doubt to die, without a fight. Much better to die quickly and cleanly, than to lie in darkness and captivity like a captured animal, waiting for the keepers to put it out of its misery. Thoughts of Renee filtered through his escape plan, possibly death with her would be preferable to any kind of life without her. His resolve set, he awaited the Maguires' next move almost anxiously. When it finally came, he was ready. They had approached noisily which gave him extra time to prepare and when the light from their lantern poured in, it showed him to be unconscious, seemingly near death. Frank crawled in and moved to Marshall who lay on his side against the far wall. After Frank took a quick look at his captive, he turned to call out to Wes who was waiting outside. Marshall whipped his hands up and caught the stunned Frank around the neck with the short length of chain that bound his wrists. Frank panicked and his eyes bulged from the pressure that Marshall put on his throat. He gagged noisily as Marsh held the cold chain tight, its links biting mercilessly into his neck. Frank clawed at it trying to loosen its hold, but Marshall gave him no quarter.

"We're going out slowly," Marsh told him quietly. "If you don't want to die, then move easy, right out that hole."

Frank could make no sound and inched toward the opening with Marshall keeping the chain taut.

"What the hell's taking so long?" Wes called irritated. "Is he dead or not?"

As Frank and Marshall emerged, Wes drew his gun.

"Forget it, Wes, or your brother will be dead before you can fire," Marsh told him coldly.

"You ain't goin' anywheres, Westlake. You're a dead man."

"You think I don't know that? I have nothing to lose. But you could lose your kin here, so make your choice and make it fast."

Wes looked indecisive for a minute then threw the gun aside. Marshall edged Frank away from the hole in the wall.

"Get in," he instructed Wes.

"No."

"Climb in there, or I'll kill him now. I want you both out of my way. Now, move!" he pulled the chain even tighter almost strangling Frank and Wes hastened to comply.

"You're not free yet, Westlake," Wes threatened. "There are still three men out there."

"Shut up and move."

When Wes was inside, Marshall quickly released Frank, who was fighting for consciousness, and shoved him in, too. After he pushed the barricade back in front of the opening and secured it, he grabbed Wes' gun and moved as quietly as possible down the tunnelway toward the main cavern. He hid behind a boulder trying to locate all three of the men who were supposed to be there. He counted only two. Nervously, he looked around but he could not spot the other man anywhere. This was his only chance and he had to do it right; there would be no second chance. He checked the gun and made sure it was loaded before inching forward from his hiding place. He waited for their attention to be distracted before gaining a better vantage point and opening fire. He was deadly accurate as he eliminated one of them with his first shot. The other outlaw tumbled out of his line of vision, calling for help as he returned Marshall's fire. Marsh could hear them shouting to each other as they readied for the action.

"He already used three shots . . . Frank was unarmed so he's only got Wes' gun . . . Try to draw his fire . . ." the voices called back and forth to each other.

When they least expected it, Marshall moved forward again, trying to get close to the guns and ammunition that were stored nearby. He knew he could make it unless it came down to a siege. He had to move and move quickly, though, before they realized his situation. He ran toward the rifles stacked negligently against the wall and grabbing one, he dove for cover. He rolled painfully behind a pile of rocks as a series of shots rang out and nicked the cave wall by his head. He was no closer to the entrance but he did have another weapon and that improved his odds. One of the gunmen tried to run across the open cavern while shooting at him and with one smoothly squeezed off shot, Marshall dropped him. He bared his teeth in a feral smile. He was now the killer and they were the hunted. Emboldened by his success, he moved ever forward, eager to be outside away from the killing and the stink of death. Shots rang out randomly at his movements, but he felt no imminent danger as he neared the main entrance. He could almost smell the fresh air and it urged him on. When finally he could see the light just beyond him, he paused, getting his bearings and trying to pinpoint the location of the man who was shooting at him. This was his chance—this was it. Readying his rifle, he ran toward the cave entrance, firing at the last known position of the gunman and staying close to the walls. Glancing over his shoulder as he sprinted through the opening and into the sunlight. He had no time to congratulate himself for trained upon him were the barrels of two shotguns.

"Jes' lay down those guns real slow, Westlake. Take it nice and easy," one of the men spoke derisively.

Later, he couldn't remember how it actually happened, he just knew that he charged at them, wanting them to shoot when someone hit him from behind. It didn't take him long to realize where he was when he regained consciousness. He was surrounded by the damp darkness, alone again. Marshall was confused as he lay there, unable to form a coherent thought. He had a vague recollection of being dragged back inside and of Wes and Frank gloating over his failed escape attempt, then blackness. He closed his eyes against the pounding pain in his head and gave in to the need to retreat from reality.

She was in his arms before the fireplace, pressing against him, calling his name in her passion, wanting him as he wanted her. He could almost feel the heat of her silken body next to his, arching and thrusting beneath him, encouraging him to take her, to make her his own. He groaned aloud and pushed the thoughts from his mind. He was losing touch with reality completely. At first, he'd tried to banish all memories of his time with Renee, just to preserve his sanity. They only led to the final scene, the ending that no matter how he tried to avoid it, was there facing him always. Her death, but more so than that release which he himself would now welcome, her degradation at their hands. His mind provided all the details too clearly for him whenever he let his guard down.

As time had passed, he was almost accustomed to living in this void. It was as if he didn't really exist and the few times when Wes or Frank chose to humiliate him no longer mattered. He knew full well the impotence of his situation and the lack of control he had over any function of his life. Guilt at having been responsible for Renee's fate and frustration at his inability to change anything had taken their toll. There was no logic to his thoughts and so his mind wandered, bringing to him, not only the horror of her death, but bittersweet memories, too, in such crystal clarity that he sometimes felt he was living them.

Philip DeGrande gazed down at Julie, adoringly, as she lay beneath him sated by their lovemaking.

"My darling," he breathed in between kisses. "Have you decided when we're to be married?"

"How does Christmas sound to you, Philip?"

"If that's what you want . . ."

"By that time, all this upset about Westlake should have blown over and we can have a big ceremony without feeling foolish. Do you agree?"

"You're certainly wise about that, I haven't heard anything else at the clubs."

"I know, it's so depressing. And poor little Renee, it must be so terrible to lose your husband after only a week of wedded bliss," Juliana's tone was cold, calculating. "What did Maguire plan to do with him anyway?"

"Really, Julie, there's no need to discuss this now!" Philip said in disgust, rolling away from her.

"But Philip, I just want to know if Marsh is dead or not. Did Maguire tell you what he planned to do?" she asked again.

"I truly don't know. He didn't say and I certainly didn't ask!"

"Philip, I want to know."

"Nobody knows except him and he hasn't been seen since Marshall disappeared."

"Oh," Juliana was disappointed. "Well, no matter. If Marsh was going to get back here, he would have made it by now. I just wonder what the rest of the family think Maguire's up to," rolling closer to Philip she smiled. "I suppose it's time I went to see them. It's been awhile."

Philip groaned and pulled her against him, "Just don't say anything that'll make anyone suspicious."

"I'm not stupid! No, I'm just going on a friendly visit. Mrs. Westlake likes me. I'm sure she'll be glad to see me."

"Let's don't talk about them right now, darling," Philip coaxed, smoothing Julie's golden hair back from her face. "I'm not interested in what the Westlakes are up to and I certainly don't think right now is the proper time to speculate."

"Um . . ." Juliana agreed as Philip pulled her down to him but in her mind she was rehearsing the conversation she would be having with the Westlakes the following day. And the smile on her face that Philip thought was from his caresses was in reality from the thought of what she would say tomorrow to the young abandoned bride.

The routine at Elise's house was as near to normal as the situation allowed now, six weeks after Marsh had disappeared. Jim had gone back to the *Elizabeth Anne* over his own protests. George had insisted. There was no point in continuing the search. They had done everything possible. Now, they would wait to see if Maguire would show himself in town. It was painful, but it was all they could do. Helplessness weighed heavily on George's mind. He went to Marshall's law office and took care of any pressing business but the hours still dragged for him. At Martha's prodding, he finally returned to Cedarhill to help there and the women of Elise's house were glad to see him go. With her mother's approval, Dorrie attended the parties and balls that were being held now that summer was almost upon them. Elise took Renee out shopping for a new summer wardrobe but was not encouraged at all by the listlessness that haunted her niece. Renee spent most of her days in her room. Her appetite was gone and she lost weight. She seldom spoke and then only when spoken to. They fretted over her but to no avail. She seemed lost, suspended in time somewhere beyond their ability to reach her.

Elise, a worried frown upon her face, knocked lightly at Renee's door, "Renee, I must speak with you."

"Yes, Elise?" Renee answered lying in bed, the drapes pulled.

"We must talk. I can't let you make yourself sick."

"I'm fine, really," she replied softly.

"Well, sit up and prove it to me," Elise argued hoping to get some sign of life out of her.

Renee sat up wearily, blinking at Elise as though she was just waking up.

"You seemed to be doing so well for the first few weeks, but now you're so withdrawn."

"I know. I can't help it . . ."

"What's happened?"

Renee looked wildly around the room, "I don't

really want to think about it. . . ."

"If you tell me, maybe I can help . . ."

"No one can help me! No one but Marshall and he's . . ." the words sobbed from her.

Elise took her in her arms and hugged her tightly, "He's not dead. You must believe that."

"But how can I? There's been no word, no clues in over six weeks. Surely if he were able he'd come back to me!" Renee cried.

"Darling, maybe he's trying right now. You must be brave. You can't give up!"

"Oh, Elise, I did believe for so long . . . but now, I just saw the doctor. . . ." she wept, broken as she had never been before.

"The doctor? Why did you go to the doctor?" Elise was frantic thinking something drastically wrong.

"I'm . . ." Renee gulped and tried to speak evenly. "I'm having Marshall's baby."

Elise couldn't speak. Relief that no illness had overtaken her made Elise sigh gratefully.

"A baby? This is wonderful."

Renee didn't speak at once, "I thought so, too, but I'm so alone. To raise a child who'll never know his father. . . ."

Elise understood what Renee was feeling. Her sense of total despair.

"The thought that Marshall will never see his own child is more than I can bear . . . Oh, God. What should I do?"

"Have you told anyone about the baby?"

"No."

"Good. We'll tell Martha tonight. I'm sure she will be thrilled."

"All right. I'm just so confused. . . ."

"Would you like to go to L'Aimant? Perhaps a trip would do you good. I'll come with you. Martha and Dorrie were planning on going back to Cedarhill soon. So when they go home, we'll take you home," Elise said.

Renee looked up at Elise questioningly, "Could we?"

"I'll speak to Martha tonight and we'll make our plans accordingly. And don't worry about Marshall —when he comes back they'll send him straight to you!" Elise answered Renee's unspoken fear.

Renee felt much better after Elise left the room and she went downstairs in time to find Juliana at the door. Julie, with arms outspread, came to Renee.

"Oh, my dear, how you must be suffering!" she exclaimed hugging Renee, thinking smugly how terrible she looked.

Renee, bewildered by this sudden concern from a mere acquaintance, held herself stiff in Juliana's embrace.

"Won't you come into the parlor?" she led Julie into the front parlor.

"Have you any word at all? I've been just frantic with worry! But dear Philip told me to stay away, so I wouldn't upset you."

"No, there's been no news," Renee stated bluntly, wondering at Juliana's belated concern.

"Nothing?"

"Jim and Mr. Westlake searched for almost four weeks but they found nothing," her voice was flat.

"Well, you'd certainly think they could have found something," Juliana said disgustedly.

Hard put to stand Julie's obnoxious presence, Renee shifted uncomfortably, biting her lip to control her anger.

"What does his family think? I had hoped to visit with Mrs. Westlake while I was here," Julie said.

"She's out at the moment . . . Perhaps if you called later?" Renee started to rise to show Juliana out.

"Do you suppose Marsh is dead? I mean, after all, Maguire did try to kill you and why else would he take Marshall with him? If it was for ransom, you'd surely have heard by now."

Renee sat down abruptly at the questions and before she could speak Julie rushed on.

"Have you planned any kind of memorial service? Surely you must be thinking along those lines now. So much time and no hint of his being alive."

Renee's face was taut in leashed fury and pain. Her eyes dark with seething emotion, "Juliana, I really think you should go. Your morbid views of our distressing situation don't help at all. Why, if Mrs. Westlake were to hear you speak this way—Please, you must excuse me," she rose, her back stiff with tension. "You know your way out, I presume?"

With a flash of skirts she was gone, leaving Julie smirking. Juliana pulled on her gloves leisurely and left the Fontaine home unnoticed. She had accomplished her task. She had nurtured that seed of doubt in Marshall's young wife. Pleased at her ability to manipulate, she strolled slowly, confidently, to her carriage and headed back to the shopping district.

Chapter Twenty-four

Renee finished dressing and pulling her hair into a neatly arranged bun at the back of her neck, she moved to leave her cabin. In the three weeks since she'd decided to go home to L'Aimant, her attitude had improved considerably. With George and Martha's encouragement, she felt brave enough to leave St. Louis and return to the place of her birth. Jim had been overjoyed at the news that he was to be an uncle and solicitously took care of her needs whenever he was in town. He made a concerted effort to keep her spirits light, bringing her small presents for the baby each time he returned.

Renee and Elise had taken their time closing up the house and after Martha and Dorrie returned to Cedarhill, they booked passage on the *Elizabeth Anne*. Although her early memories of St. Louis were happy, the most recent ones were painful and she wanted to free herself from their constant reminders.

Renee entered the grand salon and gracefully walked its length to Jim's table. Elise was already there and Jim, his eyes upon her affectionately, rose and seated her. The conversation was light due to the numerous interruptions and the meal was spent pleasantly.

"We'll make L'Aimant sometime late tomorrow morning," Jim told her as they enjoyed an after-dinner coffee.

"Good," Renee replied brightly. "I've missed it so."

"It will be good to return home," Elise remarked.

"How long have you been away?" Jim asked Elise.

"I moved to St. Louis almost twenty five years ago," she told him.

"Why did you leave?" Renee asked impulsively.

"My maternal grandmother, your great grandmother St. Sauvin, lived alone in St. Louis, and it was thought best that I join her," Elise replied evasively.

"But why? Surely Grandmother St. Sauvin could have moved to New Orleans with you and Father. L'Aimant hadn't been built yet but you both were living in the family home in the Vieux Carre," Renee continued.

"She owned extensive property and wanted to stay near her friends. She was well established socially, you see."

"Oh," Renee answered, not completely satisfied with her aunt's explanations but dropping it temporarily. "I think I'd better get some rest now."

Jim offered them each an arm as they pushed away from the table, "Would you like a short walk on deck?"

"That would be lovely," they agreed.

The moon was bright and the night clear as they strolled easily along the promenade.

"If you watch you can catch a glimpse of some of the plantation houses. They're usually well lighted and quite beautiful at night," Jim told them as they paused by the railing.

They caught sight of a large illuminated house twinkling in the darkness.

"How lovely," Elise said. "And I'm sure L'Aimant's every bit as beautiful from the river."

"Absolutely," Renee said. "It's the most beautiful house in the world."

They wandered down the deck until they neared the cabin doors. Renee gazed up at Jim, "I can't thank you enough, you've been so wonderful."

"I only wish there was more that I could do," he answered earnestly.

"You've been my closest friend these past weeks. I couldn't have come this far without you and Elise," she said, smiling at her aunt walking sedately on Jim's other arm.

"You're important to me," he replied and then changing the subject. "Is someone meeting you tomorrow?"

"Yes. Alain will be there. We wrote him as soon as our decision to return was made."

"Good. Then he'll have the house ready for you. I don't think it would be wise for you to do any sort of work right now."

She grinned at him, "Don't worry. I won't do anything to endanger my child."

"Well, I'll leave you two here," Elise said as they came to her cabin door. "See you at breakfast."

After Elise had gone in, Jim and Renee continued on to her stateroom. They were alone in the moonlight. Jim felt again the familiar desire to take her in his arms and crush her to him. He fought it down, singlemindedly ignoring his body's demands. They stopped at her door and stood silently for a moment.

"Renee, I wish . . ."

She put her fingers to his lips, "Please, don't say it. I couldn't bear it."

He took her hand and kissed it, keeping any emotion from his expression, "If there's any news, anything. I'll send word on the first packet I see."

"Thank you," she murmured, her eyes closed against the tears that threatened to come. It would be so easy to go into his embrace and let him take care of everything. Jim was strong, just as Marshall had been. . . was?

"You'll join me for breakfast, then?" He bent and kissed her lightly.

"Fine."

He watched her safely into her room and then went to lose himself in his work. Jim didn't hear Renee's composure break down as soon as she closed the cabin door behind her. She lay on the bed, sobbing.

Celia found her that way moments later when she came to help her undress.

"Miss Renee, can I help you? Shall I get Miss Elise?"

Renee sat up, slowly, embarrassed at having been caught in a moment of weakness, "I'll be fine, really. I guess I'm just tired. Everything seemed so overwhelming for a minute."

After Celia helped her into her long nightdress, she sank down on her bed. When the maid had gone, Renee lay in the dark, staring up at the ceiling, trying to get her emotions under control. She was angry with herself. She shouldn't burden anyone with her twisted feelings. It was unfair to look to Jim for comfort when he, too, had suffered a most grievous loss, his only brother. Peace was what she needed, not happiness.

Happiness was lost to her, as her husband was, so she would settle for a certain calmness in her life. A quiet space to care for her child. A child who would be surrounded by love and free from fear. L'Aimant was that place. She would live there, secure in the knowledge that her father had raised her alone and she could do it, too. Much thought had gone into her decision to return and at first Martha and George had been reluctant to let her go. They wanted to be close-by while Renee carried their grandchild, but they realized a change of scenery might improve her health. They aided all they could in the preparations for the trip and promised to visit as soon as possible. Renee sighed, more relaxed, as things came into perspective for her. Her next months would be a time of rest and waiting. She would wait for her husband's and her child's arrival.

Caring for Jim as she did, she wouldn't give him deliberate false hope that her deep affection for him had turned to love. Marshall was her only love, and there was no doubt in her mind about that. She rested then, comforted in the resolution of her thoughts.

The following morning was, as she'd hoped it would be, bright and warm. Renee was ready for breakfast before eight and was waiting on the deck by her stateroom door for Elise to appear. The lush Louisiana foliage hugged the banks and she knew a thrill in her soul at being almost home again. Jim found her there, leaning on the rail, totally absorbed in the passing scenery. He was tempted to go on up to his cabin and clean up before meeting her, for he had been up all night. Unable to sleep after his encounter with Renee he had met Ollie in the bar, shared a few drinks and buried himself in paperwork until sunup.

Renee caught sight of his tall lean figure as he came up the companionway and hurried to meet him.

"Good morning," she began, but noting his haggard appearance, added. "Are you feeling well? You look terrible."

"Thanks," he grinned and she blushed. "You, I might add, look lovely this morning. The thought of reaching L'Aimant must please you."

The bright relaxed smile she gave him tore at his heart and he looked away, frowning.

"Oh, yes. In just a few hours we'll be there!"

"I was just on my way up to my quarters to clean up before we breakfast. Would you like to wait for me in the pilothouse?"

"That sounds exciting," glancing at the door to Elise's quiet stateroom, Renee added. "I don't think Elise is stirring yet, so I won't miss her if I join you."

She took his profferred arm and he escorted her to the pilot's domain where he introduced her to the pilot on duty, Lou. Jim departed, leaving Renee sitting demurely on the bench behind the pilot. It was a good half an hour before Jim returned and found her in lively conversation with Lou about plantation trade on the lower Mississippi.

"You watch this little lady, Cap'n. She knows her business."

"Good," Jim stated. "Now that she has connections in the shipping world, we can help her cut costs and keep her expenses at a minimum. Are you ready to eat?"

"I'm famished. Thank you, Lou," she called as Jim led her from the room.

As they entered the grand salon, Renee glanced up at the lifelike portrait of Elizabeth Anne.

"She was so lovely," Renee said, studying the small blonde woman portrayed there. "I often wonder about her."

"Elizabeth was lovely on the outside," Jim agreed. "But if you'd known her you might have changed your opinion."

"Oh?"

"She was very spoiled and self-indulgent."

"That's a shame. You'd think someone that beautiful would be different."

"On the contrary, she got so much just by looking that way, that she never had to develop any of the sturdier personality traits."

"Well, at least I hope she made Marshall happy while they were together."

Jim looked at her in something akin to amazement and then led her off to his table where Elise was waiting.

Almost an hour later, they were finishing the last of their coffee.

"When did Martha say they were coming down to visit?" Elise asked Jim.

"Mother said that as soon as you two were settled-in, she would like to make the trip and stay just a few weeks. Then when it's time for Renee's confinement, she'd like to come for an extended visit."

"I'll enjoy that. I can't wait to show you L'Aimant," Renee told Jim excitedly.

"Shall we check with Lou and see how close we actually are?"

"Let's go," Renee agreed and they hurried up to the

pilot house.

A short time later, Renee gazed eagerly out the windows anxiously searching for the first sign of L'Aimant. Home! She watched as the top floor of the house came into view when the boat churned around a bend in the river. Just barely visible over the tops of the trees were the dormer windows of the third floor of L'Aimant. A thrill coursed through her. At last, a return to the familiar and, hopefully, some power over her own destiny. It seemed for so many months now she'd had no control over the events that had shaped her life, but now she would take charge.

Happily, Renee and Elise hurried down to the promenade deck to await arrival at the landing. With Elise at her side, she waved happily to Alain as he stood waiting for them there. Jim escorted them to the main deck where they impatiently watched the lowering of the plank and Renee was in Alain's arms almost immediately.

"Ma petite, it's so good to have you home. Elise, you look wonderful. Jim, good to see you," Alain greeted them all, his eyes lingering a moment longer than necessary on Elise. "Shall we walk? I thought you might enjoy seeing the grounds."

"Wonderful," Renee told him gazing about her, her expression rapt.

Jim and Elise followed Alain and Renee as they led the way along the path toward the main house. Jim was impressed at the state of the well manicured lawns and carefully tended flower gardens. The house itself was close to overwhelming. The three story home stood majestically before them, waiting to welcome them.

"I can understand why you've missed your home. It's lovely, Renee," Jim stated, obviously taken with the home that Roger Fontaine had constructed those many years before.

Renee smiled warmly and set about giving Jim the tour of her home. She noted with thanks that Alain had seen to everything and all of the rooms were in perfect order.

"How can I thank you, Uncle Alain?" she asked, hugging him. "Everything is just perfect."

"Just be happy, little one," came his heartfelt answer.

Jim parted after a cool drink and they watched sadly as the *Elizabeth Anne* backed out into midstream and moved off into the flow downstream to New Orleans.

After seeing Elise to her room, Renee decided to walk the grounds. It was still early, the noon heat had not yet made an appearance and the gardens were in full bloom, beckoning her with their fragrances. She met Alain on the gallery and together they strolled the short distance to the gate.

"Elise is looking well, wouldn't you say so?" Renee asked coyly.

"Why, yes, she is," Alain returned trying to sound casual.

Renee grinned in genuine amusement, "I may have been a bit preoccupied while you were visiting St. Louis but I did notice that Elise missed you terribly after you'd gone. Dare I hope the feeling is mutual?"

"My dear child, you have never failed to amaze me with your perceptive powers of observation," Alain chuckled.

Flashing him a sidelong glance, trying to gauge his discomfort at her remark, she led him over to a shaded bench surrounded with roses full in bloom. As he sat next to her, she asked innocently, "Were you and Elise acquainted before she moved north to live with great grandmother?"

"Yes. Your father and I were friends from childhood."

"I wasn't asking you about Papa," she teased him as he attempted to change the direction of her thoughts. "You must have been a young man when she left."

"Yes, as I recall, she left about the time my father died," he said almost bitterly. Pausing he looked at Renee earnestly for a moment. "Elise didn't tell you any of this?"

"No. I got some non-committal answer about being needed in St. Louis, but frankly I didn't believe her. Were you two in love?"

"Very much so, then."

"And now?"

"Now, I can only hope that with time we can learn to care for each other again, as we once did."

"I hope so, too. I love you both so much."

Alain hugged her, "If it's meant to be, it will happen. All those years that we could have, should have, spent together. . . . It seems so senseless now, looking back. . . . I wanted her all to myself. I declared my intentions right away, but there was a conflict with my father. He was a hard, calculating businessman and thought I'd be better married to a wealthier girl. He had just the one picked out. He arranged it all behind my back and when I refused, he presented me with the unfailing evidence that I had to marry her. Our plantation was in debt to her father for an outrageous amount and as a wedding dowry, he promised to cancel that debt."

"What did you do?" Renee was clearly upset at this news.

"Elise heard that I was betrothed to another and left without seeing me and allowing me to explain. I was young and I must admit, headstrong. I refused my father's ultimatum and set about working at Windland to repay the money. Father died shortly thereafter and it took me almost two years to clear Windland from debt and restore it. I wrote to Elise constantly for the first six months, but she refused all of my letters. Even Roger tried to talk with her but she wouldn't listen. So, I turned my attention to the plantation and made it a profitable enterprise."

"That's true. It's beautiful, you know. Perhaps you should show it to Elise one day soon."

Alain smiled and agreed, "Maybe I'll do that."

They sat in silence for a long moment.

"Tell me what has happened in St Louis since I left," he inquired.

At those words, her reason for being here came to mind and she felt an overwhelming sense of loss. All that had led to her being home again was loss. Loss of her father and now . . . she struck that thought from her mind quickly. She would not give in to that awful conjecture of Juliana's. She could not. In her deepest heart, she knew he was alive and that some day, somehow he would come back and she would be waiting for him, here.

"How have you been? I've worried and I've written Elise at every opportunity to find if there was any

305

news. Was anything ever found? Maguire never showed up anywhere?"

"No. Nothing. They searched for almost a month but they never found anything, it was as though they disappeared from the face of the earth," she sighed heavily. "But, that's not all."

"What else is there? Something I can help you with?"

"Yes, I will need your help and support over these next months. You see, I am to have Marshall's baby," she turned to face him then, tears falling freely.

Alain was stunned. This thought had never occurred to him—a baby! He could not at that moment decide if it was a blessing or a curse for one so young to be burdened with the prospect of raising a child alone.

"I see you are speechless. I was, too, at first. I was thrilled to have a part of Marshall still with me. Something that no one can take away. But the thought of raising a child alone. . . . I was afraid until I remembered that Papa did it. I know now that I can, too."

"You sound so positive that he will not return to you. Surely you have not given up hope?"

"No, but I must be realistic. As the weeks went by, I knew that the chance of his return was less and less. If he could have gotten away he would have. You see—the last time I saw him he was unconscious. Maguire had hit him and that's when I started to run. I tried so hard to get help . . . But I didn't do very well, did I?"

Alain pulled her against his broad chest, "Cry it out, ma petite, as you've always cried with your uncle."

306

And there in the safety of her garden with her closest friend, Renee let go all of the flood tide of emotions that she had held back since the ordeal had begun.

Later, when they returned to the house for a light lunch, Elise joined them. They made plans for trips into town before the weather got hot and Renee's pregnancy became too advanced. Elise seemed to sparkle under Alain's attention and so she left them to visit and went to her room to rest, feeling much more content knowing that the two people she had left in the world cared for each other and would help her through the next difficult months of waiting.

Chapter Twenty-five

Darkness. It was black. Always black. Not like a night when the moon is hidden, but an absolute pitch of darkness that no light ever seemed to penetrate. He wondered idly if his eyes would work if he, by some chance, got to go outside. That was a stupid thought, he decided. There would be no chance of that. He was too weak now. What did it matter if he died in the dark or in the sunshine? He'd lost track of the days as they had blended into weeks. He'd lost track of a lot of things. There was not much to sustain a sane thought here.

Marshall reasoned that this cave was only a meeting place for Wes and his followers. They were gone much of the time, their arrivals and departures erratic. Often he would hear their loud drunken boasts and claims of the number of banks they'd robbed. They had returned over a week ago and left the same day. Wes had thrown him a small piece of boiled meat and a chunk of hard bread along with his half bucket of water and without a word sealed him back in. It occurred to Marsh that this was the longest that they'd ever been gone. He'd learned early on to conserve what little water they gave him. Needing a drink, he moved across the room to the bucket. "Room?" The thought brought an odd sound from him. He hadn't spoken in days and the noise startled him. He supposed it could have been a laugh, but it wasn't funny, or was it? Hope? What had happened to his hope for help? For Renee? There was no room for hope in his life. There was only darkness and the release that sleep could give. Strangely, sleep didn't come often any more. He tried not to think at all but whenever they brought his meager rations, memories were forced upon him. Searing hot memories that burned and branded his soul with hate and desire for revenge. Revenge for Renee's death, revenge for the torment he was going through and that of his family. But then the memories died, forced from his mind by the necessity of staying alive.

They had been gone a long time this trip. He imagined if he were careful the water would last for another day. Marshall took a small drink and then rested on his stomach. He was used to the feel of the cold damp cave floor beneath him. His back was healing slowly but it had ceased to matter to him. He only existed now. The hours of confinement along with the inactivity had taken their toll. Only that once had he attempted to force his way out. Too much time had passed and he had little strength left.

Now, Marshall anticipated their return because it meant food and fresh water. He focused on that only in his daily life and when he heard them enter the cave much later, he was almost glad. But as he listened, he realized that they were not settling in, they were running from something.

When he heard the horses leave the cave, he panicked. Struggling to the door, he pounded with the chain as hard as he could. Abruptly the barrier was pulled free and Marsh shrank from the fierce light of the lantern.

"Well, well, you still got enough strength to move around, eh? I guess this time we won't leave you anything to eat or drink, that should slow you down and keep you quiet. You know, guards don't like to be disturbed. Ain't that right, Frank?"

"Right, Wes. Ask him if he's got any messages he'd like us to deliver in town?"

"I'm sure he does . . . but I think we're gonna be too busy. We might stop off and visit that purty little gal that helped us out . . . what was her name? Chandler? Yes, she sure did me a favor by letting me know where I could find you all alone. Why do you suppose she did that, Frank?"

Marsh was silent, listening to the conversation between these two, yet not understanding all of it. Juliana? Why would she do that? It didn't make sense. She was happily engaged to Philip. Was that all a cover? Marshall was totally confused and his mind balked at trying to reason.

"I ain't gonna ask him nothin'. Let's go. We got some hard riding to do."

The barricade slammed shut in his face and Marshall crouched in silence for a moment before erupting in violence. A last desperate effort on his part to free himself of this bondage. He sprang at the door with all his might but it didn't budge. Screams of rage tore through him and he relentlessly pounded on it only to hear the Maguires' laughter fading as a distance came between them. They were going and he was alone.

The moon was bright in the night sky, painting false shadows in the alleyways of the St. Louis riverfront. Noise came from all directions as the roustabouts and riverboat men had their good times in the many hell-holes this backwater area had to offer. Within one half-lit smokefilled saloon, Wes and Frank stood drinking whiskey and enjoying the company of several overpainted, underdressed women. A tall, buxom, dark-haired saloon girl hung on Frank's arm, rubbing against him.

"Hey, Wes," Frank spoke loudly to his brother who was occupied with a redhead of similar proportions.

"What d'ya want?" Wes answered, irritated at being distracted from his purpose.

"Wes, you think my friend, Suzie, here, looks like Westlake's wife? That girl sure was a looker," Frank slurred.

"Only if you close your eyes," Wes said cruelly, ignoring the woman who pawed on Frank.

"Well, I think that she does. I'm going upstairs and have me a party."

"Fine, but don't forget to be careful," Wes ordered and Frank dismissed him with a wave of his hand.

"Suzie, honey, you got your own room?" Frank said, running a hand over her ample breasts that strained against the tight fitting dress of scarlet silk and black lace.

"I sure do, sugar, but I don't come cheap," she took Frank by the hand and led him to the stairs, ignoring the hoots of laughter that came from the rest of the gang.

"My name is April, you game?" the redhead challenged Wes.

In one fast move, he twisted her arm and pinned her against the bar, his lower body pressed intimately to hers.

"So, you're a big, tough guy. You like to hit women?" she egged him on and Wes backhanded her across her mouth, splitting her lip.

"That's not all I like to do to women," he snarled and then, shoving her ahead of him, pushed her up the steps. Below, the rest of his men watched, enjoying the scene.

"I'm glad he didn't want me," another of the girls remarked as she came to the table occupied by the Maguire gang.

One of the men grabbed her and pulled her down on his lap, fondling her openly in front of his friends.

"That was a real man," he told her, gesturing toward the steps.

"Who was he?" she asked, trying to keep him from pulling her bodice down too low.

"That's Wes Maguire. Meanest bastard west of the Mississippi," he told her proudly.

She recognized the name and shivered as she remembered what she'd heard about him.

"Hey! Belle! We need more drinks!" voices bellowed at her and freeing herself from the outlaw's embrace, she moved to wait on her customers.

Setting up beers to a group of rivermen at the other end of the saloon, Belle whispered to them, "Which line you work for?"

"Westlake, why?" they looked at her questioningly.

"That's what I thought. Listen, you better get the sheriff, 'cause that's the Maguire gang over there!" she kept her back to the other men.

"How do you know? You sure?"

"That's what they said," she moved away trying to be casual. Two of the deckhands swigged their beers and left the bar, as indifferently as possible.

John Randolph was in his office, drinking strong coffee, trying to stay awake. It had been a long boring day and he badly needed some sleep. Someone pounded on the door and he came jerkily to his feet, surprised by the noise.

"Hurry up, Randolph!" a voice yelled at him and he threw the door open.

"What's the problem?" he asked, instantly alert.

"There's a gang down at the riverfront in Slidell's claiming to be part of Maguire's men. He might be there, too, we're not sure," they told him.

John paused only long enough to strap on his gun, "How many?"

"Could be as many as seven. You want help?"

"Yeah. Meet me in back of the bar in ten minutes with as many men as you can get. I want these bastards," John ground out and rushed off to get help.

Wes stood as he buckled his belt and then reached for his holster.

"Quit cryin' 'fore I give you somethin' else to cry about," he snarled at April.

April raised up to look at the animal standing before her, "You are filth!" She hurled at him, her mouth swollen, her face and body bruised from his attack.

"You were paid to please me, bitch," he said coldly, tossing money on the mattress next to her.

She cringed away from his coins, feeling they were contaminated by him. Wes enjoying her fear, slapped her again with such force that she fell back on the bed. Then smiling to himself, he headed for the hall door.

The shots rang out before he could reach for the knob and he froze. The fighting seemed to be coming from the barroom below and he turned viciously to April.

"How do you get out of here without going downstairs?"

She pointed shakily toward her window that opened onto the lower porch's roof. Wes climbed out onto it and crouching low, he crawled the length of the building to the roof's edge. As he made to jump, a voice rang out from below him.

"Hold it. There are six guns aimed at you right now, mister. So just throw down your gun and then jump after it."

Wes could see the glint of steel in the bright moonlight and could make out at least a few of the gunmen below. As he saw it, giving up was death without a fight for he would surely hang. He drew his gun easily as if to throw it down, then quickly, rolled back the way he'd just come, firing. He moved to climb back in April's window, but she rushed to it and shoved him back with all her force. The silhouette he made against the brightly lighted window set him up as a perfect target, and a hail of bullets slammed into his back. He lurched, losing his footing and fell, rolling off the roof. Wes landed in the alley, unable to move or feel.

"Wes!" he heard Frank's voice calling from

somewhere above and the volley of shots that silenced his brother.

Rough hands grasped his shirt-front and shook him. "Now, Maguire, where's Westlake?"

Maguire managed a smile that was more of a gimace, "Do you really think he's still alive after all this time? He's dead, just like his wife!" he sneered, coughing.

"Where? What did you do with him?"

Wes laughed at Randolph's questions, "You're stupid if you think my dying is gonna change anything. It was worth it . . . after what they did to me. You tell George Westlake . . ." Wes coughed again, spitting up blood. "Tell him, I'll see his son in hell! He's dead and you ain't never gonna find him!"

John jerked him up closer to him, but Maguire's head lolled limply to one side and he threw him down disgusted.

"What about his brother?" he called upstairs.

"Dead, we got him clean in the throat."

John looked disgustedly around and walked away. The prospect of telling the Westlakes weighing heavily on him.

Chapter Twenty-six

It was late afternoon when John Randolph rode up the lane to Cedarhill. Dorrie had been sitting on the porch when she saw him come through the gates and immediately ran to the stables to get her father. George greeted the deputy with a stern expression, noting the pained look about John's face.

"I've some news, George."

"Come in the house, John. Let's have a drink in my study. I think I'm going to need one."

John followed the older man into the study and the door was closed firmly behind him. George poured himself and John a straight whiskey and he downed his while John stood nervously holding his hat and his drink.

"Please sit. Now, what have you found out?"

"Well, late last night there was a group of wild ones down at the riverfront. Talking wild. Throwing Maguire's name around. So we went down to round 'em up. If nothing else, for disturbing the peace," he paused and took a long drink.

"Go on. Was it Maguire?"

"He was hiding upstairs with one of the girls. We got him and his brother trying to sneak out the back."

"Let's leave right now. I've got to see the man."

"You can see him but he can't tell you anything. We had to kill 'em George. They came out shooting. Most of the others got out of town but Wes and Frank were caught in the alley."

"Oh, God. Did they say anything? Anything at all that would help us find Marsh?"

"I'm afraid so," John said looking down into his glass before meeting George Westlake's eyes to tell him that he'd lost his first born. "Wes was laughin' sayin' that at least if he had to die, he knew Westlake had beat him there, and to tell you that he was glad he did what he did. In fact, he seemed to think that Mrs. Westlake was dead, too. I didn't have time to ask him much. Just that Marshall was dead and that we'd never find him, no matter how hard we looked."

George turned to the window his shoulders slumped, a defeated man. But Maguire was dead and he would do no one any harm ever again. "What about the rest of them?"

"I think they'll probably scatter now. There's nothing to keep them together."

"Yes. You're right about that."

"George, I'll go now. If there's anything I can do, please let me know."

"John, there is one thing. Jim is due back in, some time early tomorrow morning. Would you see that he gets word as soon as he docks? Then send him home. I'm sure his Mother and I will need him."

"Of course," John solemnly let himself out and met the searching faces of Martha and Dorrie in the hall.

"John?"

"Mr. Westlake will tell you everything, ma'am," he said gently and left quickly.

"Have they found my boy?" she demanded of her husband who stood with his back to the room staring out of his study window.

"Martha, sit down, please. The news is as we expected and is not good."

She sank into a wing chair and grasped her daughter's hand tightly. She knew what was coming but she had to hear confirmation from her husband before she would truly believe it.

"John and some of his men found Maguire in town last night and there evidently was a fight of some kind down by the river. Wes and Frank Maguire were both killed during the shooting. Marsh was not with them. Wes said as he died that Marshall was dead and that we would never find where he'd left him."

Dorrie broke down completely and fell into her mother's arms weeping. George could no longer control his grief and went to hold both his wife and daughter as they comforted each other.

Martha Westlake looked up at her husband as he came to bed much later that night. George was worn from the ordeal he had been through.

"How do you propose we go about telling Renee?"

"I'm not sure. I think the thing to do would be to let Jim decide what's best. He's been seeing her regularly and I feel he'll know what to do."

"Of course, you're right. It's just that she of all of us seemed to hold on to some hope. And with Marsh's baby coming. We must help her all we can. Oh, George, I know it must be awful for her to be all alone."

"I remember how Marsh was after Elizabeth died.

318

I'm sure we'll have to spend time with her to help her . . . even if Elise and Alain are close at hand."

"You're right," Martha choked back a sob. "Was he happy?"

"Martha, he was a grown man. We couldn't make this happiness for him. I know she loved him. I think that is the most important thing and we do have his child to look forward to. Now, let's get some rest. Tomorrow is going to be a long, painful day."

They fell asleep in each other's arms.

Abruptly Jim turned back to John, his face a cold unfeeling mask. "You must excuse me now. I have to get home as soon as possible."

"They asked me to tell you to hurry. That's why I met you."

"Thank you."

As Jim watched John leave, "Oh, John."

"Yeah, Jim?"

"Thanks for killing Maguire. If I'd been here, I'd have done it myself."

"I understand."

When John had left them, Jim turned to Ollie, "Are you ready to leave now?"

"There are a few more things to attend to. You go on. I'll ride out later. Your folks need you now more than this old packet does."

Jim didn't answer. Not trusting his voice to his old friend. He merely turned and hurried from the saloon to make his trip home.

Jim was grateful for the long ride to Cedarhill, it gave him time to compose himself before he met with his parents—his mother in particular. His father had assumed, after their thorough searching all those weeks ago, that there was little hope of finding Marshall, so the reality of it wouldn't take as big a toll on him as his mother. She had seemed convinced that somehow her eldest son would come home. Now, she knew the awful truth.

When at last, he turned into the drive he had managed to contain himself and maintain an unfeeling facade. He only hoped it would hold up. They had been waiting for him and rushed onto the porch when he started to climb the few stairs.

"Mother," he managed before she was in his arms hugging him to her and tearfully comforting him at the same time.

He knew his attempt at control was lost and he gave himself in to his own grief that he had tried with all his might to subdue.

Much later, after a small meal, they were in the parlor resting and trying to plan the next few months ahead. George and Martha had already decided to have a small memorial service at their church. Jim agreed. The sooner, the better, so they could at last bring some semblance of order and sanity to their much disrupted lives. But their unspoken worry about Renee had to be discussed. As George had suspected, Jim agreed to take the news to her personally. They also knew how torn she would be with the finality of it all.

"Jim, do you think we should go down to spend some time with her?"

"I think that would be wonderful, Mother, but I'd give her a few weeks before you go. I'm sure she'll need that much time to adjust to what I have to tell her."

"I wish there was more we could do for her."

"I think that your being there will mean everything to her," Jim paused to sip the brandy his father had poured for him. "I don't think I'll stay for the memorial; I'll head back downriver tomorrow, freight or no freight."

"She does deserve to know as soon as possible," George concurred. "I only wish I could spare her the pain . . ."

Jim paced his cabin relentlessly. The days since learning the news of Marshall's death had dragged by. He had kept himself constantly busy, not wanting to dwell on the upcoming scene. Now, in a matter of hours, he would have to confront Renee and tell her everything; there could be no holding back. Conflicting emotions filled him. Jim knew that he had to tell her and yet, the realization of what those words would do to her, tore at him. He loved her and with that love came the desire to protect her from all the ugliness of life. To save her pain whenever possible. He only hoped that Renee would recover from this cruel act of fate. Her child, his brother's child, would need all the love and affection it could get. Jim wanted to be there to help when she needed him. He walked almost angrily from his quarters, as he heard the whistle announce their arrival at the L'Aimant landing.

Renee was lying in bed resting late the morning she heard the familiar whistle of the *Elizabeth Anne* coming. She flung herself out of bed wondering at Jim's return. When he had passed last week, he hadn't planned to return for at least fourteen days and here it had only been nine. The thought that he brought news spurred her on and calling Sara, her maid, she dressed rapidly and ran down the stairs past a gaping Elise.

"It's Jim and he's back early. Marshall must be with him! Jim promised if he ever got news he'd come straight back here, either to take me back or bring him to me!"

Renee didn't wait for Elise's reply, she hurried out the front door and descended to the path leading to the levee. Feeling carefree for the first time in months, she was light on her feet as she raced for the landing where the *Elizabeth Anne* was just docking. Her eyes searched for Marshall on the decks and finding no trace of him, she waited anxiously as it positioned itself. She noted, without realizing it, that the boat carried no freight. Anticipation on her face, she waited nervously for the plank to be lowered and for Jim's approach. He came to her, slowly, his face a mask. She looked at him questioningly.

"Marshall's with you? Is that why you're back so soon?" she asked tugging on his arm. Then she noticed that the gangplank was being lifted and the boat made ready to continue downstream to New Orleans.

"Let's go up to the house before we talk, Renee."

Her face paled at his tone and his manner. He took her arm and led her with great care up the path. She didn't notice the stones that she stumbled over as she followed Jim's lead, her eyes filled with tears.

"The news . . ."

"Not here."

She gasped and sagged against him and he swung

her lightly into his arms and carried her hurriedly the rest of the way. Elise met them on the gallery and directed Jim to take her up to her bedroom. Without pause he hurried up the curving staircase with Renee in his arms, weakly clinging to him. When he had laid her on the bed, he instructed Sara to bring a bottle of bourbon and to send for the doctor. He poured Renee a healthy drink straight and handed it to her as she lay back against her coverlet, eyes huge in her pinched face. She sipped the potent drink and handed it back empty to Jim.

"What have you found out? I know it's not good so please . . . don't think that you can tell me gently. You can't. If it is bad I want to know now," her tone was insistent and unyielding, giving him no quarter to soften the horrible truth.

"John Randolph met me when I docked. They had caught Maguire in town and during the fight he and his brother were killed. Before he died, he told Randolph that Marsh was dead and that we'd never find him."

"Your mother . . . how is she?"

"She seemed well. She was most worried about you."

"She is so kind."

Renee didn't speak further. She just turned her head and gazed out the window toward the river where she could see the steamer as it made the farthest turn just before it disappeared from sight.

"Jim, I'm glad you're here, but please, I'd like to be alone for a while. I'm sure we can talk more a little later but right now I feel the need to be alone."

"I understand. I'll be here as long as you need me."

"Thank you," she murmured as Jim rose from the chair at the bedside and left the room.

It was sultry and hot when Renee awoke. She couldn't remember falling asleep. The whiskey on an empty stomach had taken its toll. She knew she had lain here quietly for a long time after the doctor left and before the tears came. And still there had been no strong rush of emotion. Maybe, she had insulated herself enough over the last few weeks so that this final terrible news couldn't hurt. She sighed and rose shakily from the bed. She wondered what time it was and guessed it to be almost suppertime. Smoothing her rumpled gown and trying to comb some semblance of order to her long locks she left the room in search of Jim and Elise.

They were ensconced in the study in quiet conversation when she came through the doorway.

"Renee!"

"I'm sorry about this morning. I'm afraid I wasn't quite as prepared as I thought I was for bad news," she kept her eyes downcast as she spoke softly, not wanting to look at Jim and see the resemblance to her husband.

Jim rose and came to her and took her into his arms. "I'm sorry that I had to be the one to tell you. I really was worried for a while. Are you sure you should be out of bed already? The baby?"

Renee raised her eyes then and looked Jim full in the face, noting the gentle expression in his dark eyes and the concern showing on his features so like Marshall's.

"Jim, you are so sweet. I think I knew that, that first

night on the boat . . ." she kissed him lightly on the cheek and went to sit by Elise on the small sofa.

He seemed a bit disturbed by her mood but said nothing as he sat opposite her.

"Darling, would you like a bite to eat? I can have Sara bring you a tray since you didn't have breakfast or lunch."

"Maybe in a few minutes; I just would like to visit with you both for awhile. I feel disoriented now and I think you two are the only ones, besides Alain, who care. Elise, did you let him know?"

"I sent a message over as soon as you returned this morning, but he had gone to New Orleans for a few days and I don't expect to hear from him until the weekend."

"Oh," she answered quietly, and looking at Jim, said, "Will your mother still be coming down?"

"Mother mentioned before I left that she would like to come to you as soon as you feel up to it. She and Dorrie both miss you greatly and Father also felt the need to get away for awhile."

"Good. Tell them that they are more than welcome to come whenever they're ready. I know the more people I have around me, for the next months, the better I'll feel."

"I'll send word. I had hoped to stay and visit with you for the next couple of days though, that is if you have no objections," he said testing her.

She smiled at him, then, not a happy smile but a warm one that let him know she could not have done without him in the coming days.

The glow of the lamp sharpened the features of Jim

Westlake as he sat in the wingchair. The weak light carved harsh shadows on his face that seemed to age him. He sat unmoving, except for the tumbler of bourbon that he swirled, negligently. Raising the glass, he stared at the golden liquid, not really seeing it, then drained it in one swallow. He shook himself mentally and wondered what had possessed him to start on bourbon tonight. He always drank Scotch for it allowed him to maintain his senses. Bourbon was a potent drink to his system and as such he normally avoided it. Jim rose and moved to refill his glass. Pausing at the window, he could see a boat passing and wished for a moment that he was away from this living torture chamber to which he'd committed himself. Jim walked to the hall door and glanced up the winding staircase. All was quiet. Renee had retired shortly after dinner and Elise had gone up about two hours later. Now, he was alone and grateful for the respite. He could let down his facade of kind brother-in-law and become for a while, Jim Westlake the man.

"Damn!" he muttered under his breath and went to sit down again, swallowing his bourbon without tasting it.

Renee. How he loved her. Her grace, her beauty, her intelligence. She was everything he'd ever dreamed of in a woman. And she was his brother's widow. He didn't know how long he could stay away from her . . . maybe once it became more apparent that she was with child, then, possibly, he wouldn't want her so badly. He ached with the need to hold her and make her his own. Jim also knew that there was only Marshall in her heart and his efforts would be wasted if he tried to approach her as a lover at this time. So, he knew he had to wait, to care for her, to help her and to love her from a distance.

Finally, disgusted with himself beyond belief, he turned out the light and started upstairs. The hall was dark and the air heavy, as no breeze stirred this night. Passing Renee's bedroom door, he heard her cry out and without pause, hurried into her room.

It was foggy, humid. She was running away from the house toward the river. Meeting him. He was there just beyond her reach. Fog enshrouded. Marshall! She heard her voice calling but it seemed not to come from her. Marshall! I know you are there! She ran harder. Her breath coming in painful gasps. She would find him, sobs tore from her throat, as at last she saw him. He stood silently, watching her and as she neared him, his arms opened to embrace her. She was engulfed by the scent of him, manly, of bourbon and horses. She laid her head on his broad chest and rested. Reassuringly, she could hear the steady beat of his heart and she knew she was safe again. She revelled at the strength of his arms. Her hands traced him, caressing every inch of him, devouring him with her touch. He stripped her of her gown gently and bent his head to kiss her. Renee's heart sang. At last! He was back! She stretched out, pulling him down with her, pressing her body intimately to his.

"Darling, your clothes . . ." she whispered against his lips, not wanting to end their kiss.

He stripped off his shirt and came back to her, murmuring, "Oh, my love . . ."

She moaned at the heat of his bare chest on hers

and arched to him as he spread her thighs. He fitted himself tightly against her. Renee writhed beneath him, wanting to complete their union, to feel the hardness of him once again within her depths.

Jim was lost in a bourbon induced fog of need. She wanted him. He was overjoyed at having her in his arms. He had been patient and he had hoped that eventually she would turn to him. Love inspired his every caress as he moved his hips teasingly against her. The desire for oneness with this woman was driving him on. There was no time to remember his brother, or the child she carried in her womb. All thoughts of right or wrong were banished. It was only man and woman, coming together in a fiery explosion of want. As he pulled away for a short time to shed his breeches, Renee called out for her husband in a love-drugged voice.

"Oh, Marshall, I need you so. Please, please hurry!"

Jim froze, the emotion that overtook him left him weak with immediate self-loathing. Renee was still half asleep and didn't know what had almost happened. In the darkness of the stifling Louisiana night, she had needed her husband, the one man she loved. Jim's coming to her in the night had been the answer to her dream and she hadn't taken the time to analyze it. Grateful that he was not completely undressed, Jim grabbed his shirt and hurriedly put it on.

"Marshall?" Renee's voice came to him, more aware and a trifle frightened.

Jim sat down on the edge of her bed, "Put your gown back on."

He could feel her stiffen at the recognition of his voice.

"Jim?" he could hear the edge of hysteria come into tone.

"Please, Renee, put your gown on," he spoke flatly, his voice betraying no emotion.

In the blackness of the bedroom, she fumbled for her nightdress and pulled it quickly over her head.

"Are you dressed?"

"Yes."

"I'll light your lamp."

Renee heard the match strike and flame to life and found herself staring at Jim's broad back as he adjusted the wick. As he turned to face her, she saw the bleakness of his expression.

"Oh, Jim. I'm so sorry!"

He tried to smile, but it was impossible. "It's not for you to apologize. What I almost did was unforgiveable . . ."

"Please, I was at fault. I must have been dreaming and I thought . . ."

"I know, that I was Marshall. Renee, I'm sorry. I have nothing else to offer you. I'm sorry."

Renee took his hand, the fright that had held her moments before was gone.

"Jim, you know how I feel about you. Perhaps in time, things will work out. But right now, I'm just not strong enough for any kind of involvement."

"I understand. I was going to bed and you were calling out in your sleep . . . that's why I came in. My intentions were strictly honorable, at first," he grinned, relaxing in her presence, once again himself. "I can't say I didn't enjoy myself . . . "

She laughed nervously, "I almost enjoyed myself too much. Thank you for stopping. You'll never know how grateful I am for that."

"Me, too," he agreed candidly.

A brief light knock came at the door as it opened, "Renee? Are you all right? I saw the light—"

"She was having a nightmare. I heard her as I was passing the room."

"Renee?" Elise asked, uneasy at the expression on her niece's face.

"I'm sorry I've disturbed everyone . . ." she said painfully.

"And how were you to know that I'd be passing your door just then? It was a dream or more like a nightmare from the sound of your calls," he released her hand and stood up as Elise busily tucked her in. "Are you sure you'll be able to sleep again? Would you like one of those sleeping potions that the doctor left for you?"

"No, I took a few of those when Papa died and they only make me feel horrible in the morning. I'll be fine," she tried to smile up at them.

"Well, we'll both be near if you need anything else," Elise said comfortingly.

"Thank you, Elise," she murmured sleepily as they turned down the light and left her to sleep.

Jim and Elise went back downstairs, each worrying about Renee and how she was coping with her loss.

"Do you think I should leave, Elise?"

"Why?" Elise asked startled at his question, not suspecting his passion for Renee.

"I was just afraid that maybe I'm upsetting her more by being here. It's one thing to think about his being dead, but it's another to have to look at me every time she turns around."

"No, Jim. Your being here is very important to her. Why without your support right now, she would be completely lost," Elise told him. "She loves you as Dorrie loves you, and you can bring her nothing but happiness and security. Don't worry."

Jim reluctantly agreed with Elise, yet the feeling of Renee naked in his arms, pressed against him was burned into his mind. He downed a scotch to help ease his memory of those moments when she thought him to be his brother.

Chapter Twenty-seven

Sheriff Tanner of Harrisons Mills reined in his horse and spoke over his shoulder to the five men who followed him.

"We must be close. This is their last trail, it must be the right one . . ."

They had been chasing the Maguire gang for the last five days, since the bank robbery and the murder of the clerk. The whole town had been enraged and with good reason. Tom Tanner knew he had to get them. They had followed every trail left by the escaping outlaws and all had been false, all except this one. He was thankful that there had been no rain. Although the trail was harder to read, it was not impossible and the direction made much sense. Cave country! He was surprised that no one had thought of this before.

They came upon a small farmhouse overlooking the Meramec shortly before sundown and Tom approached cautiously. When an older man and woman appeared on the porch he was visibly relaxed.

"Evenin' folks," he said from the saddle. "I'm Sheriff Tanner from over in Harrisons Mills."

"Sheriff," the gray haired ruddy complected man acknowledged. "I'm Matthew Johnson and this is my wife, Alice."

"Ma'am," Tom said tipping his hat. "Mr. Johnson, we're looking for a gang of men and I wonder if you've seen any strangers lately?"

"No sir, we ain't seen anybody in weeks. Why? What'd they do?"

"They—Maguire and his gang—robbed our bank and killed the clerk, but they've been operatin' all over the area."

"I'm sorry I can't help ya none, but you're welcome to bed down here for the night."

"Thank you, Mr. Johnson. We're much obliged."

"There's everything you'll need for your horses in the barn. And you're welcome to join us for our evenin' meal if you care to, Sheriff Tanner."

"I surely will. I appreciate this." He rode to his men and directed them to the barn.

"What do you think, Alice?"

"He seems to be a good man, Matthew. I'll start dinner for us now and Caroline can help. Where's Andy?"

"He's down to the river, I 'spect he'll be up soon, it's almost dark."

The meal was a pleasant one for all. Tanner told them of their arduous days in search of Maguire and how the outlaws had left so many false trails that it had taken them five days to find the right one. He knew though, that he was near now. In the morning, they would start off again. Tomorrow they would find them.

Caroline Johnson found Tom Tanner a very attractive man and spent the dinner listening intently to his every word. Although she was only sixteen, she felt she was ready to marry and thought him a most interesting prospect. Tom also found Caroline to be a wonderful listener and a very attractive girl. Flattered by her attention he spoke earnestly about his town and his profession. When the evening came to an end, Tanner knew he would be stopping this way again on the way home.

The posse from Harrisons Mills was already on the trail by the time the sun made its first appearance of the day. It was barely noon when they discovered the beaten path the outlaws had made when they fled almost a week ago. Sure that they were close, Tanner and his men grew silent and with great stealth they backtracked up that trail and found the camouflaged entrance to the massive cave. They approached with a due amount of caution and were not surprised to find it deserted. They lit the few lanterns that had been left behind and began to sift through the remains of their hastily evacuated camp. Two men stood guard while two others searched the main chamber and Tom explored the tunnel which branched at an angle. A hoarse call from Tom brought the others running to him.

"What is it?"

"I don't know. Why do you suppose they sealed this area off?" he asked, confused, and then without further thought dragged the barricade away from the opening with the aid of the other men.

He entered first, bending low and carrying the lantern with him.

"God, Elliot! Jacob! Get in here and help me!" Tom called in astonishment.

The other two men entered the small room and

dragged the man back out as Tom followed.

"Is he still alive?"

"Just barely. Get him out there by the entrance. Let's see what we can do for him."

"Who do you think he is?"

"I heard tell that Maguire had kidnapped a man down in St. Louis, but that's been months ago. You don't suppose. . . ?"

"I don't know, Tom. But if we're ever gonna find out we had better do something for him and fast."

"All right, Elliott. You ride back to the Johnsons and ask them if they can come down here with a wagon or a flatboat. There's no way he could survive on horseback to their place."

"Right."

After Elliott had gone, Tom set about seeing what could be done for Maguire's prisoner. The man was unidentifiable. He was thin and wasted and the sight of his back was enough to turn the strongest stomach. They brought him water first, in small amounts, and the man seemed to respond, but Tom wondered if there was any hope for him at all. They moved him out of the darkness of the cave and into the glade beyond, laying him on a blanket beneath the trees. Tom wanted to take the manacles off but he didn't have the necessary tools.

It was late afternoon before Matthew and Andy brought the flatboat into the natural landing near the cave entrance. They judged it too late to venture back upstream and having brought some of Alice's medicines with them tried to do their best for the stranger Tom had found.

He must be dead, for he could hear birds and smell the fresh air. He rested after those thoughts. But the driving force that had kept him alive these days past without water wouldn't let him accept that. That Juliana had been involved in this haunted him even now in his near unconscious state and he would live just to get even with her. He wanted to live to see her face when he confronted her with what he knew. . . . A sound . . . He jerked his eyes open and was frightened to see tree limbs lacy with green leaves overhead. He tried to sit up but it felt as though he were pinned to the ground. Struggling he managed to free himself from the tentacles of the blanket that enfolded him like a dead weight and he lay back exhausted. What had happened? Was he really free? Had he won? A footstep sounded near his head and it took all of his strength to turn to the noise. A pair of booted feet stood near him and he followed the legs up to the face of the man standing over him. A man he'd never seen before.

"You're awake . . . Don't try to talk or move. Just rest. You've been through a lot."

When Marsh didn't answer, the man continued, "I'm Sheriff Tanner from Harrisons Mills. We were searching for the Maguire gang and we stumbled onto the hideout and found you. It looks like just in time. Would you like a drink?"

Marsh couldn't speak, but he barely nodded.

"Fine, I'll be right back."

Marsh drifted off for a minute or two and then came awake again when the man knelt beside him and held a canteen to his lips. The water that poured forth was sweet and cold and he gulped thirstily until the man restrained him.

"Take it easy. You'll have all you want, but you can't take too much at once. You'll get sick."

Marsh closed his eyes in assent and slipped off into oblivion. When he opened his eyes again, he realized he'd been moved. Now, he was lying face down on a reasonably soft blanket. Marsh managed a quick look around before the agony of the movement struck him and he groaned. Immediately, a boy he hadn't seen before was at his side offering him a drink, which he took eagerly. Anxious to know where he was going, he wanted to question the youth but already exhaustion was overtaking him and he slept. He didn't open his eyes, as he came awake slowly. Relaxing to the sounds around him, he was aware that he was on some kind of boat. He could hear the gentle lapping of the river against the sides of it. It was a peaceful, restful sound, blending softly with the hum of the insects and the chatter of the birds. He focused them, sounds he never expected to hear again, absorbing it all as if he were newly born. In truth he felt that way. Marshall could feel the sun on his face, its warm rays caressing him. The heat of it gave him a sense of well-being that he thought he'd lost forever. Opening his eyes, he rolled to his side and gazed at the lush scenery of the river bank. The actual realization that he was free thrilled him. It was an emotion that was indescribable, a lifting of his soul that, at last, insured his survival. A feeling of peace came over him and he rested, lulled to sleep by the very sounds he had concentrated on minutes before.

The womenfolk were watching the river for the return of their men. Sheriff Tanner had arrived on horseback at the Johnsons' farm several hours earlier, so Alice and Caroline knew that Matthew and Andy would soon be there. Having finished her chores early, Caroline found time to sit with Tom on the riverbank and await their arrival. Finally, she caught sight of the small flatboat as it rounded a bend in the river. She ran hastily to get her mother, while Tom went to meet them at the small landing. Matthew and Andy steered slowly into the shoreline and, after tying up, they carried the injured man up to the house. At Alice's direction, the stranger was taken into Andy's room. Matthew settled Marshall on the freshly made bed and went out in search of the tools he needed to free the man's wrists.

Caroline and Alice watched quietly as the shackles were removed. There were infected, open sores on his arms and the women wondered at the length of time the cuffs had been worn. At her mother's prodding, Caroline was stirred to action and went after the necessary hot water. While she was gone, her father and Tom undressed him and when she returned, her mother was ready to bathe him. In her life, there was no room for feminine airs and she helped her mother with his bath, unembarrassed. This was women's work and she did it. Tom marvelled at her as she set to the task and then he left the room with Matthew.

The man they washed tossed and turned feverishly under their hands. Alice stripped the original bandages from him and studied his back. Then, cleansing it as best she could, she reapplied her salve and rewrapped him in fresh strips of soft, clean cloth. After carefully shaving away his heavy, lice-infested beard, she helped Caroline wash the rest of his body with strong lye soap. Alice gave him a dose of her medicine, while her daughter disposed of the filthy clothes he had worn.

"What's happened to him, Mama?" Caroline asked coming back into the room.

" 'Pears to me that he's so weak this fever musta just took him. Your daddy said it just came up on the trip back," Alice said observing the thin, pale man lying on her son's bed.

"What about his back?"

"Somebody's been beatin' him," she said matter of factly. "Now, you go rest for awhile and I'll stay here with him this afternoon."

Caroline left the room, her heart going out to the sick man. Later that evening, after dinner, Matthew decided to check on the stranger who was now their responsibility. The tall, dark-haired man was quiet now, though his fever raged. Even Alice's remedies, which were known to be effective, had done very little to improve his condition.

"Shall I stay up with him this night, Papa?"

"Yes, but mind you, we don't know this man," Matthew said, eyeing his only daughter sharply.

Caroline nodded and took the seat close to the bed to begin her vigil, the first of many nights to come. Tom came to the door before retiring and told Caroline that he was leaving the next morning to resume his search for Maguire. She hesitated and then went to him and he promised her he would stop again on their way back to Harrisons Mills. Tom kissed her quickly lest they be discovered. When he had gone, Caroline resumed her watch over the stranger, her mind dreaming of the day of Tom's return.

Marshall passed that night deathly still. He made no sound, no movement and when Caroline awoke from a short nap she felt sure he was dead. A quick check of his breathing proved her wrong and she gave him another dose of her mother's fever medicine along with some nourishing broth for strength. Her brother came to relieve her shortly after sunup. Caroline had a final chance to bid Tom goodbye then and when he'd gone she immediately fell asleep in her bed.

The next night Marsh spoke for the first time. He carried on a one sided dialogue that Caroline tried but couldn't understand. He spoke brokenly of St. Louis and someone named Renee, who was gone, whatever that meant. Caroline tried to talk to him but he never opened his eyes. She passed three more such nights. He got neither worse nor better. The fever raged and Marsh's mind roamed freely alternately cursing someone named Chandler and begging for release. Caroline couldn't imagine what from unless it was the bonds he'd been in and they had been off for a long time now. She nursed him faithfully, hour by hour. Until on the fifth day, the fever seemed to break and he was drenched in sweat. She bathed him continuously with cool water that she carried to the house for him. She spoon-fed him and spoke to him as though he were listening. On the morning of the sixth day when she opened her weary eyes to the first hint of dawn she started to see him observing her quietly. A look of sanity was in his eyes.

"Well, good morning," she said pleasantly. "Thank the Lord you're with us at last. This has been one long week."

He didn't answer. He only stared into the flushed

face that was near his in this strange room. Closing his eyes, he intended to rest for only a moment but fell into a deep sleep, the first untroubled one he'd had.

Caroline made sure he was still breathing and then hurried to tell her parents. Her mother checked him, too, and agreed that he was indeed through the worst and it was only a matter of fattening him up now, but Matthew was worried.

"Alice, what do you make of this man?"

"What do you mean?"

"Should I send Andy to town to find out who he is?"

"I don't know," she watched her husband closely, knowing he wanted to do everything possible to help him.

"Let's give him a day or so to improve. He'll tell us soon enough what he wants done."

"I suppose you're right," he agreed, but couldn't help but wonder about the man's family.

Matthew went about his chores then, telling her to call if the man chose to start talking.

Alice remained by his bed most of the day waiting for him to waken. Since he was resting comfortably, she decided to let nature take its course and simply feed him when he was ready. There was no need to urge him to take more medicine. The wounds on his arms were bandaged and starting to heal, although she knew he would always carry scars from those. His back had seemed much improved the day before and she hesitated to wake him now just to change the dressing. She watched intently as he tossed restlessly and finally opened his eyes. He lay still trying to orient himself and when he failed at that, he rolled to one side and came face to face with her. Their eyes met.

"Thank you," he whispered roughly trying out his voice for the first time.

"You're welcome," she smiled at him. "How do you feel now?"

"I don't know yet," he answered rolling onto his back easily, staring at the ceiling. "Where am I?"

"On the Meramec. At our farm. We're the Johnsons. Sheriff Tanner found you and he and my husband, Matthew, brought you here."

"How long?"

"You've been here six days now."

"That long? I don't remember anything after the water was gone." He paused and rubbed a hand over his face. As he saw the carefully wrapped bandages on his wrists he looked at her in surprise. "I owe you much."

"You can pay me back just by tellin' me your name. We're tired of just callin' you the stranger."

"Marshall . . . Marshall Westlake."

"It's nice to know you, Marshall Westlake. Now, how about something to eat? I've been waiting all this time just to see what you'd like."

"Anything . . . anything is fine. You say I've been here six days?" At her nod he continued. "No one's come around looking for me?"

"No. We seldom see folks out this way. It was a miracle that the sheriff found you there in that cave. Usually there isn't a soul around these parts."

"That's good," he said in some relief and some of the stricken look that had haunted his face disappeared. He lay back rubbing idly at the wrappings on his arms, "I never knew . . ."

"Never knew what?" asked Alice from the door on

342

her way to get him food.

"Never knew it could feel so good to be free," he answered.

Alice started to question him further but the strain that marked his lean ravaged features held her back. That was for Matthew to do. She busied herself fixing him a hot meal and watched with relish as he ate most of it. She left him to rest then and went in search of her husband. Matthew accompanied her back to the house in order to question this man who had come into their midst. How had he come to be in chains? Why was he there in the middle of the country so far from town? Who had beaten him so severely? As he entered the room, he was amazed at the change in this man. Marshall was sitting upright for the first time, his back braced with the pillow against the wall. His eyes were clear and his expression alert.

"I understand I owe you my life?" Marsh said extending his hand.

"I did what any man would do. But Tanner, now he's the one who got you out."

"No . . . you didn't do what any man would do. I thank you," Marsh insisted earnestly as they clasped hands. "And who is Tanner?"

"He's the sheriff from over in Harrisons Mills. He was searchin' for that Maguire gang and found you in the cave. He just left a few days ago. Had to track Maguire while the trail was still good."

"Is he comin' back?"

"Said he would, now Mr. Westlake, we've been so worried all these days . . . wonderin' . . ."

"Please, I'll explain all I can."

Matthew nodded his approval as Alice made her

way from the room and shut the door. Matthew sat then and met Marsh's gaze.

"My home's in St. Louis. Are we far upriver?

"Not too far," Matthew said as he lit his pipe and drew on it.

"I'm an attorney. My family owns a farm north of town and I have my offices in town."

"Then why were you shackled up like some escaped convict?" Matthew asked.

"Maguire." Marshall paused as the memories flooded in on him and his eyes became haunted. He shook his head to clear his thoughts. "They took me after . . . after Maguire had escaped from the pen."

"You're saying some escaped criminal took you and brought you up here?"

Marshall nodded wearily, the weight of the suddenly rediscovered emotions almost too much for him. "What is the date?"

"Why?"

"I don't know how long I've been gone."

"It's June, June 20th to be exact."

"My God. They must all believe I'm dead." His voice was flat, lifeless, and for a moment Matthew worried that this had been a blow more terrible than those that had fallen on his body. "I'd like to rest now, Mr. Johnson, if I could?"

"Just one thing before I go. I'll do all I can to help you."

"Thank you," Marsh said, his voice filled with sadness.

"Do you want word sent? And you can rest here and get your strength back until they can come for you?"

"No. As soon as I'm well enough I'll head back. I'll

tell them myself."

Matthew left then and Marshall stared blankly at the ceiling until he felt reality slipping away and sleep overtook him.

"Time you got to meet the man you been nursin', Caroline. Come on up to the house. Maybe today we can get Mr. Westlake outside into the sunshine. Might do him more good than just lyin' there hour after hour."

"Yes, Ma," she followed her mother obediently up to the house.

Marshall was sitting up again and looked up sharply when the door opened. His expression softened as he saw Alice enter and behind her a younger version of herself, tall, blonde and sturdily built.

"Mr. Westlake."

"Marshall, please," he insisted smiling at them. It was his first smile in their company and the difference it made in him caused the women to smile automatically back at him.

"Marshall, this is my daughter, Caroline. She sat up with you at night when you were sick."

"I thank you, too, Caroline," he said smiling still.

"You're welcome," she said softly, slightly shy now that he was awake sitting there looking so manly despite his recent illness.

"We been thinkin' that the best place for you would be out in the sun. Caroline, bring him in some of your Pa's clothes. We'll put a chair out there under one of the trees and you can rest there for the afternoon. It's got to be more entertaining than just lying in here."

"That's true," he agreed. "I appreciate the thought.

I've been getting stir crazy in here but I doubt that I can make any distance yet on my own."

"We'll help you, we got you this far we're not gonna let you get sick again."

After Caroline returned, Marshall pulled on a pair of Matthew's trousers and a long sleeved shirt and made his way to the door, leaning heavily against the frame as he waited for the dizziness to pass and a measure of strength to return.

"Marshall, let me help you," Caroline's voice came worriedly from the porch as she rushed in to the main room and took his arm about her shoulders.

"I'm afraid you won't be able to balance me," he said trying to make the statement seem light.

"Don't worry, I'm stronger than I look and you're lighter than you think you are. You must have lost a lot of weight."

"Yes, I did," he answered quickly, not encouraging any further questions, thinking that a woman didn't need to know of the things that had been done to him.

He sat peacefully under a large spreading pin oak watching the river and the few animals that the Johnsons kept. He vowed silently to himself that when he got home they would be well rewarded for helping him. Noting the fishing poles that leaned casually against the side of the house, he decided that later in the week, when he was sure of himself, he would start catching their dinner.

When Caroline finished her chores, she went to sit by him and try to cheer him up. Something about him seemed so solemn and unhappy that she couldn't help but wonder at his past. Surely she could make him see that things weren't quite as bad as he thought.

Caroline always managed to find the happiness in every situation. She talked randomly, telling him about the years that they had lived in Kentucky before coming this far north to settle. She spoke of the boyfriend she'd left behind and of her friends. She told him how her mother and father had saved to buy this better land and how they had big plans for the future. She talked of her love for horses. She encouraged him to speak of his own when she saw his interest flicker. The only time she was uncomfortable with him was when she mentioned his family. He froze at her questions and deftly turned the conversation back to her interests. She realized he was doing it but she didn't know why.

Marshall enjoyed Caroline's chatter. It kept him from dwelling on thoughts of Juliana. He had been trying to reason out why she had helped Maguire and the only thing he could think of was that her engagement to Philip was a sham just to save her face over the fact of his marriage to Renee. Renee! The name screamed through his mind. His last vision of her tortured him. Maguire with the knife to her throat . . . then Wes laughing at how easy it had been. She was dead and all because of Juliana and her sick jealousy. Rage filled him. His face blanched and his jaw tightened. Hate. That was all he had room for now. There could be no more softness in his soul. There was only bitter hatred inside of him.

"Marshall?" a soft feminine voice came to him through the fog of his memories. He had forgotten where he was and who he was with. The voice was a worried one, an unfamiliar one.

"I'm sorry," he answered bringing his surroundings

back into focus.

"It's all right. I was just worried that you were getting sick again. Your face looked so terrible, like you were in great pain."

"I'm fine, or I will be once I'm able to get home again."

"Do you miss it greatly?"

"Caroline, for a long time I believed that I would never see it again."

"How long have you been away?" she asked innocently enough, forgetting his reluctance to discuss himself.

"Too long. It must be getting near dinner time and I have much to discuss with your mother; help me back inside, will you?" he asked pleasantly but his eyes had gone cold at the probing question.

Days slipped by and Marsh felt his strength and endurance returning slowly. He had lost most of his pallor by sitting in the warm summer sun every afternoon and he began to feel more like himself. He smiled more often at the things Caroline did to entertain him and helped Alice with what he could around the house. His fishing expeditions were successful and he spent long hours in solitude before sun-up and at dusk catching the meals they would have the next day.

He hoped that Sheriff Tanner would return before he was able to leave. He wanted to thank him, but he was anxious to return to town. He had business there. Caroline joined him one evening as the sun dipped below the tree tops and sat next to him in silent companionship.

"I suppose you'll be leaving soon."

"It will be best. There are people who are worried."

"Oh," she sounded disappointed. "I was hoping that you'd like it so much here you might decide to stay."

He looked at her in surprise. It had not occurred to him that this young girl would form an attachment to him. He wanted to remain aloof, to avoid ties here. They were good people but his life was not his own now, he could make no plans other than those concerning Julie.

"Thank you, Caroline. That's the nicest thing you could say to me," he smiled gallantly.

She smiled timidly at him. Caroline found him very attractive, despite his recent injuries and the brooding quality about him only encouraged her fantasies. The dreams that disturbed his sleep had awakened her one night and she'd rushed to his side thinking him ill. But Marshall had still been asleep, shaking from the force of his nightmare, calling out to someone named Renee. Caroline wondered who she was. He had never mentioned that name during his waking hours. Only when he had been delirious before and now during his dreams.

"Who is Renee?" she asked curiously, feeling that for a moment, she was close to him.

Marshall looked up at her sharply, "Why? Where did you hear that name?"

"You've been calling for her in your sleep. . . ." Caroline was a little embarrassed; she hadn't expected him to react like this.

Marshall caught his breath, audibly. He had no idea that he spoke so coherently when he was in the grip of those terrible visions. Visions of Renee, first loving him, then their swim and finally, Maguire ripping her bodice and touching her. He swallowed convulsively.

"She was my wife," he spoke those words without emotion.

"Was?"

"She was murdered by Wes and Frank Maguire, the day that they took me prisoner."

Caroline listened, almost unbelieving to what he was telling her.

"I'm so sorry."

"So am I," he answered bitterly. "So am I."

They went back then. The bond between them gone, he walked as a stranger beside her, withdrawn, quiet and calculatingly cold.

The moonlight poured into Caroline's bedroom. The loosely woven curtains at her window did little to block the bright mooonbeams. She tossed restlessly on her small bed. The entire evening she thought only of Marshall and what he must be suffering. Caroline got up and paced the room, her bare feet making no sound. She knew that she wanted to help him. She had to do something to make this time easier for him. She thought of the pain she'd seen on his face and knew now the cause. Opening her bedroom door, she tiptoed to Marshall's room and went in, closing his door quietly behind her.

He was asleep on the bed, his blanket kicked carelessly off. She had seen him undressed before, but somehow, now that he wasn't ill, she could look at him as a man and not as a patient. She knew he would be devilishly attractive when he was completely recovered. His shoulders were broad and his legs long and straight. Going to stand next to the bunk, she watched him sleeping. His dark hair fell across his forehead and he looked extremely vulnerable. Reaching out one hand, she brushed the errant hair back off his face. He didn't stir. Emboldened by her success she knew she wanted to touch him, everywhere. Not once questioning her impulses, she stripped off her thin cotton gown and climbed in carefully next to him.

Marshall felt a welcoming warmth next to him and instinctively reached out to pull it nearer. The skin he touched was smooth and caressingly, he ran his hand over her. The woman moved closer, searching and finding his mouth in a passionate kiss. Not opening his eyes, he savored the touch of her lips, enjoying the feel of her hard-tipped breasts against his chest and the heat of her lower body pressed against his hip. Animal reactions set in, as he hardened at the temptation offering itself to him. Twisting his body, he brought her beneath him and was spreading her thighs before he fully realized who she was and what he was about to do. He stared at Caroline through the darkness, his fingers idly tangling in her blonde hair.

"What are you doing here?" he demanded, keeping his voice down. "Do you realize what might have happened just now?"

She was surprised by his actions and said nothing. Marshall climbed off her and stalked away from the bed. Then suddenly conscious of his own nudity, he grabbed the cover and tied it about his thin waist.

"Get dressed," he ordered and Caroline hastened to don her gown, tears glistening in her eyes.

"I only wanted to comfort you . . . to help you . . ."

"There is nothing you or anyone else can do to help me now. How can you think that I would betray your parents' kindness by taking their only daughter?"

"You weren't taking, I was giving," she sobbed.

Marsh stood helplessly for a long moment and then took her in his arms.

"Caroline, you thought you were doing a very wonderful thing, but the help I need is not through physical release. It means nothing without love. It is nothing without love."

She quieted and leaned against him, "I could love you."

"But I wouldn't love you," he told her truthfully.

Marsh felt her stiffen at his rejection and he spoke quickly to ease her, "You couldn't possibly want a man who loved another woman, could you?"

"I suppose not."

"I love my wife, Caroline," he told her seriously.

"But she's dead!" came her almost childish reply.

"Death does not stop the loving," he spoke quietly and dropped his arms. "I think you'd best go back to your own bedroom."

She nodded, beginning to understand what he had told her and left him standing there alone.

In the days that followed, Marshall became more withdrawn than ever and he was relieved that Caroline had kept her distance. He did not want to hurt her, so he discouraged any overtures from her with cool indifference. He rested often, that second week, and slowly as his strength returned he took long walks in the woods. The quiet and serenity there helped him sort out his thoughts and plan what he was going to do as soon as he was able. His appetite returned and with the help of Alice's fine cooking, he put on a little weight as the second week drifted into the third. Judging himself, he figured that by the end of the third week he would be fit enough to leave. During this time, too, he became accustomed to his changed facial features. It had been a shock to him, the first time he'd decided to shave and had looked in the mirror. Though the swelling had gone down, he had still been bruised. Analyzing the transformation, Marshall realized that it was not only the weight loss that had put new angles in his face, his nose had been broken. He almost thought it amusing, recalling how Jim had always complained that he'd gotten all the brains in the family, but Marsh had gotten the looks. As he let himself think about his physical injuries, Marsh found it hard to believe that they hadn't been more serious. His ribs and nose had mended on their own and his back gave him only an occasional reminder of what had been. He was grateful for that, because as soon as he was able, he was going to take care of Juliana and then go after Maguire.

It was at the end of the third week that Tom Tanner rode happily into the yard. His posse had disbanded and so he had come alone.

Matthew greeted him and Caroline, too, came rushing out.

"Tom! It's so good to see you, it's been almost a month.

"I know, Matthew, but I've got good news. Maguire's dead. I got as far as Sinking Spring and the law there told me. He got shot down in St. Louis!"

353

"That's wonderful news! I'm sure Alice'll be glad to see you're back!" Matthew invited. "Caroline, go down to the river and tell Marshall that Tanner's back."

"Yes, Papa," she hurried away after eyeing Tom.

"How is—did you say Marshall?"

"Yes, that's his name, Marshall Westlake."

"Then he is the one. The one Maguire kidnapped in early April. I can't believe he lived through it all."

"He's comin' along just fine and I'm sure the news you're gonna give him will make him even better."

Tom settled at the table enjoying Alice's warm welcome. When he heard steps coming across the porch, he turned to find Caroline entering, followed by the man he had pulled from the depths of the cave. Tom rose and took the hand offered him, all the while studying him.

"It's a pleasure to meet you, Sheriff Tanner," Marsh said with sincerity.

"Tom, please. I'm just glad to see you're alive."

The man actually looked recovered. The bruises were gone, his color had returned and he walked easily as if his back didn't bother him.

"You're all right? Your back. . . ?"

"Thanks to Alice, it's almost healed. I'm just about back to normal," Marsh let the sentence drop.

"Well, I've news that will help. Maguire and his brother were both killed in a shoot-out in St. Louis just about a month ago. Seems a deputy—"

"John? John Randolph?" Marsh interrupted.

"Yeah, I think that was his name. Anyway, he caught up with them down around the levee and let them have it. Seems the whole state is celebratin'."

"With good reason, too," Matthew added.

They breathed a collective sigh of relief and Alice and Caroline set about making a celebration dinner. Matthew got out his rarely used bottle of bourbon and the men went out on the porch to enjoy a drink. The meal was a lively one as Tanner regaled them with tales of his search for Maguire. Marshall was glad to find that Caroline was attracted to Tom, who seemed to care for her also. When the dinner had ended Marsh excused himself and went outside to sit alone by the river. Dusk was a melancholy time for him and he listened to the locusts chirping in unison and the splashing of a big fish as it top fed, solemnly. So Maguire was dead, not only Wes, but Frank, too. No doubt, they were satisfied that at least Renee and he had been revenged. It was a weight off him to know that he only had to repay Juliana for her treachery. Dealing with her would be easy, he had his plan already worked out. As darkness came Marsh rose and made his way back inside. His decision was made. He would leave as soon as possible.

Dawn, the following morning, was a watery one. Black, heavy rain-filled clouds hung low over the hills and everything seemed hushed, muted by the drumming of the downpour. There appeared no break in sight, so Marshall settled in for a long boring day, waiting, anticipating, ready for the moment he could leave. Late that afternoon the storms turned to drizzle and finally tapered off by sundown. The rising river had given them cause to worry, but with any luck at all it would be down the next day.

It was clear and bright, the early rising sun bearing promise of a hot summer day. Marshall had arisen before sunup and had gone down to the landing to check the Meramec. The river was lower than the evening before and he smiled grimly, eager to be on his way back to town.

Breakfast was relaxed and happy, as the Johnsons were glad that Marshall was well enough to be on his way and Tanner satisfied that his search had not been totally fruitless. It was agreed to take him by boat to the nearest town where he could pick up supplies and a good horse for his cross country journey. The trip to St. Louis could be made twice as fast by trail than by boat.

Marsh said good-bye to Alice at the house and moved down to the landing where the rest awaited him. Caroline stood, watching his approach with tears in her eyes. He looked at Caroline for a long moment and felt a surprising stirring within himself. Marshall came to her then and took both of her hands.

"Thank you for everything."

"Thank you," she said with emphasis and a quick look at Tanner a few feet away talking with her father and brother. Though she still had deep affection for Marsh she knew her future was with Tom. Marshall weakened at the sound of her tone and pulled her into a warm embrace.

"Take care of yourself," Caroline told him, returning the hug.

"I will and you be happy, all right?"

She nodded and he set her from him.

"Goodbye, Marshall Westlake," she said, smiling, and kissed him on the cheek.

Marsh turned and shook hands with Tanner, thanking him again before moving to where Matthew and Andy waited on the boat. As they shoved off,

Marshall felt very empty inside, as though all emotion had deserted him. Watching as the trees hid Caroline and Tom from view, he envied Tom the happiness that his future held for him with Caroline.

Chapter Twenty-eight

George and Martha were thrilled when they received word from Jim that Renee wanted them to come and visit. Dorrie was happy, too, at the prospect of seeing her friend again. As soon as they closed Cedarhill, they made the trip downriver on the *Starbelle*.

Dorrie was stunned by the beauty of Louisiana. The lushness of the growth and the endless flowers were beyond compare. When the *Starbelle* docked at the landing, they were astonished at the view before them. L'Aimant, built so many years before, was once again in its splendor. Renee spent many hours over the last weeks revitalizing the grounds and the gardens. The house shown brilliant white against the green back-drop of magnolias and dogwoods. A carriage met them while Renee waited with Elise and Jim on the gallery of the mansion. Her pregnancy not yet in evidence, Renee stood tall and slim in her mourning dress. She was a vision of beauty and Martha hurried up the steps to hug her tightly.

The welcome was warm and tearful. She graciously showed them to their rooms a few minutes later so they could freshen up.

"I can understand why you wanted to return home, my dear," Martha said after she'd entered the bedroom where she and George were to sleep. "Everything is so lovely."

"Martha, I'm so glad you understand why I had to come back. And now that Uncle Alain has finally declared his intentions for Elise, things are working out beautifully."

"Alain and Elise?" Martha exclaimed. "How wonderful!"

"It seems that they were very close years ago and have rekindled the flame, so to speak," Renee laughed happily. "I've been trying to get them married ever since I came home. They didn't decide until just last week, so I thought I'd save the news until you arrived."

"That news is most welcome."

Renee left them to settle in and went to her room for a short nap before dinner. She'd found it almost impossible to stay awake the entire day. She slept later and later each morning and often found herself yawning right after her noon meal. The doctor insisted she rest whenever she felt tired and Jim and Elise kept close watch over her so she wouldn't disobey his orders.

As she rested on the bed, Renee recalled her conversation with Elise when she had finally told Renee about her earlier relationship with Alain. They had just finished breakfast one day, that first week back, and were enjoying a cooling river breeze on the front upstairs gallery.

"It's going to take some getting used to," Elise remarked.

"What is?"

"This humidity and the heat! Why it's like August

in St. Louis here right now and we're barely into the summer!"

Renee smiled widely, "I suppose you'll just have to rest every afternoon. That's the only way to get through the summer down here."

"I remember, Papa always moved us upriver out of New Orleans when the heat got bad and the fever threatened."

"Did you know Alain then?"

"Oh, yes. He and your father were very close even as very young men."

"Did you like him?"

Renee's question took Elise by surprise and she flushed, "Of course, he was always very nice and a perfect gentleman." She added the latter a little bitterly.

"Why did you blush?" Renee asked pointedly. "Did you care for him?"

"There's no need to discuss this."

"Of course, there is!"

Elise looked quickly at Renee, trying to understand what she was getting at. "Why?"

"I just want to know what really happened and why you really went to live with Grandmother St. Sauvin."

"I've already told you why."

"And I don't believe a single word of it," Renee insisted. "You're much too beautiful not to have married. And look at Alain, he never married either!" Stubbornly Renee stated her suspicions. "Were you two in love?"

Elise looked irritated for a moment and then sighed, "I suppose it won't do any harm to talk about it now. I haven't for so many years. . . ." Renee was silent, waiting for the explanation to come. "It was all so long ago . . . I was so young and naive. I loved him very much and he loved me, or so I thought. He proposed and I accepted."

"That's wonderful, I thought so," Renee said, trying to sound as if it was newly discovered information.

"I thought it was wonderful, too, for a little while. But before he talked to my father, I found out that he was already engaged to Celeste Beauvaise."

"What?"

"I had gone shopping with a friend and I overheard Celeste talking about it to her mother in a shop. . . . I've never been so humiliated in my life."

"How horrible! What did you do?"

"That's when I came north. I was too young to stay and take it gracefully. I fled."

"Didn't Alain try to stop you?"

Elise looked wistful for a moment. "He wrote, but I returned all of his letters unopened."

"You didn't give him a chance to explain?"

"No. What was the point?" Elise said sadly. "He had used me while he was promised to another . . . I could never forgive him. . . ."

"But Elise, did you ever find out the truth about what really happened?"

"I know . . ." she began.

"No, you don't."

"What?"

"Alain told me the whole story. I know what the truth is. Do you want to hear it?"

Elise was speechless. Renee had manipulated the entire conversation just to come to this point and it left her aunt furious. She rose with all of the grace of a great Southern lady and gave her niece an icy glare.

"I know what I heard that day. I think this discussion has gone on long enough. If you'll excuse me, I do have things that must be done. . . ."

As Elise turned stiffly away to move into the house, Renee called, "He still loves you. He always has."

Elise froze at the door and turned to look at Renee, "If he cared so much, why did he waste all these years?"

"A man like Uncle Alain can only take so much rejection. According to him, he wrote you for six months and you never once gave him a chance to explain."

"I see," she said coldly.

"Don't you think it's strange that he didn't marry that other woman? I mean, if they really were betrothed?" Renee could see doubt come into her aunt's eyes. "It was Alain's father. He was in debt to Beauvaise and Beauvaise offered to cancel it if his daughter married Alain."

"So why should this prove anything to me?"

"Because," Renee spoke slowly in emphasis. "If Alain had loved her he would have married her. But instead, he took over running Windland and made it a success. In two years he'd paid off that debt and now Windland is a prosperous plantation. His father died shortly after you left and so he really couldn't get away. That's why he wrote you. He was heartbroken when you didn't respond. Why, he even sent Papa to talk to you, he was so desperate!"

Elise paled and came back to sit down by Renee, her movements jerky.

"He still loves you," Renee emphasized again.

"How could he still care, after all this time?"

"He does."

They both were silent, watching the river flow by in a distance. Renee was wondering at the impact of her words and Elise pondering the misunderstandings that had plagued her relationship with Alain. It was all so senseless. All those years that they were separated when in fact she could have been with him, making him happy. Elise blinked back burning tears.

"I think I'll rest in my room for a while," she said and left Renee sitting on the porch, a small smile touching her lips.

The situation between Elise and Alain changed almost immediately and Renee made an effort to give them plenty of time alone. It was only after a visit to Windland alone with Alain a short time before, that they finally decided to marry. Renee smiled broadly and curled on her side, her hand on her belly. She was content that they had found their happiness at last.

When she awoke, the heat was heavy and suffocating, typical of deep south summers. Renee had often been grateful during her growing years that her room faced east and the river to save her from the burning afternoon sun. Rising slowly, she went to her washstand and bathed her face with the cooling water from the pitcher. How good to have the Westlakes here. They had come to mean so much to her during her months in St. Louis that she now, in fact, considered them family. Marshall crossed her thoughts then. She saw his smiling face as he had looked that last day on their picnic. Tanned and fit, he had been a most handsome man and she doubted that she would ever feel that way about anyone again. She had tried to keep herself as busy as possible so that Marshall wouldn't haunt her but it had been useless. Wherever she went he was there, each vision a different expression. Each thought another remembrance of how much she had lost and the pain was still great within her. She had presented to Jim and Elise a calm and reasonably happy exterior these past few days since her nightmare. But when she was alone her mind brought his image before her and she would sink into despair with the weight of her loss. The only thing that kept her from total despondency was the knowledge of his child growing within her. Marshall's son or daughter was the mainstay in her life now and she would do all she could to raise his baby with love and a deep sense of family ties.

Wearily, she rang for her maid and with Sara's help she dressed in her black summer weight gown. How upset Marshall would be if he could see her. He hated these dreary clothes. She sighed as she left her room and made her way down the wide hall to the Westlakes' room. Knocking lightly, she entered when Martha called out to her.

"Did you get some rest, Martha?"

"Yes, darling, thank you. Do you have a few minutes to visit with me? George is off with Dorrie and Elise in the gardens and I'd like to talk to you about a few things."

"Of course, any time. I'm so happy you're here. You're my family, you know," she said smiling at Martha.

Renee settled in the overstuffed chair while Martha sat on the bed and opened the small trunk beside her.

"Renee, I brought these things not to upset you but because I thought that they would be important to you."

"What are they?" she asked, her eyes widening with her curiosity.

"Marshall's things. I think they belong to you, now."

Renee looked stricken, "But he was your son. You feel you can part with them?"

"I feel that his wife and child are entitled to them. Surely you realize that you don't even have a likeness of him. How will your child ever know what his father looked like?"

"Oh, Martha, you are so wonderful!" Renee went into her arms and they cried together.

Then as the tears dried, they went through each item lovingly. His important papers, a small portrait of the family when they were much younger, a small daguerrotype of him with Elizabeth, Renee supposed from their wedding and another daguerrotype taken more recently of him alone. Martha gave her jewelry that had been his and a few books that had been special to him; one was the book of Byron's poems.

"There are more things still at Cedarhill . . . if you have a son I will bring them to you . . . his guns . . . and tack," Martha's voice faded. "You know, Renee, I never really believed him gone until John Randolph came to tell us about Maguire. It's still hard for me to believe that any man as vital and full of life as my son could be . . . dead."

"I know, Martha, I didn't believe it either. Jim tried to be kind when he told me all of it but it still came as such a shock. There are even days now when I swear if

I turn around he'll be there with me. It's as if he's with me always no matter what the distance. . . ."

They packed the things away lovingly and Renee carried the trunk back to her room so she could go through them again when she was alone. She took out the latest picture and placed it on the small table by her bed. He looked so carefree, caught there by the camera. She stared at the likeness for a long moment before she went again in search of the others.

Chapter Twenty-nine

He was tired from the ride. He was tired from everything, the only thing alert about him was his mind as he rode into the outskirts of St. Louis. He had to make his way unnoticed to his office, so he could get himself cleaned up without any interference. He had no room in his carefully made plans for anyone to get in his way. He was going to deal with Juliana. He was going to give her the shock of her life and it would be the last one she would ever receive. He set his jaw against the thought of what would happen to him once he had finished with her. Although he didn't have documented proof of her involvement in this whole ordeal, he knew it first hand from the Maguires. His family would understand his need for revenge. And if he destroyed himself in the process it didn't matter. He had nothing left to live for now. His morbid thoughts had pounded at him the entire ride back to town. His mood matched his looks as he scowlingly made his way down the road. It was late evening and he was glad for the darkness as he reined in in front of his office. He knew the thick growth of beard he had cultivated these last days did much to disguise him and so he casually dismounted and tying the horse to the post moved to the office door. To his unpleasant surprise, it was boarded up. There was no notification of reason or other explanation—it was just locked up. He went to the back and tried that door but to no avail. Managing to rub a clear spot on the back room's window, he saw that all of his personal things were gone. It was as if he had never existed. His stomach twisted sickeningly at the thought. Never existed. Ceased to exist. Dead. He turned, frustrated, from the door and thought fleetingly of returning home to his parents. To warmth, comfort, security. He forced the thought away as soon as it came. He couldn't just let Juliana get away with it. With murder. As sure as she'd pulled the trigger herself. He could have forgiven her for himself but to know she was responsible for Renee's death, it was more than he could bear. He debated with himself for a moment, there in the darkened alley, and then decided to go to Elise's house. He knew it would be painful to return there but she could at least give him refuge while he readied to face Juliana. There would be no time for Elise to contact his parents or Jim either. No one would stop him. He strode purposefully back to his mount and headed toward Elise's. To his further anger and frustration, her home was closed, too. There was no one around, not even the servants. Cursing, he went back down to the waterfront and, after purchasing new clothes, he went into one of the public bath houses to clean up. He was even more grateful for the extra money Matthew had forced on him now. It hadn't occurred to him that his office would be vacant and the Fontaine house, too.

Clean and freshly shaven, he dressed unnoticed in the rear room of the bath house. Then leaving by the back door, he quietly made his way uptown to the Chandler mansion. He would watch and wait until the time was right before he made his move. That he didn't have a gun meant nothing to him. He wanted to kill her with his bare hands. It would be easy, the shock of seeing him would probably do half of the job for him and at that thought, his mouth twisted into a cold smile. He tied the horse down the street and settled back into the shadows to watch and wait directly across from the Chandlers.

Hours passed. He had seen Juliana leave in a carriage with Philip and her father departed soon afterwards. He doubted that they were attending the same social function. If Juliana was to marry Philip DeGrande any time soon, he was sure they were not spending their time at any useless parties or political gatherings. He judged it to be close to midnight when he finally moved from the safety of his vantage point. With ease, he climbed the railing at the back of the three story house and pried open the window to the bedroom adjoining Juliana's.

Marshall knew the house well. He knew that no servants waited up for their mistress and that no one was about after eleven or so at night. He relaxed in a wing chair before a dead fireplace in the small extra bedroom. It was the same. Nothing had been changed. He let himself into her room and surveyed the familiar bed. No, nothing had changed, only himself. He now knew her for what she really was. That she could plan another's death and continue on with her life uninterrupted, rekindled the fury that had lain dormant within him for these past hours. He managed not to think of it in order to remain calm and in control, but now as he stared at the satin sheets and black negligee thrown carelessly across the bed, rage burned within him uncontained. What tomorrow would bring he didn't care, he wanted to live through this night and worry about the rest later. Sounds of their carriage in front drew him to the windows and he watched from behind the heavy drapes as she descended to the walk. He was thankful that Philip remained in the carriage. He didn't doubt that he could take DeGrande in a fight but he preferred to face Julie alone.

Minutes later, he heard her in the hall beyond her room and he moved behind her drapes quickly, quietly.

Opening the door, Juliana was relieved to be finally home. Her evening with Philip at a family party had been boring in the extreme. Tossing her evening wrap onto a chair, she sat at her dressing table to take her hair down and remove her jewelry. She was lost in her thoughts as she slid her gloves off and kicked off her shoes. The maid would take care of all of her clothes tomorrow so there was no need to worry about them tonight. All she wanted to do was to collapse on the bed and sleep. She noticed a movement in the drapes but thought idly that the window must have been left open and so went on about discarding her clothes until she stood clad only in her chemise with her hair flowing loosely about her shoulders.

"You're quite a lovely sight, Julie," the voice came from nowhere and everywhere.

She gasped and her hand came up to her mouth in fear and surprise. She couldn't move, she knew that voice . . . was it her imagination? When silence reigned for the next few minutes, she thought that she must be going crazy and went to pull on her nightdress.

"No, you didn't imagine me," the voice said to her, a cruelness in its tone.

"Marshall? How? Where?" her own voice was faint and she clutched dizzily at the bedpost as he moved out from behind her velvet drapes.

"Good evening, Juliana," he spoke quietly, no inflection in his words.

"My God!" the words came unbidden as she fell to the floor in a faint.

When her eyes opened, he was standing over her. His face expressionless. She wondered why he'd let her lie there if he were really alive. Juliana's head throbbed where she'd hit the floor and she sat up slowly dazed by the force of her fall and the sight of this man she'd thought long dead.

"You're really here?"

"Yes, Julie, I'm really here. You mean you didn't expect me?"

"What do you mean?" she questioned, a hand at her throat as she swallowed convulsively.

"I mean, haven't you been looking for me?"

"You're supposed to be dead. Why should I look for you?" she asked, her tone rising hysterically.

"That's the point, my dear. You planned this so very conveniently that no one would even suspect you. Did you make your condolence calls too?"

"Yes. Your . . ."

"Shut up!" he demanded menacingly. "Your plan didn't work though. I'm quite alive as you can see and only a little worse for the wear." He touched his face.

She didn't speak as he paced about the room. His actions were much like a caged beast of the wild. Tension was in his every movement. He turned to her suddenly and caressed her hair softly.

"Such lovely hair . . ." his voice was deceptive luring her into a sense of safety. "I've often thought of it these past weeks."

"You thought of me? What of Renee?"

With a violence he didn't know he possessed he threw her from him, "Don't you ever speak of her to me again."

Juliana cowered in the corner where she'd sprawled, "Get out of here. You must be mad . . . I'll scream if you come near me again."

"Such threats have no effect on me, Julie, rest assured. I've been threatened so many times lately that it's become part of my daily life . . . or should I say existence?"

Juliana rose of her own power, wondering at the changes in this man she thought she'd known so well. Deciding to try a new approach she moved toward him.

"What are you doing here?"

He advanced on her slowly, keeping her distracted so she wasn't aware until his hands were on her neck just what he intended.

At first Juliana thought he meant to caress her. But as his fingers tightened she swallowed convulsively and met his eyes with hers. Then, in that moment, she knew what he meant to do and she panicked, fighting against his overwhelming strength. She kicked out at him but her barefoot assault had little effect on him as he was driven by demons who had haunted him for months. Juliana felt herself about to black out, her hands tugging at his wrists were losing their power. She tried to listen to what he was saying to her over the roaring in her ears.

"You killed her as sure as you pulled the trigger," over and over he repeated himself as he watched her struggle for breath.

She was almost limp now, sagging against him, her eyes trying to tell him something, but he didn't want to look at her. He didn't want to think about what he was doing, he just had to do this to pay back all the pain . . . Suddenly Marshall dropped his hands to his sides and stood looking down on Juliana's crumpled form at his feet. She was sobbing as she tried to draw breath through her bruised throat.

"I can't. I thought I could but I can't," he felt shattered within himself. There was nothing for him to grasp, to focus himself on. He just had to be away from Juliana. He couldn't kill her. God knows, he wanted to. He turned to go back out the way he'd come. To lose himself somewhere in the hell of this city he called home.

"Wait . . ." the word came out croaking from her tortured throat.

Marshall walked on into the extra bedroom and made to climb back down when he heard her again as she stumbled after him.

"Not . . . dead . . ." she was calling. "Not . . . dead . . ."

He turned to her as she swayed in the doorway of the room.

"No . . . I'm not dead. You didn't dream this," Marsh made to go when Julie lurched toward him.

"Not . . . dead . . . Reneel" she choked.

He watched her pale face with total disbelief, "You never stop, do you? You never give up? Lies . . . always lies."

His stomach turned at the unfairness she was shouting at him. He felt sick and only wanted to be rid of her presence.

"Ask Philip," she stated and moved back into her bedroom to fall weakly on the bed.

He left quickly, wondering where to go and what to do. He had a few dollars left and decided to lose himself on the riverfront. Marshall rode off with the intention of never seeing Juliana Chandler or her kind again.

Chapter Thirty

Renee sat up in bed with a start. She had broken out in a cold sweat and was shaking. That dream was so real. She tried to concentrate on reality. Not on what her mind had just given her in her sleep. Visions of Marshall. A haunted Marshall, searching for her, lost beyond hope of recovery. Calling out to her . . . She shook her head and climbed out of bed quietly. Moving to the floor to ceiling window at the front of her room she gazed out at the slow moving river. The moon was full this night and she could see clearly all details of the bank and the landing. It was beautiful, a sight that she would never tire of.

She shivered at the dampness of the night air. Somehow this night he was so real that she felt he was with her. If only she could see him, just once more to tell him of their child and of her love. Sighing, she turned back to her solitary bed, aching for the warmth of his arms and the feel of his big body next to hers. Irritated with herself for thinking such thoughts, she threw back her lightweight covers and stretched out again trying in vain to recapture the sleep that now eluded her.

Chapter Thirty-one

The bowels of the city. For some reason that phrase rang through his mind. Aptly described, he thought as he gazed around his squalid surroundings. These bars were the dives where the riverhands took their leisure. A fleeting thought of being recognized crossed his mind as he entered a small establishment but he soon banished it. He took a small table in the dark to the rear of the saloon and sat with his back to the bar. Presently, a barmaid made her sensuous way over to the newcomer and slinkingly asked for his pleasure.

"Whiskey and bring the bottle," he answered curtly.

She moved away a little put off by his abruptness, after all she did the most business of all the working girls here. But undaunted, she came back, a smile pasted on her brightly painted mouth, with his bottle and a dirty glass.

"Buy me a drink, too, big guy?"

He looked up at her, his senses sharp. He had no desire to be with a woman. Especially one who looked well used. The only woman he could envision in his arms was buried somewhere nearby. Tomorrow he would have to find her grave, at least he could be that close to her. . . .

"Well?" she demanded.

He tossed a coin at her, "Here buy yourself one at the bar and make sure I'm left alone the rest of the night."

She stared at him in shock for a moment and then moved off happily. Sure, he was a good-looking fella but he sounded mean and she didn't need that kind of trouble.

Hours passed. He finished one bottle then started another. Somehow his mind would not cease to function. He wanted to sink into oblivion. To awake tomorrow morning with all of his decisions made. But all the liquor was giving him was a pounding headache. He poured himself another stiff drink and downed it abruptly, not even pausing to breathe. He had no idea of the time but the crowd had gone and even the ladies had retired for the night. He noticed the sky lightening out the grimy window at the front of the tavern. Grimly, he continued to drink. There had to be a way to get past this feeling that clung to him. This feeling of failure and loss that sickened him.

Some time later, the door at the front of the bar swung open and a group of rowdies newly docked at the levee entered. They sidled up to the bar and ordered loudly. The tired barkeep greeted them all as old acquaintances and set the drinks up rapidly for the thirsty men.

"What's new on the boat?"

"Nothing much, Harry," the deep voice answered.

"Same as always, huh?"

"Yep. Everything as close to normal again as possible," there was a pause while the owner of the voice drained his drink. "Fill it up again, would ya?"

"Sure enough," the sound of liquor being poured followed.

"Who's your friend in the corner?" the voice asked Harry.

"Don't know. Came in hours ago with the sole intention of getting sloshed all alone. Seems he's close to his goal. Ain't heard a peep out of him in over an hour," Harry paused to pour another drink for someone. "Why you curious?"

"Looked familiar for a minute."

"Oliver, my friend, you been looking so hard your brains rattled. You ain't gonna find Westlake, especially sitting here in my establishment drinking himself to death. Man, you've got to accept things the way they are. He's dead. Why don't you give up?"

"I can't help it. He was too close to me. Meant too much. . . ."

"How's the family?"

"They're gone. Downriver for a spell. If you could just see that little gal of his. . . ." Ollie's voice broke.

The figure at the table moved; the man's head lifted but he didn't turn.

"Must be feelin' sick," Harry motioned to the man. "Ain't no wonder after all he's had. Now, what were you telling me about?"

"Just how bad things are . . . This is morbid."

"Sure as hell is. Who cares any more anyway? It was big news for a while, when he turned up missing and his wife was shot but after she left town and Maguire was killed . . ." the bartender got no further.

The strange man in the dark back corner of the bar stood so abruptly that he turned his table over. He staggered toward the bar searching the group for the owner of the voice he had been listening to through his fog. The man whose identity had finally come to him. Ollie. Marshall saw him standing at the end of the bar.

Ollie's graying head was averted trying to ignore the drunk who was making his way toward him.

"He looks like he wants trouble, Ollie," Harry said quietly. He watched the man who'd downed almost two full bottles of his best whiskey weaving purposefully toward them. "And he's headin' for you. . . ."

Ollie sighed in exasperation; the last thing he wanted was to have a showdown with some waterfront drunk. He turned challengingly in the man's direction, his jaw tight expecting trouble.

"Look mister . . ." Ollie began, then his mouth dropped open and he choked on his next words.

Before him stood Marshall Westlake. A changed Marshall but still the man he had searched endlessly for. Ollie's eyes took in his weight loss and the difference in his features.

"My God!" was all Ollie could say before he took charge and hurried to support Marshall's weight before he lost his balance.

Marsh had wanted to speak to Ollie, to ask what he'd said. How much of the conversation had his mind invented? No words came. Only sorrow and loneliness and great bitterness at all that had befallen him. He clenched his fists in frustration that now of all times the liquor would numb him and he allowed Ollie to steer him from the saloon. Ollie led Marshall through the narrow winding streets, talking to him the whole way, to the *Elizabeth Anne*. He took him aboard to the Captain's cabin. Marsh had mumbled disjointedly in answer to Ollie's many questions. Ollie could make little sense of anything he said. The older man managed to get his friend into bed and pull his boots off. But before he could tell Marshall any news, Marsh had passed out. In his stupor, Marsh had not heard Ollie telling him of his wife and how she had just gone home for a rest.

There were whistles blowing at an ear splitting pitch that grated through his benumbed senses and the light was horrendous. He cursed loudly and sat up suddenly. He immediately regretted his action. Marshall sank back down on the pillow holding his head. Now, he recognized the sounds. The levee, and it must be near noon judging by the heat and the glare that surrounded him. He vaguely remembered running into Ollie last night or was it this morning? He couldn't recall exactly but he was sure Ollie would tell him. Marsh wondered how much of a fool he had made of himself last night. The last coherent thing he could remember was wondering how much longer it would take to get drunk. Obviously now, from the state of his head, he had managed it quite successfully. Groaning loudly, he knew he had to rise, to get cleaned up and most important to talk to Ollie. He swung his long legs over the side of the bunk and rested, the effort having been taxing in the extreme. After a moment, he rose and went to the pitcher and basin to wash and rinse the taste of last night from his mouth. As he moved about and brought himself back to a functioning level, he tried to think of all that happened last night. He was still disgusted by the whole scene with Juliana. Logic dictated that she wouldn't open her mouth about the incident at all. In fact, she probably wouldn't even mention it to Philip except that he would undoubtedly see the bruises on her neck. He didn't regret not killing her, it really made it easier for him today not to have to justify what he'd done. The fact that he knew and she was aware of it was enough. Why he felt differently today, he didn't know; Marsh only knew that if he had not stopped himself he would have regretted it this morning. That, in itself, justified his actions.

Marshall had no desire to leave the cabin yet. He knew when Ollie was ready he would come in. Maybe Ollie had ridden out to Cedarhill after he'd bedded him down. Marsh settled himself gingerly on the edge of the bunk and stared around Jim's cabin. Everything was the same except Jim's clothes were gone. In fact, Marsh wondered where Jim was. It was unusual for him to move everything out just for a stop over in town. He didn't dwell on this long, though, for the door flew open and Ollie came in burdened by a small trunk.

"You're up at last!" Ollie dropped the trunk, slammed the door behind him and went to Marshall.

He eyed him for a moment in thoughtful silence and then as Marsh rose, Ollie threw his arms around him and hugged him fiercely, tears coming to him. He forced them away before he let Marsh go so as not to embarrass him and moved over to the trunk.

"You have much to tell me, of that I have no doubt. But first I imagine you'd like to get into some of your own clothes."

"So that's where you've been. Why didn't you bring

Father and Mother back with you?"

Ollie looked at him quizzically, "Reckon you didn't take in too much of what I told you on our way back here to the boat last night."

"Frankly, Ollie. I don't remember a thing. Only trying to get drunk enough to wipe everything out of my head."

"Then you haven't been out to the house yet?"

"No. I came to town first . . . to settle things, but the office was closed and Elise's house was empty . . . although I don't suppose it would have made sense for her to stay there after . . ."

"After what?" Marshall's statement had confused Ollie considerably.

Marshall looked up at Ollie with such agony on his face that for a moment he said nothing.

"I think we had better talk before we do anything else," Ollie said.

Marsh moved away from Ollie and sat on the bunk again, his head in his hands. This would be the first of many times he would have to tell his story and the thought unnerved him. He didn't want to dredge it all up again. It was best forgotten. Ollie deserved some explanation, though, so after drawing a deep breath Marsh began. He told Ollie of finding the tracks at Cedarhill and having no success in trailing them. He told him of the picnic the following day and their plans for a honeymoon trip to L'Aimant.

"We were racing back to the glade when Maguire jumped us. He had Renee before I even knew what was going on. God! Ollie the last time I saw her alive, Wes was holding a knife to her throat and Frank had a gun on me. I think I dove for the gun . . . the next thing I remember I was slung over a horse like so much pack. We rode for days, never saw a soul. When we got to the cave . . ."

"A cave? No wonder we didn't find you. You were that far southwest of town?" Ollie moved to the cabin window, his back to Marshall, wondering at the terrible things that Maguire must have done to this man. Ollie could sense the tension behind his words.

"They had me locked up until the middle of June. They left on one of their trips and never came back. Luckily, Sheriff Tanner found me while he was searching for them. He left me with a family, the Johnsons, and I was with them until I could travel."

"And when you got back you couldn't find anybody, right?"

Now it was Marsh's turn to look confused. "They aren't out at Cedarhill? I just assumed that Elise had gone out there to stay and closed her house," he paused, his expression growing fierce, yet bleak at the same time. "As soon as I make myself presentable I want you to take me to the grave."

Ollie's eyes looked at him questioningly, "Grave? What grave? Did you think they put up a marker for you?"

Marshall felt rage well up inside him at Ollie's apparent stupidity. He couldn't understand his friend's answer.

"No. Not my grave. Renee's!" he said bleakly.

Again Ollie was speechless, "Renee's?"

"Is she buried here at our family plot or did Elise want to have her buried with her parents?"

"Whoa! Marsh, she ain't dead. You little gal is just fine."

Marsh stared at Ollie in numb confusion, "She's alive?" A burning, searing hot burst of joy shot through his soul.

"The shot Maguire took at her just grazed her."

Marshall didn't move. His whole being was trying to absorb the most wonderful news he'd ever heard in his life.

"Where is she?" the words came from him in a sob.

"About the first of June, she and Elise moved down to L'Aimant. She was just too upset to stay here. When we heard from Maguire that you were dead, Jim went down with the news. Your folks went down right after. They've been there for all this time, that's why I thought you'd already been out to Cedarhill and found there was no one home."

"So you didn't see anybody this morning?"

"Not a soul. I just rode out to the house and brought back some of your things so we can head downriver today."

"Thank you, Ollie," Marsh moved mechanically to the trunk and started to pull his clothes out. "There's only one person in town that I want to see before we leave. Would you find John Randolph for me?"

"Right away and as soon as you've talked to him, we'll shove off."

Marsh's reunion with John was a warm one. Each man knew the other's feeling so there was no need to put it all into words. John knew just by observing Marshall, that he'd been through hell.

"I don't usually rejoice when someone dies but when Tanner told me that you'd shot both Wes and Frank . . . well, John, thanks," Marsh managed as they shook hands solemnly.

"Your brother said just about the same thing. You take care. I'll see you when you get back."

It was late afternoon when the *Elizabeth Anne* finally moved away from the levee and out into the sluggish current that would take them on what would seem to be the longest journey of his life.

Chapter Thirty-two

Renee felt listless. Something was bothering her. She didn't know what it was but she could find no rest this day. After her nightmare of the night before, she had been tired and now when it was her rest time sleep was elusive. Vaguely, she wondered if there was something wrong with the baby. But instinct told her that this was just a mood and she would have to live with it. Tossing on the large four-poster bed, she tried to find some comfort in a different position but rolling over only brought her face to face with Marshall's picture. She had put them both on the night table. In the one with Elizabeth he looked so young that she found it hard to imagine the strong self-possessed man she had known ever looking so carefree. The other daguerrotype must have been taken shortly before they'd met, for that one was a sterner visage, much like the man she remembered. It didn't matter, of course, she loved them both, they were the same man and he would always be the only one in her heart. It was reassuring that as her child grew, he would learn what his father had looked like. She went slowly to the window and watched the river flowing by. It looked dirty brown and rather foreboding this afternoon.

There had been little river traffic today. The whole day had been as slow-moving as the Mississippi seemed and Renee found it almost impossible to cope.

Too many idle hours allowed her to think of things she didn't want remembered. She was grateful for the company of the family. Always it seemed someone was there with something to ask her opinion about or to show her, thus keeping her occupied. Jim had told her that on Ollie's return from St. Louis he was going to resume his duties onboard. She agreed that he had been landlocked far too long and made sure that he felt no guilt about returning to his normal way of life. Dorrie was enjoying the freedom of living in the country. The parties and balls she was missing seemed unimportant as she adapted to Louisiana life. George and Martha were grateful to be able to relax together for the first time in months. They had been separated first by the move into town and then by the long weeks when the men had been gone on the search. They spent long hours walking the grounds and just enjoying each other.

Renee had reassured herself that if she came home everything would be all right. And yet she found no contentment here. For a time, a measure of peace and rest had been hers it was true, but her longing for Marshall had not stopped or diminished; in fact it had grown these past few days. It seemed now that she was obsessed with him, for every waking moment he was there in her thoughts. Renee turned from the window weary of the worry of it all. She dressed for dinner and went down to enjoy a full meal before retiring early this night. She felt the need to be alone with her dreams.

"Can't you make this pitiful excuse for a packet go any faster?" Marshall demanded.

Ollie laughed at him from behind the bar, "No, afraid not. I'm only the part-time captain and the full-time bartender. What the pilot does is his concern and I'm sure his concern is that we don't end up on a sand bar or burn to a crisp when the boilers let go! Calm yourself and have a drink," Ollie poured him a short whiskey. "You're far too worried. Relax. We'll be there day after tomorrow, probably early in the morning if the weather holds."

Marshall grunted at that statement, thinking two and a half days to Baton Rouge was slow time, but saying nothing. He took the glass of bourbon Ollie offered and moved away from the bar to the saloon door. From there he could observe the portrait of Elizabeth. She had been a beautiful woman. And it was amazing how much Renee resembled her in the face; he shook his head and looked at Ollie who was busy behind the bar.

"I think once I'm finished with my honeymoon, I'm going to have a talk with my partners and change this steamer's name," Marshall smiled then and left the room to roam the decks.

The moon was full and the forested landscape was caressed in silver light. The effect on him was much like walking in a dream, except Marsh knew that this was real. And although he could feel the boat beneath his feet and knew what Ollie had told him was true, he felt restless and caged. The sensation wasn't pleasant for him and his nerves stretched taut. He knew that physically his wounds would heal. There would be scars but he had accepted that. What he couldn't control yet was the terror still locked inside himself. It was with him always, just below the civilized veneer he maintained, constantly theatening to break through. He wanted to sleep this night but he knew it would be hard to do. Marsh knew he had to face down his fears head on but right now they seemed overwhelming to him. He thought of the reunion to come. In just a matter of hours she would be in his arms again. His hands shook at the thought and nervously he finished his drink. Would she be glad he was back? He. shook his head in disgust, wondering why that question entered his mind. Ollie had told him over and over of her sorrow and unhappiness. He could not doubt Renee—she was not like any woman he'd ever known. He sighed to himself, reassured. She had been the one person who'd refused to give up, even doubting Maguire's admission. The truth of the matter, Marshall thought more clearly, is I'm afraid to face her as the man I've become. Not only was his face different, he had changed inside, too. Retiring to his cabin, he decided sleep would do more for him than worry and he settled down, hoping for some rest.

The following day brought no respite from his constant anxiety. Ollie gave him paper work to do to help pass the time but the miles seemed to crawl by and Marshall cursed each fuel stop. As evening drew on, Ollie managed to get him involved in a poker game. The companionship and drink seemed to lighten his spirits considerably and after winning $20 he excused himself from the game and turned in. Sleep eluded him. Tomorrow . . . tomorrow . . . his heart pounded in expectation. Renee would be there.

And Mother and Father and Jim and Dorrie . . . their faces flashed before him as he lay on the bunk. There would be no rest tonight for him. Adjusting the light in the cabin, he went to the small shaving mirror. Had he changed so very much? He didn't know, he would have to judge by their reactions . . . idly he rubbed his wrists where the scars were still an angry red. He would have to wait . . . Marsh strode quietly from the room. Dawn found him in the pilot house watching the river mist settle over the land slowing their progress considerably.

Renee felt chilled. An eerie sensation seemed to cling to her. Unknowing, she thought she might be getting sick and she spent the day in her room fighting off thoughts of Marshall. She even went so far as to turn both daguerrotypes face down on her table. She reasoned if she didn't look at him so often she wouldn't think of him so much. She read most of the day. Why she picked up Byron she didn't know, she only knew that she found herself reading 'When We Two Are Parted' . . . If I should meet thee after long years. How should I greet thee? . . . Tears ran down her cheeks and she closed the book angrily, turning to needlework she sewed until her eyes grew strained at the intricate stitches. Her stomach felt nervous so she skipped dinner and retired early. Elise didn't object, knowing rest was the best thing for her.

Although she fell asleep quickly due to the emotional drain of the past two days the tranquility didn't last. She came awake abruptly, her sleep-drugged mind filled with images of Marshall and they were not restful thoughts. Renee lay still, listening to the night sounds of her home. It was warm and safe here and had she awakened anywhere else panic would have seized her. In her dreams, he had been there again . . . in pain . . . in anger . . . in frustration. It was as though he was so close she could touch him. Despair gripped her and she turned her face to her pillow to muffle her sobs. Much later, she rose from her bed and moved to stare out the window. The full moon glinted off the river and had she not been so tormented Renee surely would have thought it was a most romantic night. As it was, Renee only saw darkness, a darkness so vast it threatened her whole being. She picked up his pictures from the table and smiled at them. Surely, this melancholy would pass with the morning light and she could go on with her life. Settling back in her bed, she held the pictures to her heart and waited for the reassuring glow of morning.

Renee rose from bed when her mantel clock chimed six. She was bored with lying in bed and needed to get out of her room. Dressing quietly and tying her hair back with a ribbon, she went down stairs and out the side door to the kitchen building which was separate from the main house. Ivy, the cook, was already busy preparing breakfast and was startled to see her young mistress up at such an unusual hour.

"You sick, ma'am?"

"No, Ivy, just restless. Is there something I can eat now? I didn't eat at dinner last night and I fear I'm quite famished," she asked seating herself at one of the big tables in the cookhouse.

Ivy brought her a cup of hot tea and some fresh biscuits and then went back to her work. Renee nibbled a few bites but could not force any more. It seemed as though her stomach was tied in knots this morning. The tea soothed her jangled nerves some and thanking Ivy she left the kitchen. The ground fog was heavier than usual this morning, obscuring the river from her view as she walked the gallery surveying everything within sight. All was quiet, secluded, tranquil and comforting as she gazed about her home. She had loved L'Aimant all those years with her father and she loved it even more now. It was her refuge.

Leaving the porch, she wandered aimlessly through her gardens marvelling at the beauty of the roses in the mist. It had a fantastic quality to it, this morning. Light-headed from a lack of sleep she seemed to perceive things more clearly, to appreciate the beauty of small things more deeply. The sounds of a steamer on the river surprised her. When the fog was this heavy the boats usually tied up and waited for it to lift. Whoever it was must certainly be in a hurry to reach New Orleans, if they came down river on a morning like this, she decided as she sat on a small iron bench in the center of the walks. When she didn't hear the boat move on in the next few minutes, her curiosity overtook her and she strolled slowly in the direction of the landing. Not wanting to be seen, she went up the incline to her favorite willow tree where the view of the river was the best. Winded from the walk she rested against its sturdy trunk and tried to see what was happening below her. There was definitely a packet docked at L'Aimant and it looked to be the *Elizabeth Anne*. Staring intently, she tried to make out the name on the side of the sternwheeler but the haze was just too thick. Surely something must be wrong for Ollie to return so soon after his departure. Sickeningly, she remembered the last time Jim and Ollie had returned ahead of schedule. She knew she had to wake Jim and she hurried down the hill to the main path. Catching up her skirts, she ran toward the main house eager for company, so she wouldn't have to face this alone.

Marshall almost ran down the gangplank. Ollie had told him to follow the path directly in front of him and it would take him up to the house almost a mile distant. He was glad they'd traveled in the fog. It had been risky but getting here early in the day was important to him. He had washed, shaved and dressed carefully and now felt as prepared as he could be for the moments to come. Forcing himself not to run he walked briskly up the walk. Suddenly ahead of him he saw a flurry of skirts, black skirts, that rapidly disappeared in the mist. He sped up, rubbing at his eyes, knowing he was sober and that he hadn't imagined it. He could hear the rapid sound of footsteps as someone ran away from him.

"Wait!" he called to the retreating figure.

He listened noting that the footsteps had stopped.

The voice came from inside her head, Renee was sure of that. There could be no one on this path but herself. She hadn't seen anyone leave the boat. She started on again.

"Don't run," his voice called. "I'm quite lost in this fog."

Tears sprang to her eyes. It couldn't be. This was all part of the dreams and nightmares she'd been having, soon she'd awake to find herself in bed shaking from the emotion of it all. She turned back to the voice so deeply ingrained in her that it was part of her soul. If this was a dream, so be it. She wanted to hold him, and see him and tell him everything. If she woke up to find Jim in her arms today she just didn't care anymore. She was too tired to fight any longer. Closing her eyes momentarily, she swayed by the force of what she was feeling. When she opened them again she saw him as she knew she would. He was standing in the mist watching her silently. Why didn't he come to her? This was her dream and she wanted that to happen.

"You're here?" she whispered.

The figure she spoke to didn't answer. A dream, I suppose, for if he were really here he would have answered. She watched then as her vision moved closer. His slow steps brought him nearer and she was afraid that at any moment she would awake and find him gone.

Marshall had come upon her so quickly that he was stunned by the sight of her, so well remembered. He should have known when he saw the black skirts that it was her, but what was she doing out here at such an early hour? He wanted to rush to her but the pallor of her face gave him hesitation. She was weaving slightly and he feared she would faint, so he said nothing but moved toward her slowly so as not to frighten her.

"I'm here," he said quietly, just soft enough for her to hear. "I'm here."

She swallowed as his words came to her. A dream? Torn between the desire to run for the safety of the house and the safety of those imaginary arms she did nothing.

"Renee? Are you all right? Come to me, darling," his tone was husky and full of hope.

"Are you real?" she whispered frantically, her feet leaden, her mind spinning. "Touch me. Please, touch me!"

He covered the final distance between them in one movement and pulled her to his chest. She was shaking against him. Not looking up but burying her face in his shirt, she listened to his heart and heard the rumble of his voice as he spoke softly, comfortingly to her. After a moment the tears came. He was real. He was here. But how? Pulling back she stared up at him, wanting to ask the questions but not wanting to spoil this time of reunion.

"Marshall . . ." she breathed and his mouth covered hers in a kiss unlike any other she'd ever received. He clung to her in desperate need. Melting together, her arms were around his back caressing every inch of him she could touch.

They broke apart, laughing almost hysterically. Then they were in each other's arms again in a fury of longing.

"Your face. . . ?" Renee asked tracing his features gently. "What happened?"

"I'll tell you later," he said kissing her to distract her. "The house?" he asked huskily moments later, embracing her and not letting her move away from his side.

"Just a little farther," she pointed breathlessly up the walkway.

Leaning against him, she felt faint at the joy that seized her. She must know how he came to be here, at her side, warm and loving, but all that could wait. She only needed his nearness, now.

Marshall held her against him, relishing the feel of her. He was having trouble speaking so he said nothing. His heart felt alive at last. They reached the gallery and he admired the beauty of L'Aimant for the first time. Kissing her again at the foot of the steps, they went up hand in hand to the front door and entered the main hall.

He took in the curving stairway and the crystal chandeliers on first glance and then looked down at his wife.

"We'll wake everyone later?" he asked her in a whisper.

A smile lit her face and she led him quickly upstairs to her room. Renee locked the door behind them as he drew the drapes. He paused momentarily, wondering if she wanted to make love. She had shown no hesitation in his embrace and her kisses had been hot with desire, but what of Maguire? What had they done to her? How should he treat her now? He shook with emotion as he shed his clothing in the deep shadows of the room, wanting only completeness with Renee, wanting to once more to be joined to her as he had dreamed these past months.

Renee undressed, a bit shyly, and wondering at Marsh's hesitation went to him, quietly and slowly. Her movements were even more erotic to him, for she seemed floating, a phantom from his imaginings, who would disappear when he reached out a hand. Taking a chance, noting her willingness to come to him, he touched her cheek lightly and she turned her head to kiss his palm. They came together in a rush of passion. Soon they were one on the wide bed in a surge of heated desire that blended them together. Urgently his hands slid over her smooth skin, exploring every inch of her, testing his memory of all of her. He stopped his stroking when his hand caressed her stomach. Marshall pulled up to look at her. The question was in his eyes and she read it well. She nodded, smiling at him tenderly. A thrill shot through him. A child. His and Renee's. Almost painfully, he bent to her to kiss her. A gentle, special kiss. One that she would remember forever. Their lips touched lightly, tenderly. She sighed against him, wrapping her legs around him, moving sensuously, caressing him within her.

"I love you," he whispered against her mouth.

"I love you," she returned, not wanting to talk, just wanting to feel.

He explored her fuller breasts, enjoying the changes in them. She felt the fire within her growing out of control and moaned as his mouth found hers in a deep, searching kiss. The sensual movements of her body pushed thoughts of fatherhood from his mind and he gave himself over to his passion. Calling her name as they gained their release, they sank into blissful unawareness together.

She rested, eyes closed, her head on his chest, listening to the slowing of his thunderous heartbeat. Her hands grasped him still, as if she were afraid he might disappear from her sight. When he'd caught his breath, he opened his eyes and flashed a wide smile at her.

"It's so hard to believe you're alive. . . ."

"Me?"

"Maguire told me that they'd killed you," as he said the words, he frowned as he remembered what else Wes had said they had done. How could she be so uninhibited with him after what they had put her through? He wanted to know, but was afraid to say anything and let the moment pass.

"I'm alive, but not for a lack of trying on their part," she told him. "Wes shot me, but I was lucky. It just grazed my head." She brushed back her hair to show him the small scar.

Marshall groaned when he saw it and pulled her up to him, kissing her healed injury.

"I'm sorry I wasn't able to protect you. You'll never know how responsible I feel for everything you've gone through," Marsh said, running his hands down the length of her.

"Everything's going to be fine, now, I know. I have you and the baby. I'm so happy!" Tears fell and dropped on his shoulder.

"Stop crying," he teased. "You're getting me all wet!"

She laughed and kissed him, sniffling all the while. His hand rested on her stomach feeling the fullness of his child within her.

"How soon will I be a father?"

"The doctor said around the New Year, possibly. From the nearest he can figure, I probably got pregnant at Cedarhill."

When she said the words, he physically flinched and none too gently moved away from her embrace. His mind went in fifty different directions at once and came back with the same conclusion. The child who would bear his name could have been fathered by Wes or Frank Maguire! Marshall's stomach churned. Had he eaten, he probably would have been sick right then. He swung his long legs out of bed and sat on the edge, breathing deeply, trying to fight down the feelings that threatened him. No wonder she'd come South. Probably to hide the fact of her pregnancy. No doubt they all knew of her predicament and that's why they were here. That's why no one had waited at home for him. Hate filled him for the Maguires who even in death had left a most vicious mark on him and his family. Marshall was oblivious to Renee's reaction. She was confused by his sudden withdrawal from her and guessed that it was the mention of Cedarhill. Maybe, too, the idea of a baby so soon upset him, too, so she tried to ignore the change in him.

"Do you want to sleep for a while or stay up?" she asked conversationally.

Groping for his voice, he replied, "Ollie might come up to the house shortly, so we'd better get dressed and wake everyone before he does."

Renee, understandingly, began to dress and looked up to find Marshall watching her as she tied her chemise and reached for her dress.

"Please, wear something pretty, no black," he said seriously.

Quickly, she hugged him and then threw open her wardrobe doors and selected a brightly flowered gown. When he nodded his approval, she stepped into it and presented him her back to button it. Instead, his hands reached inside the fabric and rested on her slightly rounded stomach. He hurt with the feelings of dread and frustrated anger that tormented him, but he fought them down, focusing on what she was saying.

"You're back! I can't believe it! I'm so afraid I'll wake and find you gone."

"No, my love, it took a while but I'm here and I never intend to leave you again."

Turning into his arms, she embraced him. He looked up and saw the frown marring her expression.

"What is it?"

"What happened? Your face and the scars?"

"My nose," he said indifferently. "Was broken. It's healed now."

"It doesn't hurt you?"

"No. Not now."

"And. . . ?"

"I'm fine," he dismissed her question curtly.

Renee hugged him to her again fiercely wanting to absorb all the pain he'd suffered into her own body. Then when he'd finished buttoning her gown, she moved away.

"We'd better wake your parents before Ollie does."

"Shall I?" he asked, pulling on his clothes.

"I don't think that's the best idea," she laughed remembering her own shock at seeing him. "I'll get them."

They left the room minutes later, seemingly more composed than when they'd entered, yet within Marshall now burned a barely contained rage that had to be suppressed. As they started down the hall toward the guest bedrooms, Jim came out of his room and stopped in midstride stunned at the sight that greeted him.

"Marsh!" the shout came uncontrolled from him and he threw his arms around his brother in an emotional embrace. His shout roused the entire family and moments later George was the first into the hall with just pants pulled on over his nightshirt.

"Martha, hurry, he's here. My God! He's here!"

Not even bothering with a robe, Martha ran from her room and straight into his arms, sobbing. Dorrie was but a second behind her mother and Elise soon came from the other end of the corridor. Renee stood quietly aside while he embraced his family, holding his mother tightly the whole time. Martha went straight to Renee, when she finally had her wits about her, and, crying, took Renee into her arms.

"How did you find him?"

"I had gone for a walk . . . I couldn't sleep all night," she replied gazing at her husband. "I heard a boat at the landing and he was on the path coming up to the house . . ."

Martha and Dorrie were laughing and smiling and all the while crying heartily. Elise hurried down to order a special breakfast and sent a messenger to the *Elizabeth Anne* to invite Ollie, too.

For all of his great happiness at seeing his family, Marshall was miserable. He wondered, meanly, when or if they would get around to telling him of the rape. Sarcastically, he wondered to himself if they all thought they were protecting him. He noticed a change in Renee, as the next few hours passed, she

401

seemed to be almost afraid of him. He didn't attribute that to a response to his actions, he illogically concluded that she was trying to hide the ugliness of her attack from him and so was feeling guilty.

Renee watched worriedly as Marshall began drinking during the meal. Everyone exchanged covert glances, but said nothing as he drank a considerable amount of bourbon at his breakfast celebration. Taking it in stride, she didn't repulse him when he embraced her in front of everyone and kissed her wetly on the mouth. Renee blushed at his display, yet because she thought she understood his needs, she didn't discourage him. She stood quietly in his arms while he gazed thoughtfully, quizzically at her.

"You can't hide anything from me," he stated firmly.

Renee blanched at his words, thinking that he knew about her night with Jim, "I . . . ," she stuttered.

"We'll talk about it later," he commanded, the smell of bourbon assaulting her early in the day. He dropped his arms and walked into the study where George and Jim awaited him and closed the doors.

Renee joined Martha and Elise and Dorrie on the gallery. They were all just about recovered from the shock of the morning and had decided to relax for a while. Ollie had just gone back to the boat and now that Marshall had secluded himself in the library, she would have a moment of respite.

"Renee, how can you just sit there?" Dorrie asked, her eyes glowing.

Renee smiled, remembering her few moments alone with Marshall before everyone awoke, "Well, Dorrie, it's not easy."

"I can imagine," Martha agreed with her daughter's excitement. "So you were out walking and heard the steamer at the landing?"

"Um," Renee answered dreamily as the memory of her reunion with her husband came to mind. She knew those were memories she would treasure the rest of her life. "I couldn't sleep. I'd been up most of the night and you know how badly I felt yesterday. So when it started getting light I just stayed up. I was in the garden when I heard the boat so I went down by the willow to see if I could make anything out."

"How exciting!" Dorrie said.

"It is now but then I was scared. I saw it was the *Elizabeth Anne* and I panicked. I was running back to the house to wake you when he found me on the path. I heard him call and I thought I was dreaming again . . . Especially as thick as the fog was this morning."

"It's just so romantic that way," Dorrie sighed.

"Yes, it was after I got over the shock of really seeing him. It was so hard to truly believe he was there!"

Martha reached over and patted Renee's hand, "He's here, honey, he's here."

A calm silence fell over the group.

"What happened? Can you talk about it?" George asked giving Marsh the option not to discuss the entire incident if he didn't want to.

"I told Ollie most of it on the way down," Marsh paced to the french doors that looked out to the river. "It gets easier with every telling, I guess."

403

Nervously he moved to where the liquor was kept and poured himself a bourbon, then he came to sit on the sofa that faced the desk. George had been watching his eldest son's movements for some time now and he knew Marsh was close to the breaking point.

"Don't worry. We've time. Whatever you feel you need. . . ." Jim put in, sensing Marshall's strain.

"I'll be all right, now," he said almost too calmly.

George said nothing and there was a companionable peace among the three men.

"On the Meramec," Marsh finally said as he finished his drink.

"That's where you were all this time?"

"Yeah. Ollie told me where you'd searched. But Maguire had this cave . . ."

"A cave? We never thought . . ."

"I'm sure he realized that before he chose that spot."

"But Maguire swore you were dead . . ." George said in anguish.

"I must have been close to it by the time he was in town . . . I know I was as close as I ever care to be . . . I would be dead now if it wasn't for Tanner and the Johnsons."

"Who?"

"Sheriff Tanner from Harrisons Mills and his posse found the cave and me and took me to the Johnsons' farm. I was there about three weeks or so . . . I've lost track of so much time . . ."

Marsh rose and paced the room, the liquor not helping his agitation at all as he began to recount the story. His voice was almost dead with the telling.

"We were having the picnic . . . when we got back to the glade after a walk, Maguire grabbed Renee before I even knew what was happening. I was so stupid . . . you don't know how I've gone over those hours, wishing I'd had sense to stay back at the house instead of going off that day . . ."

"It's over. It'll be all right, now," George said moving to stand by him.

"I hope . . . anyway . . . when I tried to get the gun from them one of them hit me and I was out. The next thing I knew they had me on a pack horse and we were riding hard. It took me a while to try to figure out why Maguire hadn't killed me on the spot. He could have so easily . . ." Marsh's hand shook as he tried to pour another bourbon.

In irritation, Marshall set the decanter down and moved away, not bothering with another drink, his hands shoved into his pants pockets.

"We rode I guess about four days. Didn't see a soul. Then when we got to the cave his whole gang was there. I tried to break free one last time but there was no way. That's when I got this . . ." he said touching his face. "It was right after that that they put me in irons but I was out cold and didn't even know it until later. When I came to, he used the strap on me . . ."

"What!" George bellowed. "Irons and the strap?"

The desire to go to this man who was his child was overwhelming but he held back seeing the tautness in Marshall's expression and the vacant look in his eyes.

"They kept me in a blockaded room in the back of the cave . . . my back took the longest to heal, and my arms . . ." he rolled up a shirt sleeve and even Jim gasped at the scars there. "The Johnsons finally got the cuffs off."

"We'll have to really reward them when we go home," George murmured.

"Maguire left me in that back room all the time."

"In a room in a cave?" Jim asked incredulously.

"Yeah. About six by four of living hell. There was no light, none. That was almost enough to drive me crazy but then to think that Renee was dead. . . ."

"Renee? Maguire thought he'd killed her?"

"Yeah, that's what he told me," Marsh paused as a fleeting memory of his despair gripped him. He shook from the force of it. "God, it was terrible."

He stared around himself blankly for a moment.

"How badly did they hurt her?"

"She was hurt but not seriously. In fact, she wanted to ride with us in the posse," George told him proudly.

"How did she get back? She told me Wes shot her?"

"She said that after they knocked you out, she ran from them but didn't get too far before Wes fired. She'd started to fall as he shot and the bullet just grazed her head. Renee was very lucky. When she regained consciousness, a horse was nearby and it took her back to the house. Packy found her," Jim told Marshall. "She was so frantic about you once we got there, Elise had to sedate her."

So, Marshall thought, she hadn't told anyone about her attack. That was good, although he was surprised that the doctor hadn't mentioned it to George. He could understand the need for sedatives, too. He doubted that there had been anything but terror in the embrace of Wes or Frank. A vision of Renee, being assaulted by them both while he lay unconscious nearby nearly drove him at a run from the room. He had to get free of that torturous thought.

"I've got to get outside . . . I'll talk to you later."

Abruptly he was gone and Jim looked at his father helplessly.

"It'll take time and patience," George said sadly.

Marshall walked blindly; the walls of the house seemed to be closing in on him. Thankfully, the fog had burned off and it was a clear sunny day. He found his way out the back door and was down the gallery steps and into the gardens before he realized it. Marshall didn't stop his urgent strides until he'd neared the center of the well laid out shrubbery, where a fountain splashed coolly and a well-shaded gazebo offered a protective resting place. He mounted the few steps and entered the shadowed shelter. A light breeze circulated there and he found it a most appealing secluded spot. Sitting down on one of the built-in seats, he wearily leaned his head back against the wall. His mind was in total confusion, as much from the bourbon as from all of the shocking news he'd had that day. Marsh knew that he was not the same man who had disappeared those months before. Was he making sense at all to those around him or was he being totally irrational, operating on tightly strung nerves and the liquor that he'd drunk all day? He felt he was being reasonable, but was he, in fact, so influenced by those long days and nights when no reasoning mattered, that he could no longer think things through logically? Trying to clear his mind, he drew deep within himself to find that part of him which could look upon the facts only and come up with a rational, thought-out conclusion. He'd never tried to analyze his own emotions so coldly before, but Marshall knew that he had to do something and fast, his depression was getting deeper as the day wore on.

The first fact, he stated to himself, was the attack on Renee. Could Maguire have been lying to him about the rape? And to what purpose? To mentally defeat him of course, he decided analytically. A glimmer of hope stirred through him, but was quickly subdued. This was no time for emotion. Renee had changed. Their passionate reunion could not be denied, but as the morning progressed, she'd become increasingly tense and nervous around him. Was it a delayed reaction to her physical encounter with him? Marsh didn't know. Could she have survived the Maguires' assault and still feel the same about making love to him? How had he expected her to act? Did he think that she should cower from his every touch? Disgustedly, he could reach no definitive answer. It remained undeniable that she had been injured.

Secondly, and even more far reaching in its effects, was the fact that Renee was pregnant with a child who would be born at the end of the year. If fact one was true, which to the best of his knowledge it was, then there could be no denying that he might not be the natural father of that child. Marshall paused. Logic, no matter how correct, could sometimes be unbearably painful. And if it was Maguire's baby, what was to stop Renee from trying to rid herself of it as Elizabeth had. What if something happened to her. . . . He closed his eyes momentarily, and as he rested, all of his mental anguish died under the onslaught of the one main truth that defied all else. He loved Renee. She was everything to him. He had just been given back his life and his love, both. She was his wife, he was her husband. The child would be theirs. He would raise the baby and love it because it was a part of Renee. A soothing, relieving peace came over him with his final assessment of his life. If she chose not to confide the horrors of her abuse, he would understand and not demand any more than she could give. Renee needed his love and tenderness now, just as he needed hers. He knew that he could not tell her of his degradation at the hands of Wes and Frank, it was too ugly a thing for a woman to be exposed to. No, they would both have their private wounds which would have to heal on their own, out of sight.

Marshall smiled to himself and took more notice of his surroundings. Renee's gardens were lush and lovely. The summer foliage was blooming in a riot of bright colors and their scents filled the air. He could see the house at a distance and took the time now to study its classic beauty. Marsh could sense that L'Aimant had been Roger Fontaine's dream come true. Someday, he hoped to establish a legacy of his own, one that would be as important to his offspring as Roger's had been to Renee. Getting up slowly, he left the small garden house and walked in the direction of the river.

As Renee began to climb the stairs to her bedroom, George came out of the study and beckoned her to join him there. Worriedly, she wondered where Marshall was. Jim had gone riding some time ago, but Marsh and George had never come out. She had assumed that they were still together in the library, talking privately.

"George, what is it? Where's Marshall?"

"I'm not sure."

"What? Did he go upstairs to lie down?"

"No. He went outside a while ago," George told her calmly.

"Oh, good," Renee was relieved. "I thought something might be wrong."

"Something is, but I don't know what."

"What do you mean?"

"He's still very upset, although I'm sure he'll be all right in no time now that you two are back together."

"I hope so. I intend to do whatever I have to to make him happy. Maybe by the time our baby comes, things will be normal again," Renee rested a hand on her stomach.

"How did he react to the good news?"

"He seemed ecstatic, at first . . ."

"At first?"

"Well, he asked me when I was due and I told him that the doctor calculated the baby had been conceived during our stay at Cedarhill. When I mentioned Cedarhill, he withdrew from me. It seemed as though he became a total stranger. It upset me. How could he be so loving one moment and so cold the next?"

"I think, until he gets more relaxed with us and with himself, we'll just have to be patient. He's had a

410

very rough time these past months. Did he tell you any of it?"

"No. Not yet."

"He will, eventually. Just avoid stressful situations."

"Do you think it was the mention of Cedarhill or the baby that upset him?"

"I think the fact that you're pregnant is what disturbed him. Did you know that Elizabeth Anne died after a miscarriage?"

"Yes. Dorrie said something about it once."

"Well, conceivably, he could be worried that the same thing could happen again."

"Oh," Renee replied and she thought she understood Marshall's actions. He had been concerned about her. He had been afraid that she'd die just as Elizabeth Anne had. It all seemed so simple, now, Renee thought naively. Slowly, she would convince him that she was perfectly healthy and that they would have a healthy, strong baby. As soon as all of his fears were laid to rest, he would be himself once more.

"Did you happen to notice which way he went?"

"Into the gardens, I think."

"Thank you, George. I'm going to see if I can find him."

Renee ventured out into the late morning heat. The sun was merciless this day and she was glad to lose herself on the cool shell-lined paths that wandered through the ornamental trees and shrubs. She searched futilely the gazebo and several comfortable benches placed strategically about the garden before heading for the landing. She saw him sitting on a grassy slope near the river's edge. He looked tired and Renee wondered at the things that the Maguires had done that George had referred to.

"Marsh?" she stopped a short distance away, not wanting to surprise him. "If you want to be alone, I'll go but you look like you might enjoy some company."

"If the company is you, you can be sure of it," she came to him eagerly as he called to her.

Rising as she neared him, he embraced her warmly.

"It's lovely here," he said, gesturing toward the vista of the river.

"You'd like my tree better," she said trying to draw him out. "Do you feel like taking a walk?"

"Fine. Let's go."

She took his hand and together they walked toward the small bluff. When they finally topped the hill, they sat beneath the willow savoring the view. The river stretched in both directions, wide and deceptively lazy. The *Elizabeth Anne* was still tied up at their landing and they could see Jim onboard now, talking to the pilot and Ollie in the pilothouse.

"Is this the place you were telling Dorrie about that day at Cedarhill?"

"Yes, I used to come here all the time."

"It's as special as the creek was . . ." he began and then quickly changed the subject. "Come here."

Marshall leaned back against the tree trunk and pulled her against his chest, his hands resting lightly on her rounded stomach. She smiled over her shoulder at him, saying nothing and putting her hands over his, holding them tightly to her. Eventually, she closed her eyes and rested contentedly.

Chapter Thirty-three

"What did he say?" Martha asked George as they too took a walk about the grounds.

"A lot," he replied.

"Well?"

"Maguire's hideout was a cave down on the Meramec. That's where he'd been all this time, imprisoned in a cave."

"Couldn't he get away somehow?"

"He tried once, but after that he was chained in a small room at the back of a cave."

"Chained?"

"I guess Maguire wanted him to have a taste of prison."

Martha didn't reply to that and a feeling of outrage filled her. "I'm glad he's dead, George. He deserved to die."

"You're right. But that's not all."

Martha looked at him expectantly dreading the news to come.

"He used the strap on him and then put him in that room and boarded it up. The bastards kept him in the dark for the whole time they had him."

She didn't answer again, feeling the despair that

must have gripped her son to be locked up in the blackness chained, for a seemingly unending length of time.

"Maguire told him that Renee was dead."

"That by itself would have been enough to hurt him."

"He's hurting, he's hurting bad. We're just going to have to take our time and let him learn to live again."

She nodded her understanding and moved to his side, putting her arm around his waist, glad for the deep understanding between father and son.

It was almost noon when Marshall and Renee returned from the river. They looked much more relaxed and Marshall was smiling.

Alain had been sent word and he let them know he would ride over for dinner so a celebration was definitely in order. The noon meal was a light one and everyone enjoyed just being together. Martha couldn't seem to take her eyes off Marsh as he ate heartily. Dorrie kept him entertained with a running monologue of their trip to L'Aimant and how beautiful everything was down here. Marsh agreed, his eyes resting on his wife. After eating, Renee decided to get some rest for the evening to come so she and Marsh retired upstairs for a few moments of privacy.

Her room was overly warm from the hot July sun, so she drew the drapes partially and moved to the dressing table.

"Do you want to rest with me?" Renee asked eager to feel his arms around her again.

"I'll lie down for a while but I doubt if I'll be able to

414

sleep. I'm still tense from everything that's happened today."

"I understand, darling," she answered softly and moved to stand in front of him so he could loosen her dress.

He helped her discard it and as she lay on the cool inviting sheets he took off his shirt and boots and stretched out next to her. Renee moved to rest her head on his shoulder and his arm went around her protectively. She knew he had no desire to speak yet so she held her questions and just enjoyed the feel of him next to her. Moments later, Marsh could tell by the sound of her even breathing that she was asleep. From what he'd gathered around the noon day meal she hadn't been eating well or gettting enough rest the past few days. Perhaps she had known in her soul that something was about to happen.

He was still feeling the strain of the last few days. The sudden news that she was alive, the subsequent trip to L'Aimant. Perhaps, he thought, if I can just put this from my mind for a few minutes I can drift off, too. He turned his face into the sweet scent of her hair and closed his eyes.

"Just a minute," she called softly and moved from Marshall's side.

Throwing on a light dressing gown, she went quickly to the door to answer the knock that had sounded. Elise was waiting outside in the hall for her.

"I'm sorry to wake you but it's already seven and Alain is here. Did you get some rest?"

"Oh, yes, Elise. In fact he's still sleeping. Is dinner ready?"

"You've got about half an hour yet."

"Fine. Will you send one of the girls up with bath water for us?"

"Of course. You take your time. I'm sure Alain can wait a little longer to see that husband of yours."

Renee went back into her room as quietly as possible. Marsh was still deeply asleep. Shedding her gown and chemise she climbed back into the bed and moved close to him, pressing kisses against the hard lean line of his jaw. He stirred and an arm reached out to enfold her against him.

"Dinner is almost ready and Alain is downstairs waiting to see you."

"Um," he murmured drowsily, his lips seeking and finding her throat.

"I've had bath water sent up for us. I thought a bath before dinner would feel refreshing, how about you?"

"Why? Do I need one?" he grinned.

"Not yet," she said mischieviously. "But I thought you might by the time the water gets here!"

"I can't imagine why," was his answer as his mouth sought hers.

There was no desperation in their coming together this time. He was gentle. Taking his time and making sure that she enjoyed it. His hands and lips caressing her softly, created within her a need that had to be fulfilled. As his mouth found her breasts and explored the hard peaks and soft valleys, Renee moved restlessly, pressing her hips to his. Eager for the consummation of her passion, she encouraged him to take her, but he held back. Controlling his own raging desires, he toyed with her, taking pleasure from her growing excitement.

"I've missed you so, please love me," she murmured breathlessly, as he finally parted her thighs and drove into her.

"I do, I do," he answered softly, kissing her.

His manhood seemed to fill Renee completely and she relished this intimate contact with him. The closeness she felt when they were one was nearly overwhelming and she answered his thrusts with eager lifts of her hips. Marsh's hands slid to her hips and lifted her slightly to increase his pressure against her. She was surprised by the erotic movement and gasped as ecstasy filled her. Marshall knew he had pleased her and gave a free rein to his own desire and took his own pleasure. They collapsed together, completely satisfied by their passionate joining, whispering words of love that meant so much to them.

When Marshall and Renee entered the front parlor some time later their eyes were merry and their mood light.

"Marsh!" Alain exclaimed, shaking his hand and hugging him in great joy. "It's so good to have you back!"

"Thanks, Alain," he answered.

"It's time to eat," Elise announced. "I hope everyone is hungry."

"Have you worked up an appetite?" Renee whispered to her husband, as they followed Elise into the dining room.

Marshall smiled quickly down at her, "I'm famished. You could wear me out, you know."

She blushed and made to move ahead of him but a quick arm pulled her back to his side.

"I love the feel of you and the way you smell," he murmured to her as he kissed her cheek.

She almost turned to throw her arms around him, but remembered where she was.

"You have to stop this," she insisted, lightly.

"Stop what?" he asked in mock innocence, one hand caressing her hip.

"Let's go in to eat, everyone is waiting."

He let her go ahead of him then and followed her to the table. Unfortunately for him, he was now head of the household and had to sit at the end of the long dining room table, opposite his wife. She smiled ruefully at him as he grudgingly took his seat.

"What are your plans, Marshall," Alain inquired after they had said grace. "Have you thought of what you want to do now with the baby coming and all?"

"I haven't really thought to much about the future. I've been taking it one day at a time since I found out from Ollie that Renee was all right."

"You didn't know?"

"No, they'd told me that they'd murdered her . . . anyway it was an unbelievable feeling to discover she was alive and living here."

"I can imagine," Alain agreed. "Well, if you want to get involved in plantation work, just let me know. I could definitely use your help here at L'Aimant."

"I will," he agreed.

Dinner was ready to be served so they ate immediately, a succulent meal of creole dishes which the Westlakes enjoyed tremendously. Conversation was general until the wedding came up and now they decided to set a definite date. With Marshall returned there was no need to wait any longer. Elise and Alain could marry and Elise would still be close by if needed. The day was chosen a month away and a toast drunk to their happiness. It was quite late when Renee and Marshall retired for the night and both were glad for the long nap they'd taken in the afternoon.

With the bedroom door locked securely behind them, they went into each others arms for the security of the embrace.

"We'll have to change rooms, soon."

"Why? I've been most satisfied with this one," he whispered in her ear.

"We can move into my parents' suite of rooms, if you like. It'll be much more private."

"I've always been a great believer in privacy."

"Um, me, too," she answered against his mouth.

Wrapped in each others' arms they stood there, lost in each deepening kiss.

"Do you suppose we should go to bed?" Renee asked.

"No, not yet, we just got up, remember?"

"I remember."

His mouth met hers tenderly, "Are you happy about the baby?"

It was a question that had occupied him most of the evening. He had to know how she felt about having this child.

Pulling back, she looked up at him questioningly, "Aren't you?"

"Of course!" he answered almost hastily, and Renee wondered at his train of thought.

She unbuttoned his shirt and caressed his chest. "We really haven't talked."

"I know," he replied, dreading the upcoming discussion. "And we won't get to talk, if you don't stop long enough for me to say a few coherent words."

"I liked the words you said to me this morning and this afternoon." She grinned at him and rested her cheek against the warmth of his chest, listening to the solid beat of his heart.

He picked her up and carried her to the bed, where they sank down together. Leaving her for a moment, he stripped off his shirt and then the rest of his clothes and came back to her.

"I should have Sara help me with all of these things."

"Why? When I'm here? I enjoy undressing you."

When she at last lay visible to him in the soft lamp light, he marvelled at her body. The changes brought about by her pregnancy made her even more beautiful. Her breasts were fuller and more firm, her hips slightly more rounded. He lay watching her for the longest time before he spoke.

"It's like a dream, being here with you. I'm having trouble believing it's all real," he said solemnly. "To finally hold you again . . . it's a miracle . . . When I found out that you were still alive, I didn't believe it. For so long, I thought you were . . . " His voice trailed off as his eyes darkened.

He lowered his mouth to hers and kissed her slowly, lingering over this closeness to her. His lips sank to her throat and then to her breasts. She ached for his possession but knew that this time was special. He was opening to her at last.

Renee longed for the ease they had once shared, for all the times when they had totally been enmeshed in one another. It would come, she knew, but it would take time. Time and patience, George had said, and now Renee felt she had both. Her senses were aware that finally Marshall was back. Not as a fantasy, but as a flesh and blood man. He had come to her as she had hoped and prayed and she would do everything she could to regain the specialness of their earlier time together. At the touch of his lips on her stomach, she arched in surprise, trying to twist away from him. He stilled her with his hands and continued his kisses, seeking and finding her most erotic places with his lips and tongue, until she cried out in a fever of ecstasy. Renee looked at him through a haze of satisfied desire, stunned by what had just occurred. He smiled and slid over her, fitting himself to her, and filling her with his hardness. She sighed contentedly as his weight came down upon her and she held him tightly to her. He moved within her steadily, increasing his pace as his tension mounted until he reached his own release and relaxed on top of her. After a moment, he lifted away from her, looking deep into her passion-drugged eyes.

"We'll start all over again, beginning right now. We've something very special."

"I know. Together we can do anything."

"Together. That sounds so good to me."

"Me, too. When I thought you were dead, all I

wanted to do was to have your child and raise him to be just like you," her arms went around his neck.

His head bent to hers and the kiss was need and love and completeness. She moved atop of him, now, and took the lead, taking him deep within her. He groaned aloud and thrust into her as desire flamed through him once again.

Much later, Renee awoke to find Marshall asleep and the lamp still burning on the small table. She moved easily from the bed and put the light out. Then curling against him, she fell back asleep feeling safe in the protective circle of his body.

Panic . . . there was a moment of panic when she could not imagine what was wrong. Marshall was not in bed . . . but he hadn't left the room for she could hear him moving angrily about. Sitting up, she leaned to the table and lit the small lamp there. As Renee turned back to the room she saw him, his back against the far wall, his expression unreadable. He looked at her almost wildly for a minute and then ran a hand over his eyes. Without looking at her again, he pulled on his pants and left the room. She heard him descend the stairs and then his steps were muffled by the main hall carpet. A sense of great uneasiness gripped her and rising from the bed, she grabbed her robe and raced after him. The front door stood open at the end of the hall and she went out to find him on the gallery. If he noticed her behind him he gave no sign. He seemed some great lifeless statue as he gazed out into the moonlit night. Renee waited nervously only a moment before she moved closer to him.

"Marsh?" her voice soft and worried.

He looked down at her, his eyes unnaturally bright and their gaze piercing her. She shivered involuntarily at this unknown she must deal with. Something had happened to him that neither he nor George had told her and it was time now for her to find out. Whatever it was she could cope with it. It was the not knowing, that would harm them. With all the bravery she could muster she took this stranger's arm and pulled him over to the chairs clustered at the end of the gallery nearest the garden. He moved with her after resisting for an instant.

"Sit down," she said firmly, half expecting him not to.

He sat wearily not wanting to look at her, keeping his face averted less she see some of the anguish he was going through . . . What a shock it had been to wake up in the dark room. He should have told her sooner, then this would never have happened. On the boat he'd let the lamp burn all night, not that he'd slept that well. It hadn't occurred to him that the dreams would happen here. He had come awake so suddenly that he'd practically thrown himself out of the strange bed. He'd tried to remember where he was but his mind had gone completely blank and he had been trapped in his hell. The cave. He'd been back in the cave again in darkness and solitude. Drawing a shuddering breath, he raised his eyes to her pale face. For all that she looked upset, she also looked determined and he knew it was time that he told her all the things he'd wanted to spare her.

"Do you want to go inside?" she asked.

"No, outside is best, now, for what I have to say to you."

Dread filled her. She had wanted to pretend that he was the same man who'd been taken from her but she knew now that he was not. Patience, George had said. Well, the past months had proven to her that she had that.

"Go on," she said encouraging him.

She sat apart from him watching his muscles move across his wide shoulders as he shifted uncomfortably in the hard chair. She waited for him to begin, knowing that he must exorcise these feelings on his own.

"I can't feel comfortable in a dark closed room now," he said simply trying to gloss over the state of things.

"I wake up to find you like a wild beast in our bedroom and that's the explanation you give me?" she raged at him. "Surely you give me credit for more intelligence than that?"

He stood and walked to the railing, then turning to her he leaned against one of the pillars.

"The entire time I was with Maguire, I was locked in a small cell in the dark in chains. It was his idea of putting me in prison to get even."

Renee digested that information, "I knew by your wrists that you had been tied some way."

"When I woke up just now, I didn't know where I was. I was dreaming. I have to admit that I was terrified. The only thing I could think of was to get out but I was disoriented . . . I'm sorry . . ." he looked away from her now, afraid to let her see too much of what he'd become.

"You shouldn't be sorry. You had no control over

424

what happened. I shouldn't have turned the lamp down but I didn't know. From this night on we'll leave a lamp burning," she said matter of factly.

"If it's inconvenient for you . . ."

"Will you stop being so civil!" she almost shouted at him. "I am your wife and soon to be the mother of your child . . ."

"Are you so certain of that?" he snarled the words which he'd thought he'd exorcized that morning.

The sound of her hand connecting with his face seemed to reverberate around them, as Renee came to her feet in outrage at his viciousness.

"How dare you doubt my chastity!" she hissed at him, her fists clenched. "How dare you!"

He grabbed her by her shoulders, his fingers gripping her cruelly. Marshall stared at her, realizing the damage he'd done by uttering the doubts he'd been harboring, but it was too late. He had to know. There was no point in trying to excuse his words.

"Well?" he asked coldly. "What really did happen?"

"What are you talking about?" she asked growing pale at this change in him. Surely, he couldn't mean the few minutes that she'd thought of Jim as her husband. How could he think that she could make love to anyone else? He had been her only man.

Marshall pulled her closer, ignoring her struggle to be free of his hurting hands.

"You don't have to lie to me. I know what happened to you," he sneered hatefully, in the grip of emotions that were boiling over uncontrollably. "After what I've been through, did you think a little more bad news would matter?"

"I don't know what you want me to say."

"How about the truth? Your side of it. I've already heard one version."

She shook her head and wanted to question him, but knew he was beyond simple reasoning. Her mind searched quickly for a way out.

"Tell me what you heard," she told him, hoping that if she got him talking, he would make sense.

He snorted derisively and pushed her back in her chair, turning his back to her.

"Frank and Wes told me everything. Everything," he said tiredly and ran a shaking hand through his dark, tousled hair.

"What? Tell me!"

"I've seen it in my mind so often and I don't really know what's true and what isn't. They told me that before they shot you, they . . . used you. . . ." the words, never voiced before tore from him.

"They what?!"

"They told me that they raped you before they killed you," he said tersely, not turning around. "They said that you didn't fight, that you really enjoyed. . . ."

He didn't say any more as Renee came to him and turned him to face her. Marshall looked everywhere but at her.

"Listen to me," she commanded. "Nothing of the sort happened. When they hit you, I broke free and ran. They didn't—*did not*—touch me, only when he ripped my dress, that was all!"

He heard her words and wanted to believe them.

"Ask your father. He talked to the doctor," Renee insisted. "If you doubt me, please check with them. I wouldn't lie to you, ever!"

He looked down at her bleakly, his eyes filled with emotions he couldn't express.

"Believe me," she told him and reached up to pull him down for a tender, chaste kiss. "There has been no man for me, but you."

As he felt her lips, first on his cheek where she'd slapped him and then on his own, he pulled her to him, his arms about her holding her fiercely. They clung together giving and receiving hope, love and forgiveness.

"All these months, that's festered within me," he began brokenly. "Finding out about the baby this morning almost drove me over the brink. . . . I'm sorry."

"You've nothing to be sorry about. These things were done to you, not by you. The Maguires just wanted to hurt you and obviously they succeeded," she held him close, her hands caressing him soothingly. "We're starting over, remember?"

He nodded and kissed her deeply, their souls touching and joining.

"Where were you all this time?" she asked, as they stood next to each other, arms intertwined, a moment later.

"It's not important," he replied, trying to bury all of the memories that had just come to mind again. "What's important is that I'm back."

"Don't you dare shut me out! I can well imagine what has happened to you over these past months

427

away from me. If you don't want to talk about it, so be it, but I am a part of your life and as such you cannot share just the good things and skip the bad. I won't let you."

"Renee . . . I didn't try to hurt you . . . I just . . ."

"Don't you think I know what you just . . . ? You think in time these problems you have will just go away. They won't. Not until you face them squarely. And I can help you do that but not if you pretend that I can't handle it. Or that I might find out something about you that I won't admire or love. I love you. I've been through too much praying for you, worrying about you, thinking you dead to let you slip away from me now, when you need me the most," she was crying when she finished, great heartbroken sobs.

He didn't move. He couldn't move for a long time. Hearing her words over and over in his mind. He knew she was right. He knew that she was entitled to his innermost thoughts. That she, of all people, should be the one closest to him. He had made that decision months ago when he had married her that stormy night. There was really no decision for him to make. If he turned from her now, their entire life together would be a wasteland of unspoken thoughts and feelings. He had told her once, long ago that if there was something bothering her she was to tell him. And here this past day he had betrayed that trust that they had exchanged. To share their troubles as well as their joys. He straightened from his stance and moved to her, picking her up easily and turning to sit down himself with her cradled against his chest.

"You're right. You're right," he whispered softly to her and kissed her hair.

She lay against him limply. Exhausted by the outpouring she had just been through, she rested there quietly. Her tears dampened his chest and she wiped at them idly.

"I can't bear not being close to you. Not knowing if you're hurting or why . . . Why won't you let me help?"

"I know . . . I know."

Resting then, they stayed there for a long while, holding onto each other firmly. When he finally started talking, she let him speak without interrupting. He told her everything. More than he had his father or Jim or Ollie. The only time she spoke was when he told her of Juliana's connection to the whole ordeal. Renee jerked upright away from him.

"If I had known . . . and she had the nerve to visit and ask if we'd had any news," unreasonable with anger, she trembled with the thoughts of what she wanted to do to Juliana Chandler.

"Don't let it upset you. I took care of Juliana before Ollie found me in the saloon."

"What did you do?" Renee asked worriedly.

"I had planned to strangle her," he said coldly. "I'm glad now that I stopped just short of the act. We'll hear no more from her."

"Thank God."

"I don't know what stopped me, at the time I truly believed you were dead. I had no hope . . ."

Renee pressed against him, "Please don't think about all of that again. Not now."

His arms tightened around her, "You're right of course, but I dwelled on that for so long. The only thing that kept me going was the thought that I would get even with Julie. For that much I'm now grateful to her."

"Tell me about the Johnsons."

"They own a nice size farm southwest of town. Been out there for a while. They moved up from Kentucky."

"How did they find you? I mean if you'd been there all along and nobody knew, how was it they found you when they did?"

"They didn't find me; Sheriff Tanner did and took me to their farm."

"You were with them long?"

"About three weeks or so. The first week I don't remember anything about. The daughter, Caroline, took care of me then. She was a sweet girl."

"How old a girl?" Renee questioned jealously, hiding her smile.

"Old enough," he answered teasing her and then bent to kiss her lips. "You have no worry with me on that account. There's only one woman I need and that's you. Even when I thought you were dead, I didn't want anyone else."

"Let's keep it that way," she murmured, deepening the kiss. "Go on now. I don't want to distract you."

He chuckled in his chest, "You definitely are a distraction."

His hands sought her, slipping beneath the dressing

gown to stroke her intimately.

"You were saying." she interrupted, pulling his hands away from her and closing her robe.

"They cut the chains off right away, I guess. I was unconscious most of that first week."

"Did your arms bother you much? Your back? The scars . . ."

"Ugly, aren't they?"

"Yes, they are," she answered him with no hesitation.

"My back was the worst . . . it took so long to heal. Once the cuffs were off my arms got better right away," Marsh wasn't disturbed at all by her honesty.

"It looks like I owe Caroline Johnson quite a lot."

"They are good people. When Father goes back north I want him to send them a substantial financial compensation."

"I'm sure they'll appreciate it although if they're as nice as you say they are they probably won't be expecting anything."

He leaned down and kissed her gently on the forehead. "It's beautiful here. I understand why you were so homesick, now."

"I love L'Aimant so. You would have liked my father, I think."

"If he was anything like you, he probably was a tyrant!"

"Hardly," she laughed. "He was a kind and generous man."

"Who runs all this now?"

"Alain. He manages the plantation with the help of his overseer. You see L'Aimant and Windland adjoin each other so it's no problem."

"I figured he must live close by. He got here on pretty short notice for dinner last night and Elise was talking about coming quickly in case we needed her when you have the baby."

"You should see his house, it's really beautiful."

"It'll be hard put to beat L'Aimant," he replied.

"I'm glad you like it here. You don't mind staying until after the baby is born?" she asked this question timidly, afraid he wanted to return to Cedarhill and his work as quickly as possible.

"My darling, the way things are now, would you mind remaining here permanently?" he querried, wanting to start a new life from this day forward with no looking back.

"Oh, Marshall, how wonderful!" she threw her arms around his neck and hugged him tightly. "This house was built for many many children and I think we can fill it up, don't you?"

"Absolutely," he agreed, wondering if she really meant what she said.

"Father built this house for my mother but she died right after I was born. He never remarried."

"He must have truly loved her," he observed.

"He did. I'll show you her portrait one day soon. It's up in father's old den off his bedroom. She was a very beautiful woman."

"No doubt if she had a daughter like you."

"Think we should go up to bed now? If we stay up much longer, it'll be dawn."

"I've got a better idea."

"What?"

"Wait here a minute," and with those words he disappeared inside. Within minutes he was back dressed carrying her slippers.

"Come on. We'll go on down to the willow and watch the sun come up."

Taking her hand, he led her down the steps and up the path that led to her private place and they watched the sunrise enfolded in each others arms, bravely facing a new day.

Chapter Thirty-four

The days that followed mellowed and blended together in peaceful harmony. Each one like the next except for the anticipation of Elise's wedding. Jim had gone back to his river, glad to be away from the worries that had beset him for so many weeks. Marshall appeared to adapt well and Martha and George now came to think of their visit as a vacation. They planned to return home after the wedding. August was upon them and the heat became quite unbearable. Many afternoons were spent lazily inside trying to find a breeze. Generally, Renee had been unaffected by the weather but with her pregnancy advancing she became more uncomfortable as she grew in size.

The wedding was a splendid affair held at Windland. All of their neighbors attended and even friends from New Orleans. Renee delightedly introduced Marshall to all of her father's old acquaintances and they met him with hearty approval.

Elise was radiant and Alain was proud. At last they would have a life together no matter how many years had passed since their youth. Renee was thrilled with her aunt's happiness, but she was upset that they were postponing their honeymoon until after the baby's arrival. They insisted that the child was more important to them than a trip. Besides Alain could use the time to instruct Marsh in the plantation operation.

It seemed the wedding was barely over when they were saying goodbye to George, Martha and Dorrie. Jim stopped on his way upriver and picked them up. They all promised to return in time for the holidays and in the meantime George would conclude Marsh's affairs in St. Louis.

Almost collapsing on their bed when they returned to the cool shadows of their bedroom, Renee groaned.

"Are you ill?"

"No, just tired," she paused her eyes widening, her hand going automatically to her stomach. "Marsh?"

He looked at her nervously, thoughts of miscarriage wildly running through his mind, "What?"

"Marsh, I . . ." she paused, her expression now changing to one of amazement and pleasure.

"What's wrong?" he came to her side and took her hand wondering if she was all right.

"The baby . . ." she put his hand to her stomach. "Can you feel it?"

He was still for a moment not knowing what he was expecting to feel. "No."

"I did!" she exclaimed and jumped up to hug him. "What a perfect ending to a hectic week."

He smiled and relaxed at her happiness. He felt so much better these last few weeks. There had been a few bad moments in those days after they had talked, but now most of that was behind them. She had helped him when she could and when she couldn't she had remained at his side giving him support. He felt fit and confident. Only his concern for her and the baby caused him any worry. He kept reminding himself that she was not Elizabeth and there was no need to drag all of those thoughts up from the depths of his mind. Now as he looked at her, he knew there had never really been any comparison in the beginning either.

In the days that followed the decision was made to move into the master suite so the den could be redecorated as a nursery. It had been closed off when Roger died and Renee had not entered it since her return. But now, with Marshall here she knew she would be putting the rooms to good use. She entered the dark rooms with trepidation, Marsh following her. He threw open the drapes and windows and surveyed the large bedroom approvingly. There was a massive canopy bed of mahogany with a matching armoire, several overstuffed chairs and an Aubusson carpet of soft hues on the floor. Marshall again was more than impressed by the home Roger Fontaine had created here for his wife and daughter. He hoped that he could do as well in the future. Renee hesitated slightly before opening the connecting door to the den.

"This is the room where Father and I used to have our talks . . . I remember you teased me about that once."

He smiled at her and came to take her hand, "Show me."

She turned the key in the lock and opened the door. It was very dark in the den and Marsh went ahead of her to draw back the drapes and open the French doors. He noted that this room opened onto the second floor gallery and stepped outside to admire the view. At the opposite side of the house from Renee's room, the view from this point afforded a panoramic sweep of the gardens. Feeling curiously relaxed and at home, Marsh turned to enter the room and stopped dead in his steps.

"My God!" was all he could say as he stared open-mouthed at the small portrait on the massive walnut desk.

"What, Marshall?" Renee turned to him stricken by the look on his face, she glanced up to see what had disturbed him. "My mother."

He nodded quietly trying to find the right words. "What was your mother's maiden name?"

"Chase, why?"

"Where was she from?"

"They met and married in Philadelphia, Father had just returned from a European trip and it was love at first sight."

"Was she an only child? Did you have any aunts or uncles in Philadelphia?"

"No. Father never mentioned anyone there. Why is this so important?"

As he started to speak, they heard a horse outside and Marsh turned to see Alain riding up. It was almost time for them to go over the plantation books together.

"I have to speak to Alain for a moment. Will you

wait for me or do you want to come downstairs?"

"I think I'll stay here and sort through a few things," she answered puzzled at his interest in her mother.

Marshall met Alain in the hall, "You've arrived at the perfect time. I've just discovered something that I don't know what to make of."

"What?" Alain asked in some confusion.

"Did Renee's mother have any brothers or sisters?'

"No. She was an only child."

"Oh," he said slightly disappointed. He had been stunned when he had seen the portait of Anne Chase Fontaine. She had been Elizabeth's double.

"So, you've seen the portrait, eh?"

"Yes."

"I knew you would come to this sooner or later. Where is Renee? I might as well tell you both at the same time."

Alain led a befuddled Marshall back up to Roger's suite and stood before Anne's portrait.

"Renee, darling, why don't you sit down while I tell you a long story your father should have told you years ago."

She moved to the settee pulling the dustcover from it and sat down. "What is all the mystery about? Marshall acts as if he's seen a ghost and you're telling me a story that my father neglected to?"

"It's important."

"I believe you, please, what is it?"

"When your Father married your Mother in Philadelphia she had already been married once, to a man named Parker."

Marshall groaned.

"She had had a daughter by this man before he was lost at sea," Alain, conscious of Renee's troubled look, hurried on. "When Roger married your mother and brought her back to live here, he also brought her little daughter Elizabeth with her."

The shock brought her to her feet and she looked quickly at Marshall to see his pale face strained at this new knowledge, "Elizabeth Parker was my sister?"

"Your half-sister, ma petite," Alain said kindly.

"But . . ."

"Let me continue, then you'll understand. When your mother died the Parker grandparents came down and took little Elizabeth back home with them. They had never approved of your father and were more than happy to get back their only grandchild. I'll never forget that day as long as I live. Roger knew he didn't have any legal claim to the little girl. The Parkers brought a whole pack of lawyers with them. There was no choice but to let go. He had no chance to keep her. I can still hear her crying and begging Roger not to let them take her. He was the only father she had ever known, it was terrible. He was heartsick. I guess that's why he spent so much of his time being the perfect father to you, his real daughter. He knew he couldn't help Elizabeth so he devoted himself to you."

"But why didn't he tell me?"

"Because he had been so badly hurt. She was so like your mother and to have her taken away right after Anne's death . . . it was almost more than he could bear. He made me promise never to mention to you

439

about your half-sister. There was no further contact over the years so we just assumed that everything went all right for little Elizabeth," Alain looked over to Marshall. "And then when I came up to St. Louis, your parents told me all about Elizabeth and I made the connection."

"And you didn't tell us."

"Would you really have wanted to know? You were so happy and I just wanted you to be happy together."

"Then it's not coincidence that you look so much alike," Marshall said gazing at Renee and finally managing to smile. He went to her and drew her into his arms.

"And it doesn't bother you?"

"At first it did but this explains it; so there's really no mystery involved. In fact this explains a lot of things about Elizabeth that I never understood," he said more to himself.

"Marshall?"

"Oh, nothing," he kissed her lightly. "Alain and I have much to do today. Shall I send one of the girls up to help with the airing of these rooms?"

"Please."

"And I think a likeness of you would be much more apropos," he said gazing at Anne Fontaine.

"Oh, I'm sure you want one painted of me now while I'm so big!" she smiled at him.

"You are beautiful to me always, remember that," he replied seriously. "I'll send some help up to you while Alain and I get our work done."

When they had left the room and Renee was alone with her thoughts, she wondered at the strange chain of events that saw her married to the same man as the sister she hadn't even known. She was sure that Marshall had been quite shocked to find Elizabeth and herself related, but he seemed to take the news in good humor. In fact, for some moments he even had looked relieved. What she didn't understand is why her father did not tell her of the existence of her half-sister. True, he must have been hurt by what had happened, but surely she was entitled to know that she had other relatives. Especially since she had never known her mother. Sighing, she knew she would find no answers. They were buried with her father. When the maids came to help her clean the rooms they found her gazing out the window watching Marshall and Alain ride off to the fields.

Later that evening as they spent their last night in her bedroom, she asked him his real thoughts about their discovery.

"I'm glad I found out."

"Why?"

"Because, and I'm being honest with you now, there were many things about Elizabeth that I didn't understand. This explains a lot of it . . . her selfishness . . . her possessiveness."

"But you loved her?"

"I loved the person I thought she was. But I don't think she loved me, knowing what I know now. I don't think she was capable of loving anyone."

"And you think being torn from my father had a lot to do with it?"

"Most definitely, my love," he kissed her then and settled back to rest. "Come here and let's get some sleep. We're going to need it if we're moving into the other rooms tomorrow there'll be a lot of things to do."

She nestled close to him and they slept contentedly in each others arms.

Chapter Thirty-five

The weather had finally cooled off and the first hint of winter was in the air. Renee was glad for the respite from the clinging heat. Her stomach had grown so that it amazed her and Marshall only laughed when she remarked on it. He kept telling her she looked gorgeous but she was beginning to think he might be crazy if his preference for women was turning to big fat ones. As November grew old, she became thoroughly disgusted with her shape and although she wasn't vain about her looks she felt decidedly unattractive. Waddling seemed the only way to make any progress and at times she gave up and sat back, letting the servants wait on her.

Marshall was more and more involved with the running of things and was gone most of the daylight hours. She grew bored and depressed and because intimacies were forbidden right now, she felt thoroughly abandoned. There were days when for no reason at all she would burst into tears. Renee knew that these moods were to be expected but it didn't make living with herself any easier.

They passed a quiet Thanksgiving with Elise and Alain at L'Aimant and then began planning for the arrival of Marsh's family. Martha wrote to expect them the week before Christmas so Renee was supervising the preparation of their rooms along with putting the final touches on the new nursery.

Marshall rode happily up to the house. The crop was in at last and it was time for relaxation and celebration. L'Aimant had had a good year and with the help of their factor in New Orleans, a substantial profit would be made. He had come in especially early this day to enjoy a light luncheon with his wife. He had seen little enough of her these past weeks and knew it was time to make amends. He had many new ideas he wanted to employ around the plantation and he needed to discuss these with her. He dismounted and hurried up the gallery steps. He felt confident this day. He was once more in charge of his life and emotions. Soon they would have a child to cherish and the thought thrilled him. She would be a wonderful mother as she was a wonderful wife. Humming, he took the stairs two at a time and went light-heartedly down the long wide hall to the master bedroom suite. Without pausing he threw open the bedroom door and stopped short. Renee was stretched out on the bed crying.

"Renee?" he was startled. "What's wrong?"

She raised her head to look at him standing there so vitally handsome and fit while she lay there so swollen with his child.

"What's wrong? I'll tell you what's wrong! And it's all your fault!"

"I don't know what you're talking about," he said with great concern, having no idea of her mood.

He crossed the room and sat on the bed next to her, taking her in his arms he held her close but she was so intent on feeling sorry for herself that she jerked away. Marshall was at a loss as to how to deal with her.

"Of course you don't, why should you?" she cried. "You don't care about me any more. All you care about is this baby. It's all your fault!"

Mindless to the fact that she had something to do with conceiving the child and that she was happy to be having his baby, she turned her back on him and missed the change and bewilderment that overtook him. His face contorted at her words . . . the exact words that had been hurled at him over five years ago. Rational thought fled as the words echoed through him. How could he have been so stupid? How could he have believed all these months that she was any different from Elizabeth? Anguish tore through him as he turned from her, fists clenched at his sides in barely suppressed fury. As he moved to the door in angry strides, his gaze focused on the small framed likeness of Anne Fontaine on the table. He didn't see Renee's mother in that smiling countenance, he saw Elizabeth and all control deserted him.

"*Damn you! Damn you both!*" he snarled throwing the picture across the room and watching it shatter against the wall.

Renee raised her head and looked at Marshall in astonishment. All color drained from her face, her eyes widened in shock. Silence hung heavily in the room and he turned with unconcealed disgust and slammed out.

"Marshall!" she called but he was already gone.

Renee was stunned, she sat up slowly, pushing her hair back from her tear-stained face. Smoothing her dress nervously, she looked at the broken portrait on the floor. What had happened? She'd never seen Marshall like this before and what did he mean by 'Damn you both'? She moved to the window in time to see him ride off. Shakily, she picked up the pieces and put them in the back of her dresser drawer. After bathing her face in cool water, she went wearily downstairs. His last words to her ran through her mind again and again, and she shivered at the memory of his face as he had stalked from the room.

Marsh was halfway to Windland before he remembered that Alain would not be home this afternoon. Reluctantly reining in his horse, he slowed his headlong pace. Riding down to the river, he watched its slow progress before following the bank back toward L'Aimant. Reason was replacing the cold dread that had filled him earlier. He supposed that she was just too young for the responsibilities of motherhood. It was just such a shock. He had thought she was happy. Guilt weighed on him, again he had failed in some way. Just as he had before with Elizabeth . . . Dwelling on her exact words he realized that he had spent little or no time with her these past weeks. In her condition, she could have mistaken his absence as a lack of interest or love but surely she understood. He would have to explain it all and make her listen. Then he would promise her a honeymoon trip as soon as the baby was born. He was certain that the thought of all that time alone together would please her. He would spoil her now as he had intended all those months before . . . Still, the thought of leaving L'Aimant didn't sit well with him. He had come to love it. There was still so much to be done . . . Alain and Elise would be leaving soon, too. He knew that Alain was counting on him to supervise Windland while they went to Europe. Marshall shrugged; he would talk to Renee about it. He knew they could solve any problem if they shared it. Satisfied with his decision, he rode eagerly to the house.

Renee heard him coming up the drive and rose with some difficulty from the overstuffed chair in which she was resting. Glancing in the mirror over the fireplace she checked her appearance and then hurried into the hall. Her hour alone had given her time to think. She knew she owed Marshall an apology. She had been cruel to him earlier and she needed to tell him that she was sorry. Standing nervously in the center of the hall, she waited for him to enter and jumped a little when the door quickly opened and he strode in.

Their eyes met, hers anxious, his searching. Marshall wanted to speak, but the sight of her so pale and subdued, momentarily struck his words from him.

"I'm glad you're back," she said softly. "I was worried."

"Why?" he answered and then scowled at his own reply.

Renee mistook his expression for irritation with her and hesitated. Marshall, exasperated, walked purposely toward her and Renee couldn't help but cringe as she remembered his violence upstairs.

"Renee . . ." he said, pulling her into his arms and holding her there protectively. "Please, don't ever be afraid of me."

"I'm so sorry. I didn't mean to make you so angry . . ." she cried muffledly into his shirt. "I just felt so miserable . . ."

He raised her face and kissed her tenderly. "I'm sorry too, I shouldn't have lost control."

He held her quietly until she relaxed against him. Then with his arm around her, they moved into the front parlor and sat together on the loveseat. She finally looked up at him and smiled.

"That was easier than I thought it would be."

"It was, wasn't it?" he agreed a little surprised.

"I supposed this was our first argument," she said. "Although, I don't think we really had a chance to argue. I'm sorry for the way I treated you."

Marshall frowned, "I should have been more understanding of your situation . . . I know these past months have been hell for you. And since I've been back we really haven't had a lot of time together. There's so much work to be done . . ."

"I know that," she insisted. "I've been so wrapped up in myself and feeling so useless and ugly . . . Now, don't interrupt me . . ." she continued as he turned to her to disagree. "Your mother wrote in her last letter that the final two months are the worst. That I should just try to relax and not worry but it's so difficult. I miss you so when you're gone all day."

He pulled her across his lap and she rested her head on his shoulder. They sat that way for long quiet minutes.

"I think we should take a trip, better yet, a delayed honeymoon, as soon as possible . . . what do you think? New Orleans? Or we could even go to Europe if you like?"

Renee lifted her head to stare at him incredulously, "Do you want to leave? I thought you liked it here?"

"I do. Why?"

"Then why would you want to leave? I'm so happy here, too. There's nowhere else I'd rather be. But if you really want a trip, I'll go just to please you," she paused trying to read his thoughts. "But what of our baby? Surely we wouldn't be able to take him with us so soon and I have no intention of abandoning our child to a nursemaid."

"You *are* happy?" he asked. "I thought you needed the trip to lift your spirits."

"Darling, my spirits lifted when you walked in that front door. I love you. I only need you to be happy."

Renee kissed him deeply and he crushed her to his chest, glad that the sense of estrangement was gone. A deep sense of inner peace stole over him and he softened his embrace. He felt, too, that familiar stirring of passion within him and he carefully held himself in check. This was no time to be dwelling on that, although the fullness of her breasts against him was more than a little distracting. Renee, aware of the desire growing within Marshall, stood up and took his hand.

"Let's go upstairs," she said a small teasing smile curving her lips.

"But I thought . . ." he looked at her in surprise.

"Never mind what you thought, I need you now very much . . ."

He stood quickly and gathered her close kissing her fiercely. Tugging at him happily, she led him upstairs and locked their door behind them.

"Are you sure it's all right?" he asked. "I don't want to hurt you in any way . . ."

"I'm sure, if we're careful. I can think of a perfectly delightful way . . . that is if you need guidance?" she

449

teased, moving from him and starting to disrobe.

Caught up in her excitement, he helped her undress. She tantalizingly slipped her chemise straps from her shoulders and let it fall, revealing her full breasts. Then turning her back, she finished by herself and slipped beneath the covers. He lay down beside her still dressed, intending to kiss her gently but Renee was too excited and she moved against him through the blanket urging him to hurry to her. Her arms wrapped around him and she returned his kiss with abandon. Sensuously her hands strayed to his shirt and she unfastened it and pushed it from him, encouraging him to undress and join her. Releasing him from her hungry embrace, she watched eagerly as he shed the last of his clothing and came back to the bed. She moved to welcome him and sighed in pleasure as his mouth found hers once again. Caressing her carefully, he was gentle with her. When she turned her back to accept him in the most comfortable position for them, he was ready and they came together in a mutual giving that left them breathless in its beauty.

Renee was pleased that he still found her desirable and Marshall was relieved that she still loved him after witnessing his unleashed temper.

"Where did you put the picture of your mother?" he asked finally noticing that it had been picked up.

"I put it in my dresser drawer. I thought it best to put it out of sight. I don't understand why you were so upset with my mother."

"Oh, darling, I didn't see your mother in that picture. It was Elizabeth."

"Oh," she said without emotion. "But why would you be thinking of Elizabeth?"

"For the same reason that I was so angry."

He rolled on his side to face her. His expression was serious, his eyes seemed haunted for a moment.

Before he could speak, Renee went on, "I know Elizabeth died after a miscarriage. Dorrie told me that much."

"Dorrie doesn't know everything."

"What else is there? Is it that terrible that you still can't speak of it?"

He kissed her tenderly and laid back so she was against his side, her head resting on his shoulder. Rubbing a hand wearily over his eyes he glanced at her.

"For so long, I've forced myself to not think about it . . ."

"Please, tell me. Perhaps if we'd discussed this sooner we wouldn't have had our misunderstanding," she gently caressed his cheek and he turned his head to kiss her palm.

"Elizabeth didn't miscarry. She deliberately tried to abort our child and she hemorrhaged. The doctor was there but he couldn't stop the bleeding."

"But why would she do it?"

"She thought I cared more for the baby than I did for her. So the simple solution was to get rid of the child."

"No wonder Jim said she wasn't as lovely as she looked. How terrible for you!"

"I had been upriver on business and when I got back, well, she was barely alive. I'm certain she thought it would look like an accident. Then we would have gone on as before and I would never have known the truth!"

451

Renee could feel him tense beside her as he remembered the pain of Elizabeth's death.

"She died in my arms and all she could say was that it was all my fault . . ."

"Oh, my God!" Renee clung to him, tears blurring her vision as she recalled what she'd said to him. "I'm sorry, I never meant to hurt you! I didn't know . . ."

Marshall hugged her and kissed her forehead, "Don't cry. It's all right now. Now that you understand."

"Are you sure?"

"How can you have any doubts after the way we just made love?"

Renee smiled, completely satisfied with his answer.

One week later, Alain and Marsh were closeted in Alain's office.

"Can you be ready to go?" Alain asked as they made plans for a short trip to New Orleans.

"Sure," he answered. "Although I don't like leaving Renee just now."

"No problem. Elise can stay with her. We'll only be gone three, maybe four days at the most."

"Fine, I'll tell her to expect you both this evening."

"When is Jim coming through?"

"He stopped by on his way down two days ago. I imagine we'll meet him once we're in New Orleans."

"Good, I haven't seen him in a while."

After agreeing to leave the following morning, Marsh headed home from Windland. He was not eager to go to New Orleans. But Alain felt it was necessary that he learn every facet of the business as soon as possible and dealing with the factor, Mr. Miller, was a major part of plantation operations. Their trip down river would take less than a day and hopefully the business could be concluded in another.

Renee met him at the door when he came in from his meeting with Alain.

"How was Alain today?"

"He was just fine." After a quick welcoming kiss, he continued. "He thinks that it's time we went to New Orleans."

"Of course," Renee agreed without hesitation. "I know father had to make the trip quite often. I'm surprised you haven't gone before. When are you leaving?"

"Tomorrow morning. I am concerned about your being all alone, so Elise has agreed to stay with you while we're away."

"That's wonderful. We haven't had a chance to visit in ages. Will you get to see Jim while you are in town?"

"Hopefully, if I can find him. I thought we could all go out to dinner tomorrow night."

Alain and Elise arrived late in the afternoon to stay the night so the men could depart early in the day. By ten the next morning Marshall and Alain were already on their way to New Orleans. Marshall had stayed on deck and watched until L'Aimant landing was out of sight. Their trip downriver was slow and uneventful with frequent stops at the plantations along the way. Once they had docked, they left the ship in search of Jim. After checking at the Westlake office they finally were able to locate the *Elizabeth Anne*.

Jim was concentrating on shipping figures and looked up with annoyance at the knock on his door.

"Come in," he called flatly, irritated by the interruption.

As the door flew open and Alain and Marshall

entered, Jim threw down his pen and rose to welcome them.

"Hard at work?"

"Always. In fact, I'm due to head back upriver late tomorrow and I still haven't contracted for a full load," Jim explained.

"Well, why don't we rescue you from all this drudgery? Alain and I still have to check in at the hotel, so why don't you meet us at the St. Louis in about two hours? Bring Ollie, too."

"Fine. Ollie and I haven't had a break this entire trip. A little relaxation might be just the thing."

They enjoyed an excellent meal at the hotel dining room and were relaxing with brandies when Jim suggested visiting some of the livelier establishments in town. Alain and Ollie both declined leaving the two brothers to their own devices. Their mood was light as they made their way to some of the more refined night spots. It was well past midnight when, more than a little intoxicated, they found themselves surrounded by a bevy of beauties in one of the bars. Jim was thoroughly enjoying himself, balancing a lady on each knee and still downing his whiskey. Marshall, however, was not inclined to such sport and repeatedly turned away the suggestive offers. Finally in good natured humor Jim suggested another time to the two women he'd been entertaining and departed with his slightly aggravated brother.

To Marshall it had come as quite a surprise that none of the women, no matter how slim or attractive appealed to him. There had been no interest stirred in him at all as the women had flaunted their charms before him. He shook his head in mock sympathy at his own besotted state, a wry grin on his face and Jim looked at him questioningly on their way back to the hotel.

"And what's the matter with you?"

"Absolutely nothing."

"Oh," he paused then trying to grasp his brother's train of thought. "I take it you've had enough of this wild night life?"

"I've got meetings first thing in the morning. I'm sure Alain won't appreciate it if I'm late."

"You don't sound at all enthused about this visit."

"I'm not. It was Alain's idea and Renee agreed. I just don't like leaving her for any length of time."

"What time is your meeting with Miller in the morning?"

"Alain set it up for nine. I just hope we can conclude all that needs doing in one day."

"Then you're planning on going home day after tomorrow?"

"Hopefully. Why?"

"I'll see how my loading is progressing tomorrow and if I can I'll take you back with me."

"Fine, you still have the fastest boat on the river and that's what I'm looking for going home."

"You are in a hurry," Jim grinned as they approached the hotel.

Marshall smiled at his brother. "It was harder than hell to leave, even the way things are now."

"So, is that what you were smiling about when we came out of the saloon?" When Marsh didn't answer, Jim continued, "I can certainly understand your feelings. Renee is very special."

"You sound like you're in love with her, too,"

Marshall said glancing at his brother.

"You know I am," Jim answered still grinning.

Marshall considered this a moment and agreed, "I wish I was at L'Aimant now."

"You'll be back in two days; don't worry. I'll get you there as fast as I can."

Time couldn't go fast enough for Marshall. He was relieved when the meetings with Mr. Miller ended shortly after lunch and he had some free time to do his Christmas shopping. He visited a dressmaker recommended by Alain as one she had frequented in the past and culminated his spree with a stop at a jeweler's to order a very special gift. Marsh and Alain rendezvoused with Jim early the next morning and were glad to feel the engines throbbing beneath their feet as the *Elizabeth Anne* backed out to mid-stream and headed north.

Renee and Elise had spent their days planning menus and making sure everything was ready for the arrival of the Westlakes the following week. They were thrilled when they heard the familiar sound of the *Elizabeth Anne* as she whistled her arrival and the women went eagerly to meet their men on the gallery. Having left the luggage behind, Marshall and Alain hurried up the path and Renee flung herself into his arms as he reached the house.

"I missed you so much!"

"Me, too," he murmured before kissing her soundly and holding her to him.

Alain and Elise were a bit more restrained in their reunion but were happy to be together. The Chenauts stayed only long enough for a brief visit and then set off for their own home.

After a quiet evening enjoying each other's company with a few more evenly matched games of backgammon, they lay together in the wide bed, Renee curled to his side.

"Did you miss me?" she whispered.

"I was so lonely without you. I was miserable the whole time," he confessed. "In the future, I want you with me."

"I'm glad you were lonely!" she stated fiercely. "I was lost without you and I definitely don't like sleeping in our bed all alone."

He kissed her on the forehead and protectively held her close, "I won't go without you ever again."

She smiled to herself and closed her eyes, secure in his embrace.

In a flurry of activity the Westlakes arrived, laden with brightly wrapped packages that were secreted away until Christmas morning. The days that followed were warm and loving establishing the perfect atmosphere for a family gathering and Renee hoped the baby would come soon to make it a perfect holiday.

Chapter Thirty-six

Christmas Eve dawned cloudy and cold; a heavy frost had settled the night before and it left no doubt that it was winter. Fires burned brightly in all the rooms and breakfast was a jovial meal. When the meal had ended George and Marsh went out to get the Christmas tree while the women waited in the front parlor. Soon the men returned with a perfect tree and they all decorated it with a myriad of small ornaments and candles. They were careful not to hang any ornaments near a candle for the fear of fire was great and when at last all were put on the tree Renee gave Marshall her golden star to put on the very top.

"It's beautiful!" Dorrie exclaimed.

"It sure is, I can't wait until tonight to light it!" Renee said excitedly and slipped into Marshall's arms.

The women spent the rest of the afternoon going over preparations for Christmas dinner. Elise and Alain were invited and it would be quite a festive occasion. Renee yearned for something bright and cheerful to wear but her pregnancy was so far advanced that she resigned herself to wearing her usual late afternoon gown. It wasn't unattractive, she just longed to be slim and pretty again. Dinner that night was a light one as they saved their appetites for the day to come.

Gathering around the fireplace, they were a comfortable close, loving group. Only Jim was missing but he had promised to be there sometime on Christmas Day. George took over the lighting of the tree and when he finished they sang carols and drank hot punch to celebrate. Much later, warmed by the punch and the love of their family they retired.

Christmas Morning! Would there ever be another as glorious? Renee was awakened by a warm tender kiss from Marsh and she laughed delightedly in anticipation of the day to come.

They hurried downstairs as fast as her body would permit, but half way down Marshall gave up and laughingly carried her the rest of the way. He set her gently on her feet at the bottom of the stairs.

"We can't take a chance on having an accident today."

She kissed him lightly and almost dragged him into the parlor. George was already up and Martha was just coming in with a steaming cup of tea when they made their way into the room. Dorrie came racing in, her cheeks pink from the cold.

"Where have you been so early?" Marshall asked.

"Watching for Jimmy. I just saw the boat. He should be here in about twenty minutes!" she exclaimed taking off her mantle.

"Good. We'll wait for him before we open the presents."

"Fine. Let's have something hot to drink while we wait," Marshall helped Renee to the settee and then poured them each a cup of coffee from the silver service brought in by Sara.

"Oh, I hope he hurries!" Dorrie said eyeing the mound of gifts under the tree.

"He will," Martha replied. "You know Jim and

459

presents!"

The family laughed, remembering Jim's excitement as a child whenever gifts were given. Marsh sat beside Renee after handing her her cup. They looked at each other adoringly and Martha smiled a knowing smile at her husband. Dorrie watched from the french doors for the sight of her brother coming up the path.

"You're looking the wrong way," George teased her. "I've had a wagon waiting for him since this morning early. Once they see the boat they'll drive down and pick him up. After all we wouldn't want him to strain himself carrying all those packages he's bringing."

Renee laughed, having no idea that George was serious.

Soon they heard the horses at the front and Dorrie ran to let him in. True to George's word Jim came in laden with gaily wrapped surprises for one and all. Renee watched in wide-eyed wonder as the gifts were piled by the tree.

"Dorrie, help me sort these out!" Jim called to her after kissing his mother and drinking a warming cup of coffee. Everyone watched eagerly as the presents were sorted and passed to the person waiting. Renee watched in amazement at the number of gifts intended for her. When they finished handing out packages, she looked at Marshall stunned.

"All of these are for me?"

He nodded and smiling, she began opening her presents. Soon colorful bits of paper were everywhere as everyone began unwrapping. Dorrie was thrilled with her many presents and was the first one finished.

"I've never had a Christmas like this and I definitely hope this is the first of many!" Renee laughed gaily after she thanked Jim for the beautiful embroidered shawl he'd given her and George and Martha for the rosewood letterbox, and she was thrilled with a small ornate hand mirror from Dorrie.

"Where are the other things, Jim?"

"I left them in the hall, Marsh. Just a second, I'll get them."

"What things?" Renee asked.

"Did you think that I'd forgotten your gift?"

"But . . ."

Jim entered just then with his arms full again. Renee took the boxes and sorting through in surprise opened the biggest one first. Within was the most beautiful gown she'd ever seen. It was a high-necked, long-sleeved evening gown of emerald velvet, trimmed in ivory lace with small pearl buttons down the front.

"Oh, Marsh, it's gorgeous! I can hardly wait to wear it."

"You must wear it tonight. I had it especially made for the holidays."

She hugged him and carefully laid the gown back in its box with the tissue paper. He handed her another and she unwrapped a long flowing dressing gown of apricot silk trimmed in satin ribbons of the same color. She caressed the smooth folds of the wrap and looked longingly at her husband wishing she could wear it now to entice him. The last box he handed her was a small one.

"With all my love," he murmured to her.

She leaned against him as she opened it cautiously. She mouthed a silent, "Oh." Inside was an emerald and diamond ring. When she looked up at him her eyes were full of tears.

"You never had an engagement ring," he said simply as he put the ring on her finger.

He kissed her gently and everyone smiled at the affectionate display. After a hearty breakfast, they retired to their rooms so Renee could rest for a while.

"Do you think your family liked the gifts we gave them?"

"Father and Jim were delighted with the rifles. Mother, I'm sure, will enjoy the books and Dorrie always loves new clothes.'"

"Good. We hadn't spoken of it so I wasn't sure what was appropriate. I'm glad that you bought the guns for Jim and your father," she moved to the massive armoire and stealthily took a small gift from within. "I didn't forget you either, darling."

She held out the precious package to her husband who was more than surprised by her unexpected gift.

"But how? You haven't been off the plantation in weeks."

She only smiled and handed him the carefully wrapped memento, "I wanted you to have this more than anything."

Marsh unwrapped it slowly, glancing at her often, trying to read the expression on her face but finding it impossible. Within the wrap was a jewelry box. He opened it to find her father's pocket watch.

"Are you sure?"

"Absolutely, you're the master of L'Aimant now. It's yours."

He held her close and kissed her tenderly. This personal gift had touched him more deeply than she could possibly have known.

Later, Elise and Alain arrived gift laden, too. Elise

even brought a present for the baby, in hopes that he would hurry and be born just to open it.

Renee looked radiant in her new gown. She marvelled at the fit. The deep green accented her eyes and they sparkled as brightly as the ring on her hand.

Dinner was perfection. Roast pork with creole gravy and rice dressing, yams dripping brown sugar glaze, stuffed mushrooms, and enough different pies to please everyone—mincemeat, pecan and lemon. Contentedly stuffed they left the dining room and went into the parlor to rest before the beauty of the tree.

"What a wonderful day it's been," Dorrie said. "The only thing missing is snow."

"I'm certainly not missing it!" Renee laughed and Elise agreed with her.

Martha played a few songs for them on the piano and all joined in singing the carols which were so much a part of Christmas. Replete and happy they said good night and the evening drew to an end.

The following morning was dreary with rain. Cold gusts of wind splattered the drops against the windows as Marshall and Renee lingered overly long in bed, not wanting to brave the cold outside. He ran his hand over the taut skin of her belly and was rewarded with a strong kick from within.

"He's feisty this morning," Marshall grinned at her.

"I'll feel much better when he's being feisty in the next room and not inside of me," she laughed.

"Does it hurt when he kicks?"

"No, not at all. It's good to know that he's active and healthy."

He nodded and kissed her briefly before jumping from the bed and tugging on his breeches. "What an awful morning. Why don't you stay right there safe and warm and I'll have Sara bring you breakfast."

As another splattering of icy drops stung the windows Renee pulled the covers up to her chin. "That sounds marvelous. I'll just rest here until she comes, I haven't been sleeping all that well lately."

"Bad dreams?"

"No, I just can't seem to get comfortable. I'm surprised that I didn't wake you last night."

"I slept like a rock."

"Obviously. Look at all the energy you've got this morning," she said enviously as he finished dressing and made to leave the room.

"I'll be back later, you stay there until you feel like getting up. I'll tell Mother and Elise to come visit, all right?"

"Fine." she said snuggling back down under the comforter.

Elise and Alain left early as they had other visits to make on their way home. Martha and Dorrie entertained her the rest of the day with tales of other Christmases gone by and it was suppertime before she finally rose and dressed. Her body felt unusually heavy as if her center of balance had somehow shifted.

When New Year's Eve arrived she was glad that the Westlakes had all been invited to Windland for a party. She had declined on doctors orders and she was more than happy to spend a quiet evening alone with her husband. They sat in the parlor till late in the evening reading and playing backgammon. Marshall finally beat her and was unduly proud of himself.

"Being vain is a sin," she teased when he bragged about his victory.

It had all begun as a small muscle spasm earlier in the day and Renee had ignored it. It seemed only a passing discomfort. But now as she rose to go to bed a cramp-like pain cut through her. She gasped slightly and waited a moment to see if it would go away. It did. She was glad Marshall hadn't seen her. He would worry and it was nothing important. She was upstairs undressing with the help of the maid when it happened again and Sara knew immediately what it was.

"It's time," Sara said convincingly.

"Will it come fast? Should we get the doctor?"

"No, ma'am. Not yet. Sometimes that first child comes real slow."

"All right," she agreed trusting Sara's judgment. "We won't tell Marshall yet. He's going to stay downstairs for a while and I think it's best if we don't worry him just yet."

"Yes, ma'am," she agreed and hastened to make Renee as comfortable as possible.

Within an hour the pain was quite real and Renee was more than a little nervous.

"Ask Marshall to come up, please."

Sara left the room in search of him. Within minutes Marsh came casually into the suite.

"You needed me?"

"I think our son does," she smiled a little painfully as another contraction began. "I think we'd better send for the doctor soon."

He paled at her words and came to the side of the bed.

"You're quite sure?"

"Yes, my love. I've been having them regularly since I left you."

"I'll send a message right away, I believe Dr. Alexander is at Windland, too."

He hurried from the room and returned a few moments later. He pulled a chair to the side of the bed

465

and sat down heavily, a worried look on his face.

"What do we do now?"

"Dr. Alexander said to try to relax and wait. The pains hurt but they're not really too strong yet."

"Then you're comfortable?"

"Yes."

As if in response to her words, they seemed to grow in strength and duration. She gulped at the strangeness of it all. To feel her stomach become hard, without any effort on her part, was a bit unnerving. Catching Marshall's troubled gaze upon her she smiled at him.

"Don't worry. I'll be fine."

"I know. You try to rest. If the doctor isn't at the party, Mother is and she'll come right back when she gets the message."

Renee nodded, not trusting her voice. The maid bustled in and out bringing fresh bedclothes and helping Renee into a more suitable gown for the birth. It had been well over an hour when they finally heard the carriage outside. Marshall ran to the front window and then hurried down the stairs to let them in. Dr. Alexander came into the hall carrying his bag while Martha followed directly behind him.

"Is she upstairs?"

"In our bedroom. I'll show you the way," he led the physician up to the suite.

Renee was relieved when the doctor and her husband entered the room. Marshall immediately went to her side and took her hand.

"All right?" he asked anxiously.

"I think so," she answered a little nervously. "Hello Dr. Alexander. I'm sorry to interrupt your evening."

"Don't worry about that, Renee," the doctor smiled. "I find babies much more exciting than parties."

Renee started to smile but gasped as a hard contraction gripped her and she clutched at Marshall's arm.

"Doctor!" Marsh ordered tersely, his expression worried. "Can't you give her something for the pain?"

Dr. Alexander looked at Renee's pale face. "Mr. Westlake, would you find your mother for me and have her come up?"

"But . . ." Marsh began not wanting to leave Renee.

"Don't worry, I'll take care of her while you're gone," Dr. Alexander grinned.

Marsh looked at Renee for approval and she nodded. He kissed her hand and quickly left the room. Martha was still in the downstairs hall giving instructions to the servants who by now were all aroused by the excitement.

"Your father and Jim and Dorrie will be along soon. I came with the doctor in case he needs my assistance," she told Marshall as he came back down the steps.

"I'm glad you're here. The doctor wants to see you," he answered, casting a worried look upstairs.

Martha started upstairs and her son followed.

The doctor looked visibly relieved when Marshall had gone.

"Now, let's see how you're doing," he said conversationally.

Renee remained silent as he examined her.

"It'll be a while yet," he said. "When did these pains start?"

"Late afternoon, but they didn't hurt until about an hour ago."

"All right. You just relax, I'll have Mrs. Westlake in here with you in a few minutes," he said as he left the room.

"How's she doing?" Martha asked as they met the

467

doctor in the hall.

"Just fine, but it's going to be a while before the baby comes. Mr. Westlake, why don't you keep her company for a few minutes while your mother and I have a cup of hot coffee?"

Martha and the doctor disappeared downstairs and Marsh hurried in to see Renee.

"What did he say?" she asked him curiously.

"Just that it'll be a while before the baby's born," he said sitting by her side on the bed. "Can I do anything for you?"

"No, I'm just fine except for the contractions."

They sat in silence waiting for the next labor pain, their feelings a mixture of fear and excitement.

"Do you suppose he'll be as handsome as you?" she asked breathlessly as the contraction ended.

"Who?" Marshall returned, his thought process a shambles in the face of Renee's suffering.

"Your son!"

"My dear, our first born could very well be a girl, either way I'm sure any child of ours will be perfect."

"Absolutely!" she agreed laughing momentarily until her stomach grew painfully tight.

Dr. Alexander and Martha entered then and against his wishes Marsh was shooed by his mother from the room. She left him standing in the middle of the wide dark hall.

"You go see if your father's here yet; I thought I heard the carriage when I was coming up," she called over her shoulder as she hurried into the bedroom to be of service to the doctor.

Marshall stared unseeingly at the closed bedroom door momentarily until he heard the voices below. Then pulling himself together, he went downstairs to

468

greet the rest of his family.

"What's the news?" George bellowed. "Is the baby here yet?"

Marsh answered as he descended the staircase, "He said it would be a while yet . . ."

"I have experience in this area," George said confidently. "There is no way that we can help that baby along, so we'll just have to sit back and wait."

Putting his arm around his son's shoulders, he led the way into the study almost dragging Marshall with him. Jim and Dorrie exchanged conspiratory glances and they followed their father.

George rattled on for a few minutes until it occurred to him that no one was listening. Marshall stood by the fireplace gazing into the flames and Dorrie and Jim were deep in a game of backgammon. Grinning to himself, George poured a drink and settled down to await the birth of his first grandchild.

The hours dragged by since Marshall had left her. Renee pushed down in agony. It hurt. She had had a vague idea of what would happen when she went into labor but she hadn't in her wildest dreams expected to feel this way! Her water had just broken and the contractions were regular and strong, sometimes doubling up on each other.

"I'm afraid," she whispered to Martha.

"Just think how happy you'll be to hold your baby. It shouldn't be much longer judging by your pains."

Renee tried to smile as another spasm gripped her. She tried breathing the way the doctor instructed but it only made the pain worse. When it finally subsided, she lay limply back against the pillows. Dr. Alexander examined her and seemed quite pleased and Renee was tempted to ask him what he was so happy about, when another contraction started and she had to grit her teeth.

When Marshall heard the bedroom door open he rushed into the hall and met his mother.

"How is she? Can I go up?"

"Calm down. She's doing just fine. It'll be a little longer. I just came to see how you were doing. Renee's worried about you."

"Oh," he answered. "Couldn't I just go in for a few minutes?"

"Doctor's orders. Now, try to relax a little. I'll let you know as soon as anything happens," Marshall went into the study with his mother.

Dorrie was asleep on the sofa and Jim and George were drowsily sitting before the fire.

"I'm glad to see Marshall has such stimulating company."

George came to her and kissed her lightly, "Everything going all right?"

"Seems to be. I just came to check on all of you."

"We're holding up. Dorrie had a little too much punch at the Chenaut's. She fell asleep right away."

Martha moved to the sofa and straightened the coverlet about her daughter, "I best get back before Renee misses me."

After walking with his mother to the bedroom, Marsh went to the sitting room at the end of the hall. It faced the east and he could tell now that the sky was beginning to brighten. Dawn, a new day. And soon, hopefully, a new life. He sat on the settee and watched the few clouds in the sky change colors as the sun nudged its way above the horizon. Just as he began to relax, Renee's scream pierced every corner of his soul. He was on his feet and running before the sound stopped and a death pall hung over the house. He was at the door before his father and brother made it to the bottom step.

Marshall stood frozen at the door. Supposing she was dead or dying! Could he face it? Horrible thoughts crowded in on him and he couldn't move. He couldn't bear to throw open the door and witness what had happened to his wife, so he stood immobile. It seemed an eternity before Jim, George and Dorrie joined him there. All looked at him questioningly.

When at last the door opened, they turned as one person to Martha who came forth with a warm bundle. Her face was filled with such joy that Marshall wanted to hug her to him.

"How is Renee? Can I see her?"

"She is just fine, and so is he," she paused and then handed him the bundle.

"He? I have a son?"

At his mother's nod, he felt the tears come to his eyes and he slumped wearily against the wall, "Thank God, I was so worried."

"You can go in as soon as the doctor comes out. I'm sure he'll want to talk with you for a few minutes, but first let's look at my grandson."

Martha drew the rest of the family close and carefully opened the blanket to show them the tiny baby. The door opened behind them and Marsh turned to the doctor after giving his child over to his mother.

"She did just fine. She's tired now but she'll be better after she gets some rest," he said shaking Marshall's hand.

"And the baby?"

"Healthy! I'm sure he'll be fine. You may go on in, but no real excitement for a few days. Let her get her strength back."

Marshall murmured an agreeable answer and went hastily through the door as the doctor went to speak to the rest of the Westlakes. He paused, taking a deep breath and then moved to the bedside.

Renee was propped against the pillows, looking lovely in the new dressing gown. He bent to kiss her, sweetly.

"You saw our son?"

"He's beautiful. Gramma and Grampa are gloating over him now."

Renee smiled and reached out to pull Marsh down beside her as the rest of the family came in.

"I have someone here you might want to keep," Martha said, laying the baby in his mother's arms.

Renee beamed as her child let out his first of many cries.

"He's perfect, Renee," George complimented and kissed her affectionately. "We'll leave you two alone now to get some sleep. It's been a long night."

"Shall I bring the small cradle in here so we can keep him by our bed?" Marshall asked after the rest of the family had gone.

"I think that's a good idea."

Marshall moved the small bed out of the nursery and placed it within reach for his wife. After placing the baby in it, he went back to Renee.

"How does Roger Fontaine Westlake sound?"

"For my father? Wonderful, thank you."

"How are you?" he asked, content that his choice of names had pleased her.

"Most tired, I'm afraid."

"Me, too. All night you did the work and yet I'm exhausted," he laughed.

"The waiting is always the hard part and we've both had our share. He was worth the wait, don't you think?"

"Absolutely."

"Will you rest with me?"

He smiled at her. His expression was at once tired and yet full of joy and he rose momentarily to undress. Renee thrilled at the look of love in his eyes and when he turned back to her she held out her hand invitingly.

"I love you."

"And I love you," he answered as his lips found hers in an intimate caress.

He stretched out carefully next to her holding her tenderly.

"I won't disturb you, will I?"

"No. I want you near me."

"Good. That's where I want to be."

They were awakened some time later by Roger's soft cries and they smiled at each other.

"I hope that he always cries this softly," Marshall told her as he picked up his son. "Tiny, isn't he?"

"Not for long," she replied, taking him from her husband as he got back into bed.

Marshall had rung for Sara who appeared moments later.

"I've been waiting to see Master Roger," she said excitedly. "Birdie is waiting in the nursery for him."

"Birdie?" Marshall questioned.

"Roger's wet nurse," Renee informed him. "I think he's ready, too," Renee told Sara as she handed her son over to her maid.

Sara cooed to him sweetly as she moved into the nursery and turned to close the door, "I'll put him down to sleep in here, so you can get some rest, Miz Renee."

"Thank you, Sara," Renee called as Sara closed the connecting door.

Renee sighed, resting on Marshall's shoulder and he cradled her tenderly.

"I think we should have a dozen more, right away," he said in mock seriousness.

Her eyes twinkling, she looked up at him, "Making them is much more fun than having them!"

"Don't!" he groaned, grinning. "It's going to be hard enough keeping my hands off of you for the next few weeks without your teasing me. Practice looking unattractive, will you?"

She laughed, "Never. I don't want rumors flying around that my husband is after every light-skirt in New Orleans because I've turned into a frump after the birth of my child."

"Don't worry, darling. There isn't a woman around who could hold a candle to you, even frumpy!"

She kissed him, "Thank you."

"It's just the simple truth," he told her. "Now, lie still, so I can sleep or I'll have to move into another bedroom."

"All right," Renee told him and nestling close against him, they were both soon asleep.

Renee was confined to bed for a full week but Roger didn't suffer any lack of motherly attention as Dorrie, Elise and Martha all vied for his time. His waking hours were few and his audience had standing room only as his every gesture and movement brought reminiscences from Martha and George. Everyone agreed too, that he looked very much like himself, not favoring either parent, much to their disappointment.

Marshall, meanwhile, was a doting father, constantly checking on his son and spending as much time as possible with him. Renee encouraged their closeness, often sharing her bed with them both for short afternoon naps.

Jim had had little time with Renee this visit and was happy to find her on the gallery alone one morning the following week.

"Aren't you chilly?" he asked as a cold breeze blew up from the river.

"A little," she smiled. "But it's worth it to get out of the house for a while. I didn't realize how restricting it would be. I guess that's why they call it 'confinement', right?"

Jim laughed easily, "The *Elizabeth Anne* will be back in a few days and I'm going to get back to work. You're always welcome to join me if you want to get away for a few days . . ."

"I'd be delighted, but I'm afraid I'm needed here."

"I think so," he told her and then more solemnly. "I'm glad everything worked out so well. You should have everything you want from life."

"Thank you," she responded, softly. "You're a very special man, Jim Westlake."

He grinned, "You're a very special lady."

Sara called her then and Renee went to care for her son, leaving Jim by himself, staring down at the river.

Later that day, the men gathered in the study to talk business.

"Alain and I have been studying the plantation records for the past few years and I've come to some conclusions," Marshall told his father and brother.

"What?"

"I've got to invest in something besides L'Aimant. All it takes is one bad crop and we could fall into debt so deeply that we'd never get out. In order to keep solvent I'm going to put the money I got from my practice in St. Louis into some sort of manufacturing venture. What do you think?"

"I think you're wise. Alain told me about quite a few families who've lost everything because of poor management," George told him.

"That's what I want to avoid. I owe it to Renee's father and Alain to run L'Aimant to the best of my abilities and it seems that investments outside of the region are the only logical choice."

"But what about the political situation? Do you think anything is going to come of all the shouting in Congress?" George asked Marsh.

"I've been following it closely, these past months since I moved here. If they're not careful, there could be trouble, bad trouble. With all the hotheads around, this talk about abolition could start many a fight. Remember last spring, when Sumner and Butler got into it on the Senate floor? And look what's happening in Kansas—all those people murdered over the slavery issue. . . . I hope when Buchanan is inaugurated, things will calm down."

"He did seem to be the most reasonable candidate. Let's hope he can keep things from falling apart," George agreed.

"What kind of investment can we make in this day and age? You aren't talking railroads, are you?"

"That's not a bad idea," Marshall responded to Jim. "They are going to be the future as far as transportation goes."

"No, we're not getting into railroads," George said noticing Jim's grimace. "We could try mining or an even better possibility, munitions. They're always in demand."

Marshall looked satisfied, "I think that's our answer."

"I'll look into it when I get back home. It does sound promising."

The decision made they relaxed over drinks and discussed plans for the upcoming baptism.

"Have you decided on Roger's godparents yet?" George asked.

"Tentatively, depending on their response," Marshall told them.

"Oh? Who?" Jim inquired.

"Well, brother, you for one. What do you think?"

Marshall asked him smiling.

Jim paused a moment, "I'd be honored."

"Wonderful, I'll tell Renee. The baptism probably won't be for a few more weeks. Renee's sent word to a priest in New Orleans who was a friend of her father's and he'll be coming up here for the ceremony."

"That sounds good, I wondered about taking the baby into town. He's awfully small yet," George sounded concerned. "Who's to be godmother?"

"We thought Elise would be perfect, but Renee hasn't asked her yet."

"Just let me know a few days ahead of time, so I can make arrangements with Ollie to cover the boat for me."

They drank a toast to the new godfather and went to find Renee to tell her of Jim's acceptance.

Renee received her response from Father Duvall and the christening was scheduled for a day three weeks away. Elise was thrilled at being asked to be Roger's godmother and accepted readily. Martha and Dorrie took over plans for the party, insisting that Renee rest and get her full strength back. When Jim went back to work, George joined Marshall on his rounds with Alain about L'Aimant. The days sped by, Renee spent most of her waking hours with Roger, delighting in his every expression and relating it all to her husband who was just as impressed.

Father Duvall arrived the day before the baptism eager for a visit with Renee and his old friend Alain. They spent a long comfortable evening talking of the old days when Roger was alive and of the days to come with a new generation.

The christening was held the next afternoon, when young Roger was awake. Dressed in his father's christening gown, he protested loudly and vigorously all of the excitement. Jim and Elise held him throughout the ceremony and were greatly relieved when he finally fell asleep toward the end. Marshall and Renee took him up to bed and tucked him in before rejoining their guests. As they moved to the door of the darkened nursery, Marsh took Renee in his arms.

"I've been longing to do this all day," he murmured softly.

"Why haven't you?" she teased.

"No time. You've been keeping me so busy, I don't have a minute left for play."

"How about now?" she asked and pulled his head down to hers.

Marshall crushed her to him, his mouth moving warmly over hers. He'd managed to control himself for the past month by working long hours, but tonight just watching her had brought back to him full force his self-imposed celibacy for she had quickly regained her trim figure. He had wondered on several occasions why he hadn't been wise enough to move into a guest room until she was herself again. It had been exquisite torture watching her undress day after day and not being able to take her when his body demanded it. Now, as she clung to him, he knew that she was telling him without words that she wanted him, too, and that she was ready. Against his better judgment, he set her from him.

"Our guests, madam."

Wanting to feel his arms about her again, Renee stepped closer, "They'll wait."

"They might wait, but another minute in your arms and I wouldn't be able to," he kissed her quickly and opened the hall door. "Later, my love, later," he promised.

Although the evening was pleasantly passed, the hours dragged as Renee anticipated the joy she would find once more in Marshall's arms. She had felt his eyes on her all evening and was glad that she'd chosen to wear one of her most flattering gowns. A sigh almost escaped her as the last person said good night and she and Marshall were finally alone. A fire was blazing in the front parlor and while Renee sat enjoying its warmth, Marshall went to the liquor cabinet and poured them both a snifter of brandy.

"I remember the first time you did that," she told him throatily as she took the glass from him.

"So do I," he answered, his voice seductive.

Marshall walked to the hall doors, closed them and locked them.

"I also remember the first time you did that," she smiled at him in anticipation.

"Good," he returned her smile, his eyes darkening with his long controlled desire. "I trust you haven't forgotten what came next?"

"Um . . . ?" she tried to sound confused. "I don't really remember, could you show me again?"

She placed her glass on the table and went into his arms. They embraced quietly for a long moment until he picked her up and carried her to the sofa. Their hands were eager as they helped one another shed their clothes. Moving together the instant they were unencumbered, their passion flared. Marsh was gentle, yet demanding, bringing her to those long denied peaks of desire that left her glowing as he moved to fill her. She arched to receive him and knew the thrill of his possession once again. Thrusting steadily within her, he was lost in the power of his love for her. Calling her name, he gained his release deep within her. They lay together in mutual fulfillment, entwined in both body and soul. Savoring the renewed commitment of their love, they knew their lives stretched ahead of them in an unconquerable vista under the warm Louisiana skies.

Thank you for shopping
The Book Rack